Son of Samson
and the Heroes of God

Zondervan

The Heroes of God
Copyright © 2009 by Gary Martin
Illustrations copyright © 2009 by Sergio Cariello

Requests for information should be addressed to:
Zondervan, *Grand Rapids, Michigan* 49530

Library of Congress Cataloging-in-Publication Data
Martin, Gary, 1956-
  The Heroes of God / series editor Bud Rogers ; written by Gary Martin ; illustrated by Sergio Cariello ; letters by Dave Lanphear.
     p. cm. -- (Son of Samson ; v. 6)
  Summary: In 1060 B.C., eighteen-year-old Branan, the mighty son of Samson,
contends with desert thieves and sandstorms in the Judean wilderness before
uncovering a Philistine plot to steal Israel's most sacred object and wield it as a
superweapon.
  ISBN 978-0-310-71284-8 (softcover)
1. Graphic novels. [1. Graphic novels. 2. Jews--History--1200-953 B.C.--Fiction. 3.
Philistines--Fiction. 4. Bible--History of Biblical events--Fiction.] I. Cariello, Sergio,
ill. II. Title.
  PZ7.7.M37He 2009
  [Fic]--dc22
                                        2008053868

Series Editor: Bud Rogers
Managing Art Director: Merit Alderink

Printed in the United States of America

09 10 11 12 13 • 10 9 8 7 6 5 4 3 2 1

Son of Samson and the Heroes of God

series editor: bud rogers

story by gary martin

art by sergio cariello

letters by dave lanphear

ZONDERVAN®

ZONDERVAN.com/
AUTHORTRACKER
follow your favorite authors

CHAPTER 1
"THE HONEY EATER"

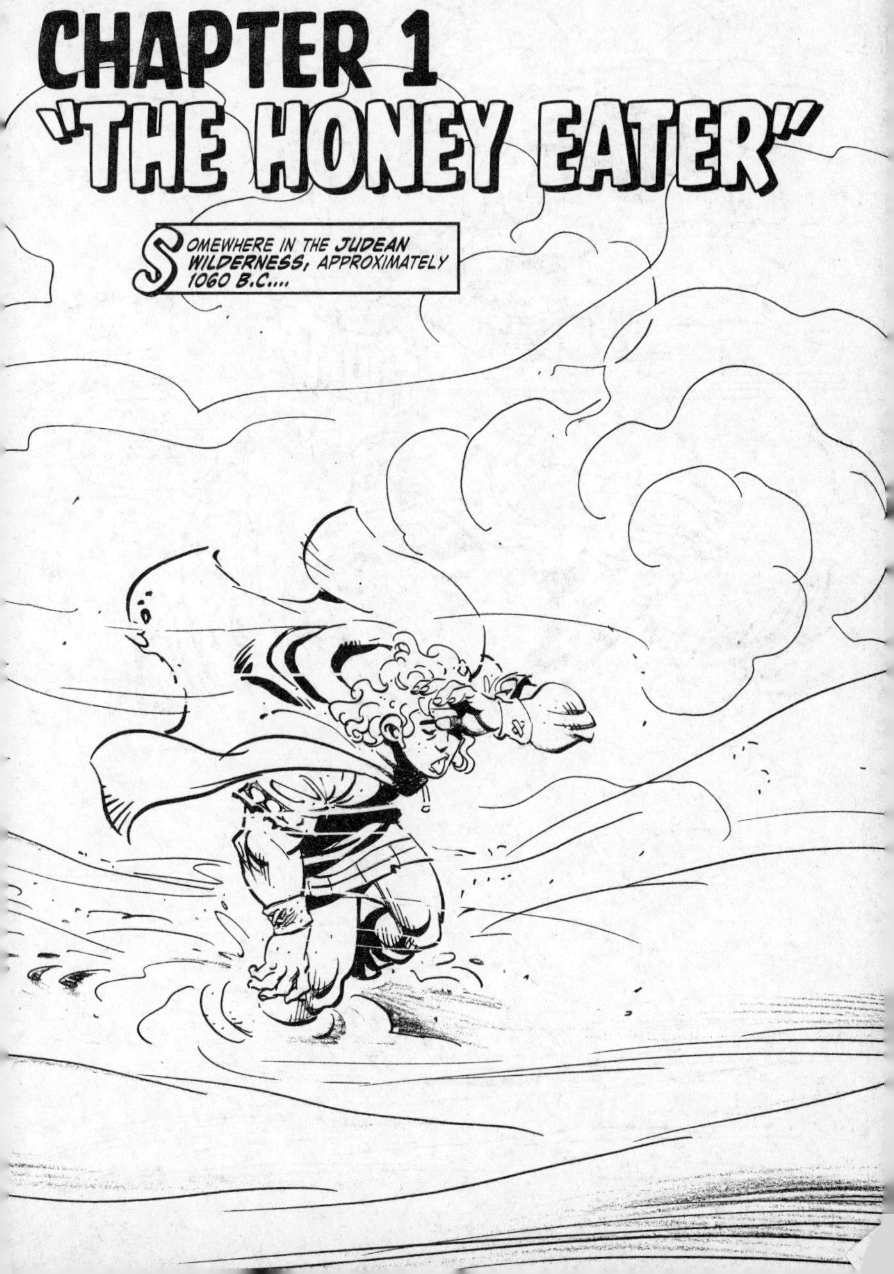
SOMEWHERE IN THE JUDEAN WILDERNESS, APPROXIMATELY 1060 B.C....

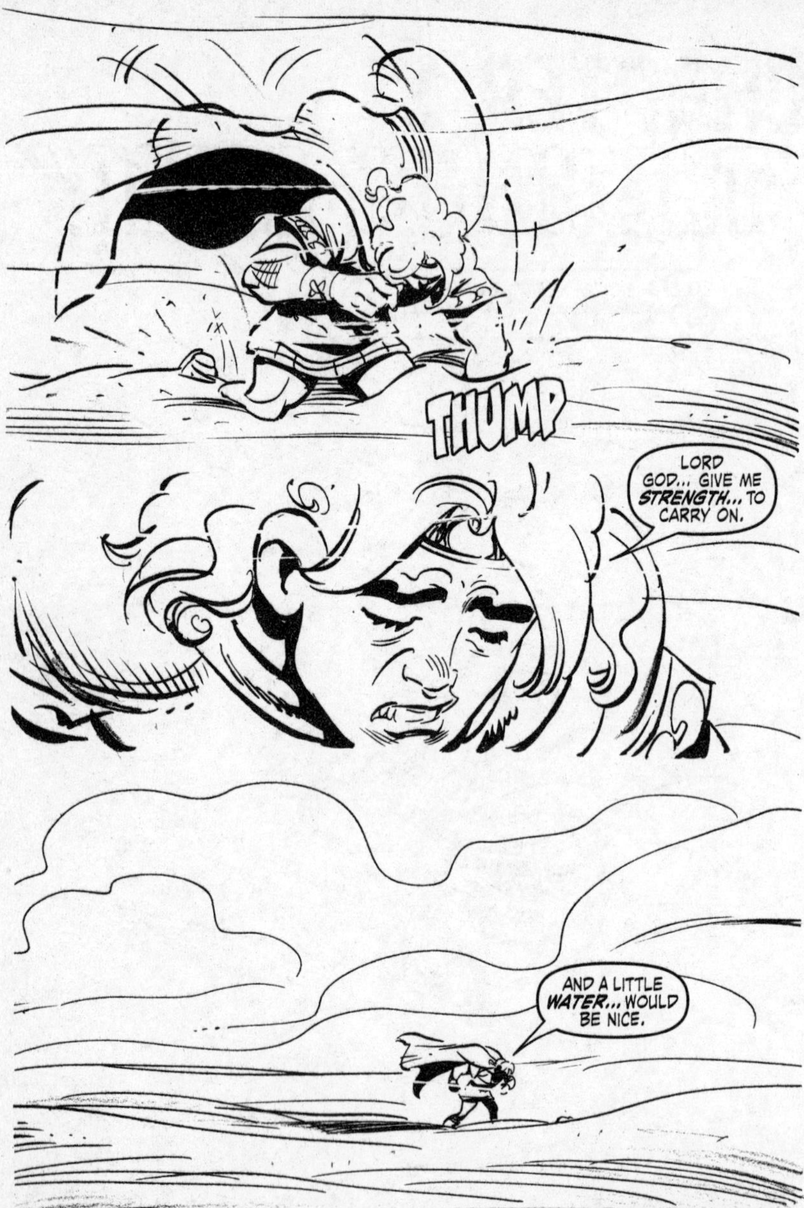
THUMP
LORD GOD... GIVE ME STRENGTH... TO CARRY ON.
AND A LITTLE WATER... WOULD BE NICE.

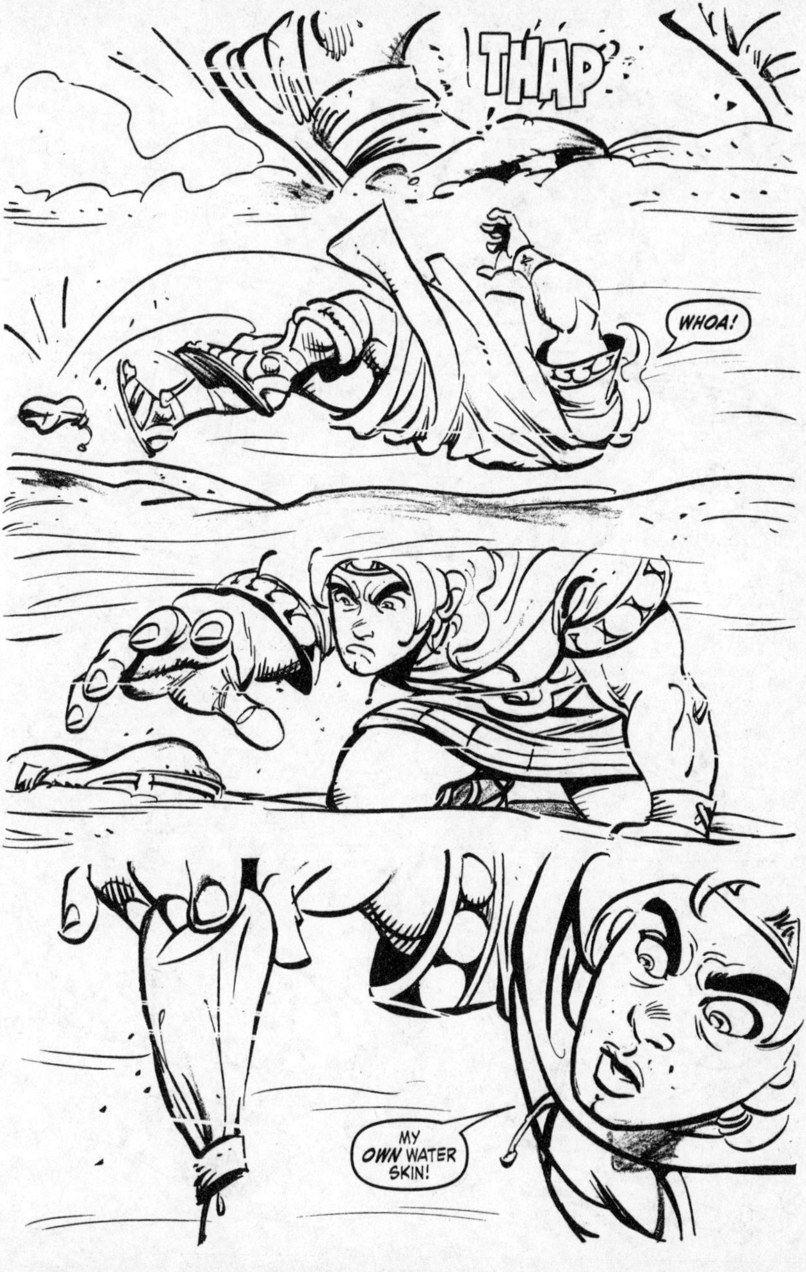
THAP
WHOA!
MY OWN WATER SKIN!

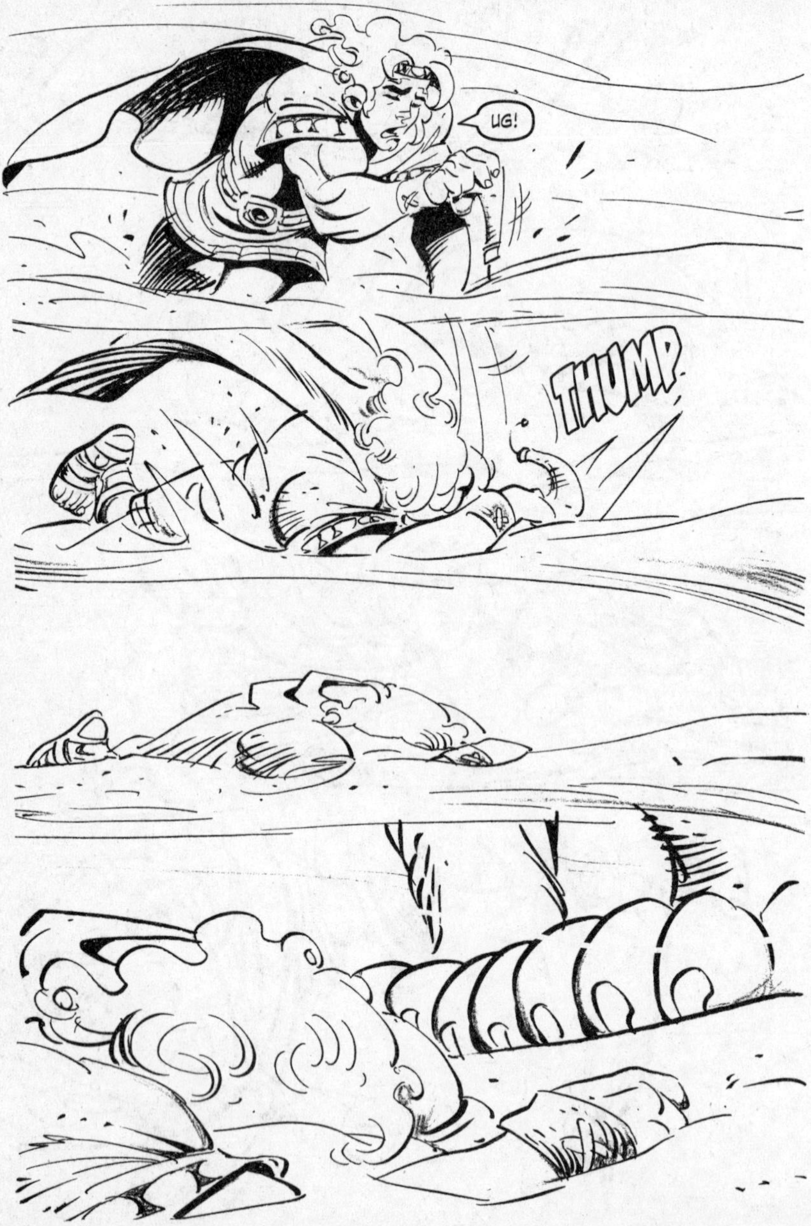
UG!
THUMP

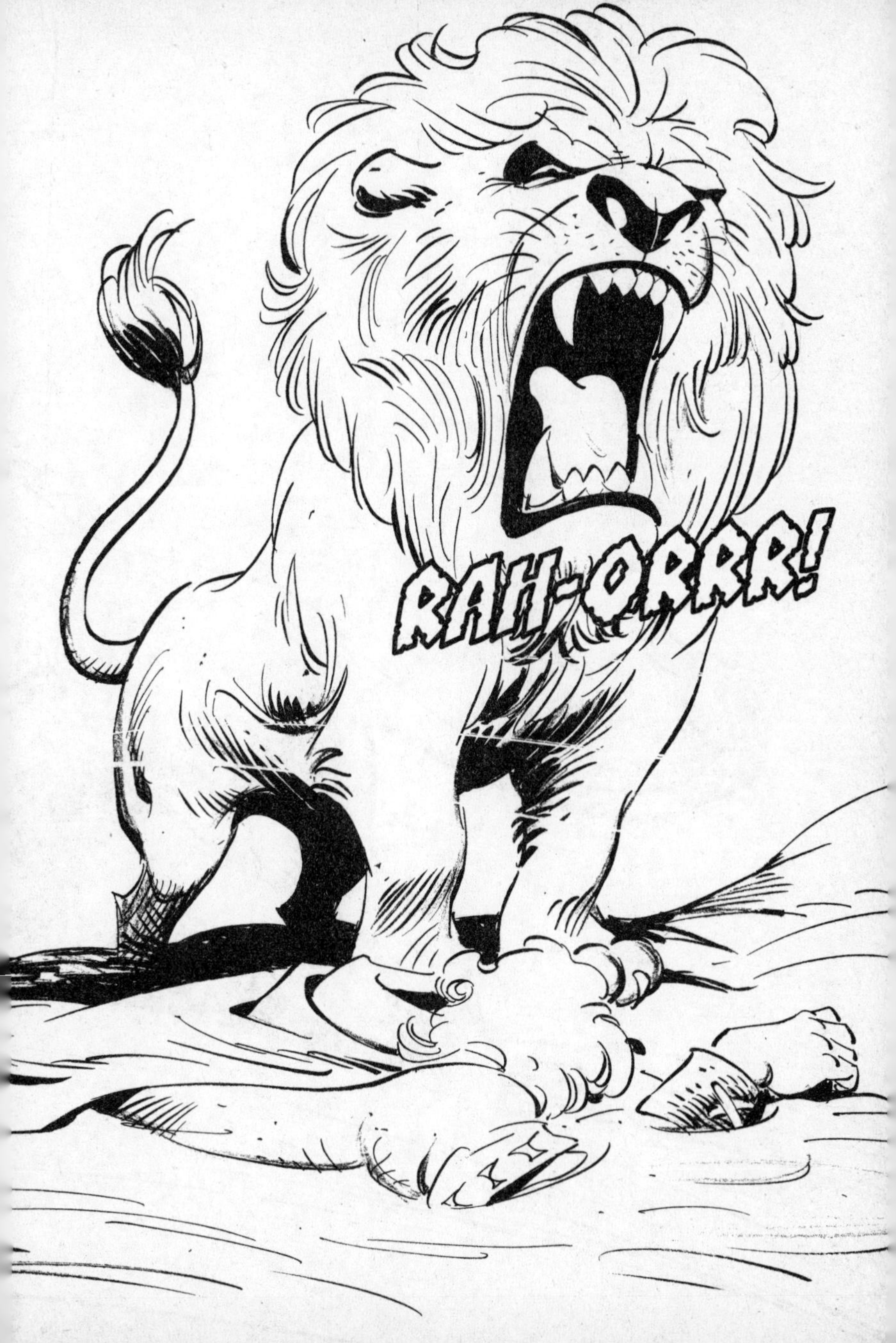
RAH-ORRR!

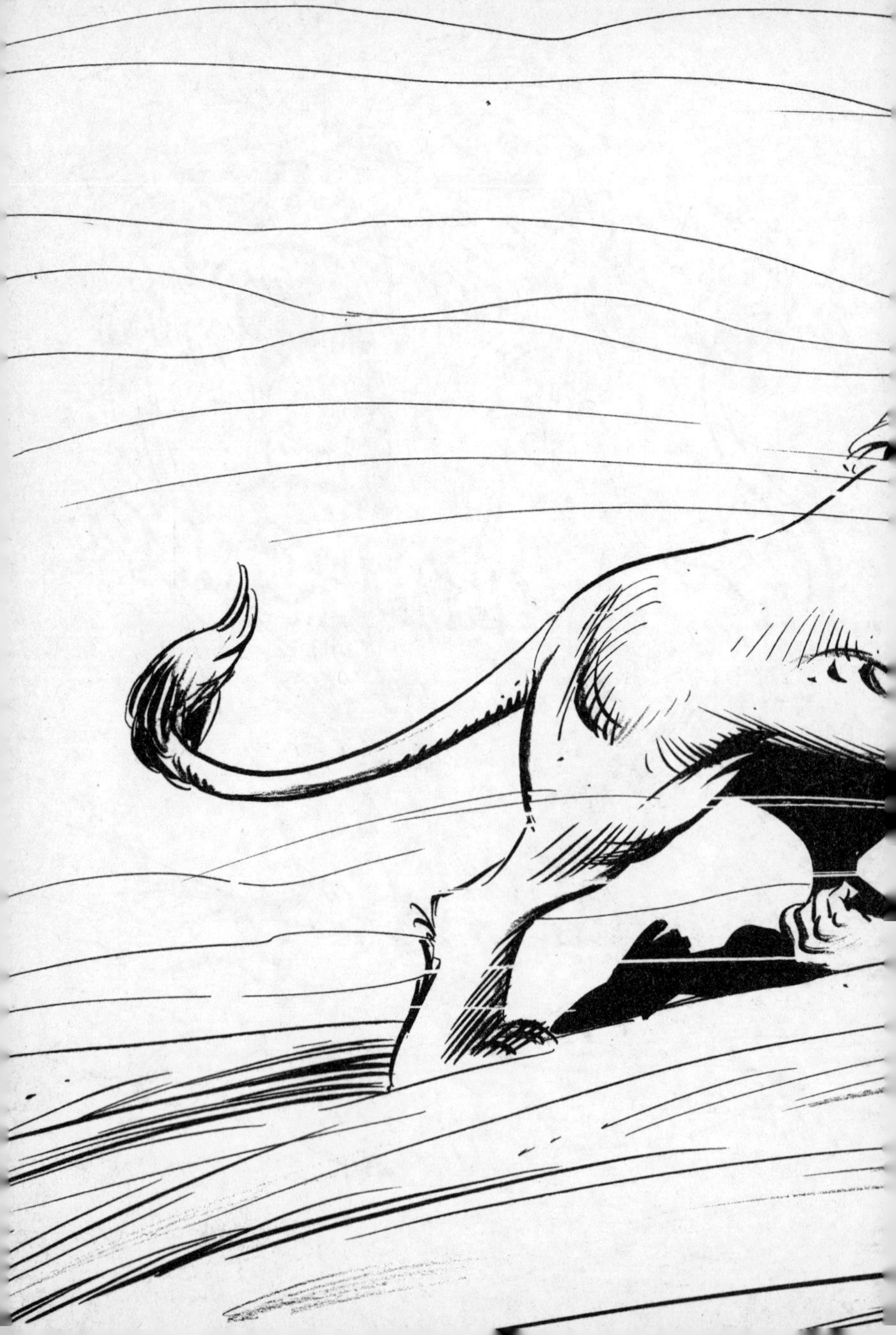

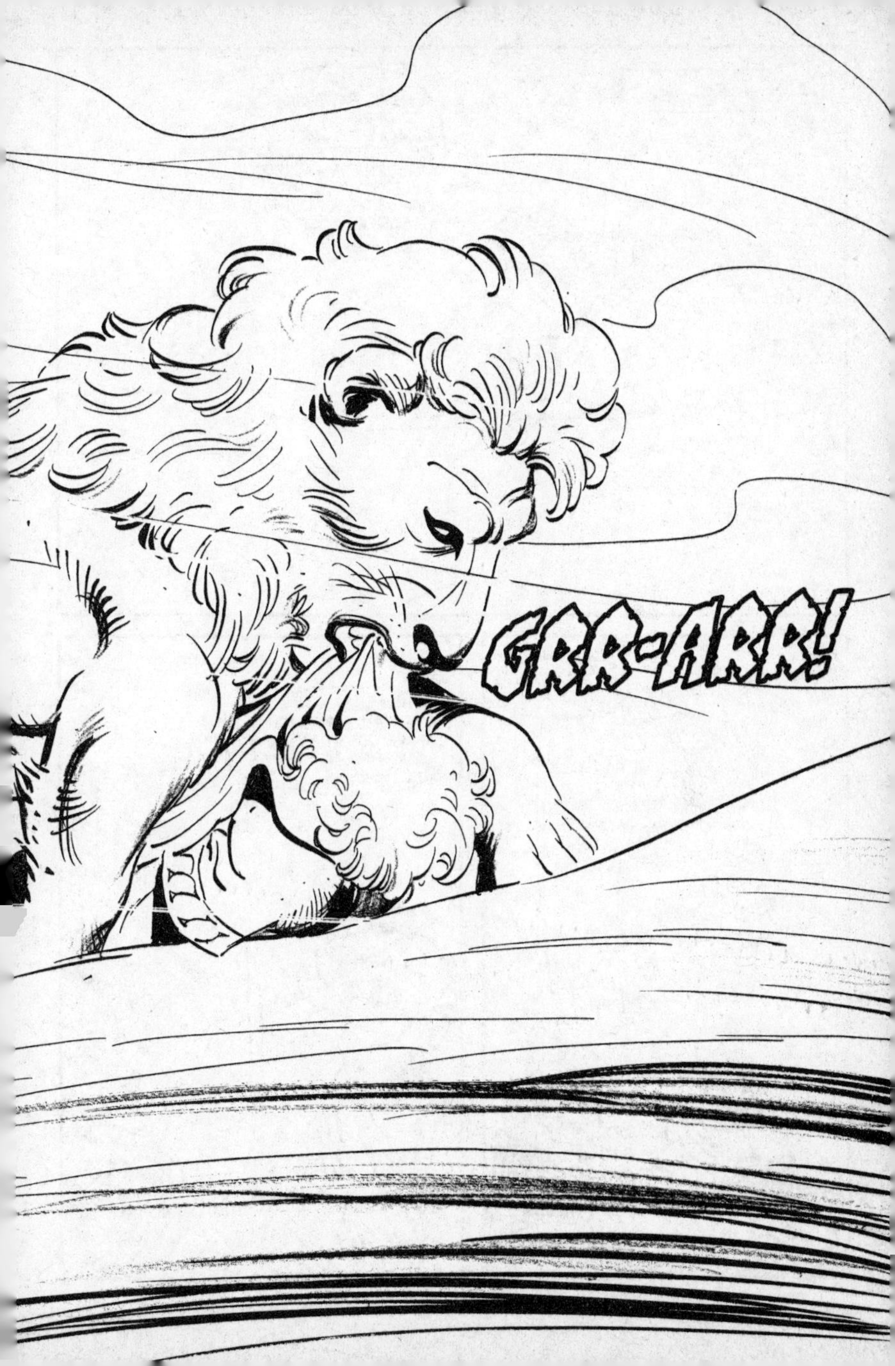
GRR-ARR!

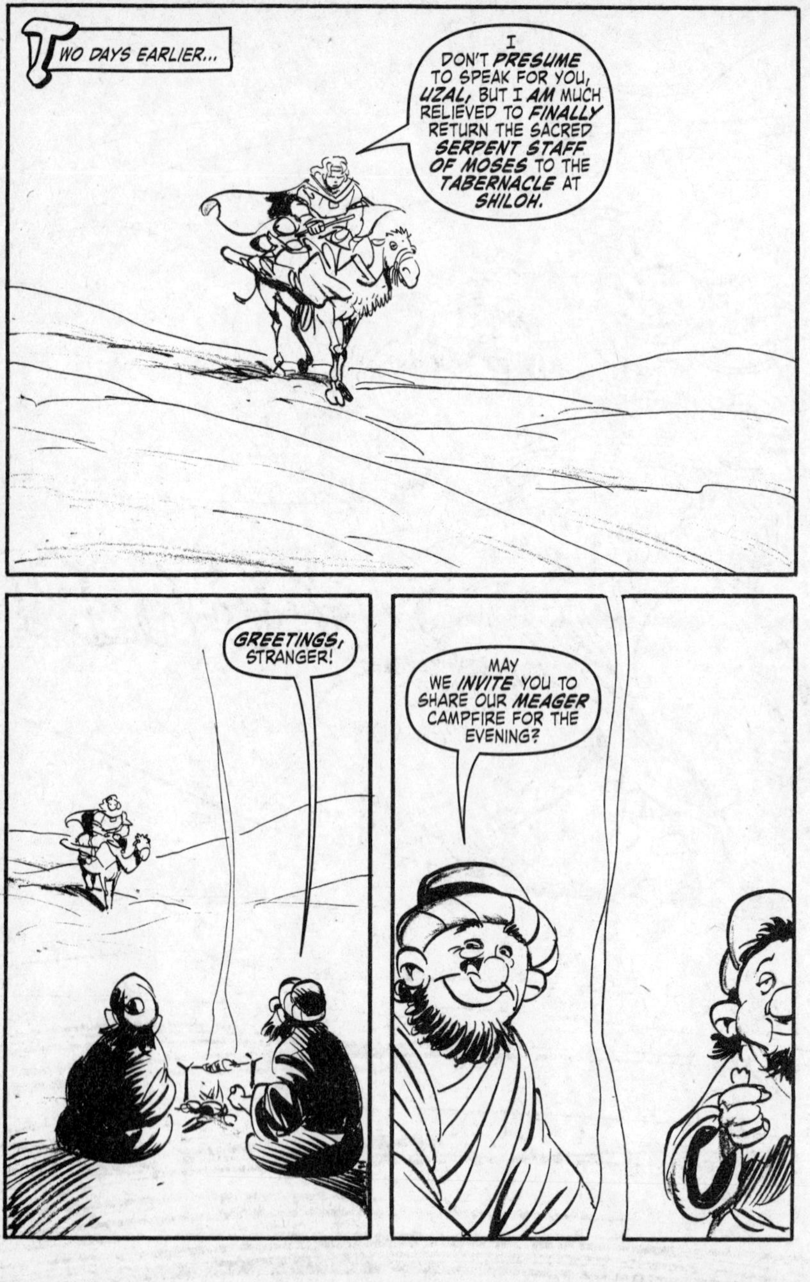
TWO DAYS EARLIER...
I DON'T PRESUME TO SPEAK FOR YOU, UZAL, BUT I AM MUCH RELIEVED TO FINALLY RETURN THE SACRED SERPENT STAFF OF MOSES TO THE TABERNACLE AT SHILOH.
GREETINGS, STRANGER!
MAY WE INVITE YOU TO SHARE OUR MEAGER CAMPFIRE FOR THE EVENING?

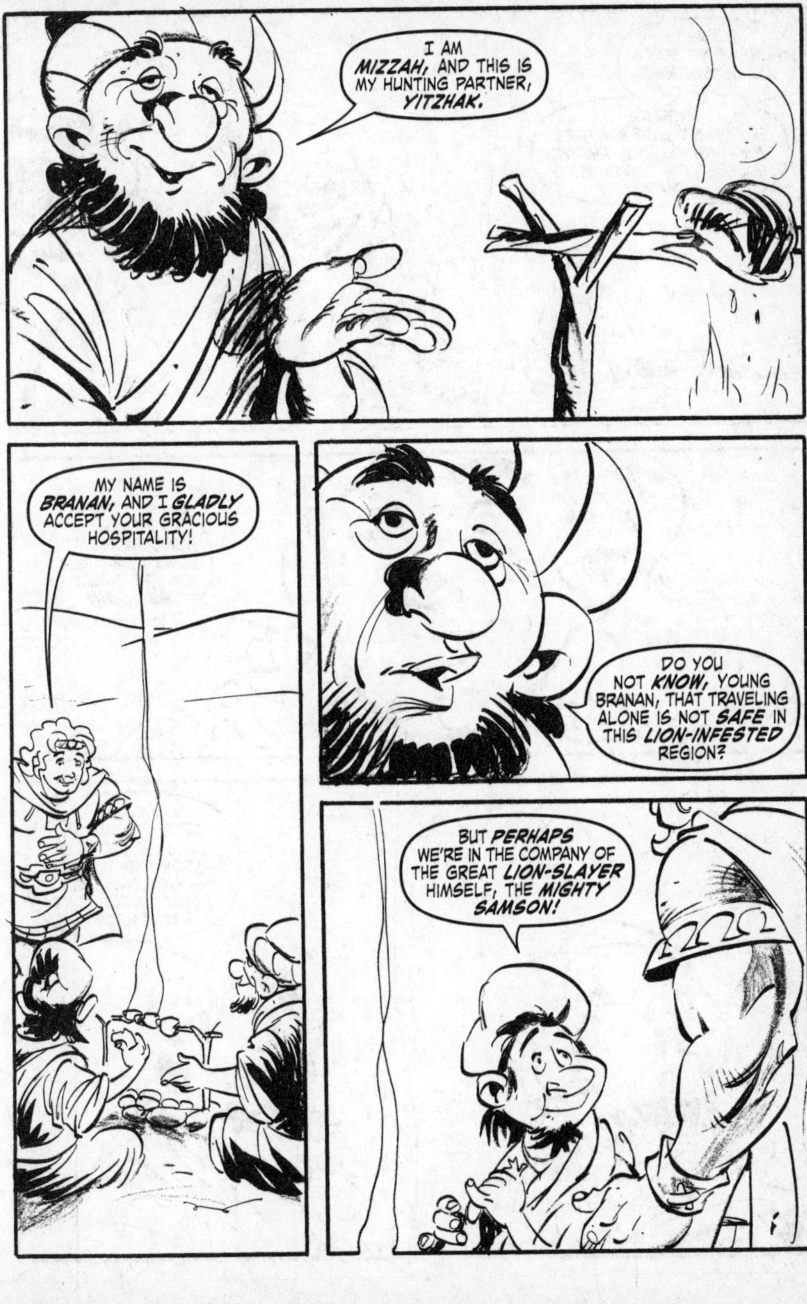
I AM MIZZAH, AND THIS IS MY HUNTING PARTNER, YITZHAK.
MY NAME IS BRANAN, AND I GLADLY ACCEPT YOUR GRACIOUS HOSPITALITY!
DO YOU NOT KNOW, YOUNG BRANAN, THAT TRAVELING ALONE IS NOT SAFE IN THIS LION-INFESTED REGION?
BUT PERHAPS WE'RE IN THE COMPANY OF THE GREAT LION-SLAYER HIMSELF, THE MIGHTY SAMSON!

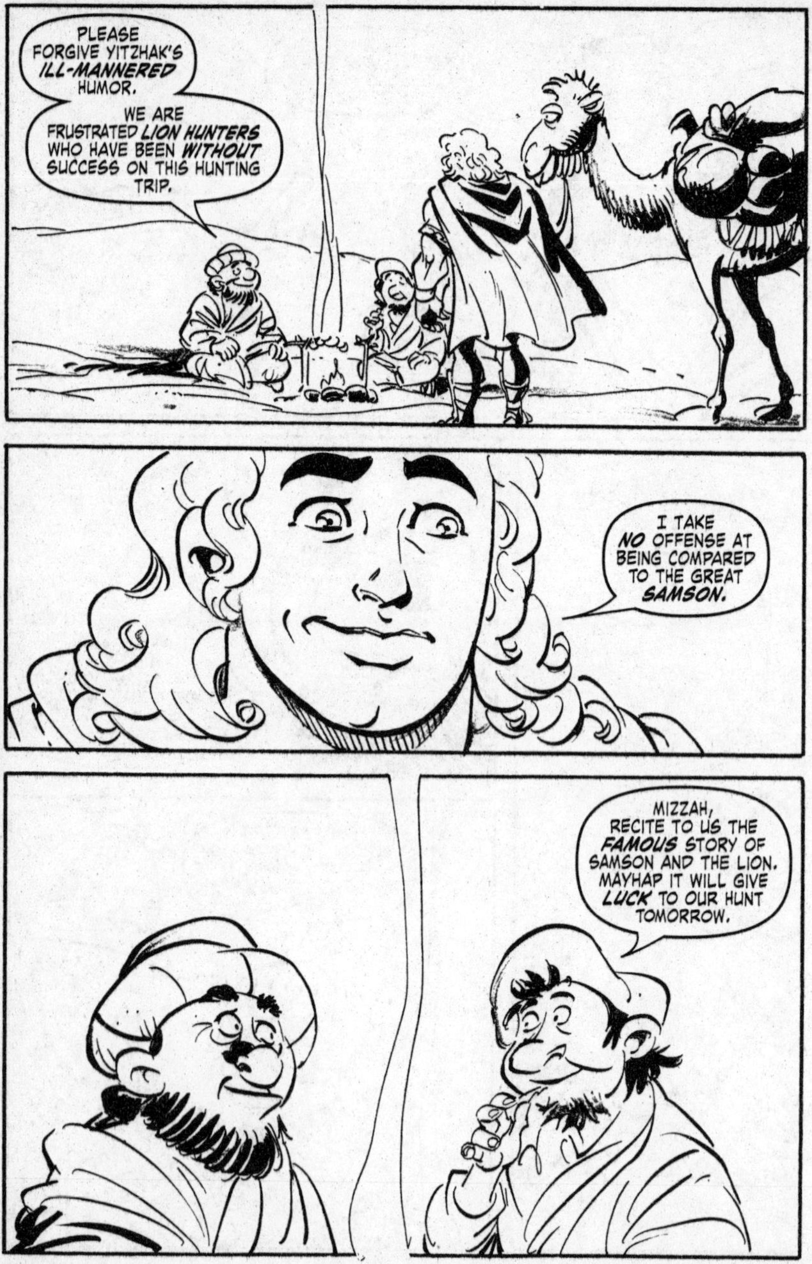
PLEASE FORGIVE YITZHAK'S ILL-MANNERED HUMOR.
WE ARE FRUSTRATED LION HUNTERS WHO HAVE BEEN WITHOUT SUCCESS ON THIS HUNTING TRIP.
I TAKE NO OFFENSE AT BEING COMPARED TO THE GREAT SAMSON.
MIZZAH, RECITE TO US THE FAMOUS STORY OF SAMSON AND THE LION. MAYHAP IT WILL GIVE LUCK TO OUR HUNT TOMORROW.

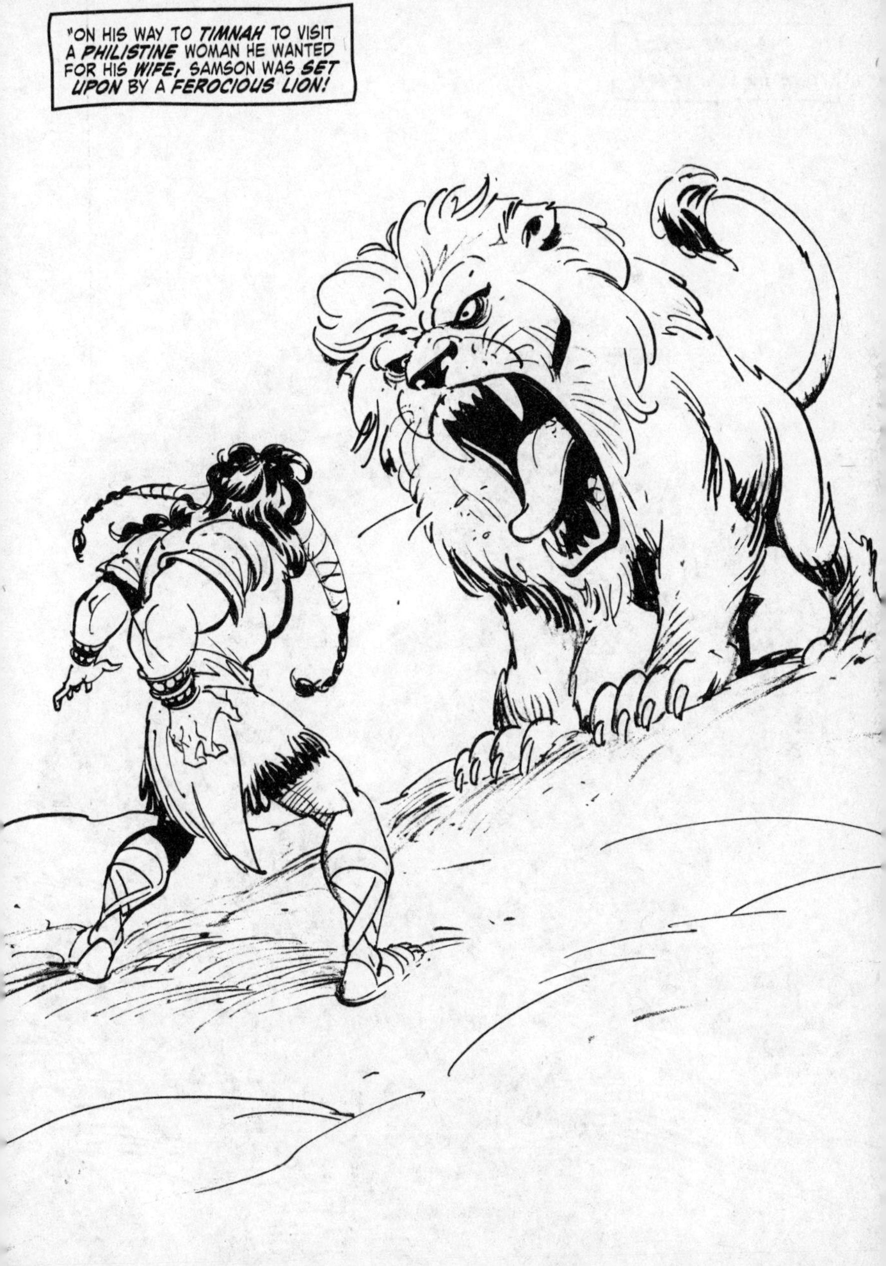
"ON HIS WAY TO *TIMNAH* TO VISIT A *PHILISTINE* WOMAN HE WANTED FOR HIS *WIFE,* SAMSON WAS *SET UPON* BY A *FEROCIOUS LION!*

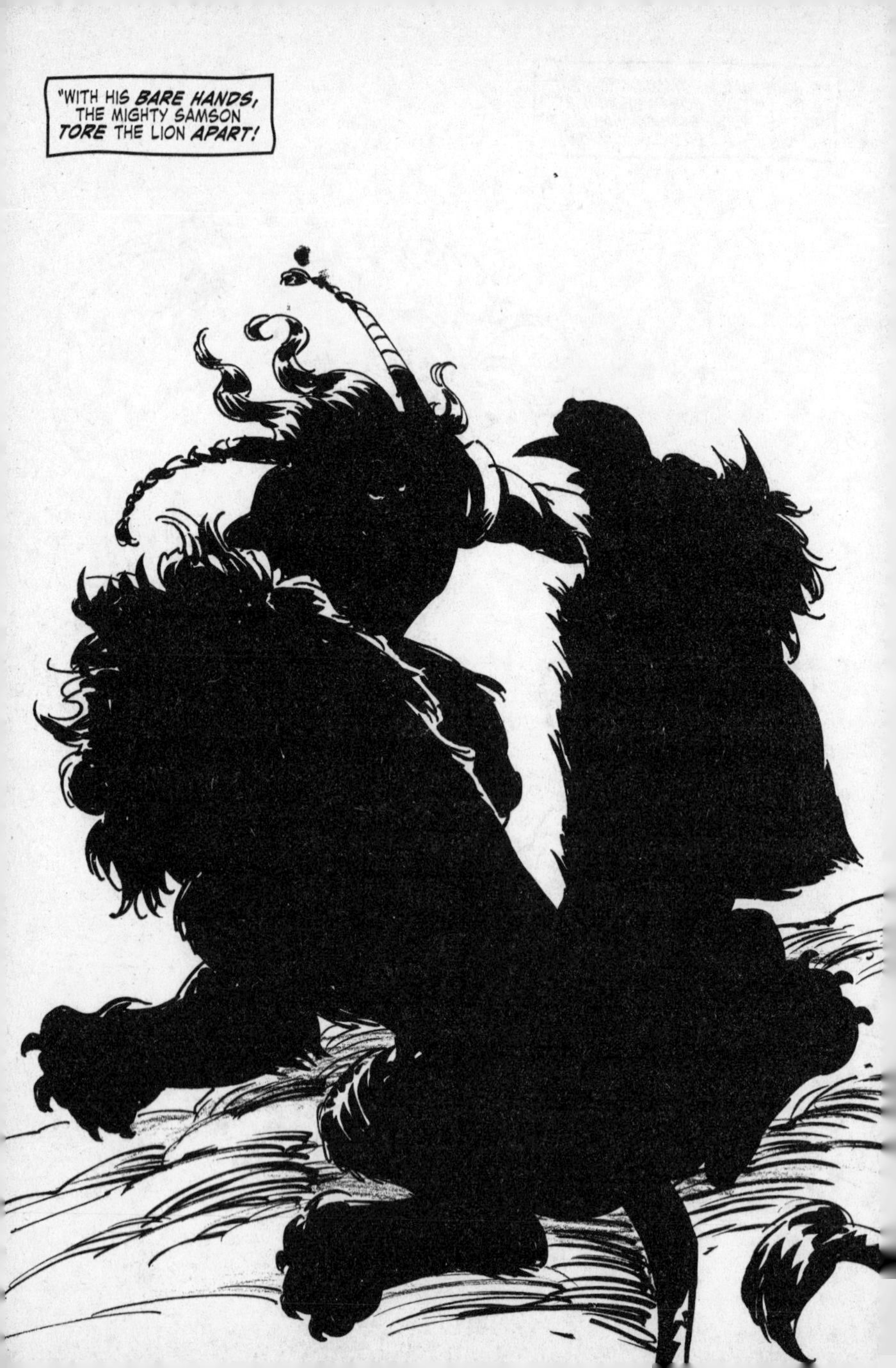
"WITH HIS BARE HANDS, THE MIGHTY SAMSON TORE THE LION APART!

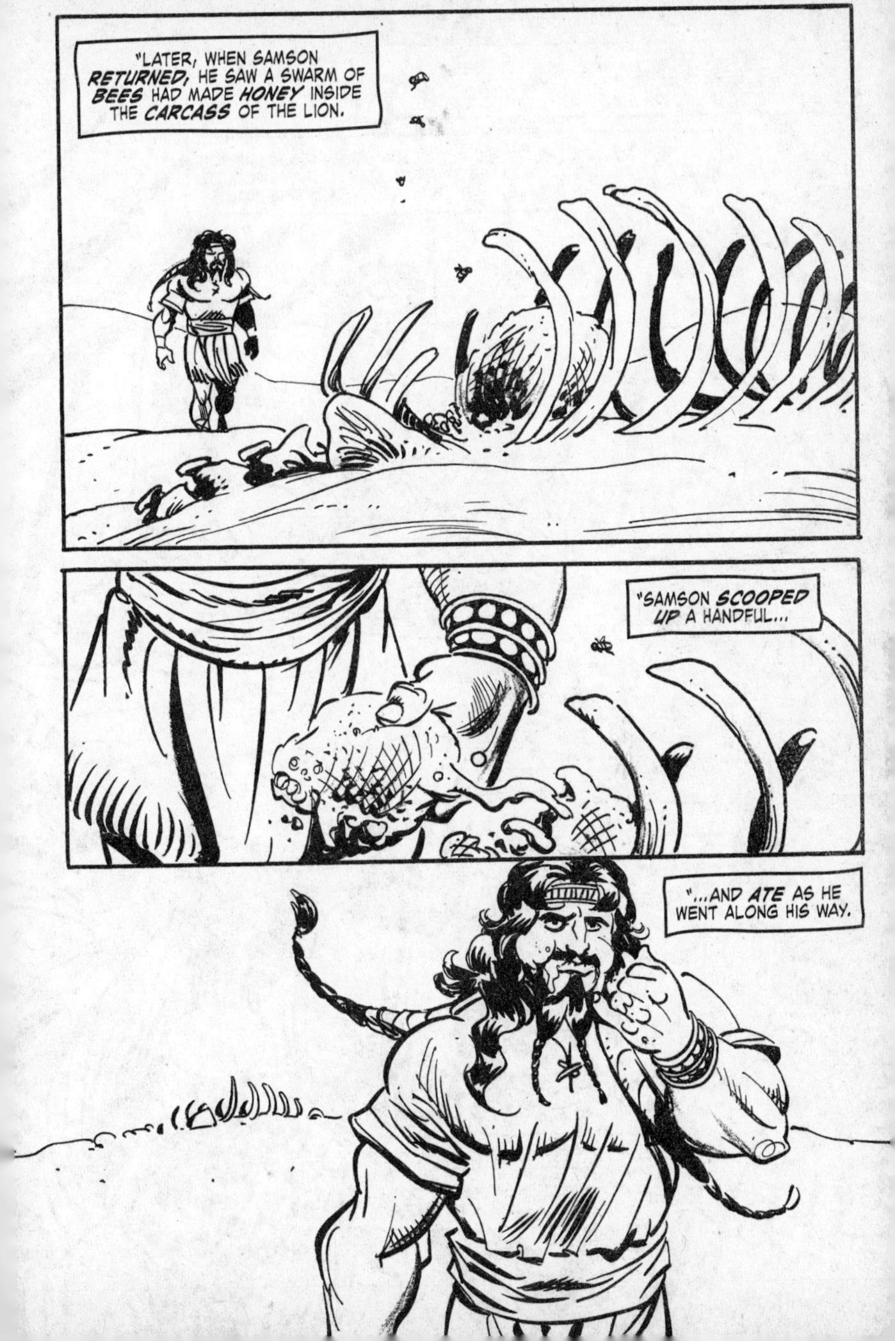
"LATER, WHEN SAMSON RETURNED, HE SAW A SWARM OF BEES HAD MADE HONEY INSIDE THE CARCASS OF THE LION.
"SAMSON SCOOPED UP A HANDFUL...
"...AND ATE AS HE WENT ALONG HIS WAY.

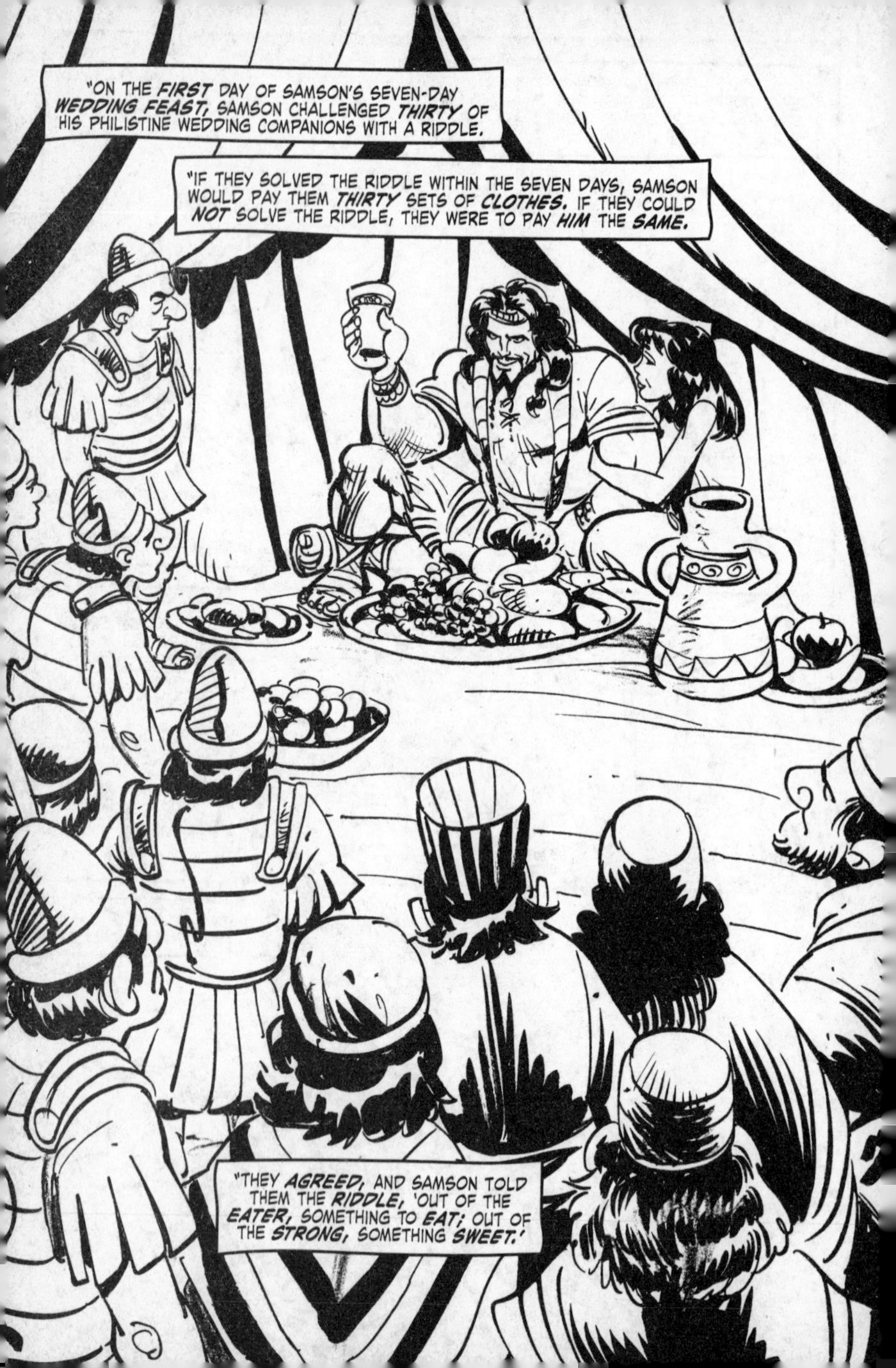
"ON THE FIRST DAY OF SAMSON'S SEVEN-DAY WEDDING FEAST, SAMSON CHALLENGED THIRTY OF HIS PHILISTINE WEDDING COMPANIONS WITH A RIDDLE.
"IF THEY SOLVED THE RIDDLE WITHIN THE SEVEN DAYS, SAMSON WOULD PAY THEM THIRTY SETS OF CLOTHES. IF THEY COULD NOT SOLVE THE RIDDLE, THEY WERE TO PAY HIM THE SAME.
"THEY AGREED, AND SAMSON TOLD THEM THE RIDDLE, 'OUT OF THE EATER, SOMETHING TO EAT; OUT OF THE STRONG, SOMETHING SWEET.'

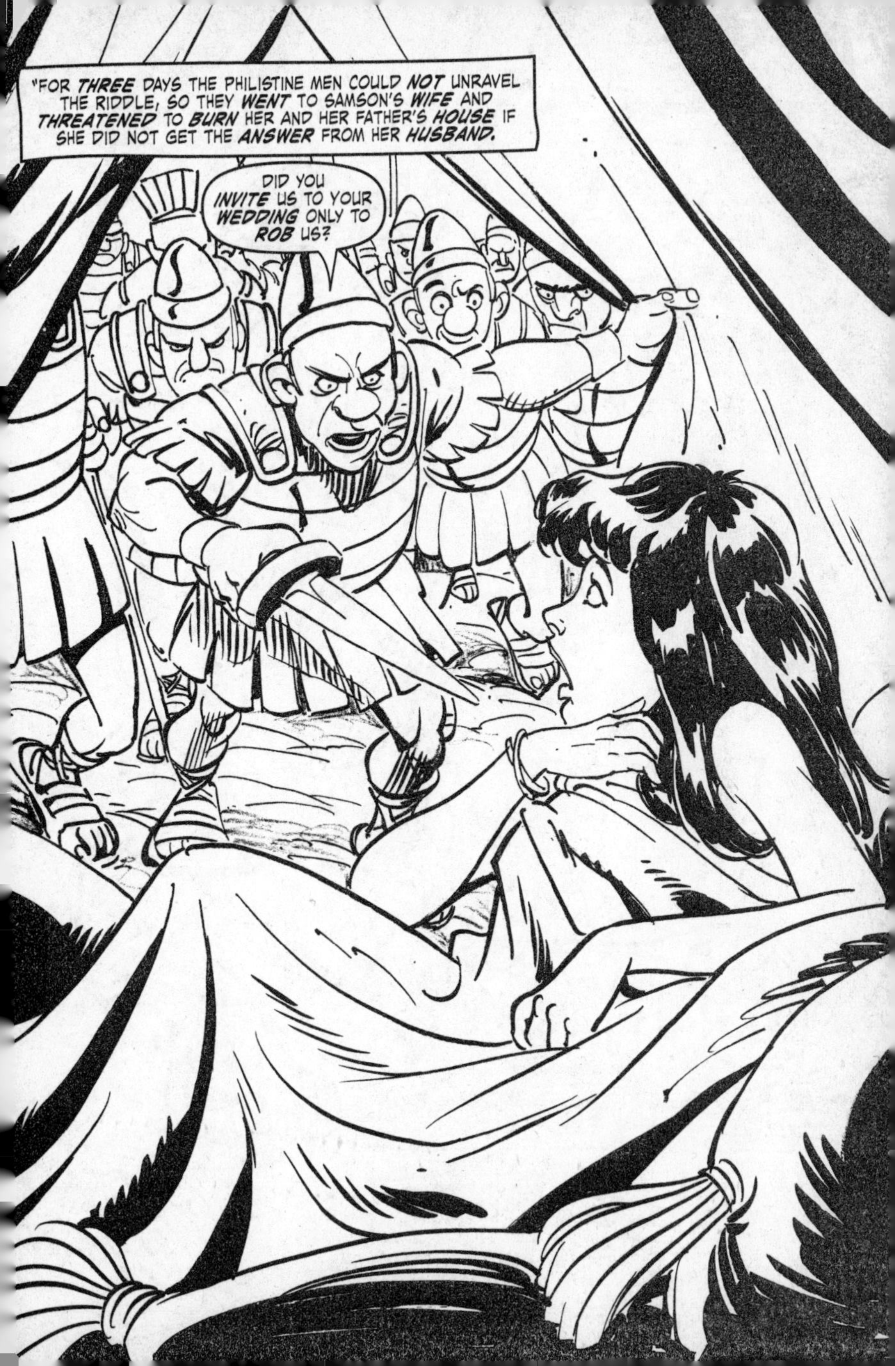
"FOR THREE DAYS THE PHILISTINE MEN COULD NOT UNRAVEL THE RIDDLE, SO THEY WENT TO SAMSON'S WIFE AND THREATENED TO BURN HER AND HER FATHER'S HOUSE IF SHE DID NOT GET THE ANSWER FROM HER HUSBAND.
DID YOU INVITE US TO YOUR WEDDING ONLY TO ROB US?

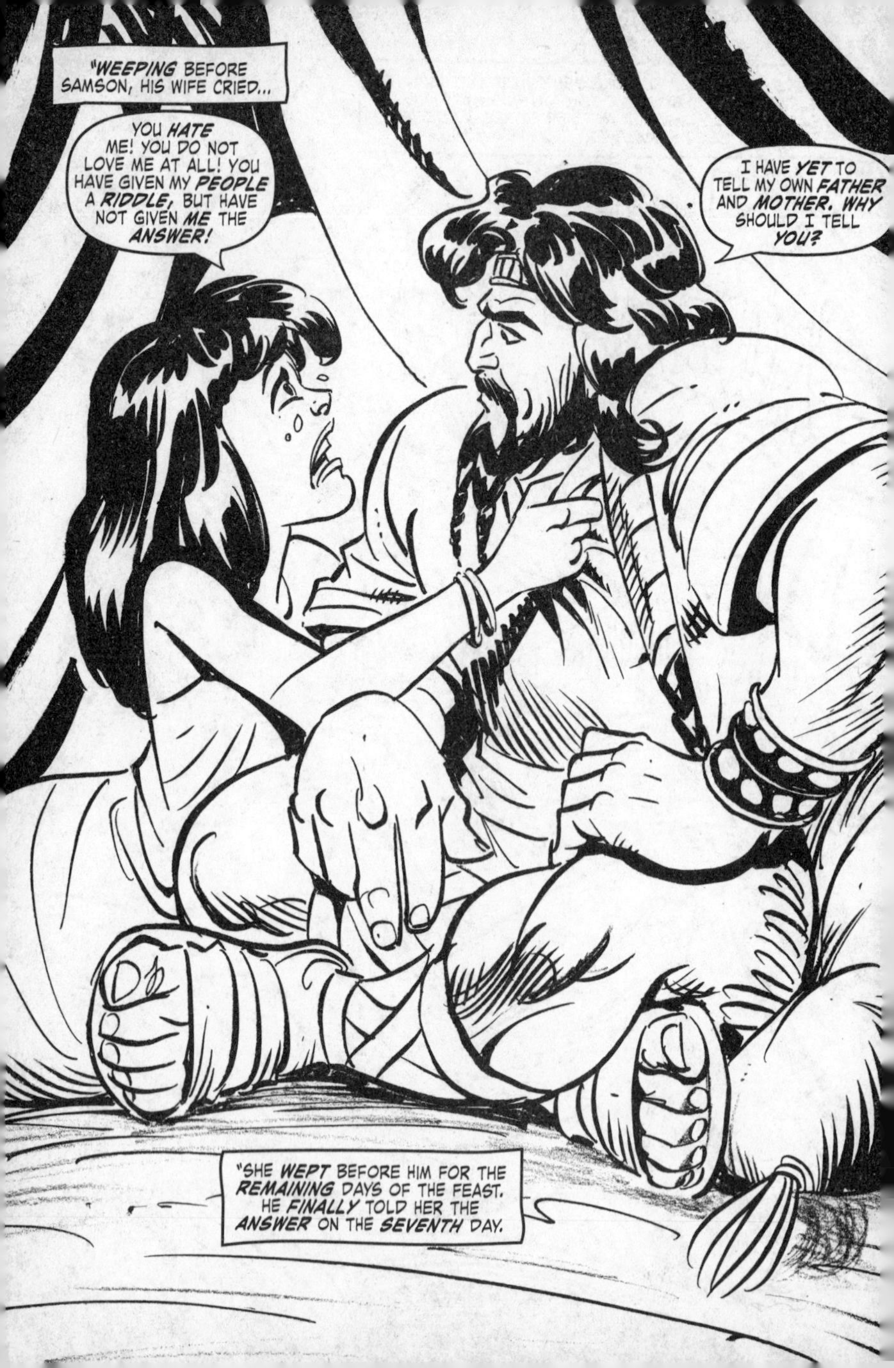
"WEEPING BEFORE SAMSON, HIS WIFE CRIED...
YOU HATE ME! YOU DO NOT LOVE ME AT ALL! YOU HAVE GIVEN MY PEOPLE A RIDDLE, BUT HAVE NOT GIVEN ME THE ANSWER!
I HAVE YET TO TELL MY OWN FATHER AND MOTHER. WHY SHOULD I TELL YOU?
"SHE WEPT BEFORE HIM FOR THE REMAINING DAYS OF THE FEAST. HE FINALLY TOLD HER THE ANSWER ON THE SEVENTH DAY.

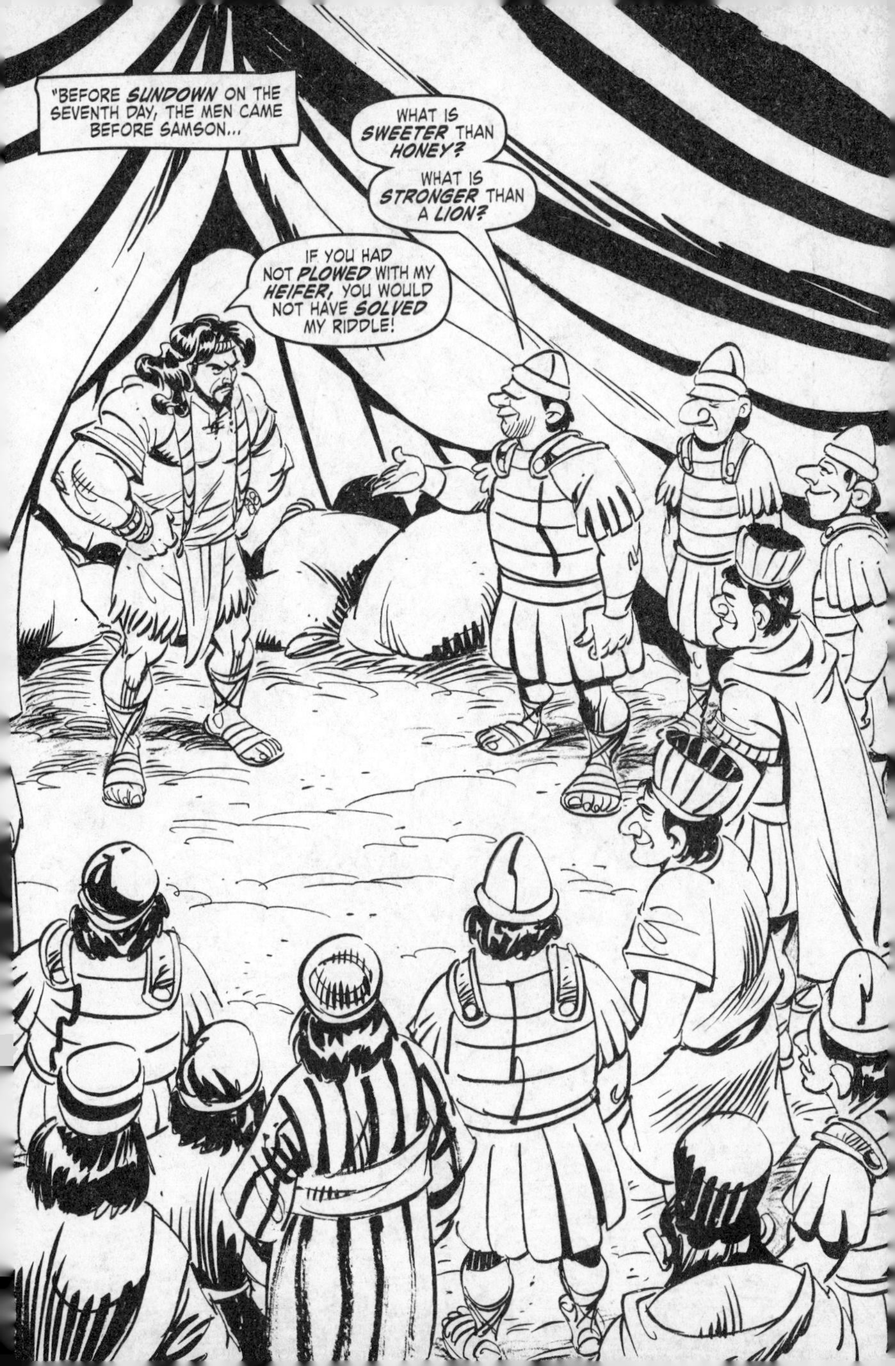
"BEFORE SUNDOWN ON THE SEVENTH DAY, THE MEN CAME BEFORE SAMSON...
WHAT IS SWEETER THAN HONEY?
WHAT IS STRONGER THAN A LION?
IF YOU HAD NOT PLOWED WITH MY HEIFER, YOU WOULD NOT HAVE SOLVED MY RIDDLE!

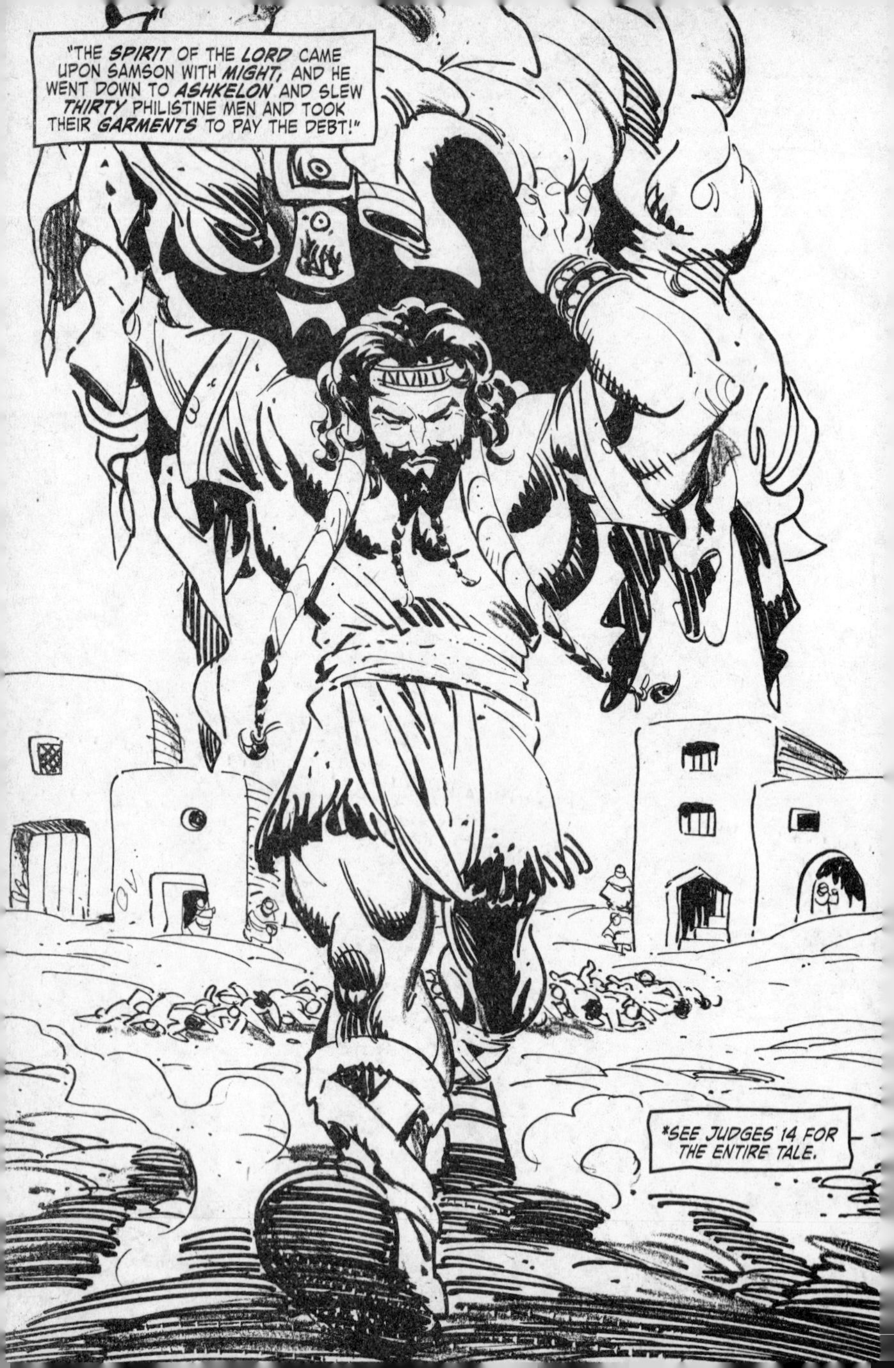
"THE SPIRIT OF THE LORD CAME UPON SAMSON WITH MIGHT, AND HE WENT DOWN TO ASHKELON AND SLEW THIRTY PHILISTINE MEN AND TOOK THEIR GARMENTS TO PAY THE DEBT!"
*SEE JUDGES 14 FOR THE ENTIRE TALE.

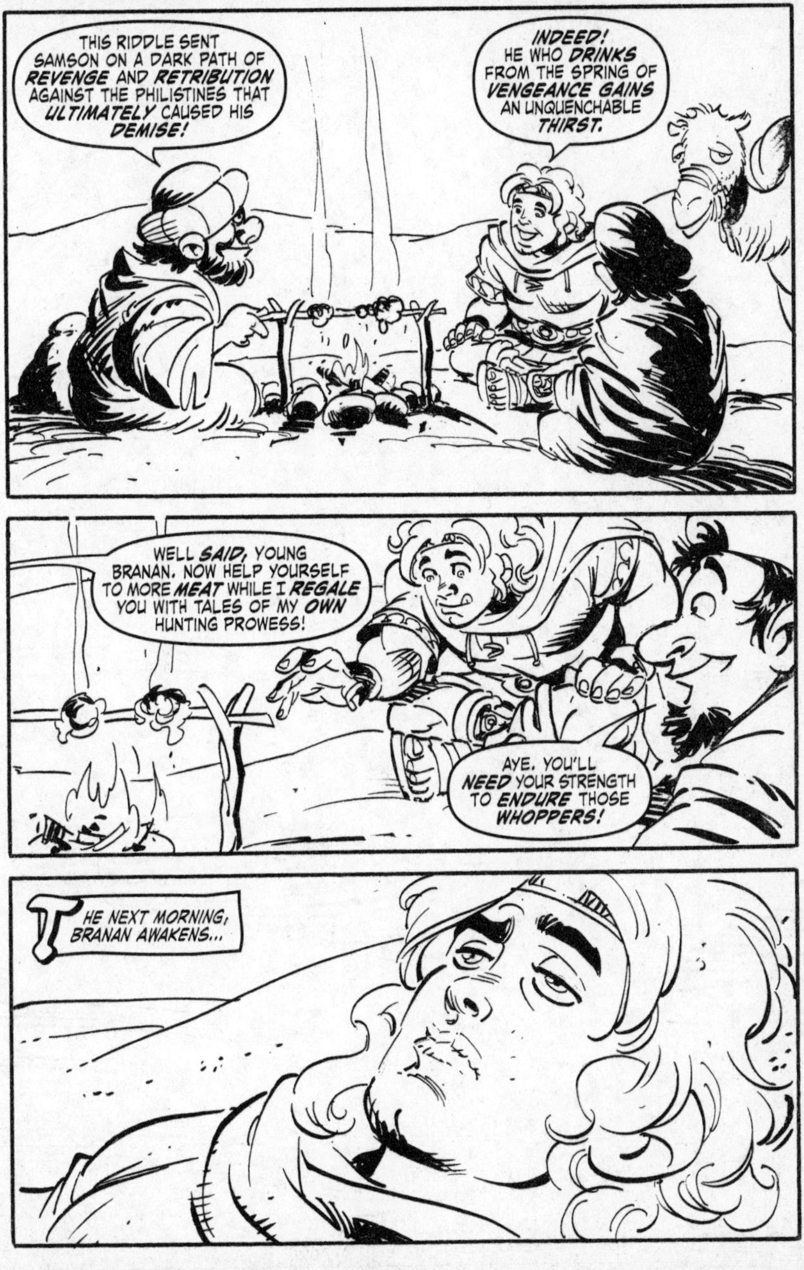
THIS RIDDLE SENT SAMSON ON A DARK PATH OF REVENGE AND RETRIBUTION AGAINST THE PHILISTINES THAT ULTIMATELY CAUSED HIS DEMISE!
INDEED! HE WHO DRINKS FROM THE SPRING OF VENGEANCE GAINS AN UNQUENCHABLE THIRST.
WELL SAID, YOUNG BRANAN. NOW HELP YOURSELF TO MORE MEAT WHILE I REGALE YOU WITH TALES OF MY OWN HUNTING PROWESS!
AYE. YOU'LL NEED YOUR STRENGTH TO ENDURE THOSE WHOPPERS!
THE NEXT MORNING, BRANAN AWAKENS...

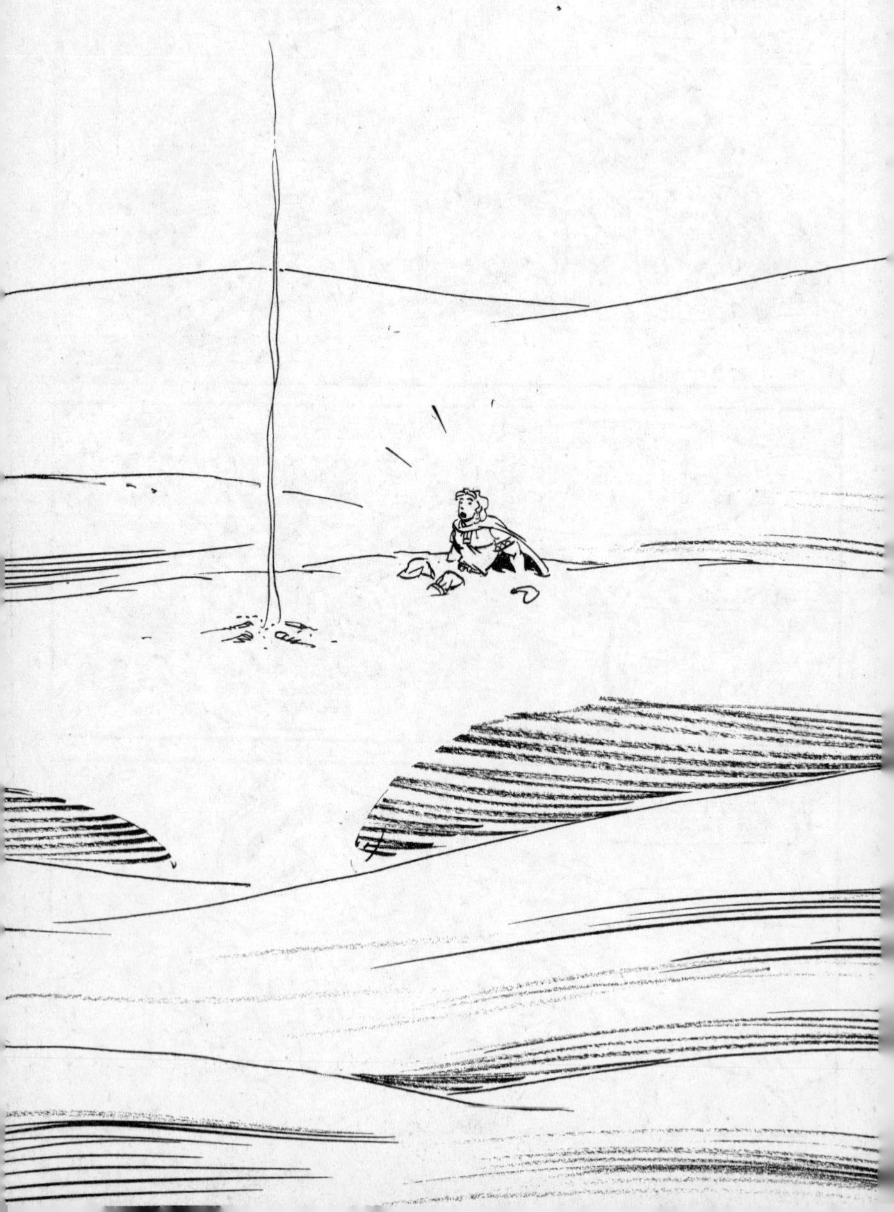

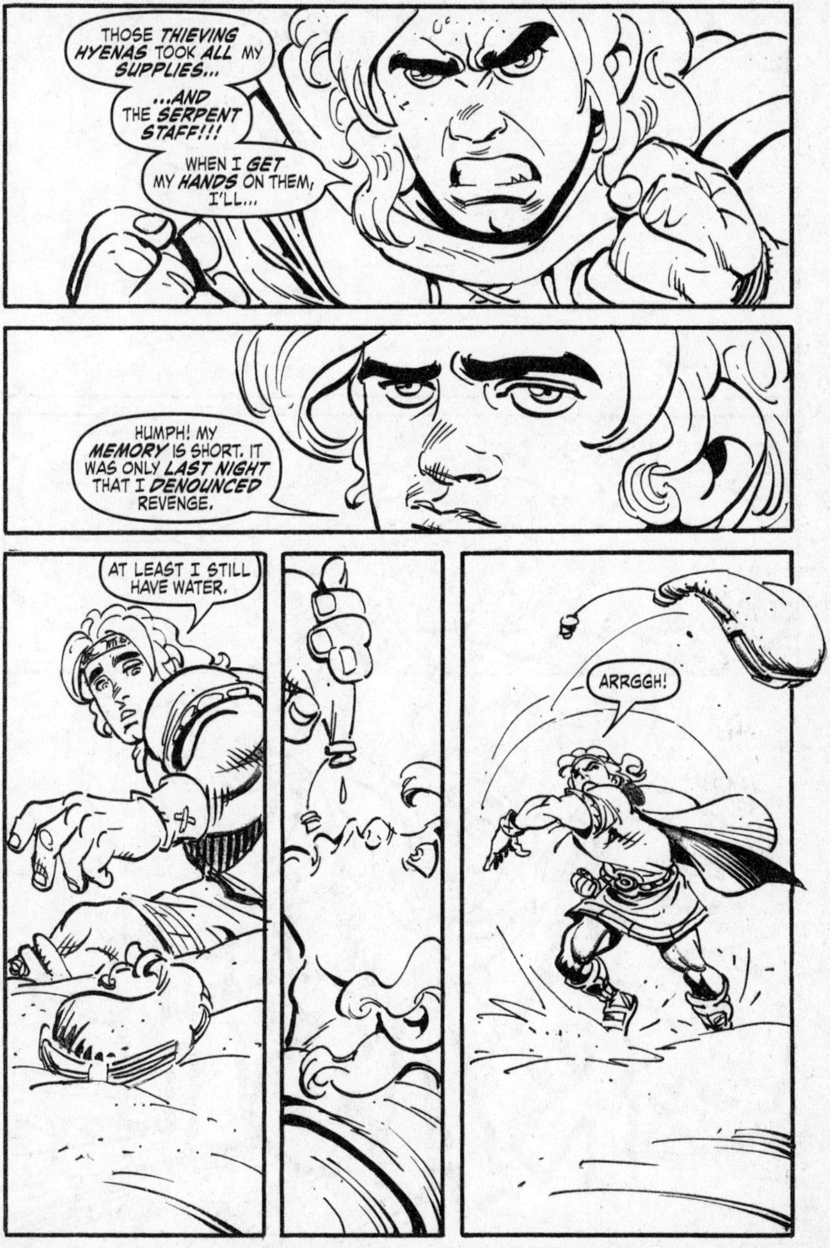
THOSE THIEVING HYENAS TOOK ALL MY SUPPLIES...
...AND THE SERPENT STAFF!!!
WHEN I GET MY HANDS ON THEM, I'LL...
HUMPH! MY MEMORY IS SHORT. IT WAS ONLY LAST NIGHT THAT I DENOUNCED REVENGE.
AT LEAST I STILL HAVE WATER.
ARRGGH!

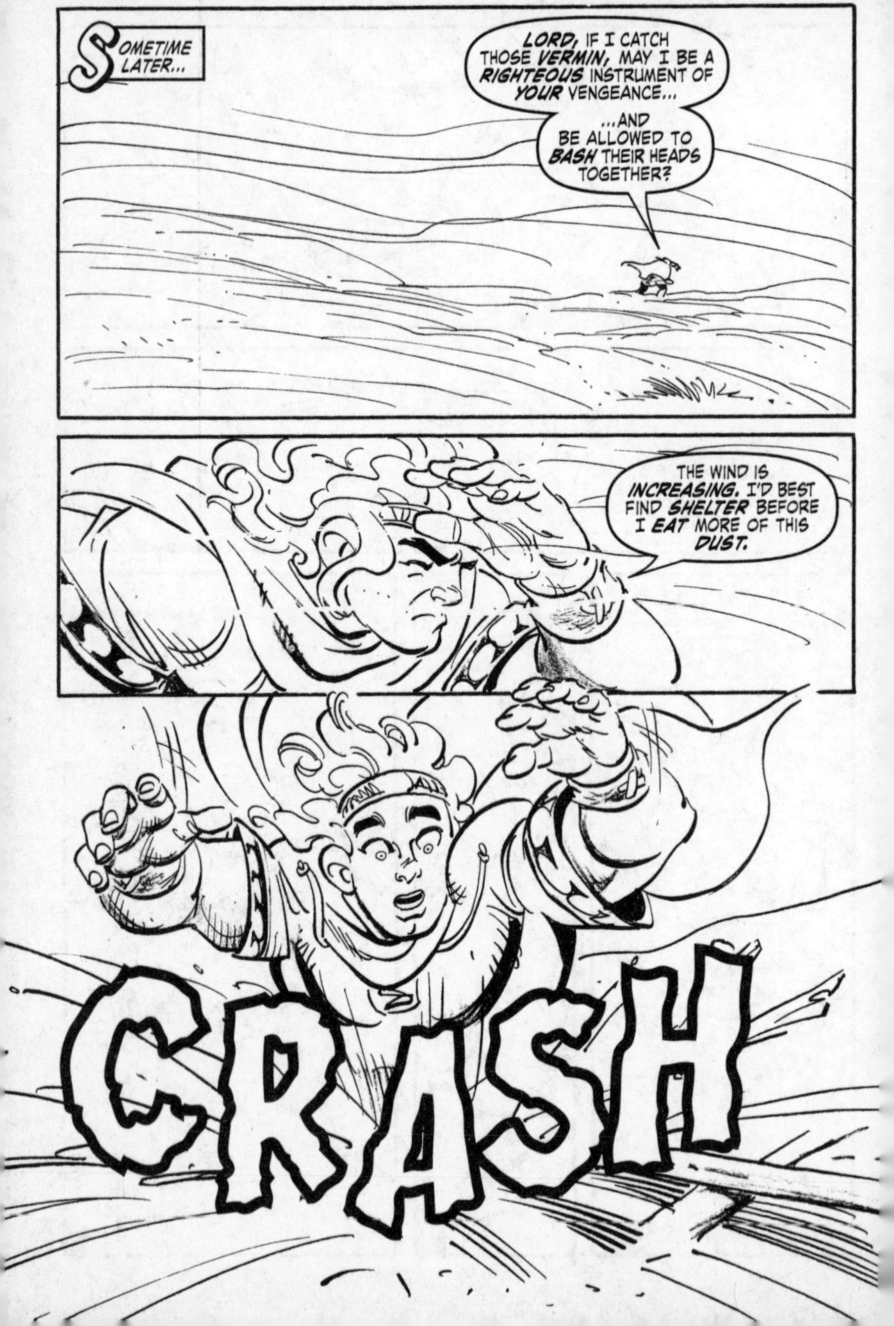
SOMETIME LATER...
LORD, IF I CATCH THOSE VERMIN, MAY I BE A RIGHTEOUS INSTRUMENT OF YOUR VENGEANCE...
...AND BE ALLOWED TO BASH THEIR HEADS TOGETHER?
THE WIND IS INCREASING. I'D BEST FIND SHELTER BEFORE I EAT MORE OF THIS DUST.
CRASH

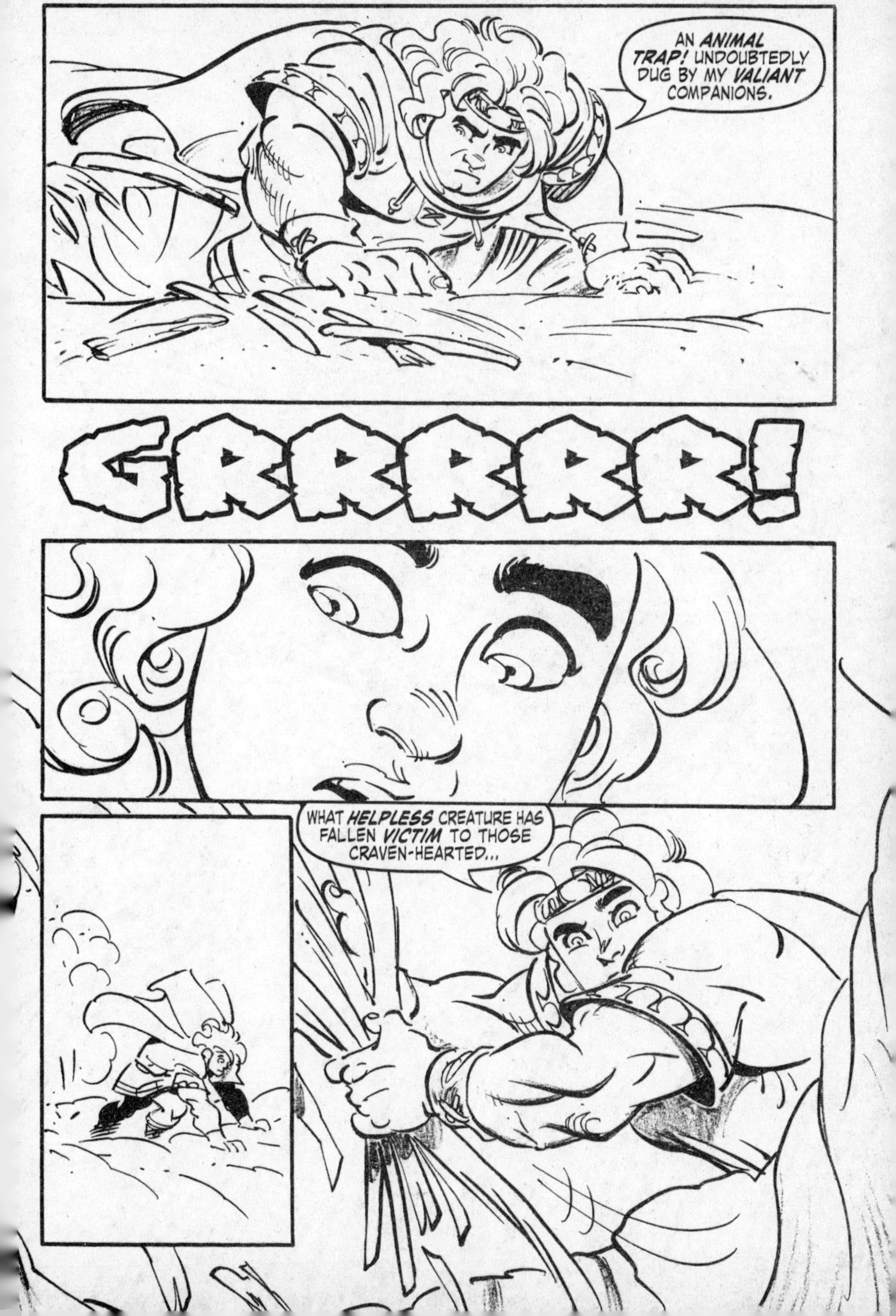
AN ANIMAL TRAP! UNDOUBTEDLY DUG BY MY VALIANT COMPANIONS.
GRRRRR!
WHAT HELPLESS CREATURE HAS FALLEN VICTIM TO THOSE CRAVEN-HEARTED...

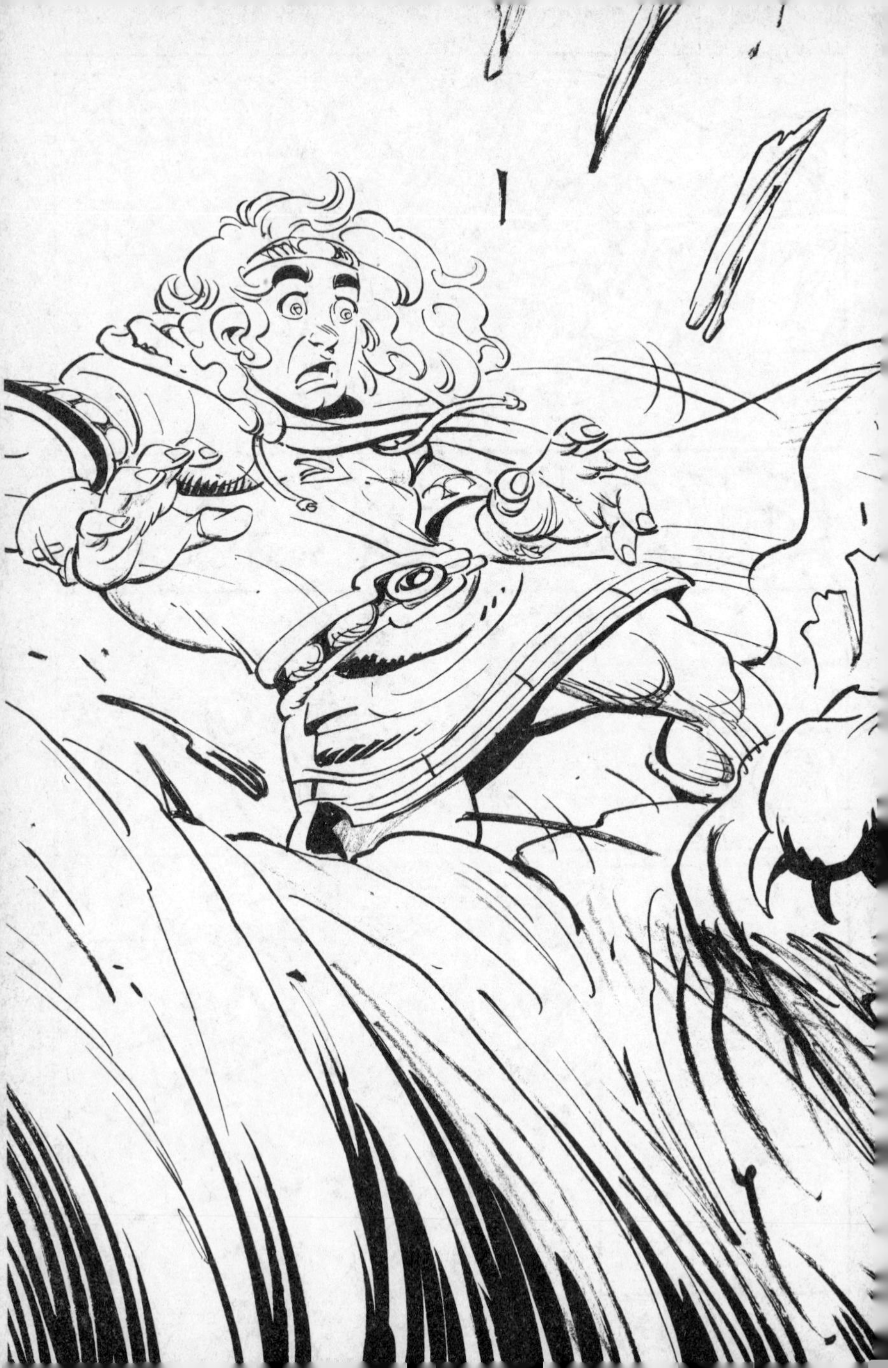

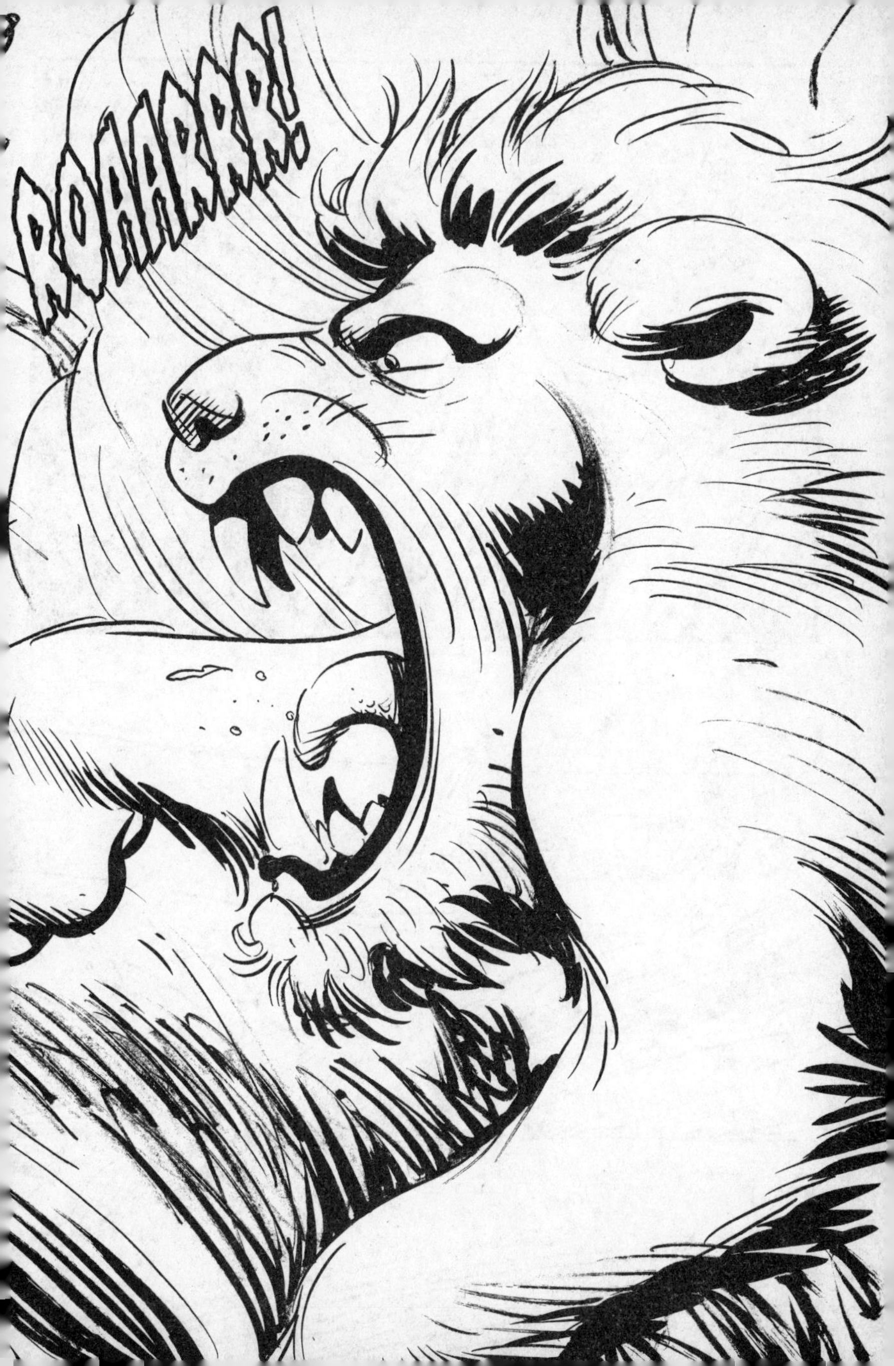
ROARRR!

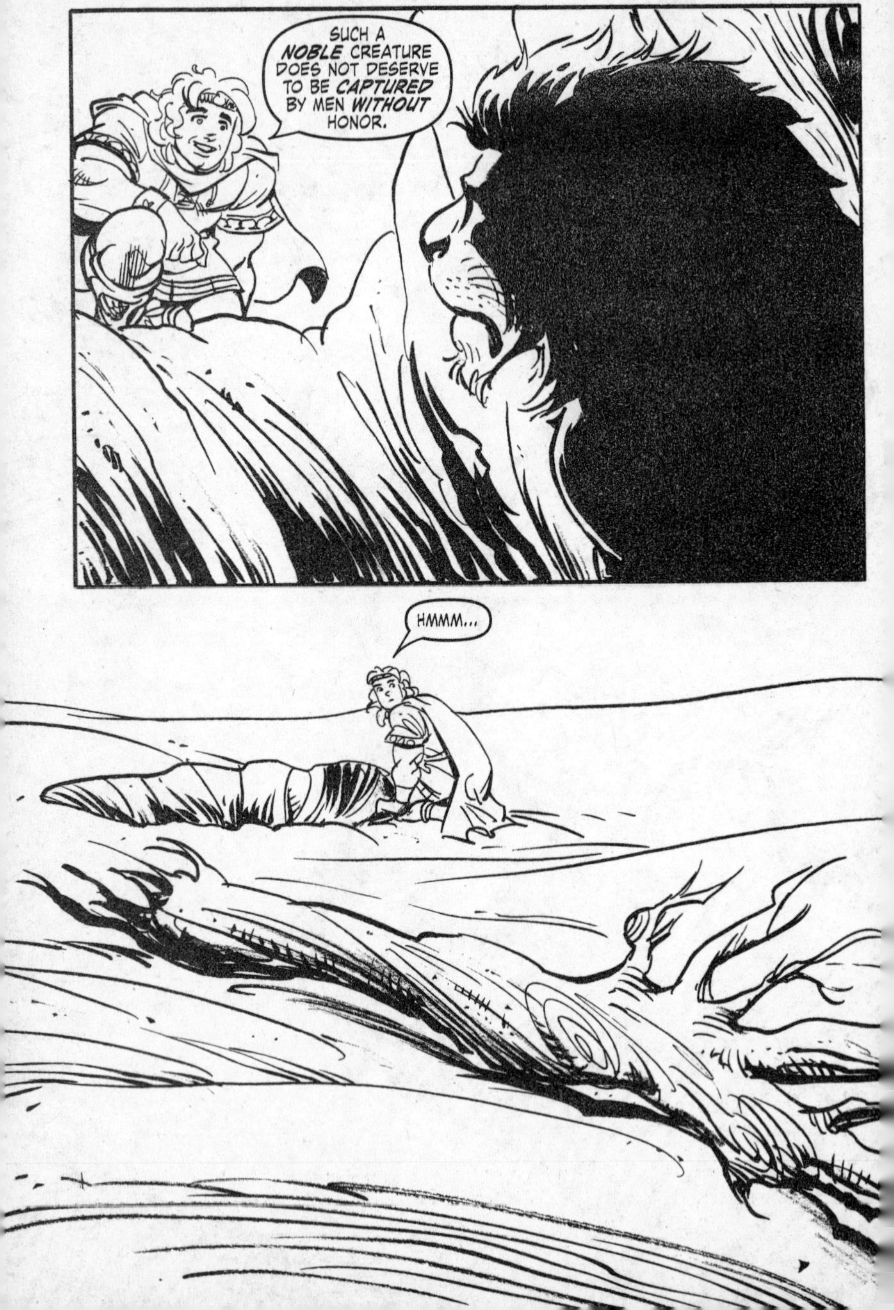
SUCH A NOBLE CREATURE DOES NOT DESERVE TO BE CAPTURED BY MEN WITHOUT HONOR.
HMMM...

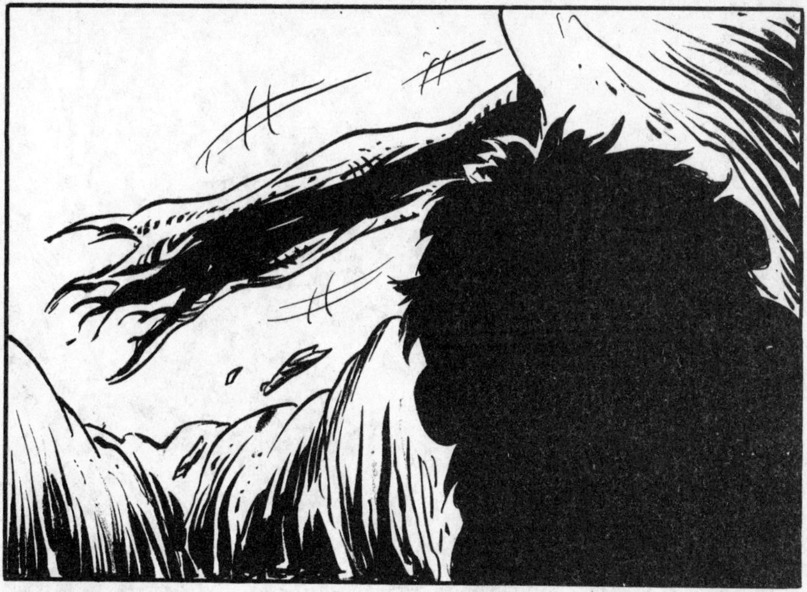

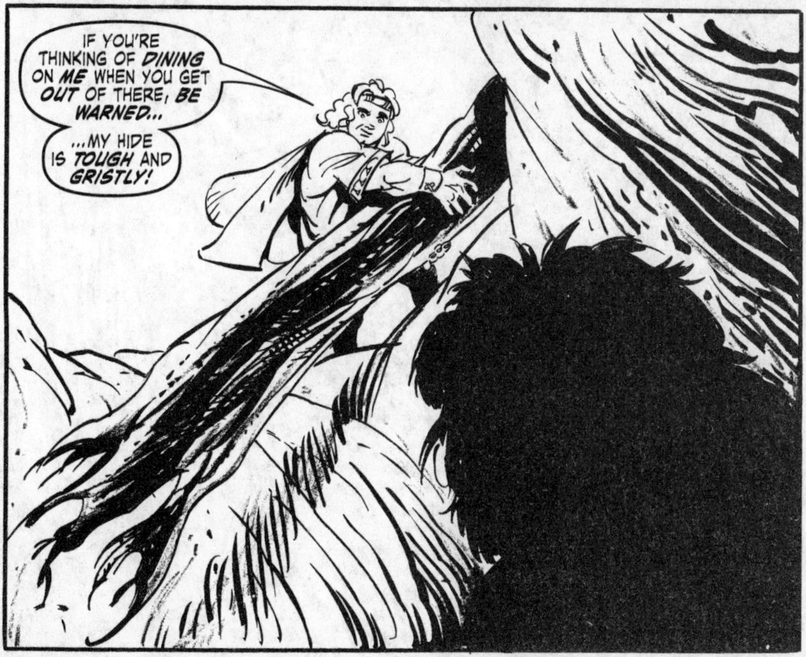
IF YOU'RE THINKING OF DINING ON ME WHEN YOU GET OUT OF THERE, BE WARNED...
...MY HIDE IS TOUGH AND GRISTLY!

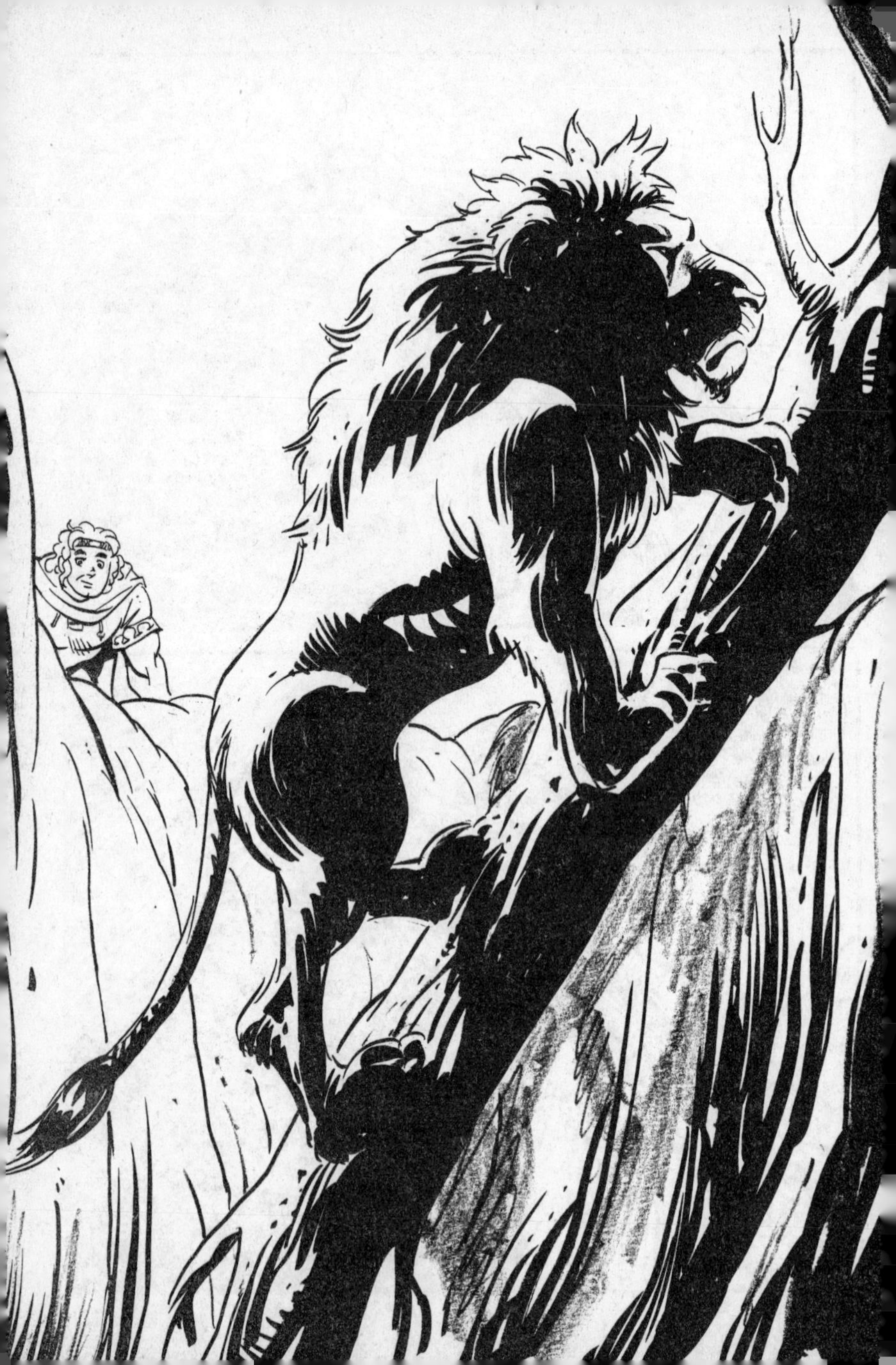

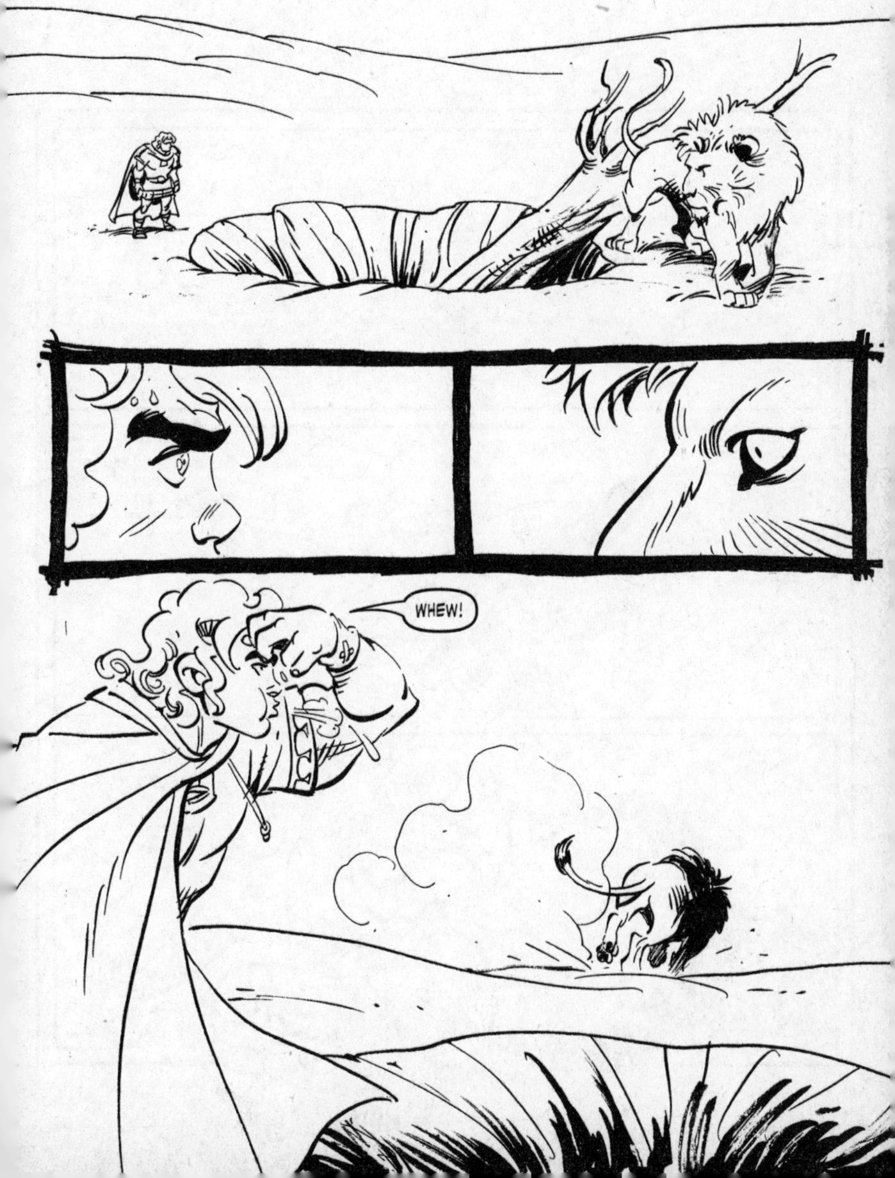
WHEW!

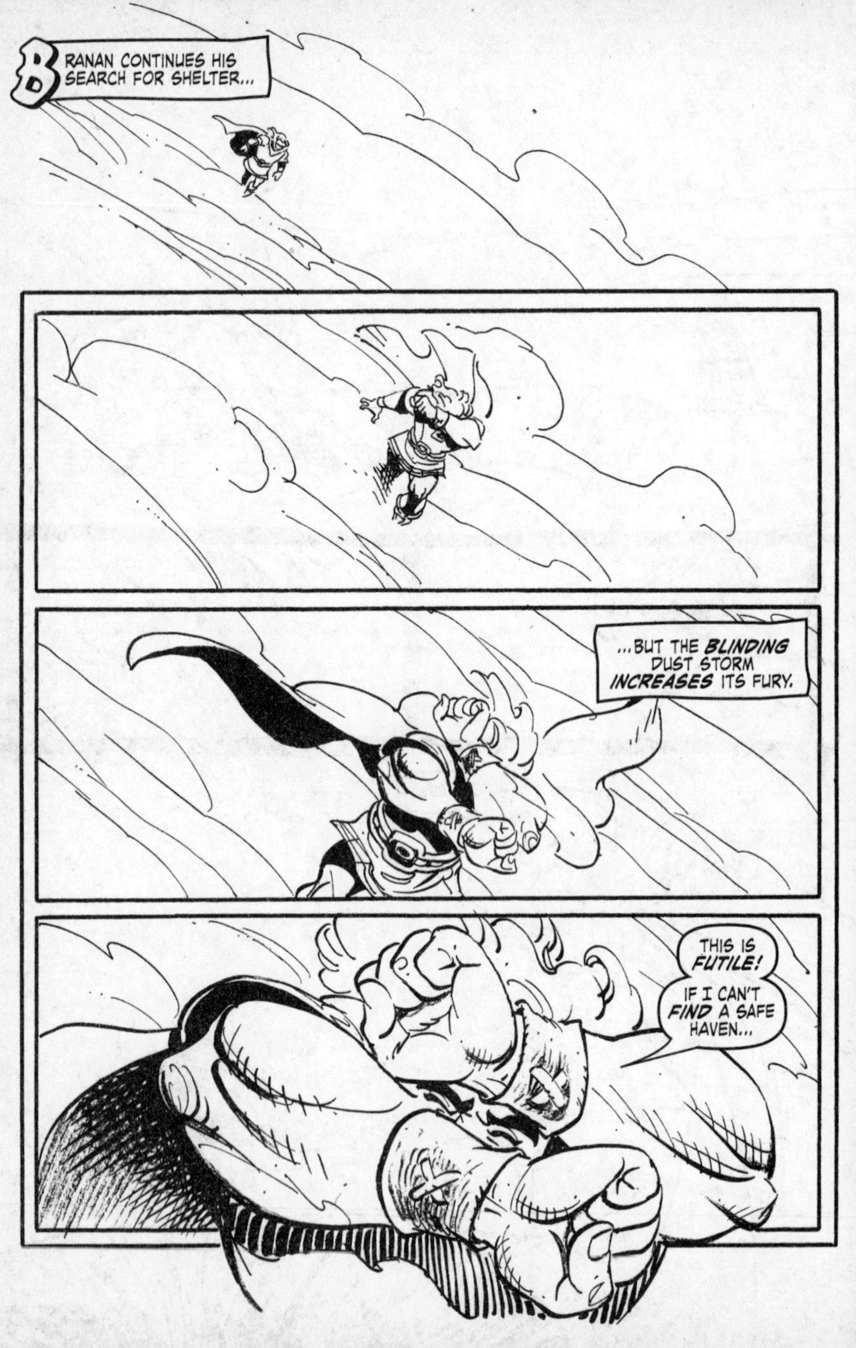
BRANAN CONTINUES HIS SEARCH FOR SHELTER...
...BUT THE *BLINDING* DUST STORM *INCREASES* ITS FURY.
THIS IS *FUTILE!*
IF I CAN'T *FIND* A SAFE HAVEN...

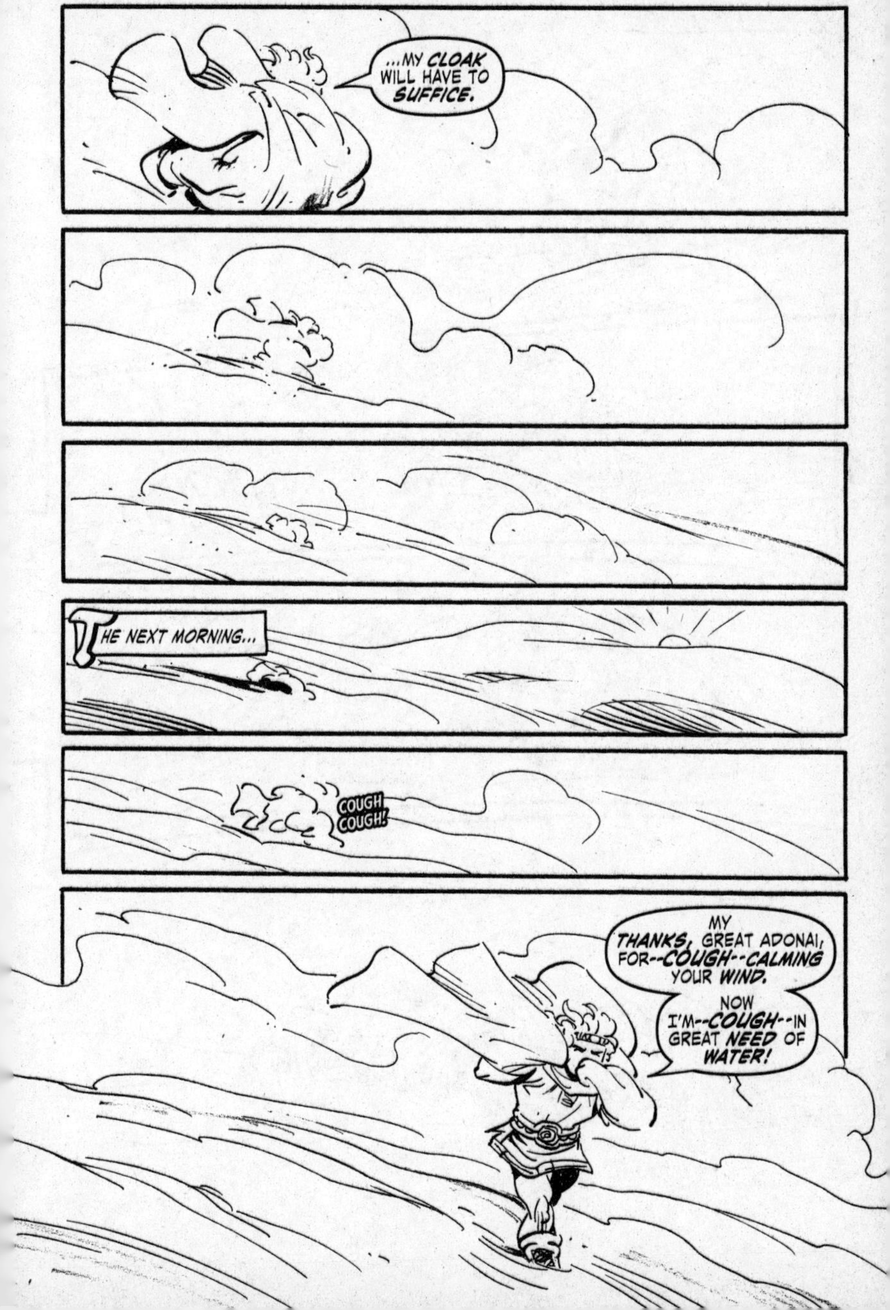
...MY CLOAK WILL HAVE TO SUFFICE.
THE NEXT MORNING...
COUGH COUGH!
MY THANKS, GREAT ADONAI, FOR--COUGH--CALMING YOUR WIND.
NOW I'M--COUGH--IN GREAT NEED OF WATER!

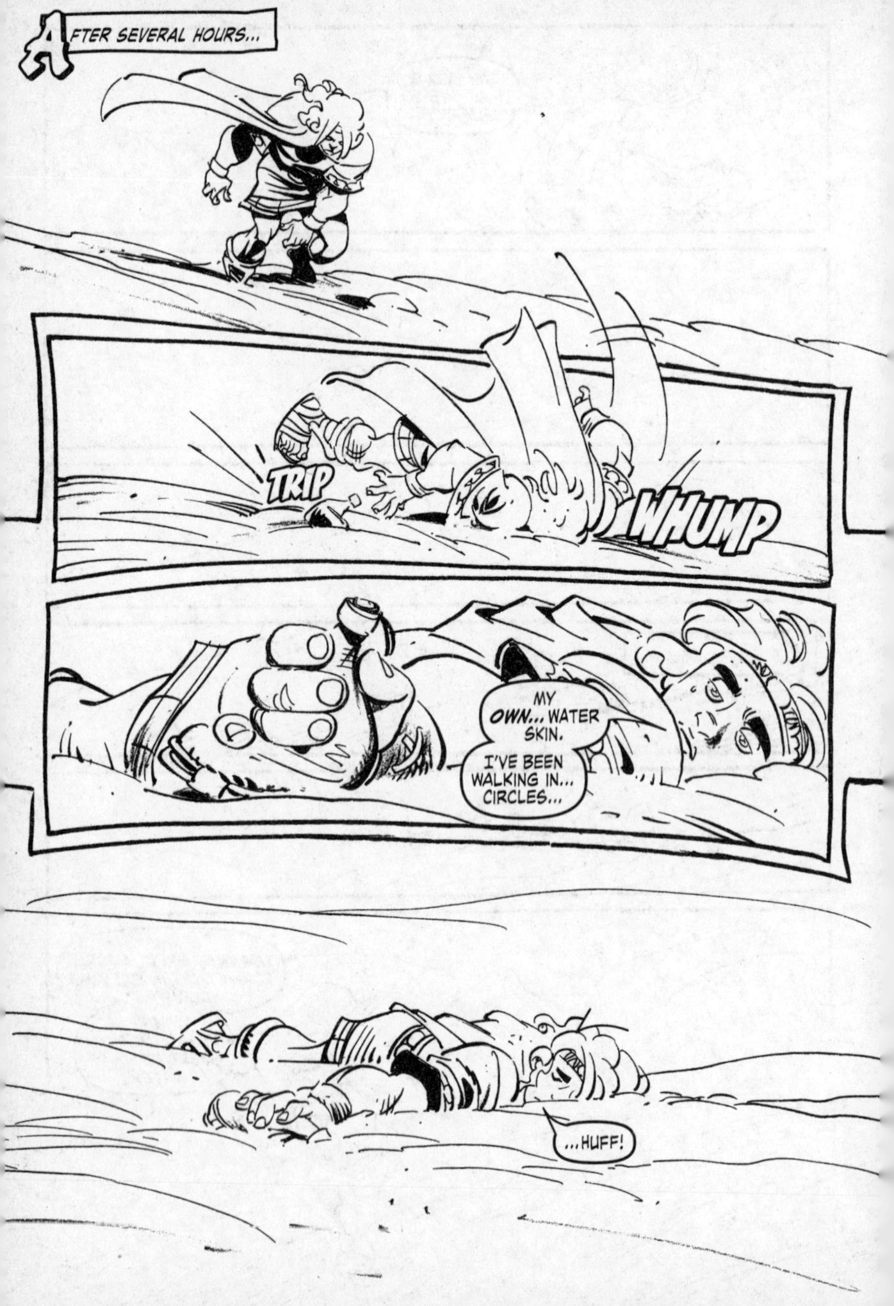
AFTER SEVERAL HOURS...
TRIP
WHUMP
MY OWN... WATER SKIN.
I'VE BEEN WALKING IN... CIRCLES...
...HUFF!

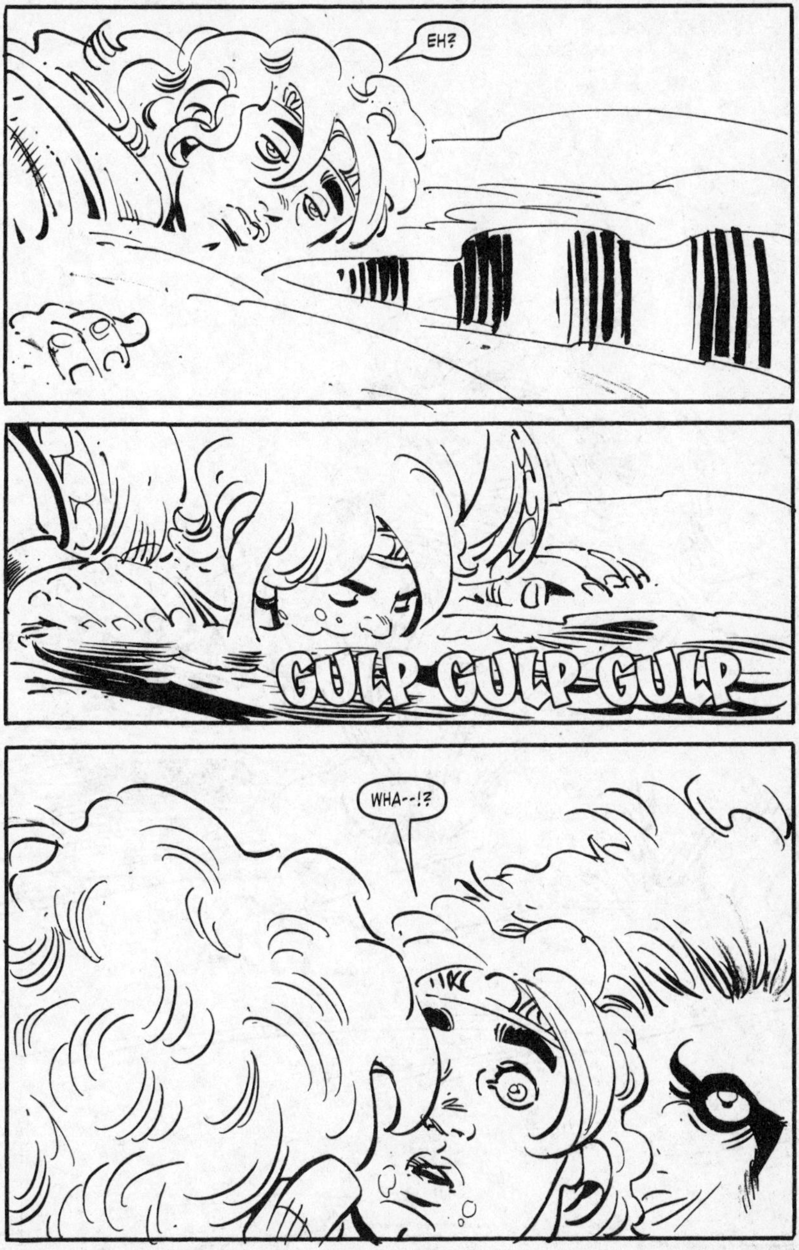
EH?
GULP GULP GULP
WHA--!?

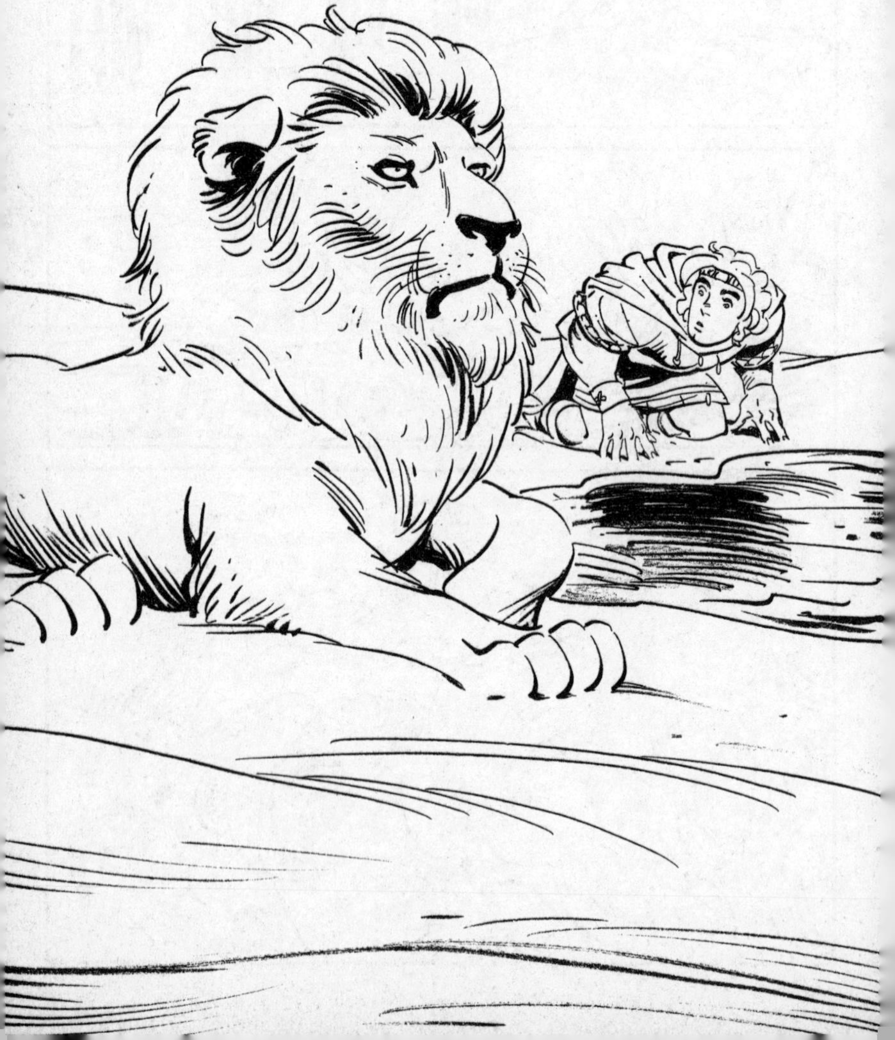

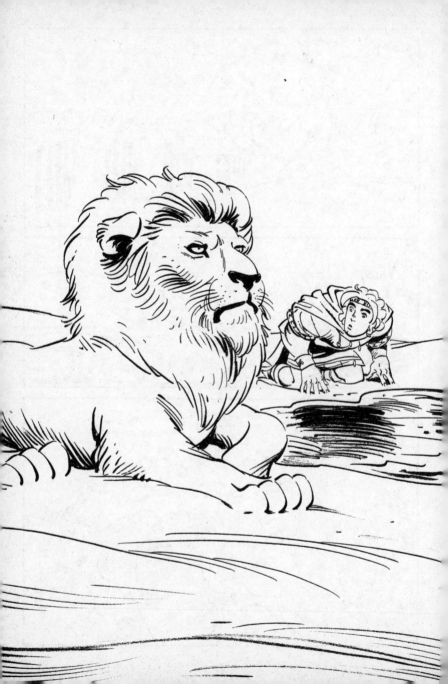

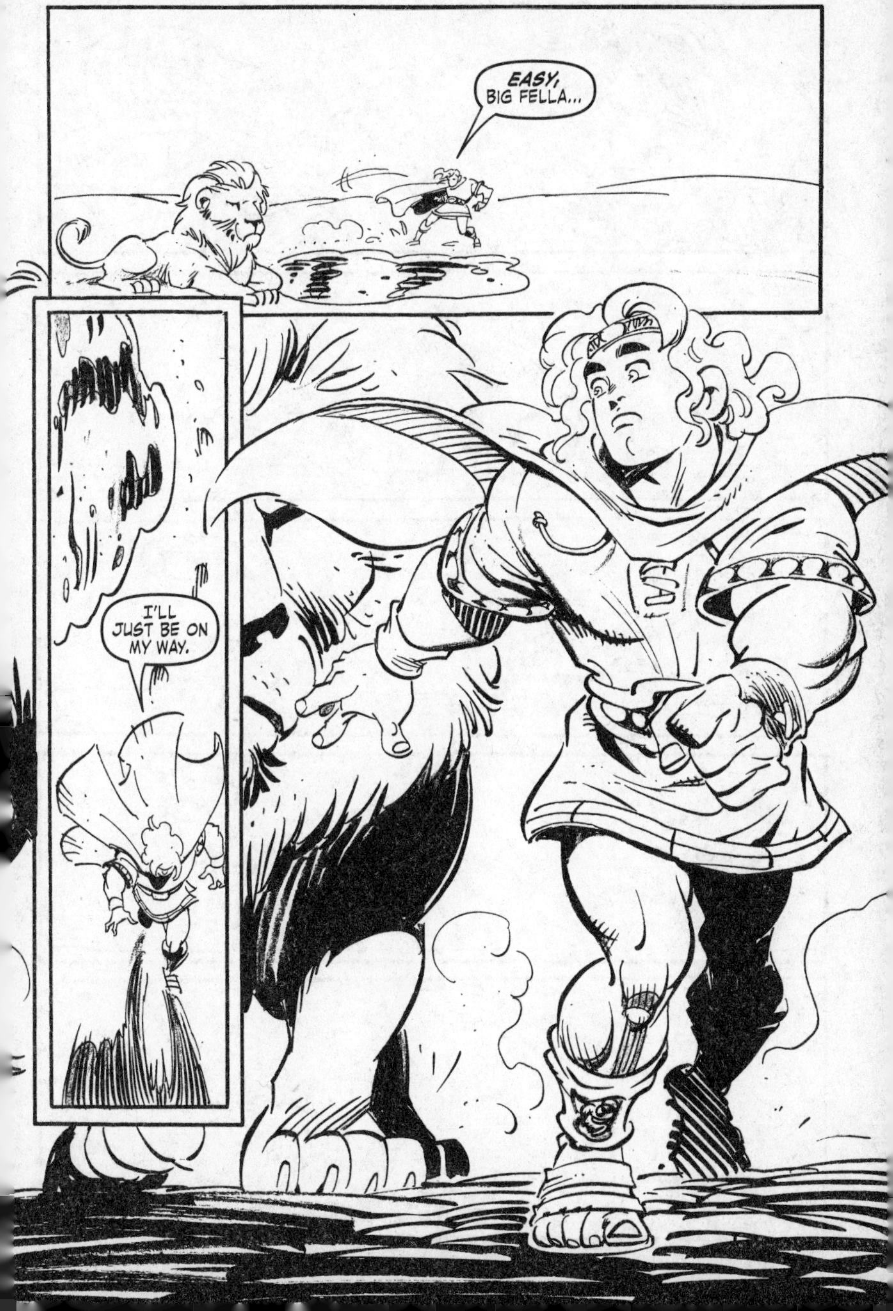
EASY, BIG FELLA...
I'LL JUST BE ON MY WAY.

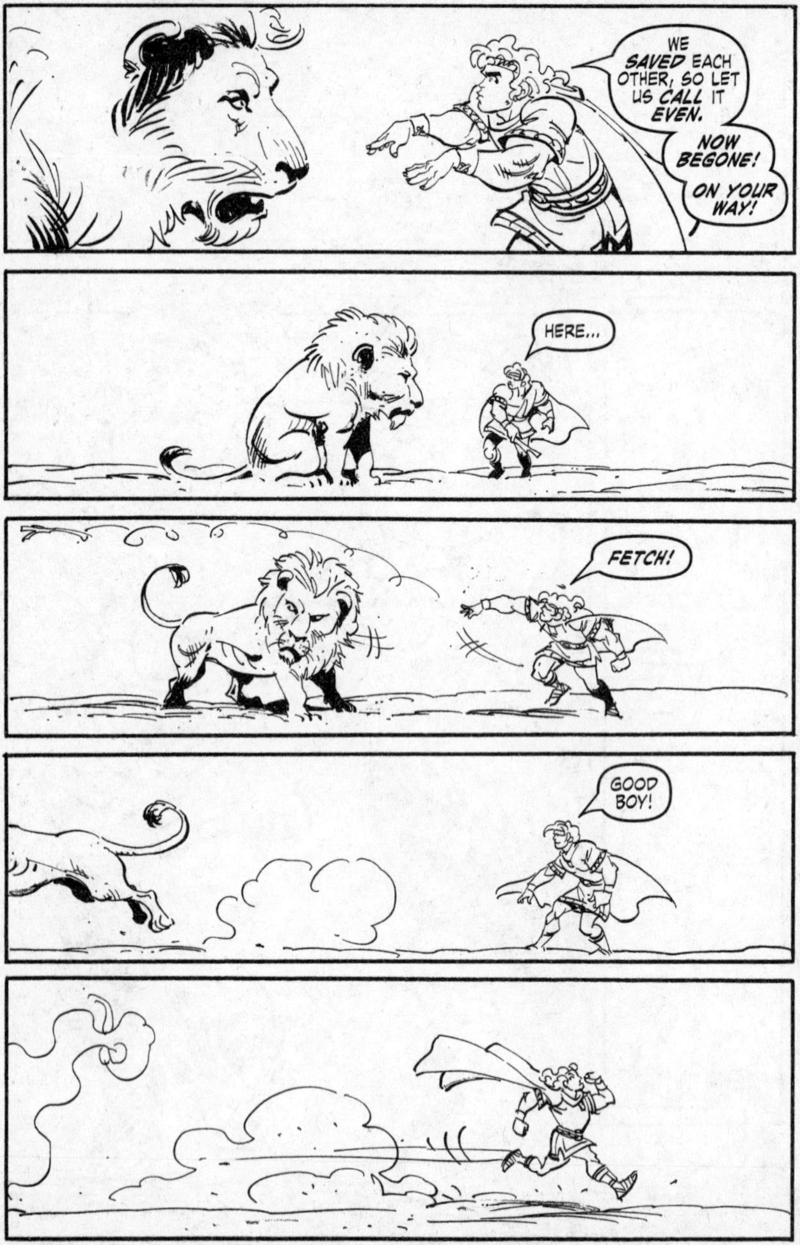
WE SAVED EACH OTHER, SO LET US CALL IT EVEN.
NOW BEGONE!
ON YOUR WAY!
HERE...
FETCH!
GOOD BOY!

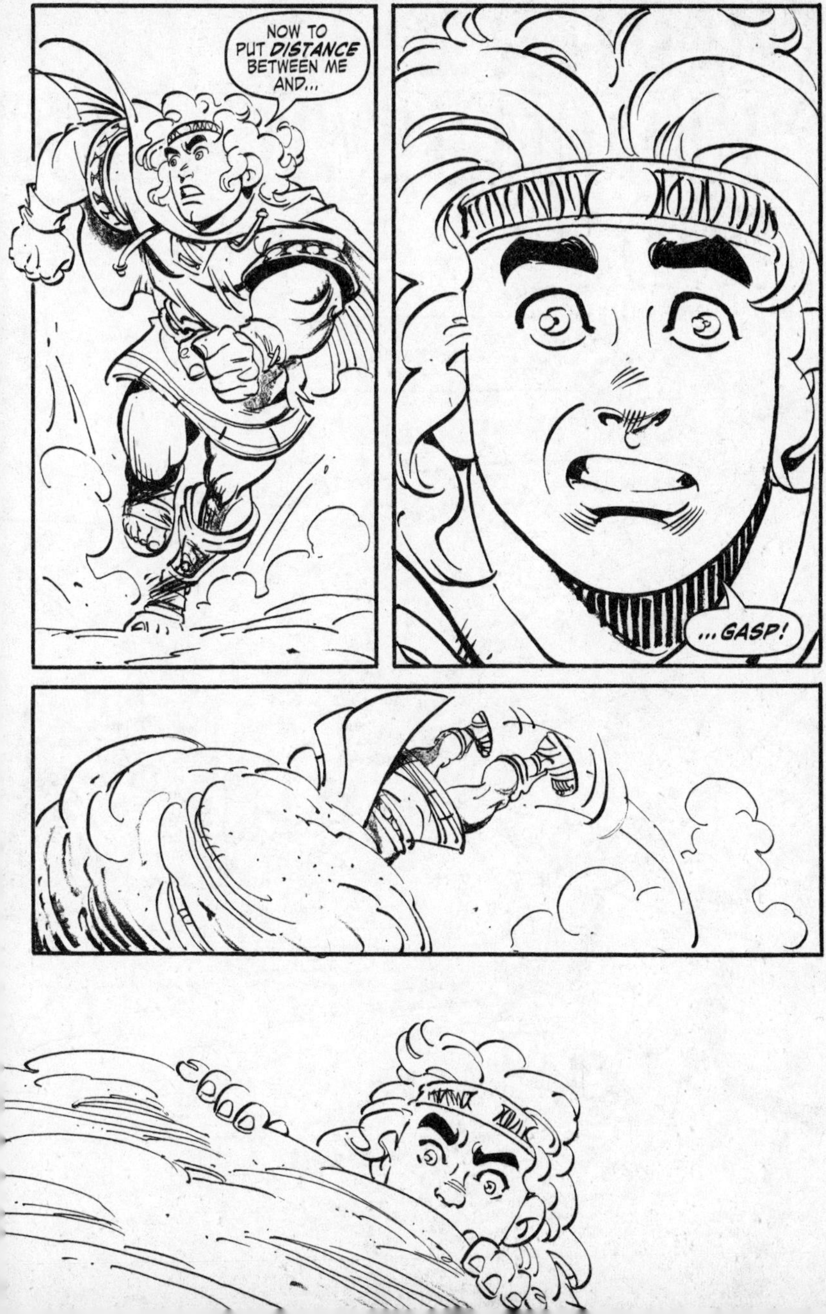
NOW TO PUT DISTANCE BETWEEN ME AND...
...GASP!

CHAPTER 2
"PLOTTING AGAINST GOD"

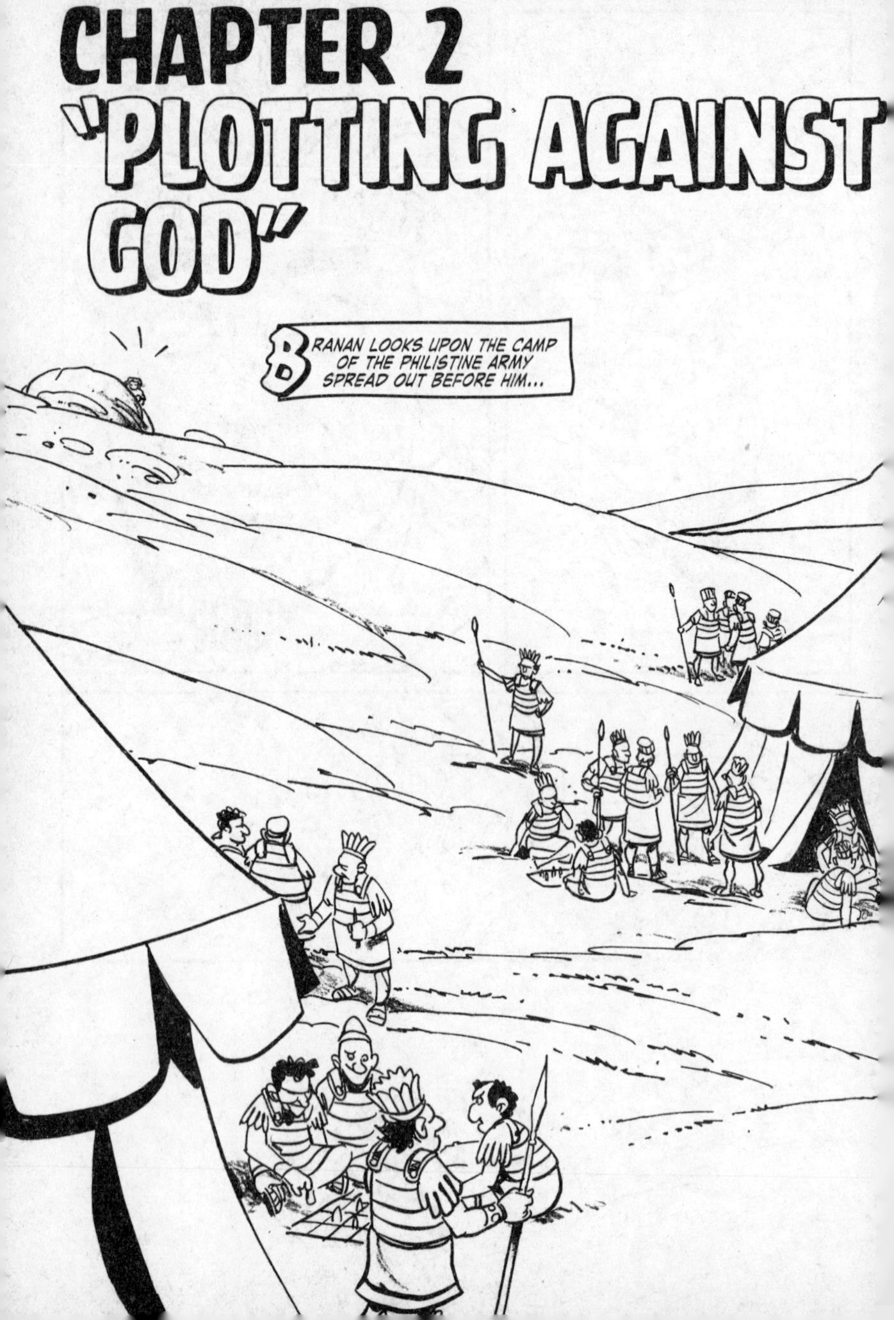
BRANAN LOOKS UPON THE CAMP OF THE PHILISTINE ARMY SPREAD OUT BEFORE HIM...

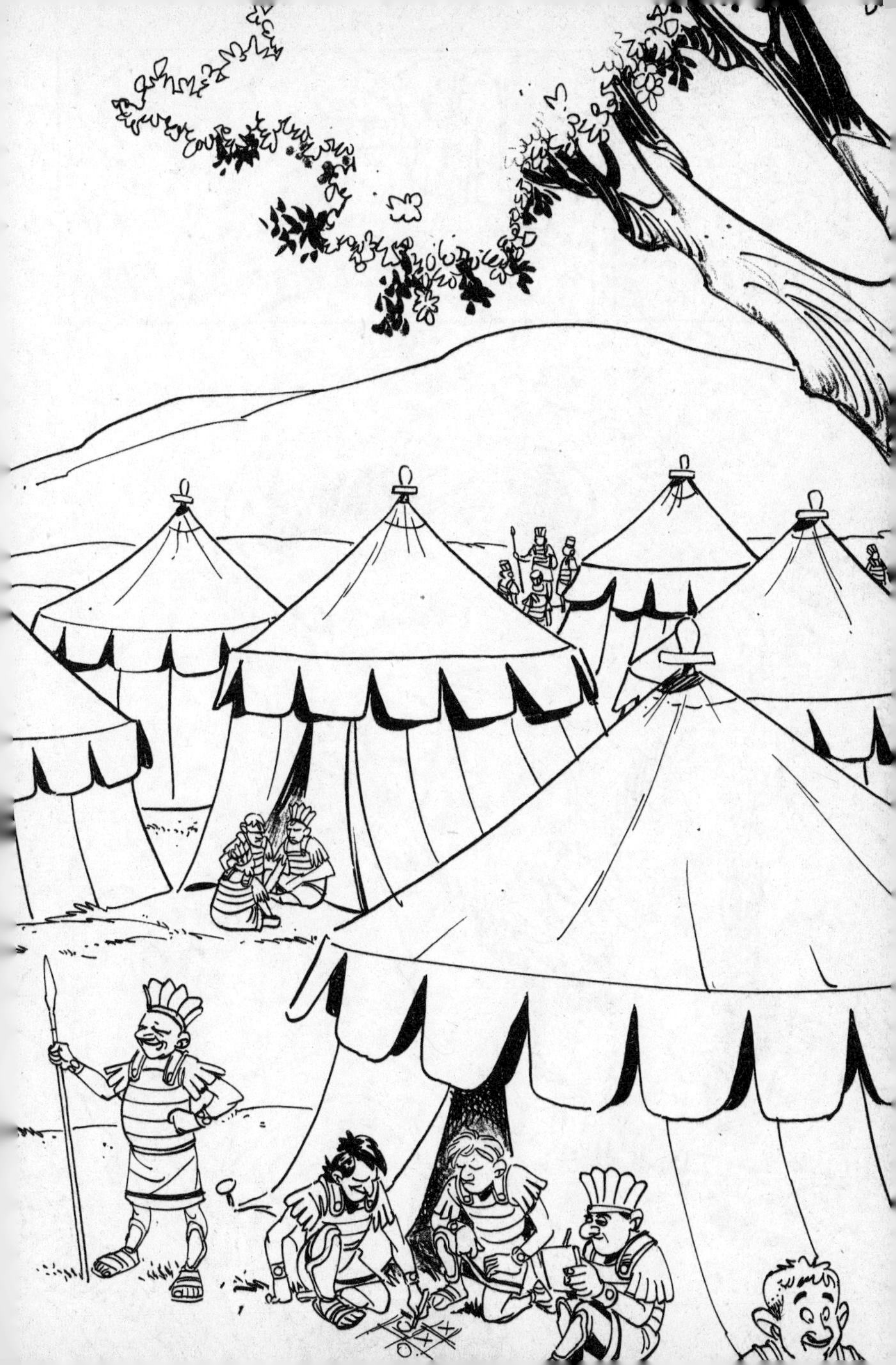

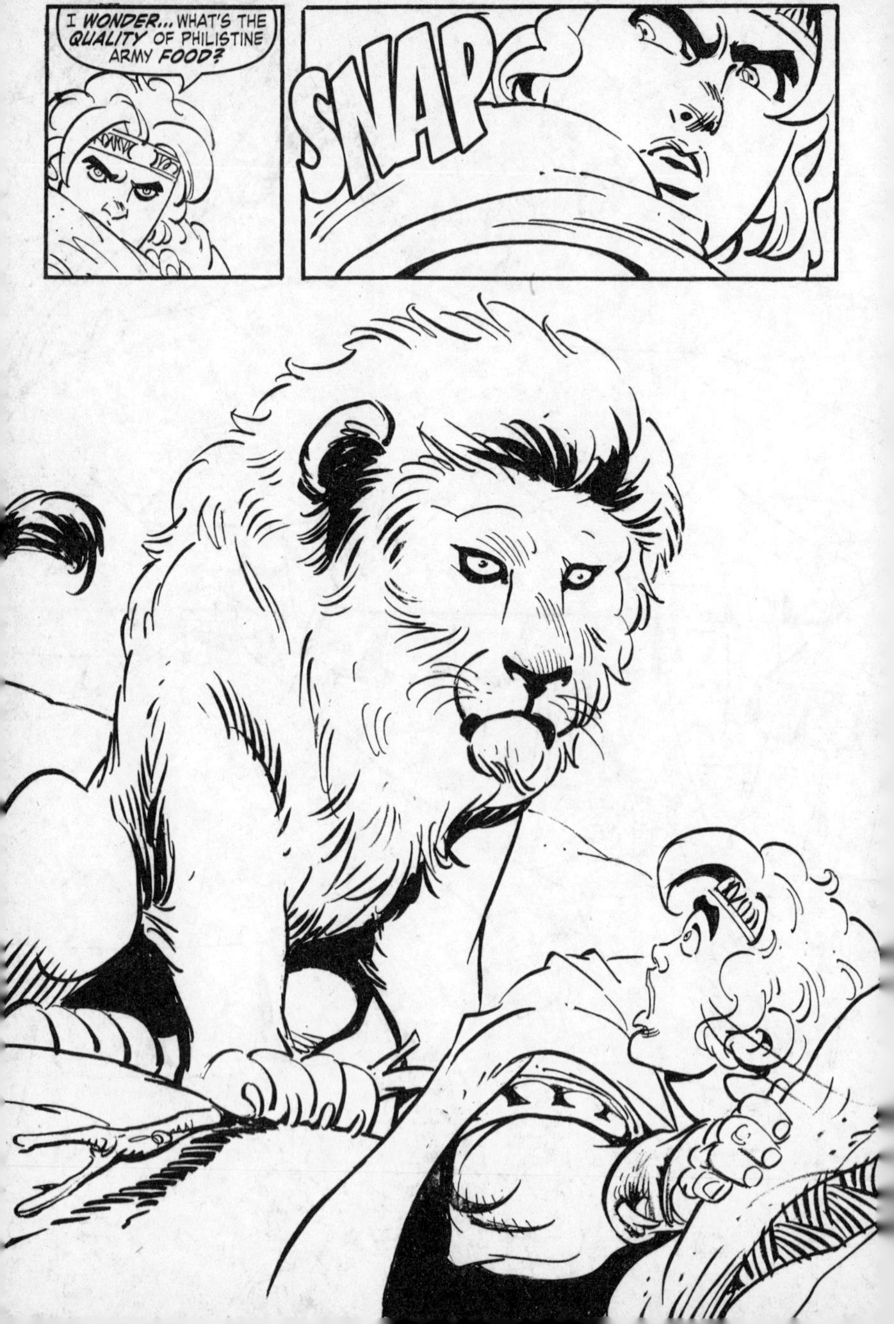
I WONDER... WHAT'S THE QUALITY OF PHILISTINE ARMY FOOD?
SNAP

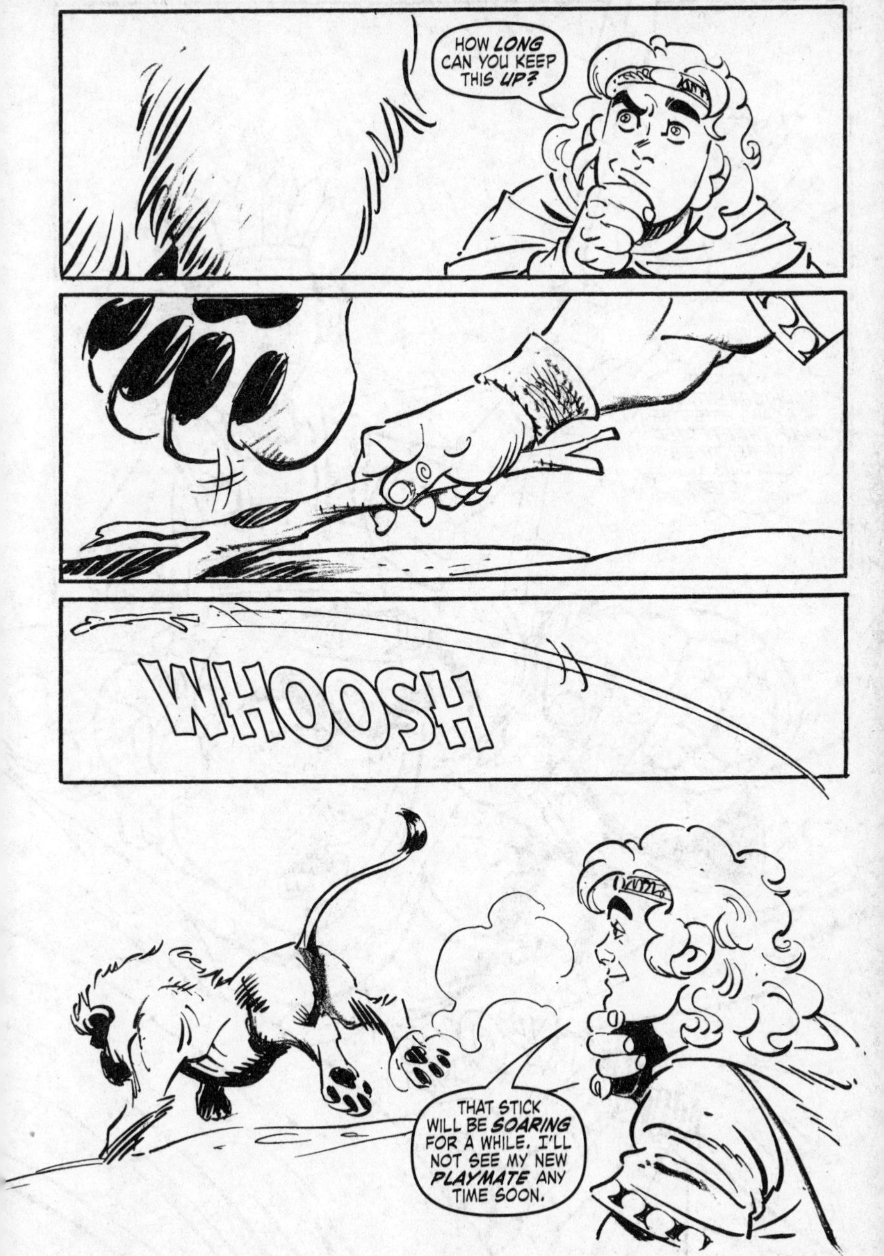
HOW LONG CAN YOU KEEP THIS UP?
WHOOSH
THAT STICK WILL BE SOARING FOR A WHILE. I'LL NOT SEE MY NEW PLAYMATE ANY TIME SOON.

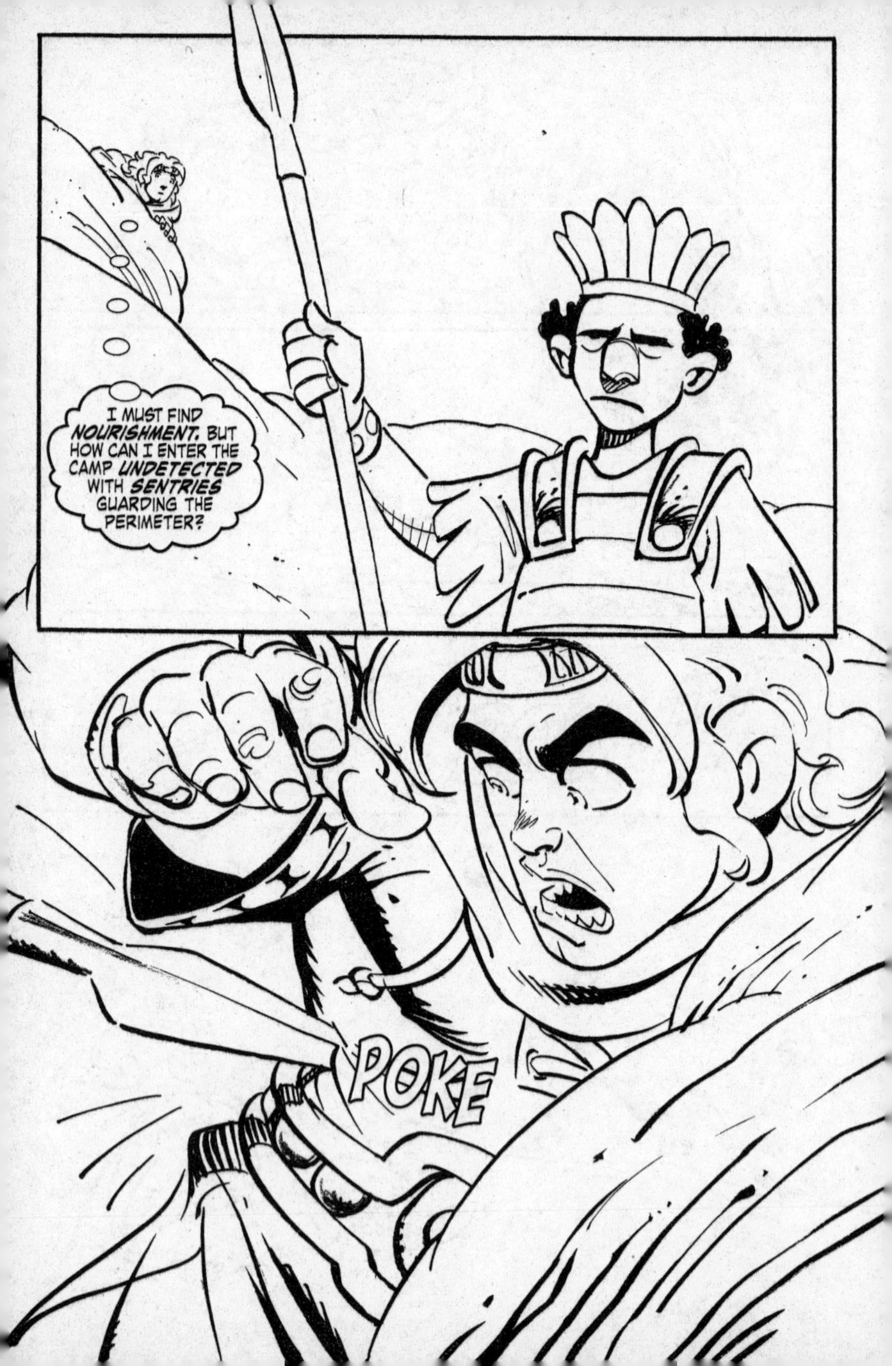
I MUST FIND NOURISHMENT. BUT HOW CAN I ENTER THE CAMP UNDETECTED WITH SENTRIES GUARDING THE PERIMETER?
POKE

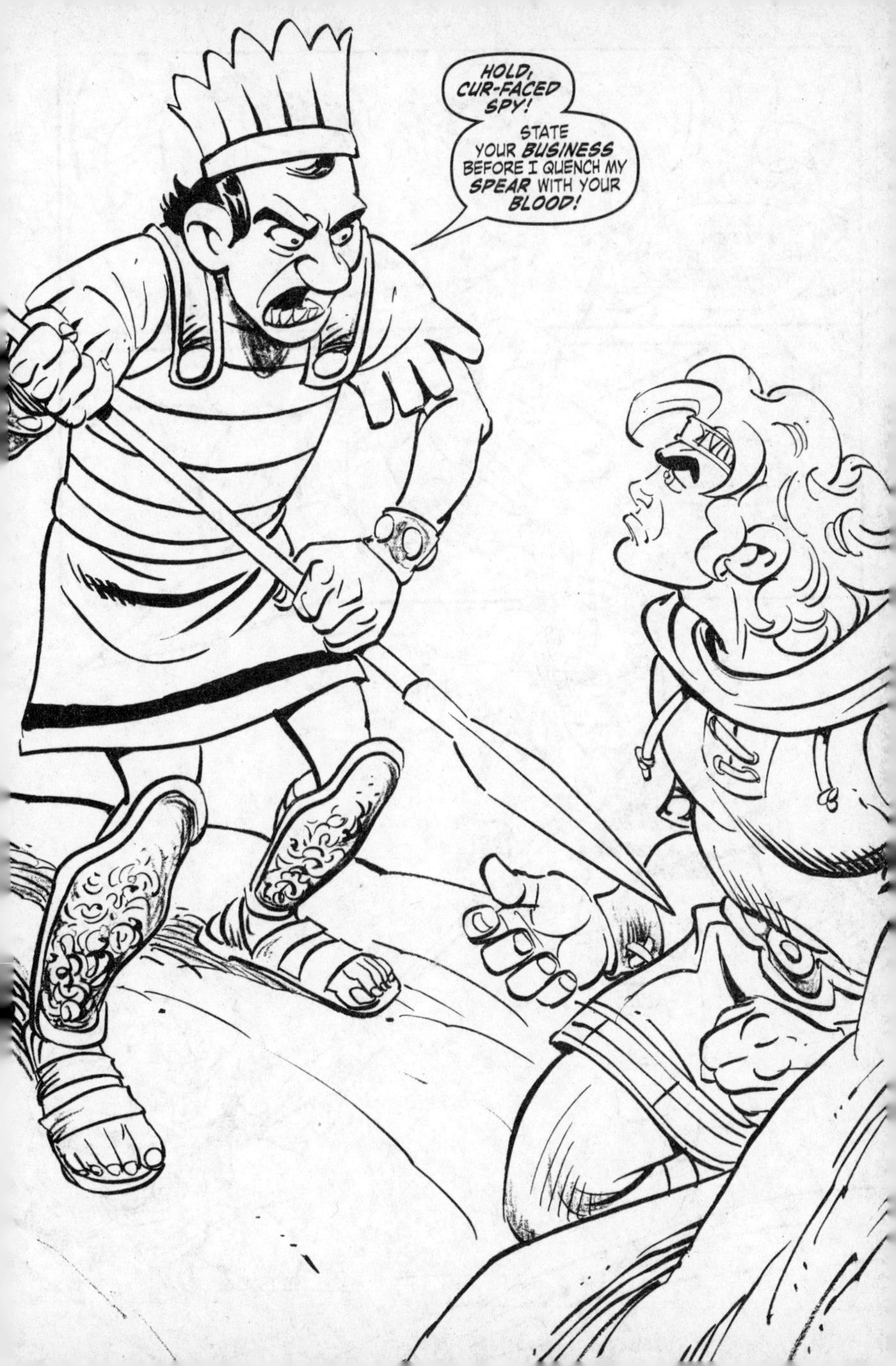
HOLD, CUR-FACED SPY!
STATE YOUR BUSINESS BEFORE I QUENCH MY SPEAR WITH YOUR BLOOD!

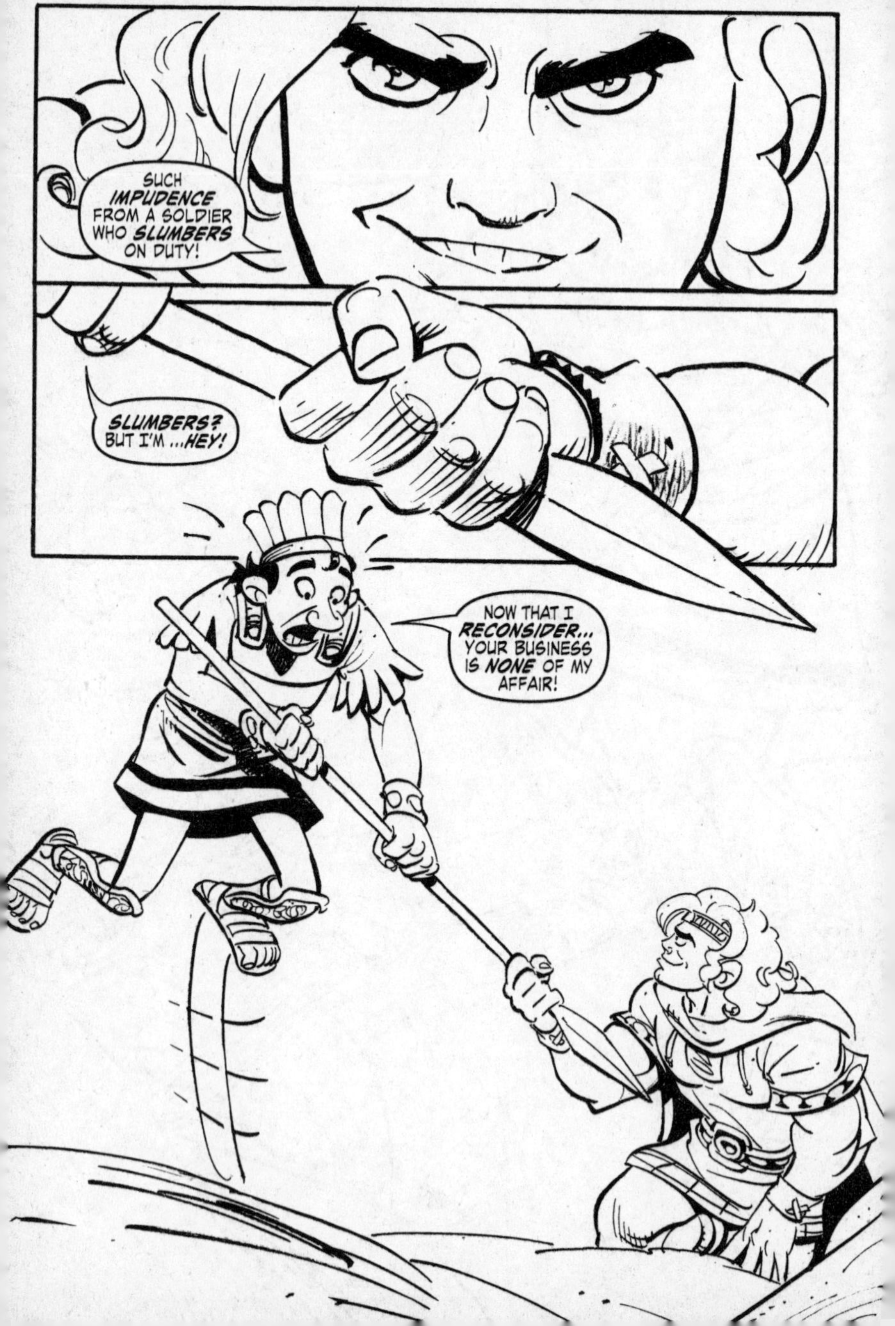
SUCH IMPUDENCE FROM A SOLDIER WHO SLUMBERS ON DUTY!
SLUMBERS? BUT I'M ...HEY!
NOW THAT I RECONSIDER... YOUR BUSINESS IS NONE OF MY AFFAIR!

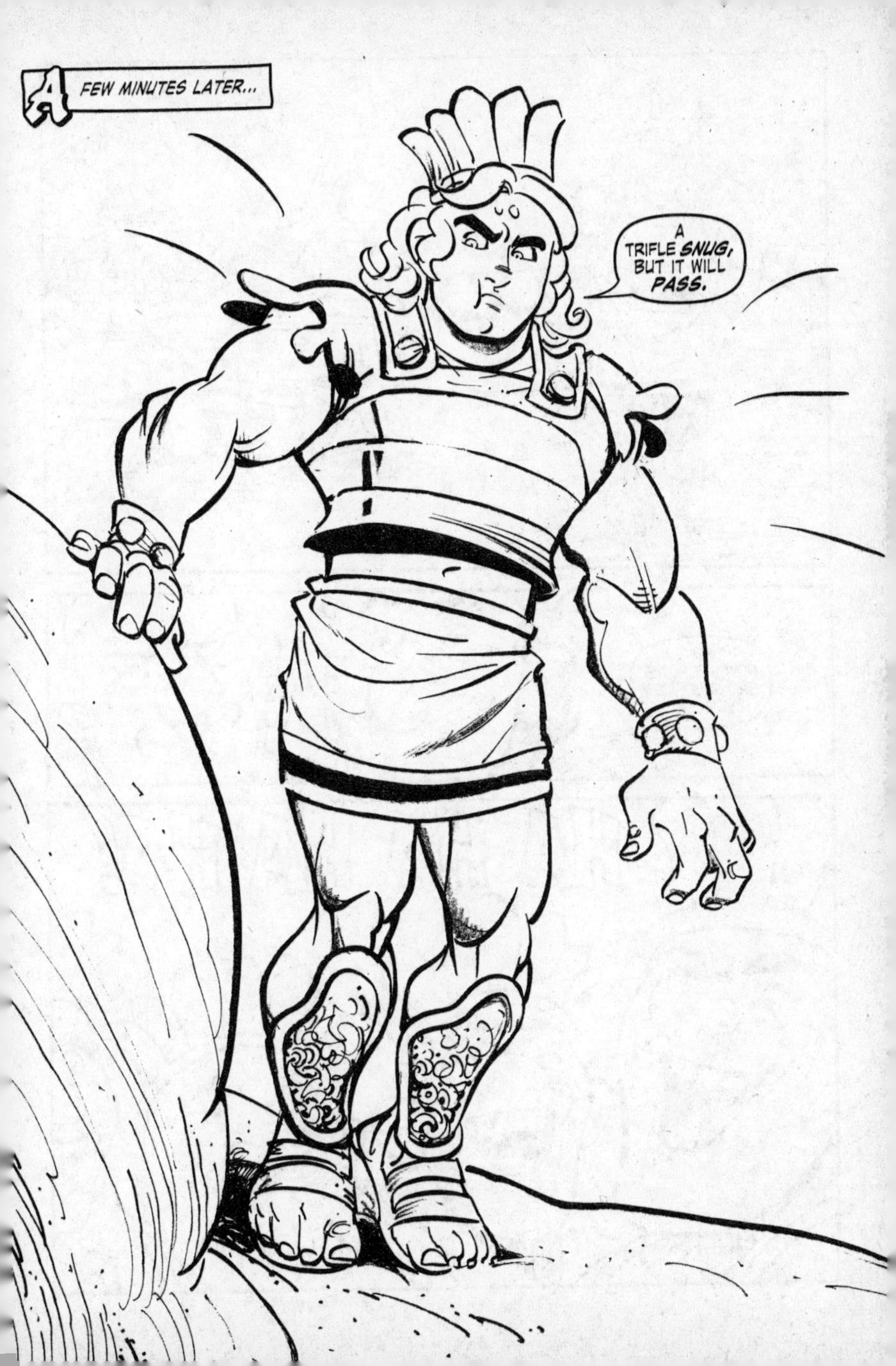
A FEW MINUTES LATER...
A TRIFLE SNUG, BUT IT WILL PASS.

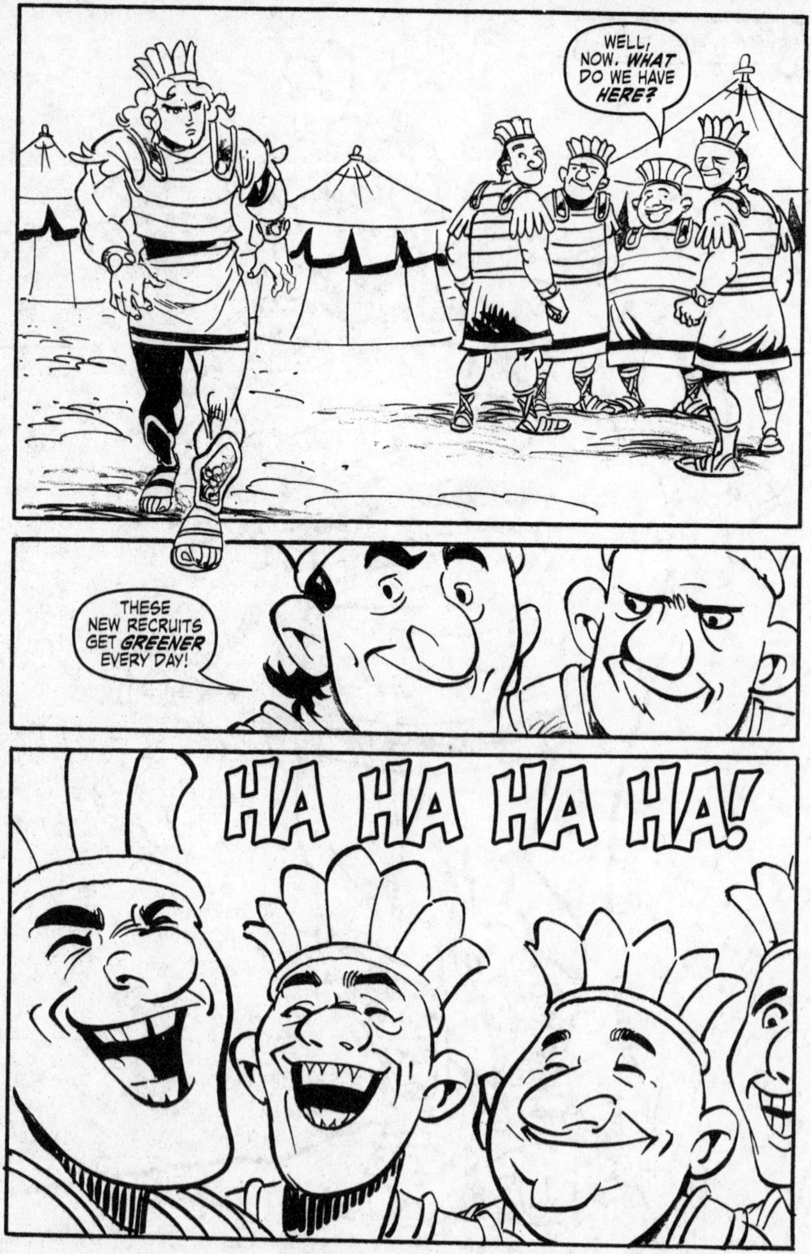
WELL, NOW. WHAT DO WE HAVE HERE?
THESE NEW RECRUITS GET GREENER EVERY DAY!
HA HA HA HA!

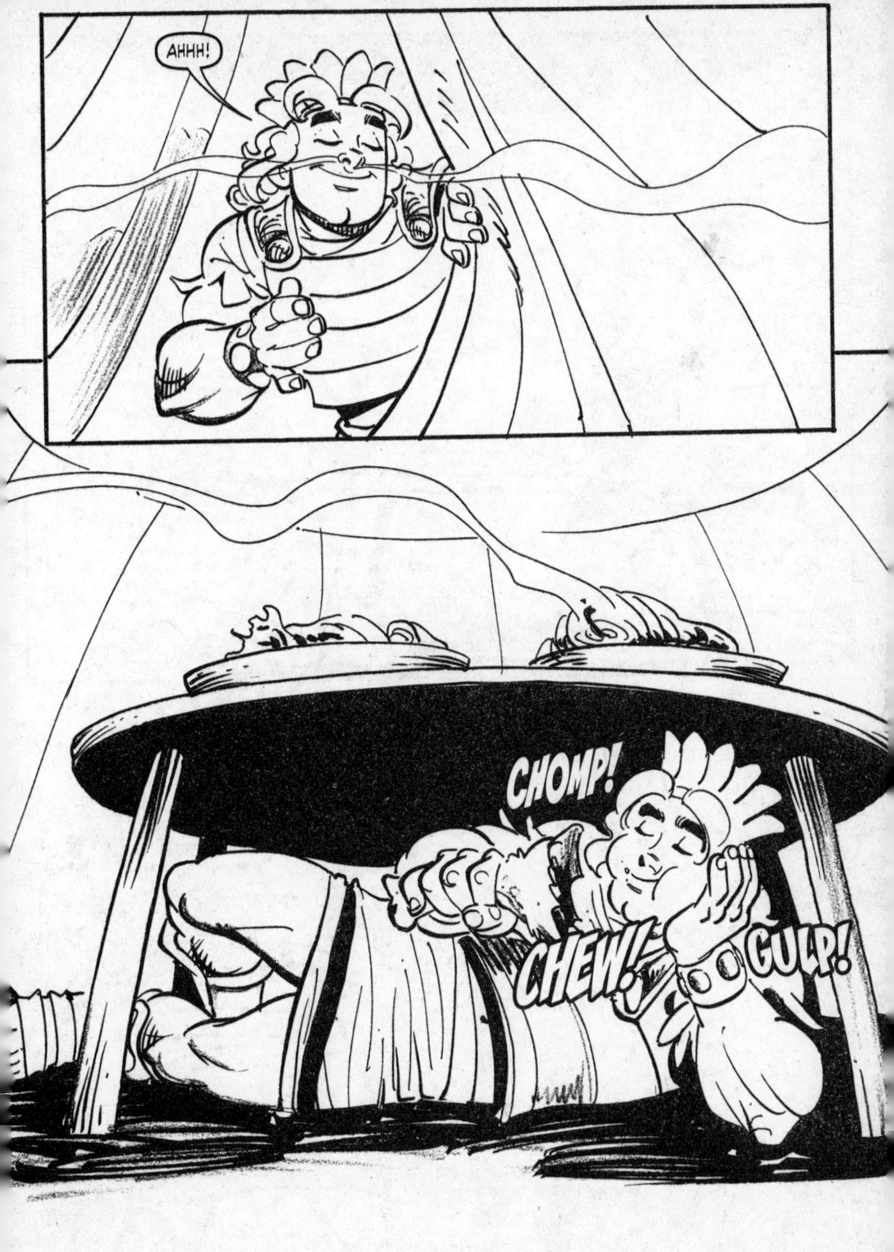
AHHH!
CHOMP!
CHEW!
GULP!

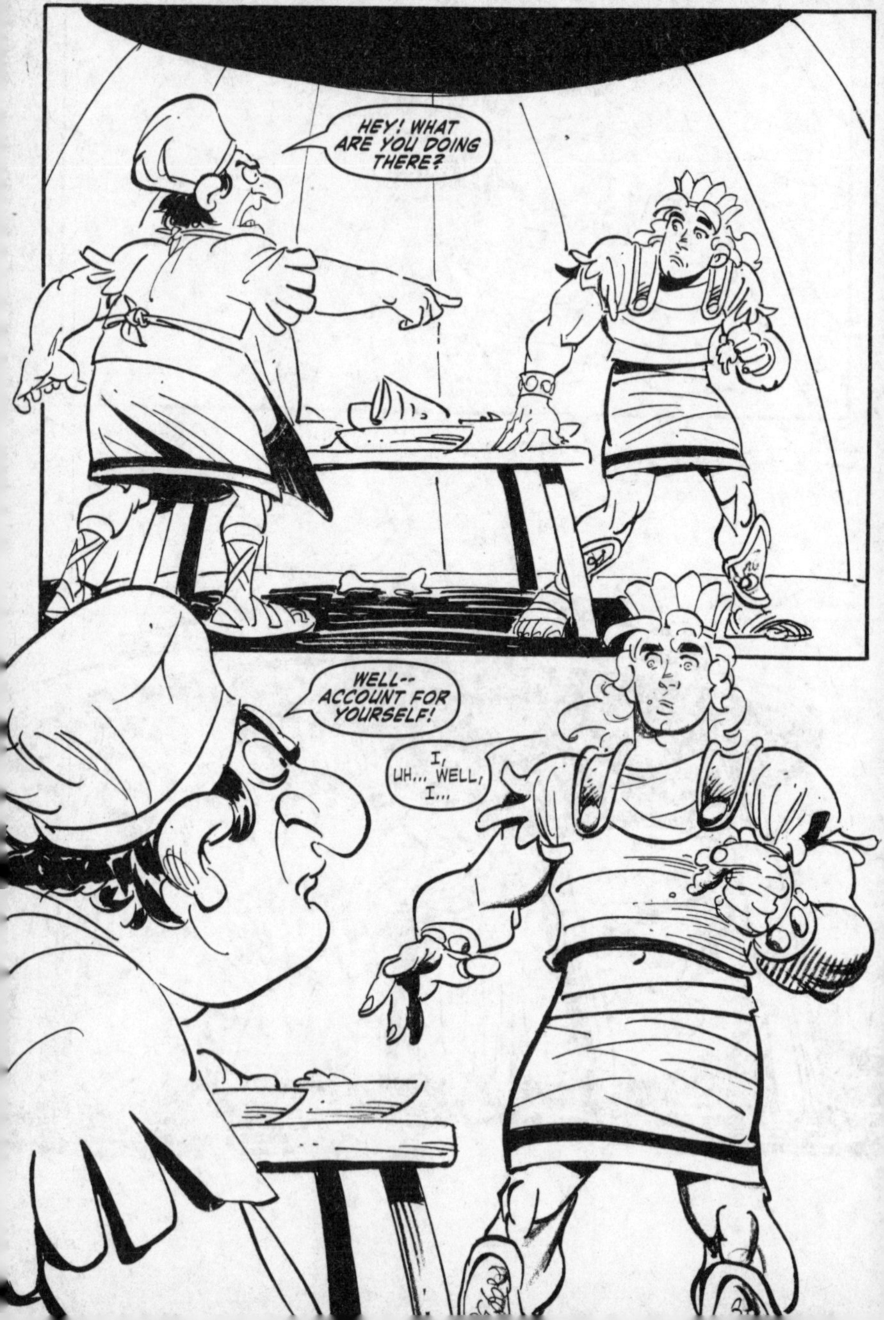
HEY! WHAT ARE YOU DOING THERE?
WELL-- ACCOUNT FOR YOURSELF!
I, UH... WELL, I...

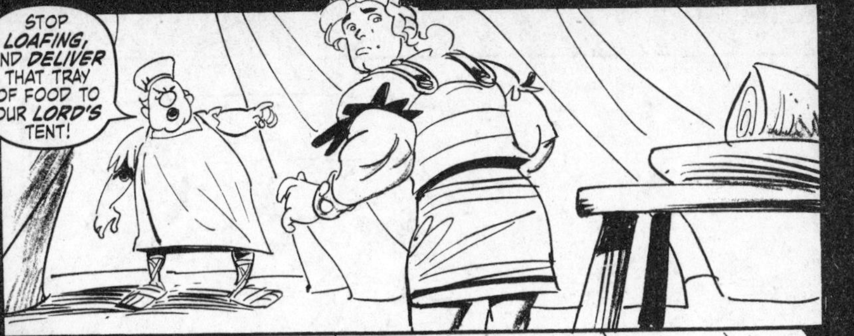
STOP LOAFING, AND DELIVER THAT TRAY OF FOOD TO OUR LORD'S TENT!

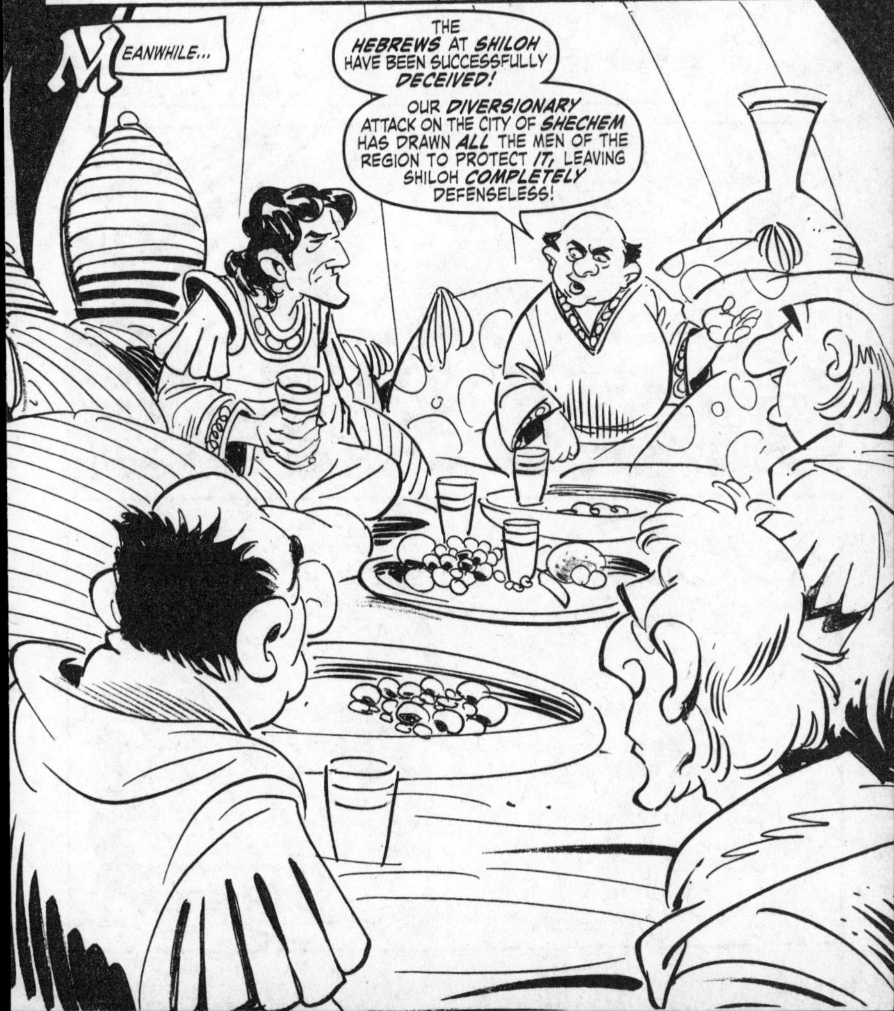
MEANWHILE...
THE HEBREWS AT SHILOH HAVE BEEN SUCCESSFULLY DECEIVED!
OUR DIVERSIONARY ATTACK ON THE CITY OF SHECHEM HAS DRAWN ALL THE MEN OF THE REGION TO PROTECT IT, LEAVING SHILOH COMPLETELY DEFENSELESS!

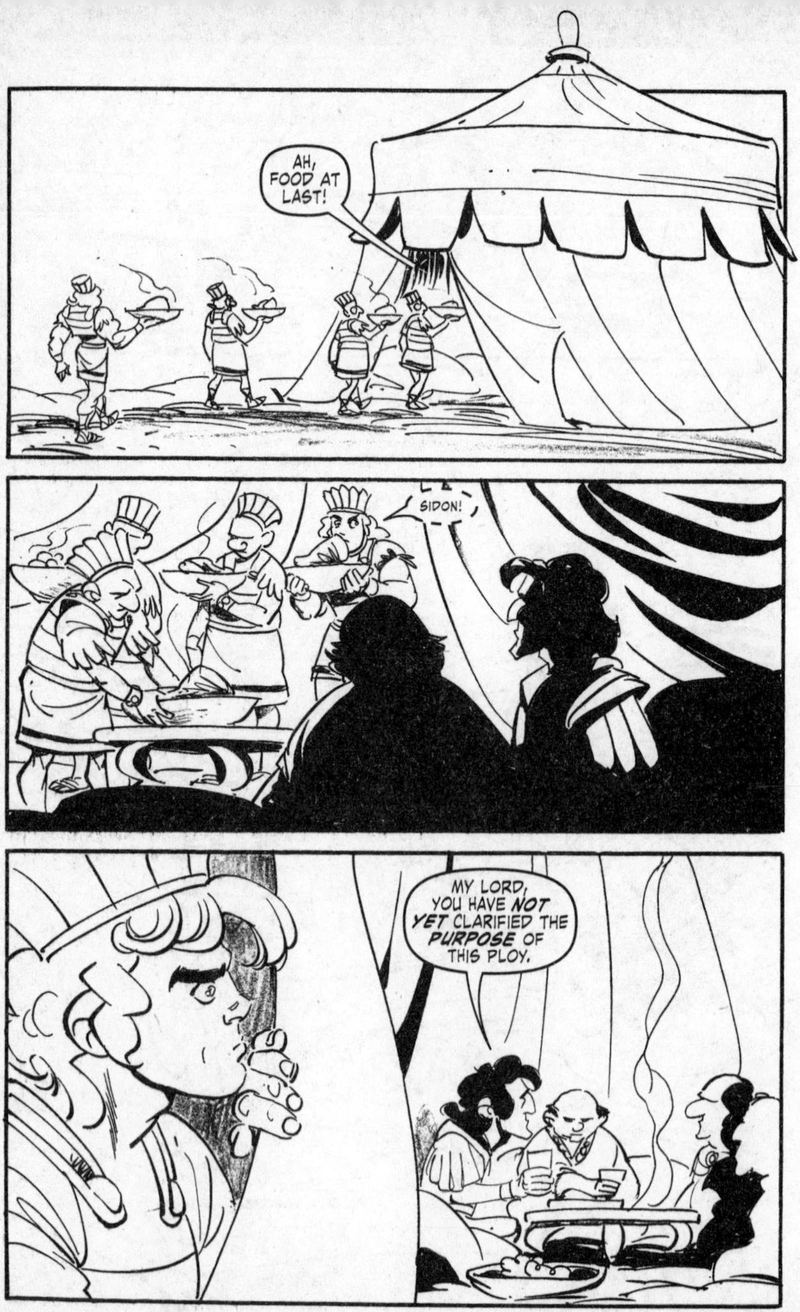
AH, FOOD AT LAST!
SIDON!
MY LORD, YOU HAVE *NOT YET* CLARIFIED THE *PURPOSE* OF THIS PLOY.

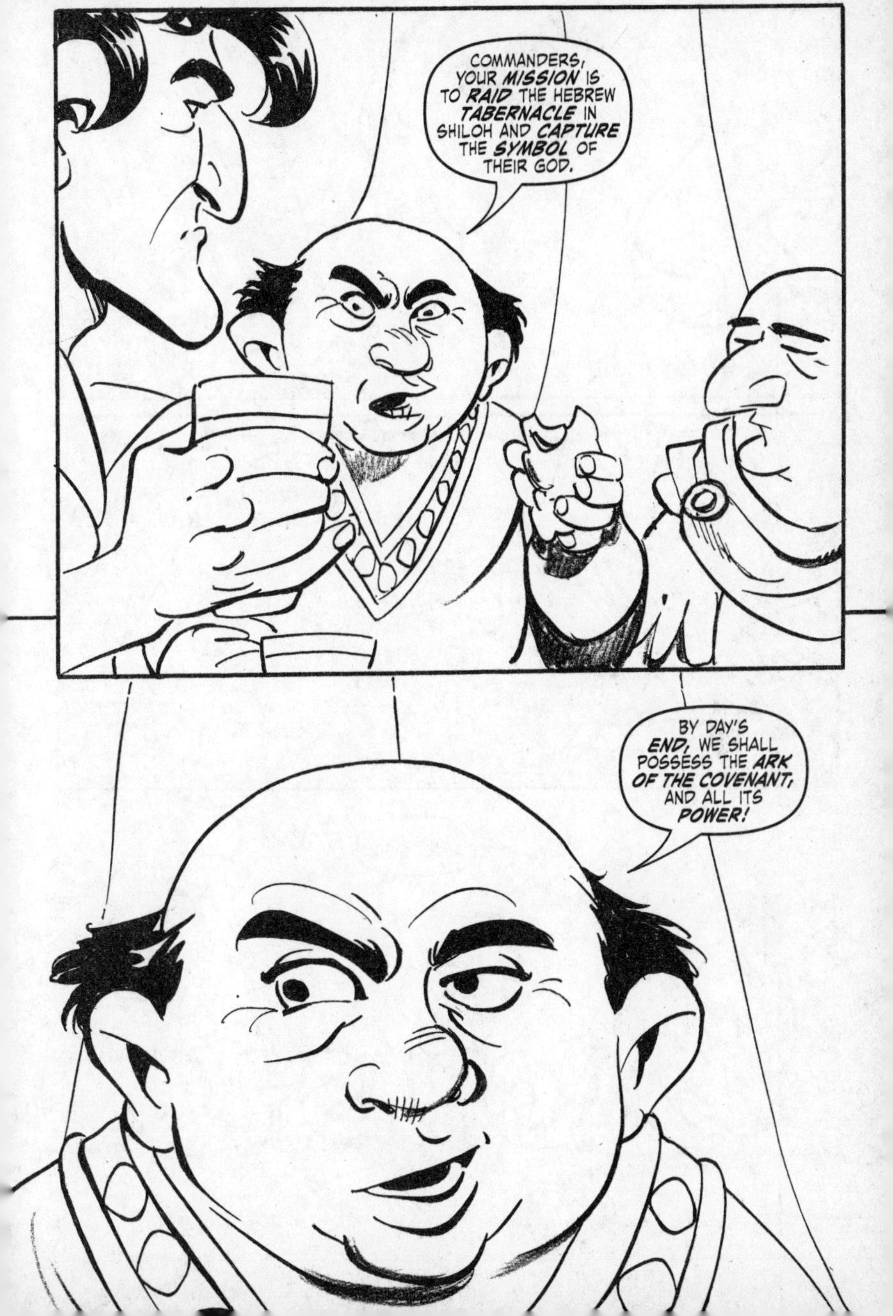
COMMANDERS, YOUR MISSION IS TO RAID THE HEBREW TABERNACLE IN SHILOH AND CAPTURE THE SYMBOL OF THEIR GOD.
BY DAY'S END, WE SHALL POSSESS THE ARK OF THE COVENANT, AND ALL ITS POWER!

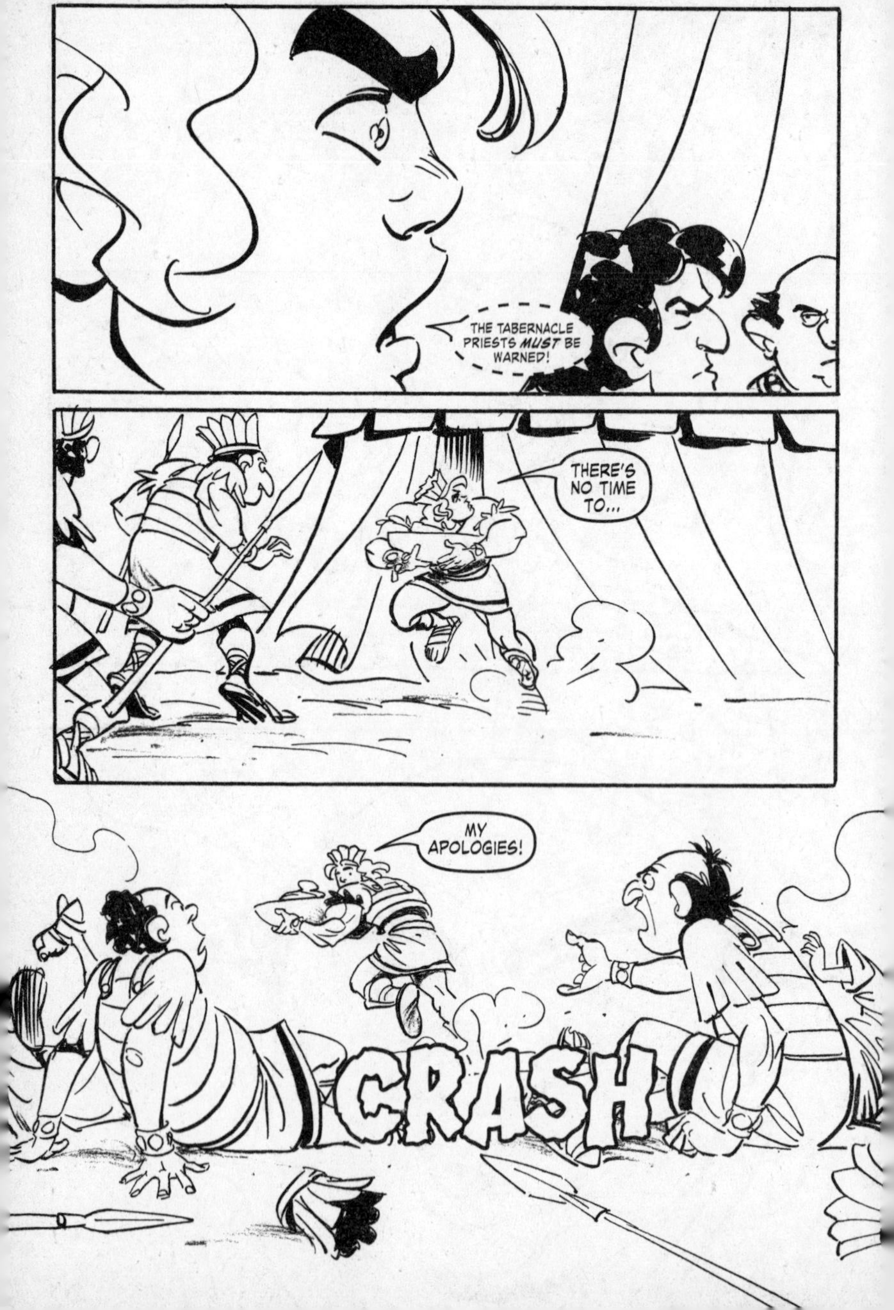
THE TABERNACLE PRIESTS *MUST* BE WARNED!
THERE'S NO TIME TO...
MY APOLOGIES!
CRASH

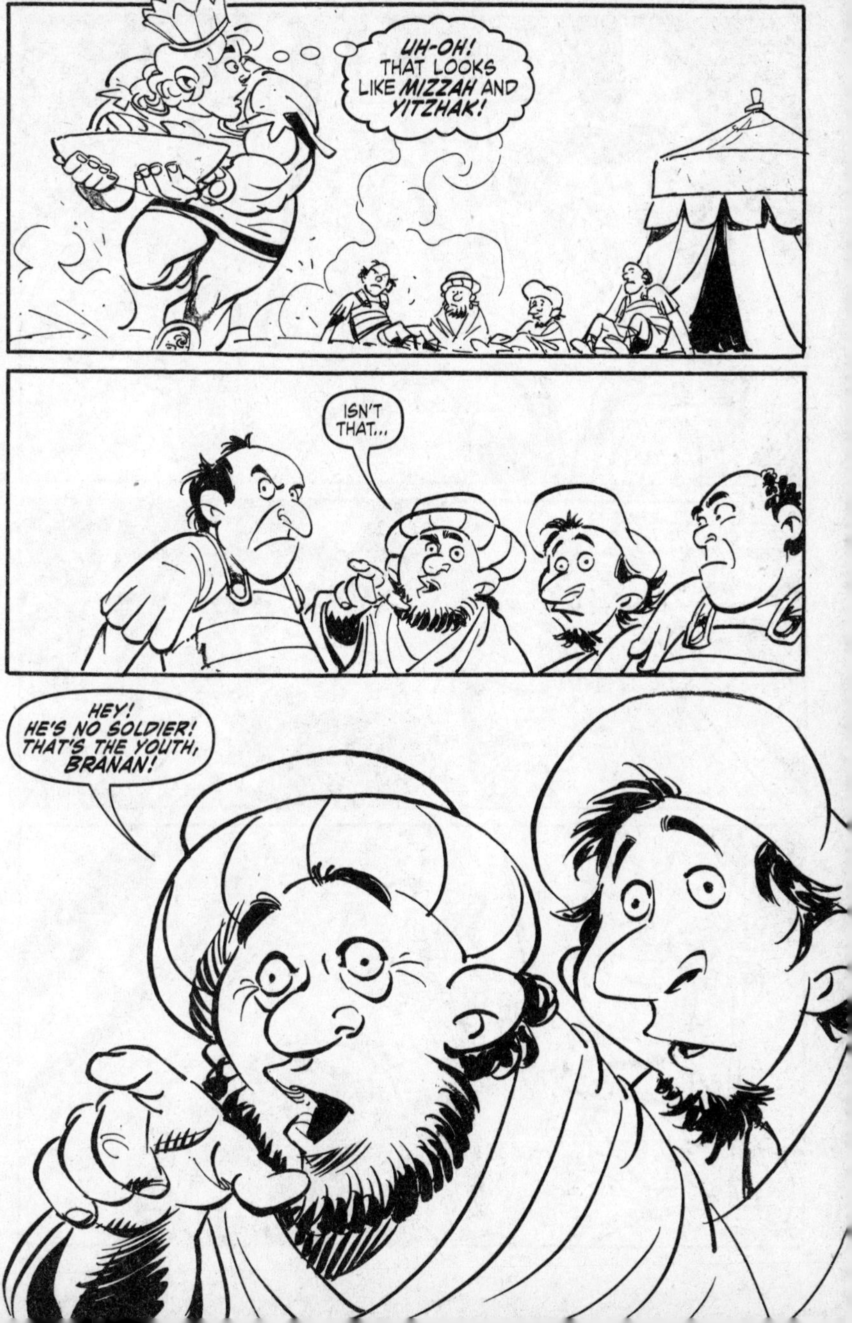
UH-OH! THAT LOOKS LIKE MIZZAH AND YITZHAK!
ISN'T THAT...
HEY! HE'S NO SOLDIER! THAT'S THE YOUTH, BRANAN!

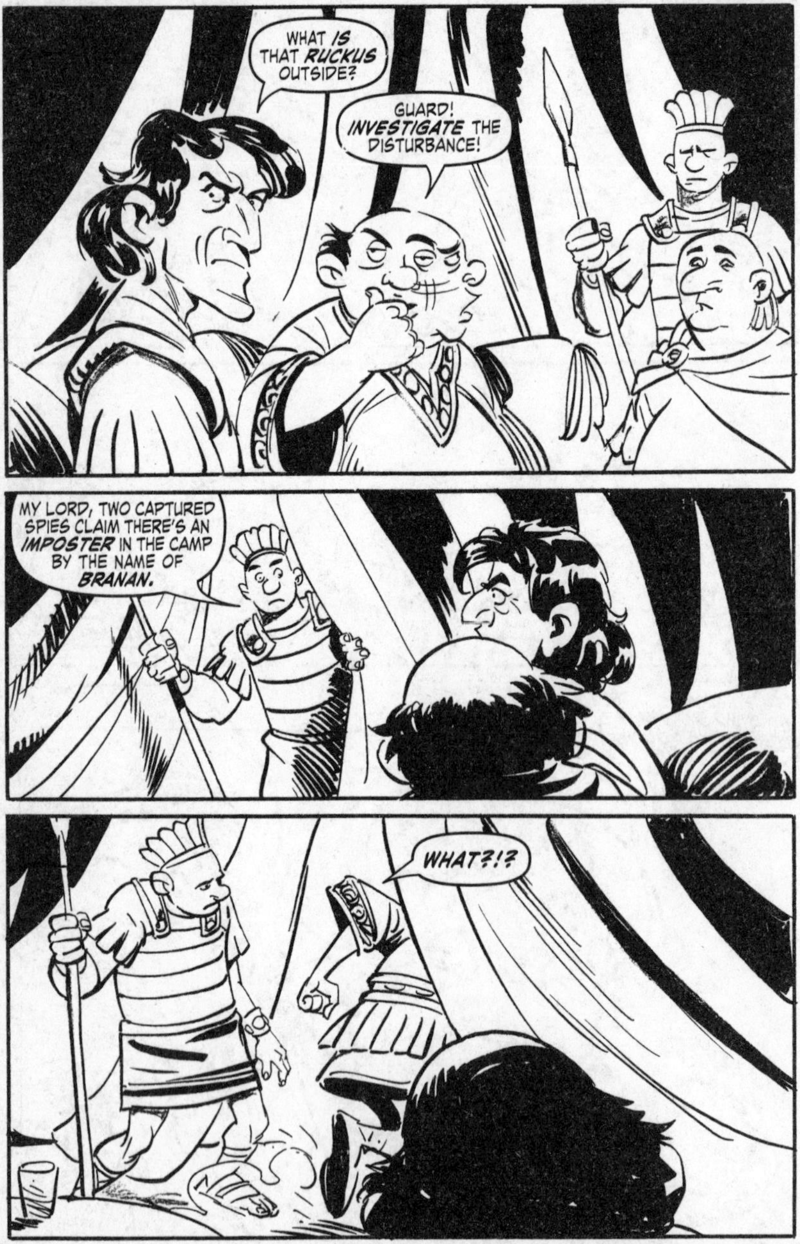
WHAT IS THAT RUCKUS OUTSIDE?
GUARD! INVESTIGATE THE DISTURBANCE!
MY LORD, TWO CAPTURED SPIES CLAIM THERE'S AN IMPOSTER IN THE CAMP BY THE NAME OF BRANAN.
WHAT?!?

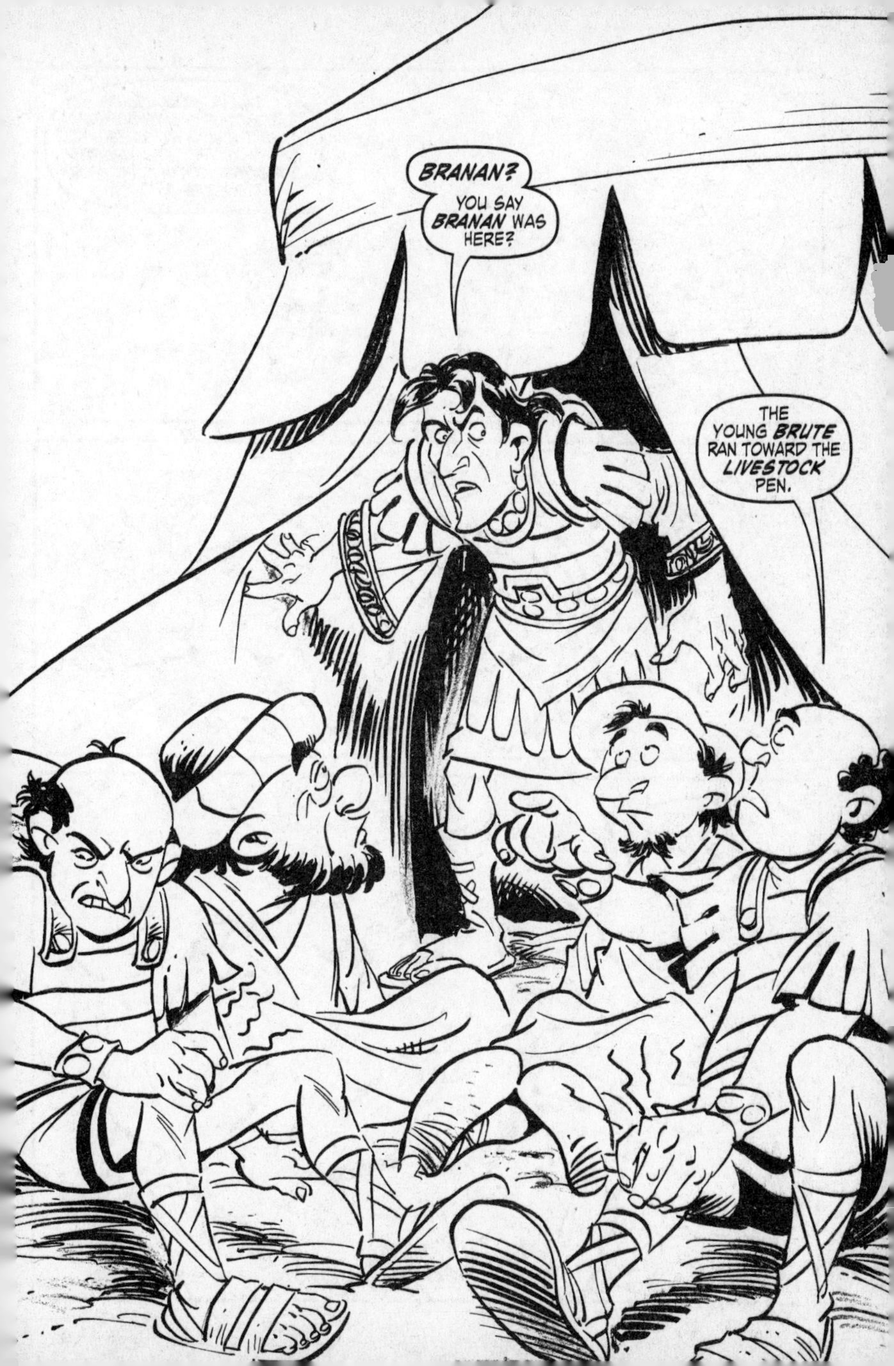
BRANAN?
YOU SAY BRANAN WAS HERE?
THE YOUNG BRUTE RAN TOWARD THE LIVESTOCK PEN.

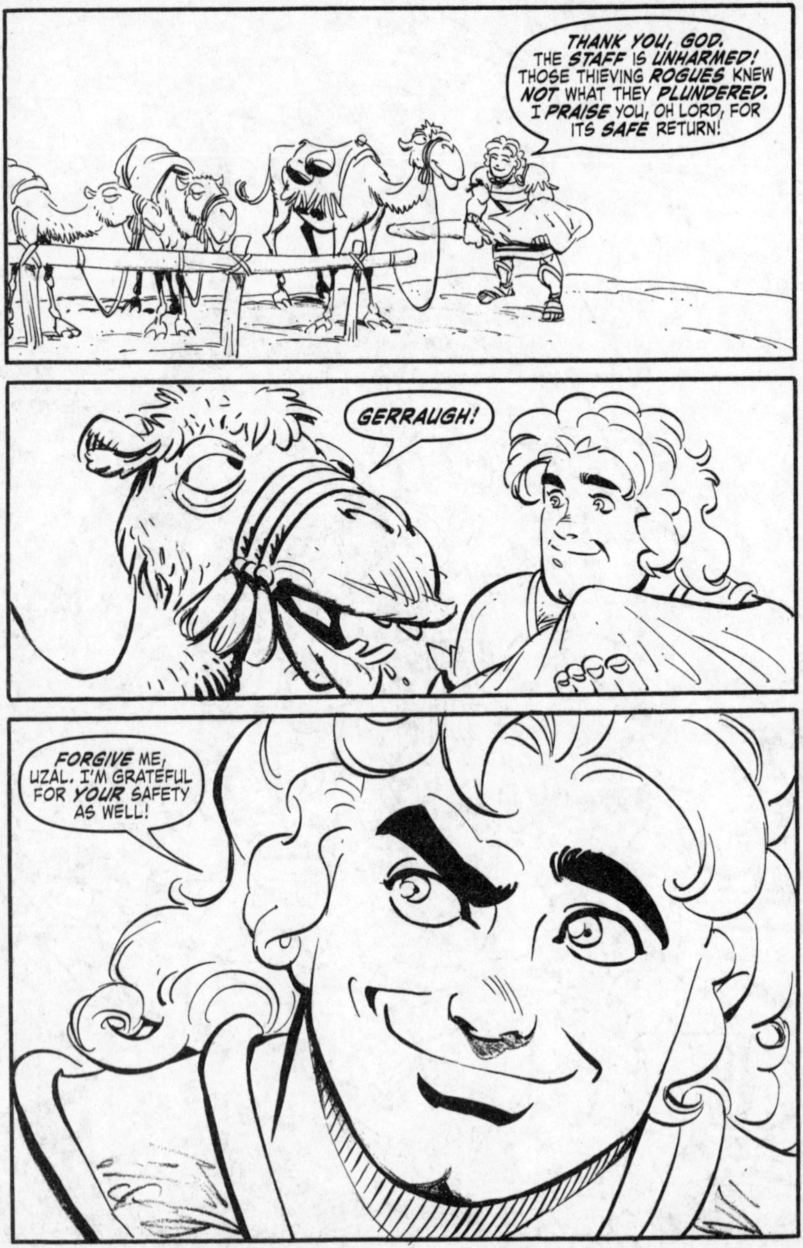
THANK YOU, GOD. THE STAFF IS UNHARMED! THOSE THIEVING ROGUES KNEW NOT WHAT THEY PLUNDERED. I PRAISE YOU, OH LORD, FOR ITS SAFE RETURN!
GERRAUGH!
FORGIVE ME, UZAL. I'M GRATEFUL FOR YOUR SAFETY AS WELL!

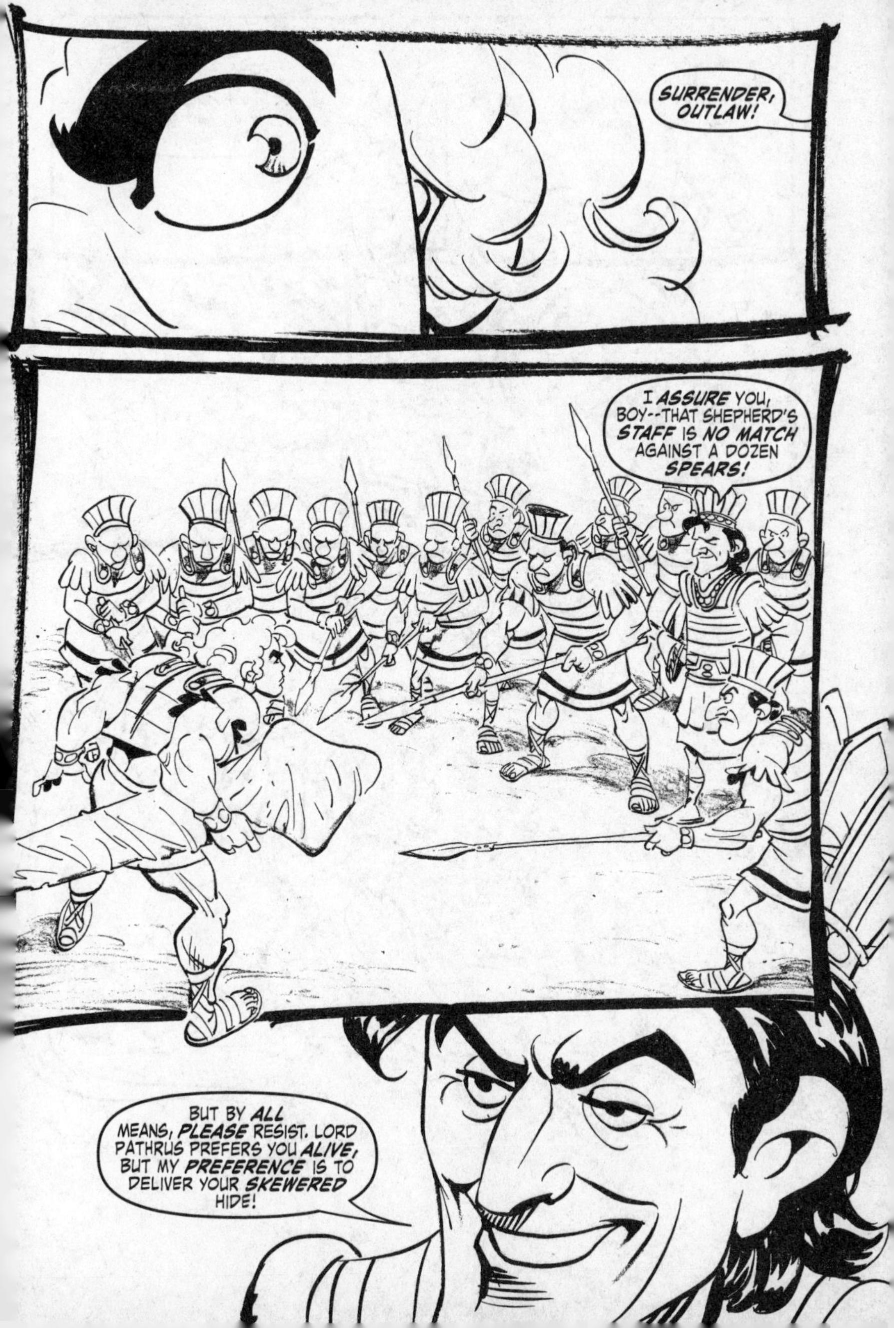
SURRENDER, OUTLAW!
I ASSURE YOU, BOY--THAT SHEPHERD'S STAFF IS NO MATCH AGAINST A DOZEN SPEARS!
BUT BY ALL MEANS, PLEASE RESIST. LORD PATHRUS PREFERS YOU ALIVE, BUT MY PREFERENCE IS TO DELIVER YOUR SKEWERED HIDE!

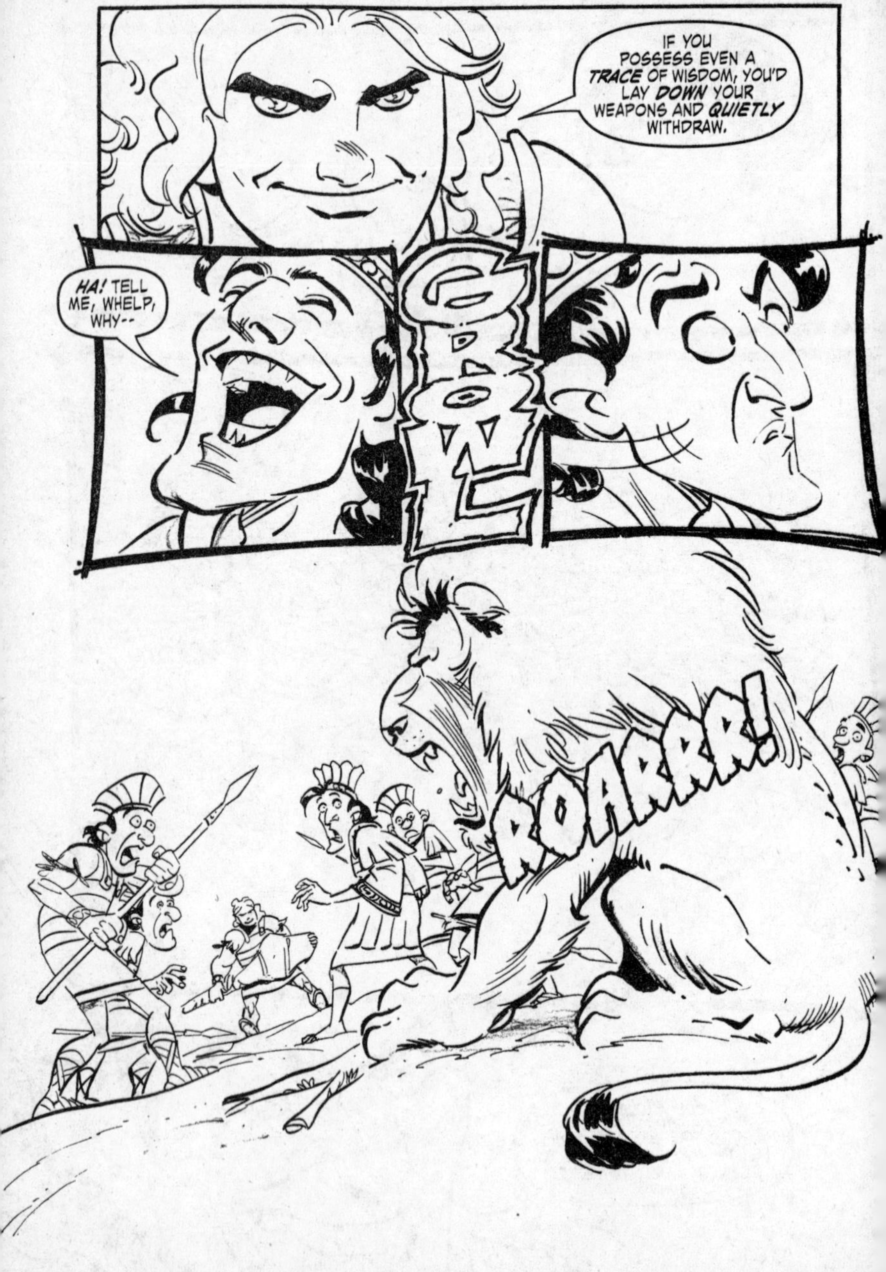

IF YOU POSSESS EVEN A *TRACE* OF WISDOM, YOU'D LAY *DOWN* YOUR WEAPONS AND *QUIETLY* WITHDRAW.
HA! TELL ME, WHELP, WHY--
GROWL
ROARRR!

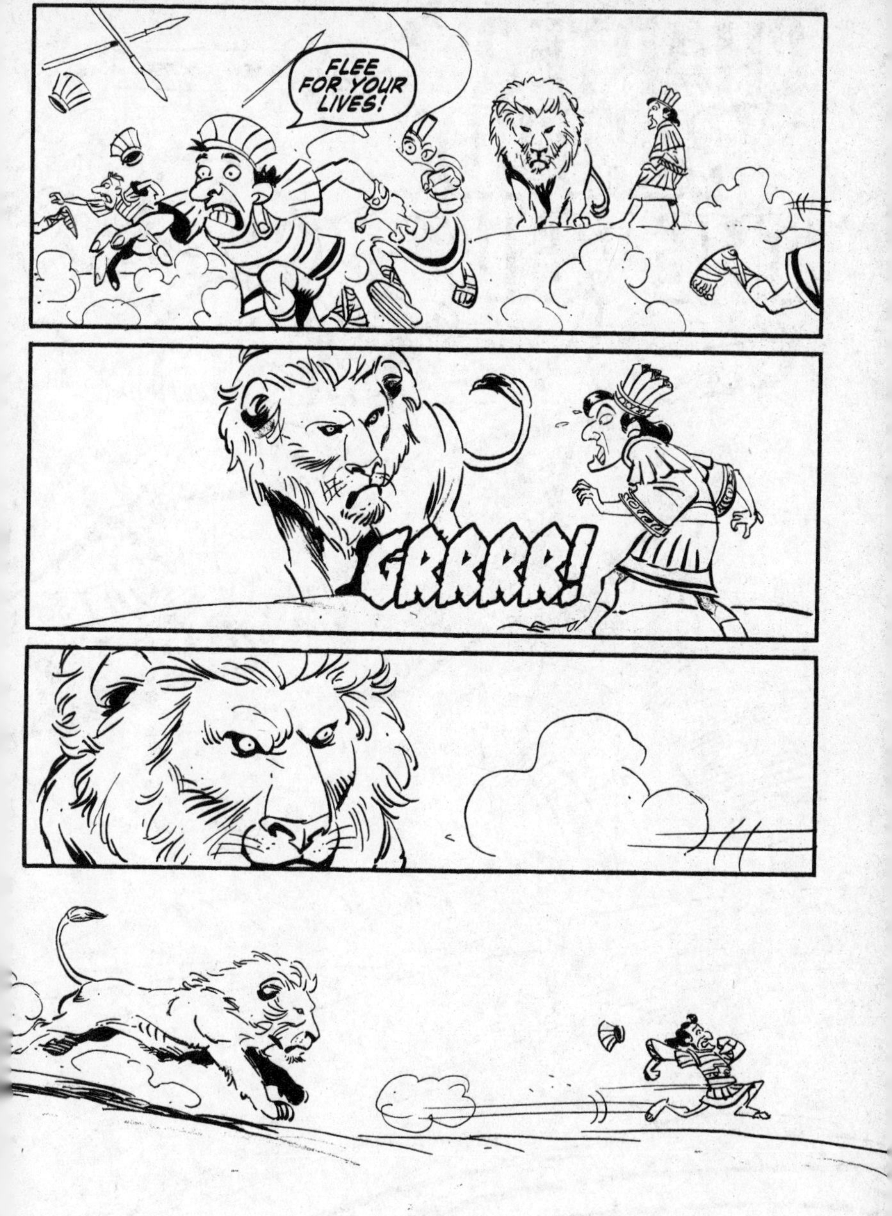
FLEE FOR YOUR LIVES!
GRRRR!

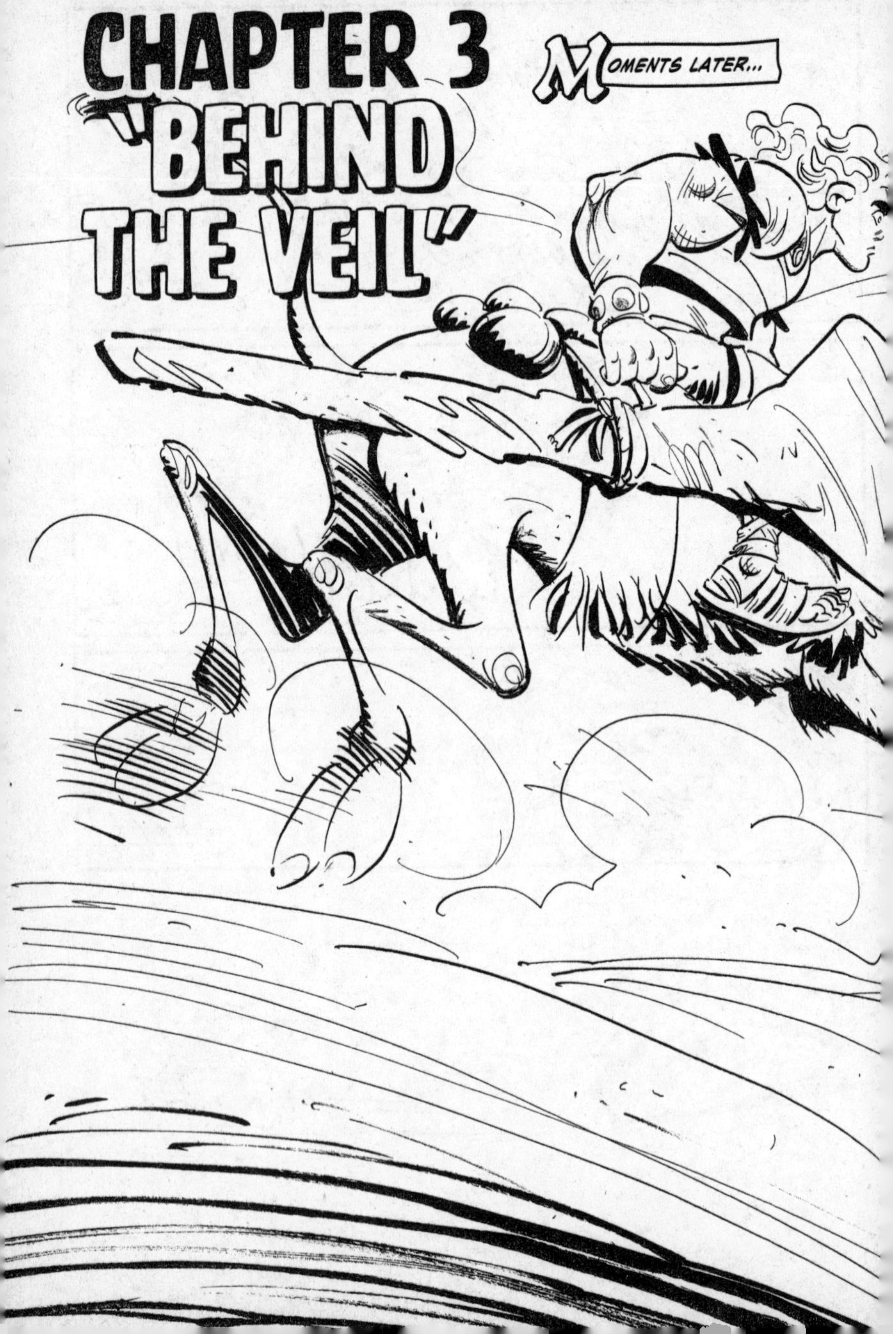
CHAPTER 3
"BEHIND THE VEIL"
MOMENTS LATER...

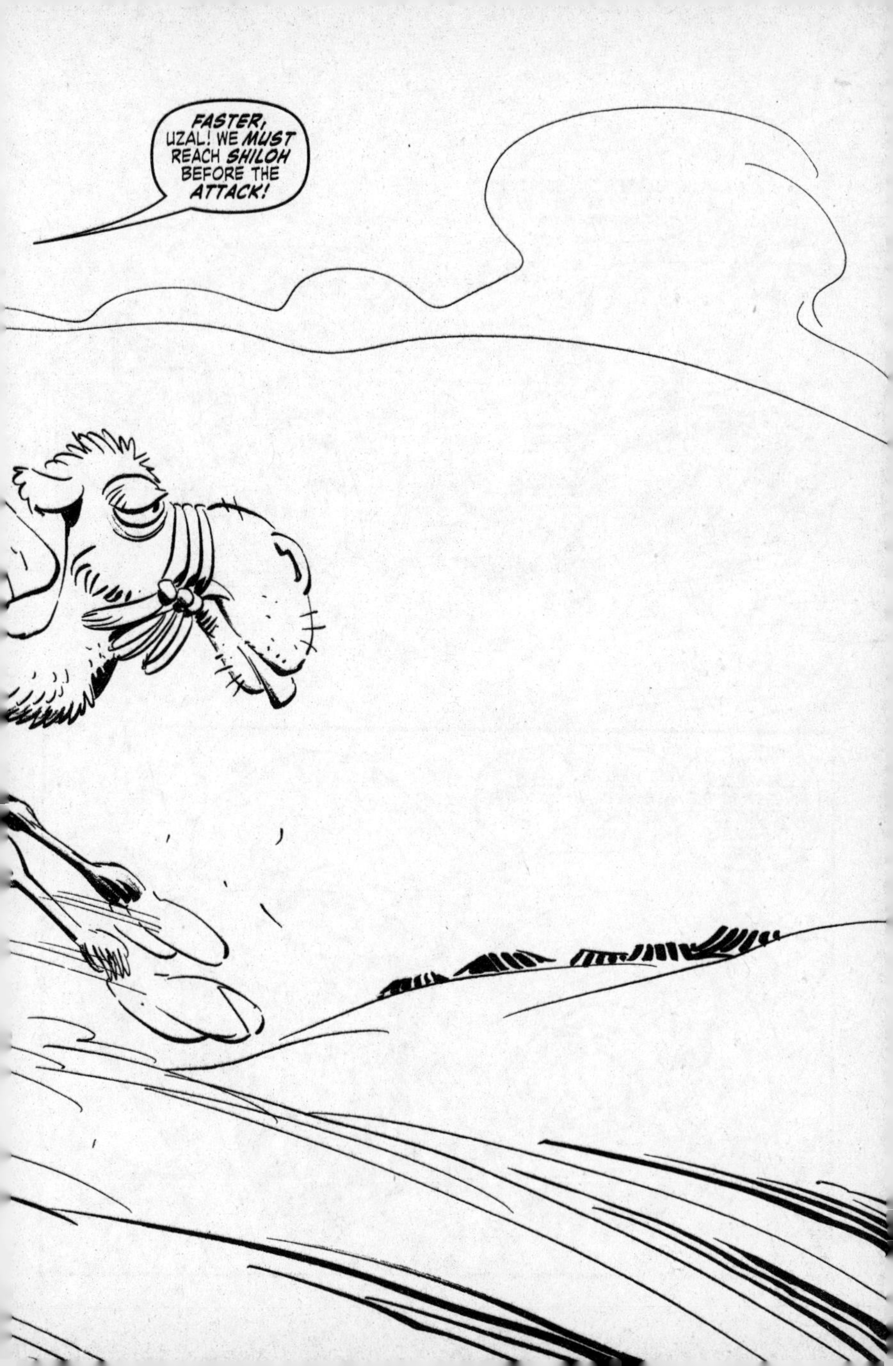
FASTER, UZAL! WE MUST REACH SHILOH BEFORE THE ATTACK!

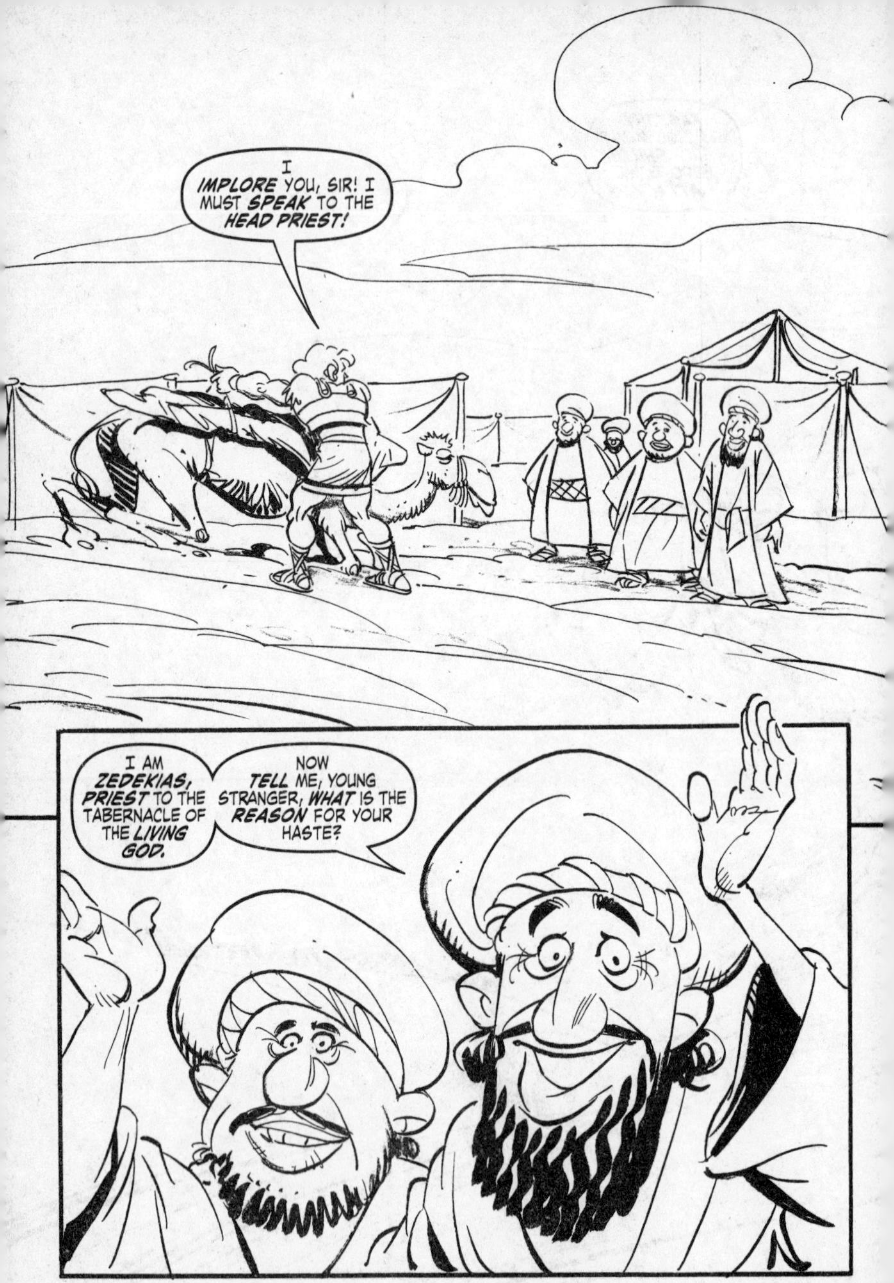
I IMPLORE YOU, SIR! I MUST SPEAK TO THE HEAD PRIEST!
I AM ZEDEKIAS, PRIEST TO THE TABERNACLE OF THE LIVING GOD.
NOW TELL ME, YOUNG STRANGER, WHAT IS THE REASON FOR YOUR HASTE?

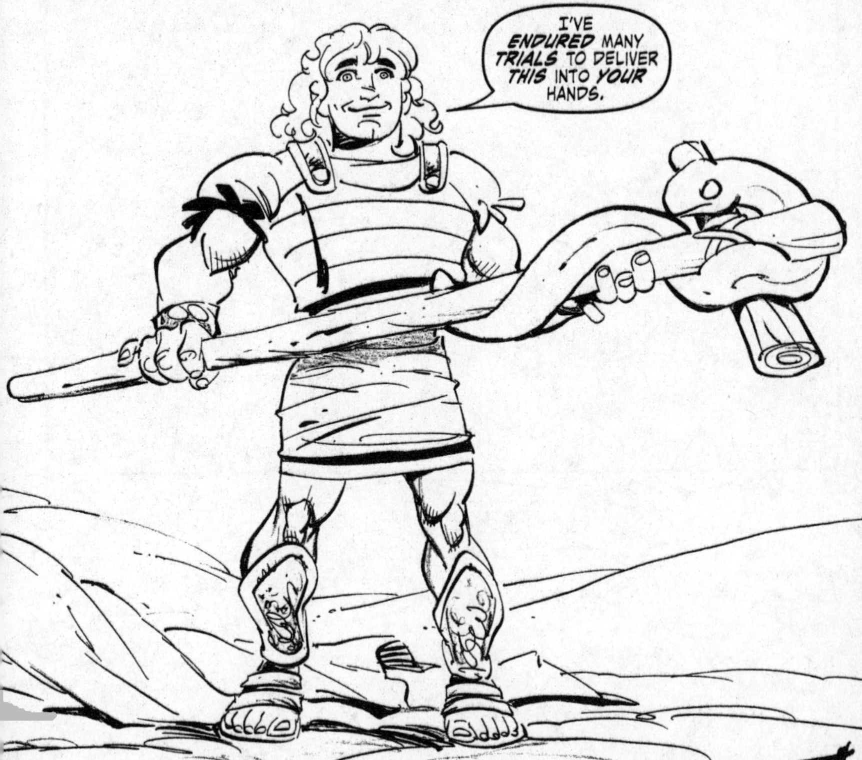
I'VE ENDURED MANY TRIALS TO DELIVER THIS INTO YOUR HANDS.

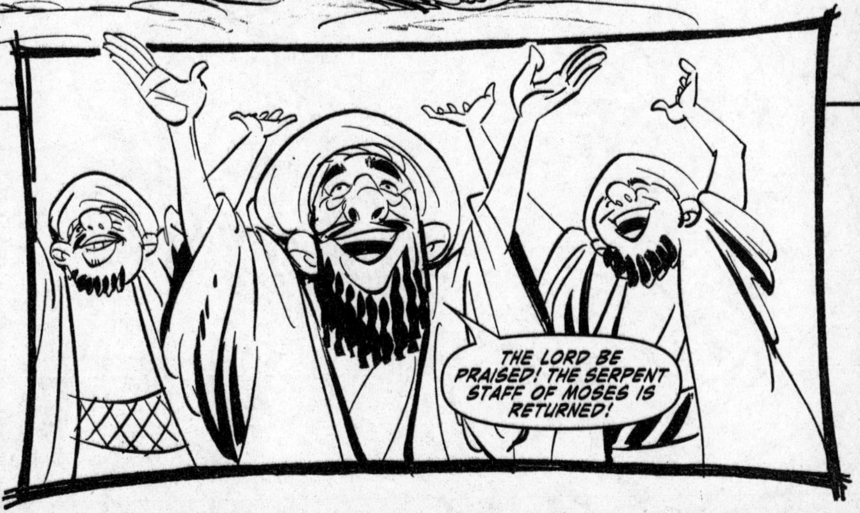
THE LORD BE PRAISED! THE SERPENT STAFF OF MOSES IS RETURNED!

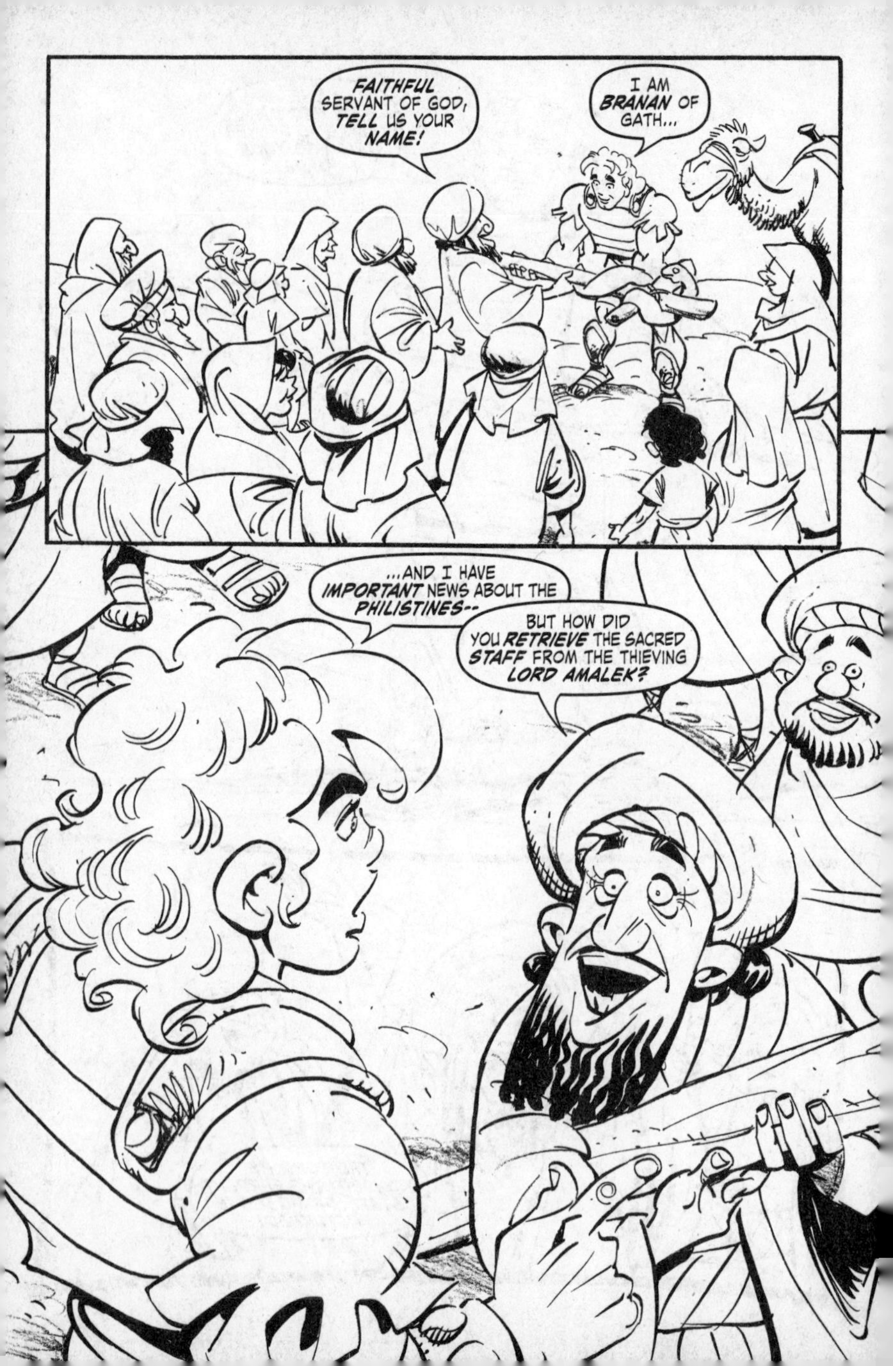
FAITHFUL SERVANT OF GOD, TELL US YOUR NAME!
I AM BRANAN OF GATH...
...AND I HAVE IMPORTANT NEWS ABOUT THE PHILISTINES--
BUT HOW DID YOU RETRIEVE THE SACRED STAFF FROM THE THIEVING LORD AMALEK?

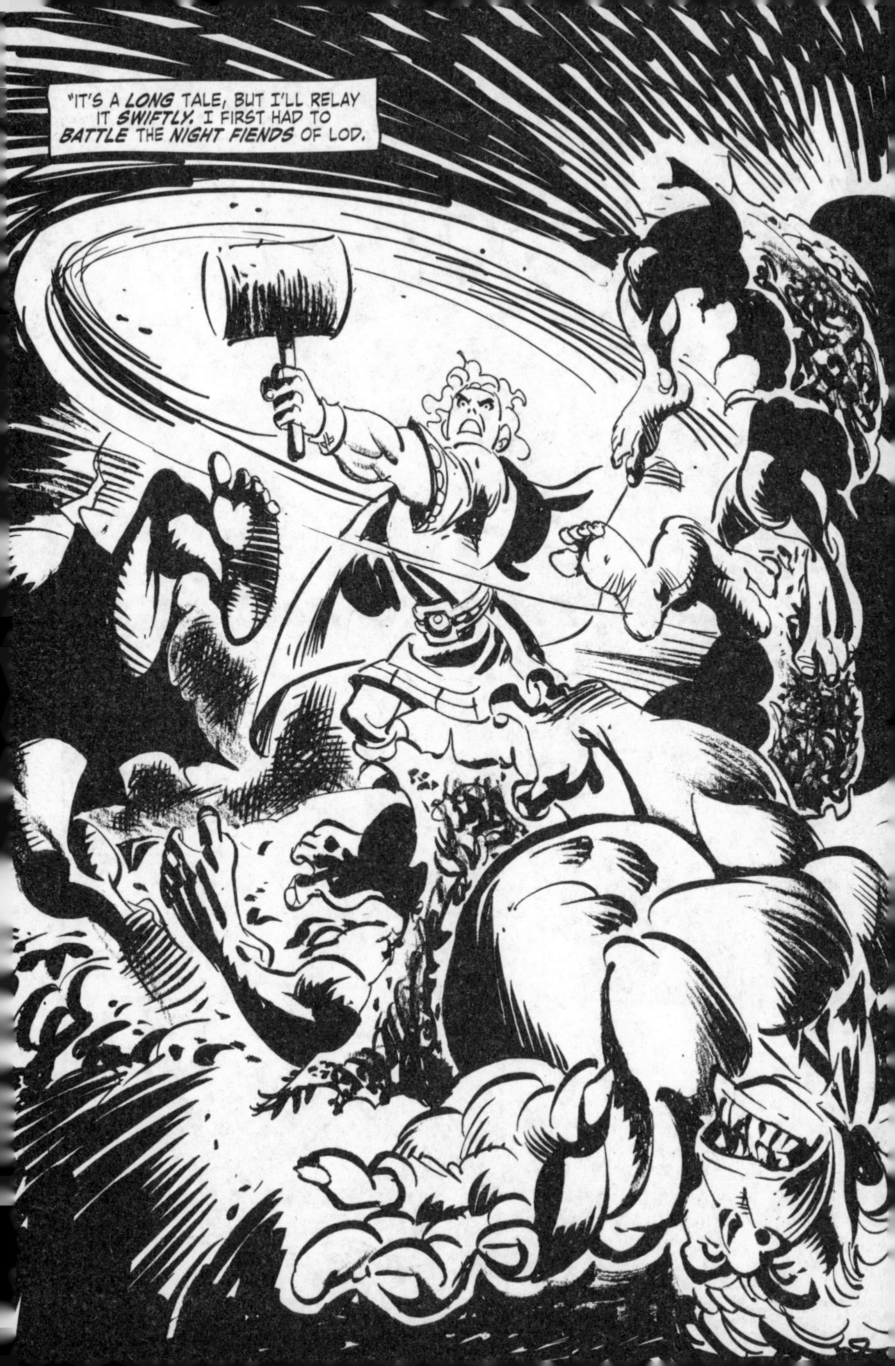
"IT'S A LONG TALE, BUT I'LL RELAY IT SWIFTLY. I FIRST HAD TO BATTLE THE NIGHT FIENDS OF LOD.

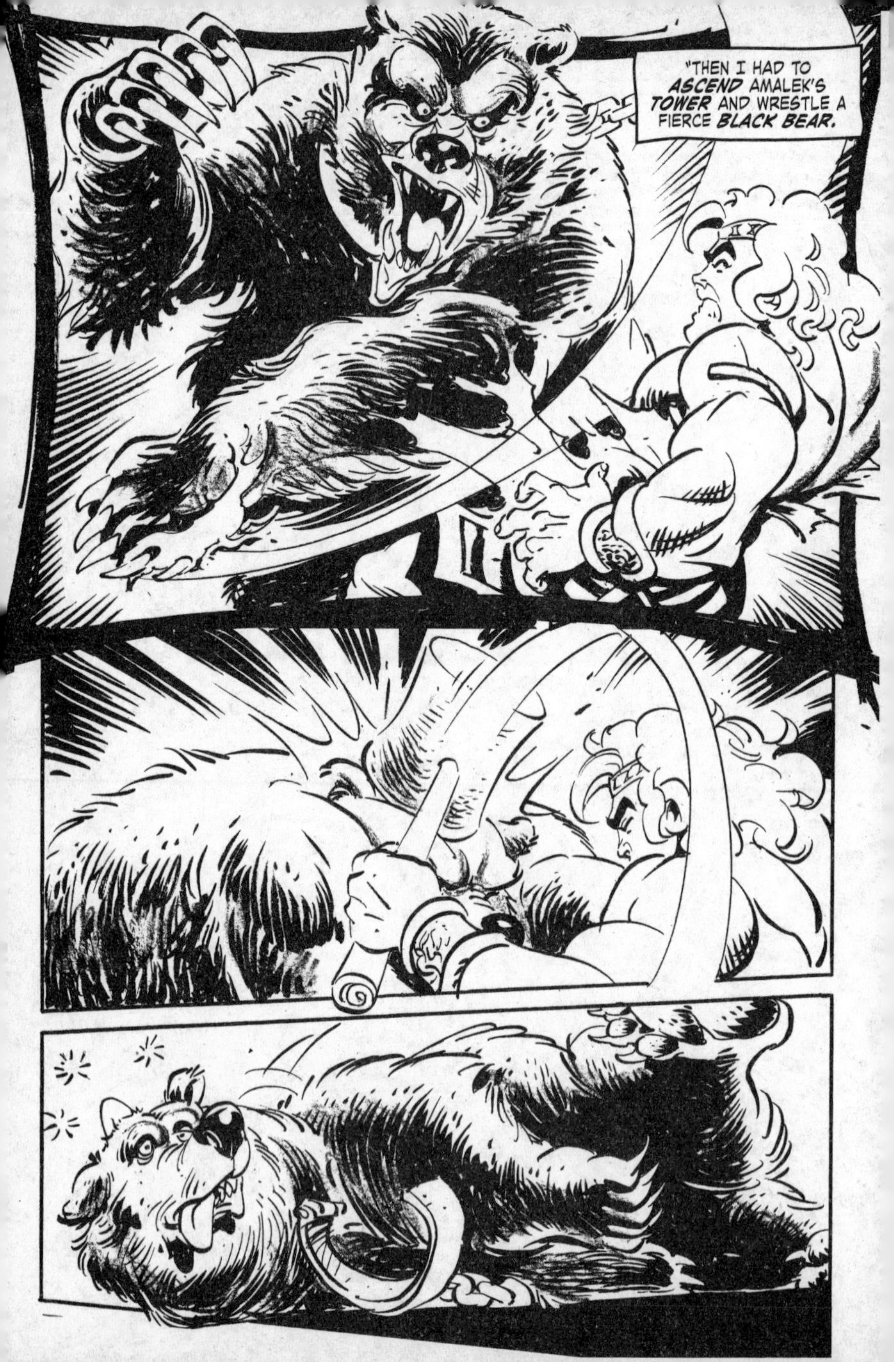
"THEN I HAD TO ASCEND AMALEK'S TOWER AND WRESTLE A FIERCE BLACK BEAR.

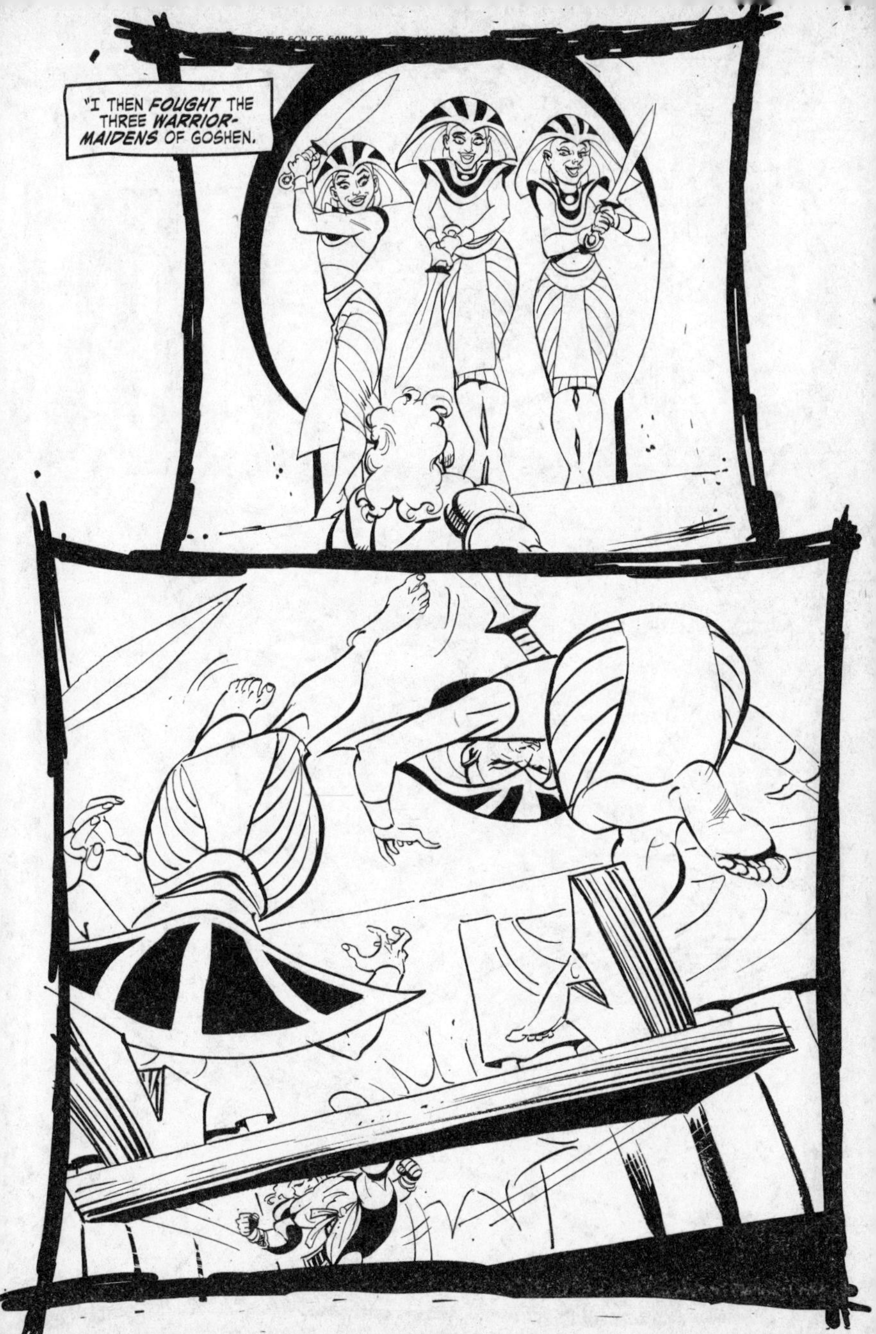
"I THEN FOUGHT THE THREE WARRIOR-MAIDENS OF GOSHEN.

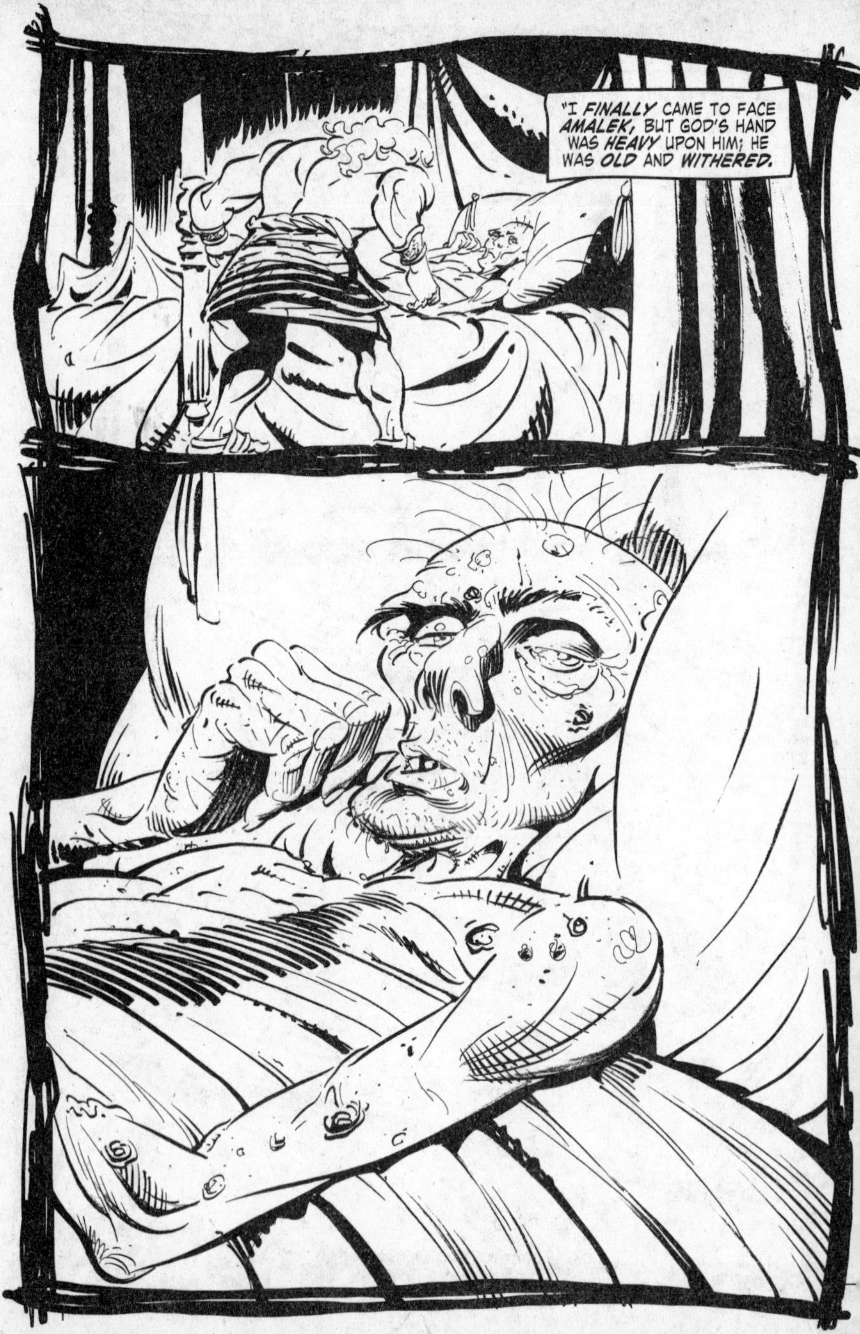
"I FINALLY CAME TO FACE AMALEK, BUT GOD'S HAND WAS HEAVY UPON HIM; HE WAS OLD AND WITHERED.

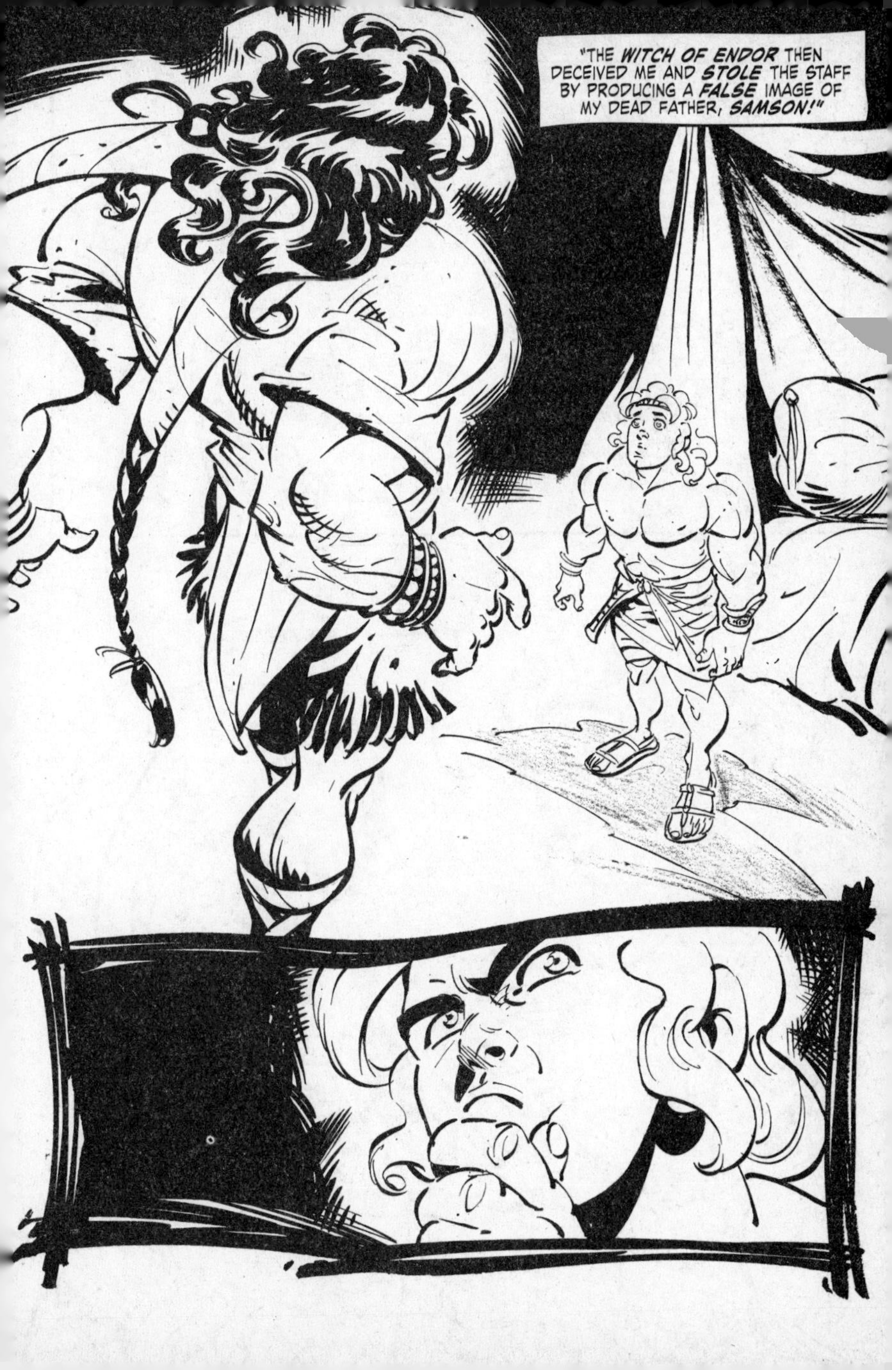
"THE WITCH OF ENDOR THEN DECEIVED ME AND STOLE THE STAFF BY PRODUCING A FALSE IMAGE OF MY DEAD FATHER, SAMSON!"

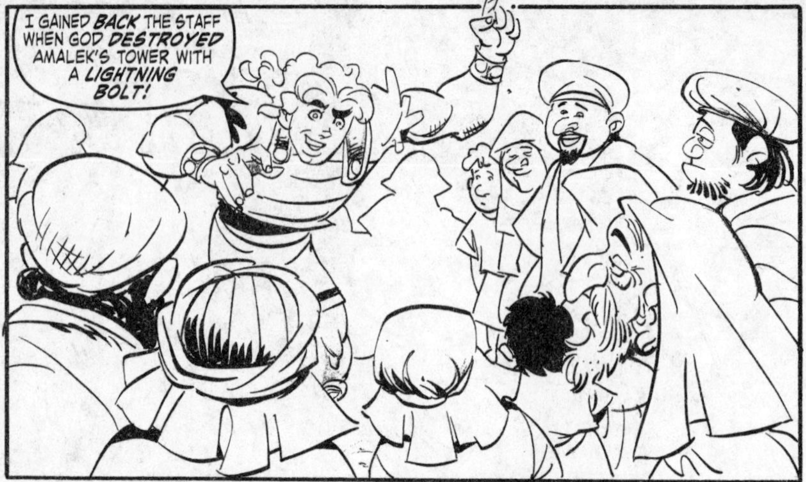
I GAINED BACK THE STAFF WHEN GOD DESTROYED AMALEK'S TOWER WITH A LIGHTNING BOLT!

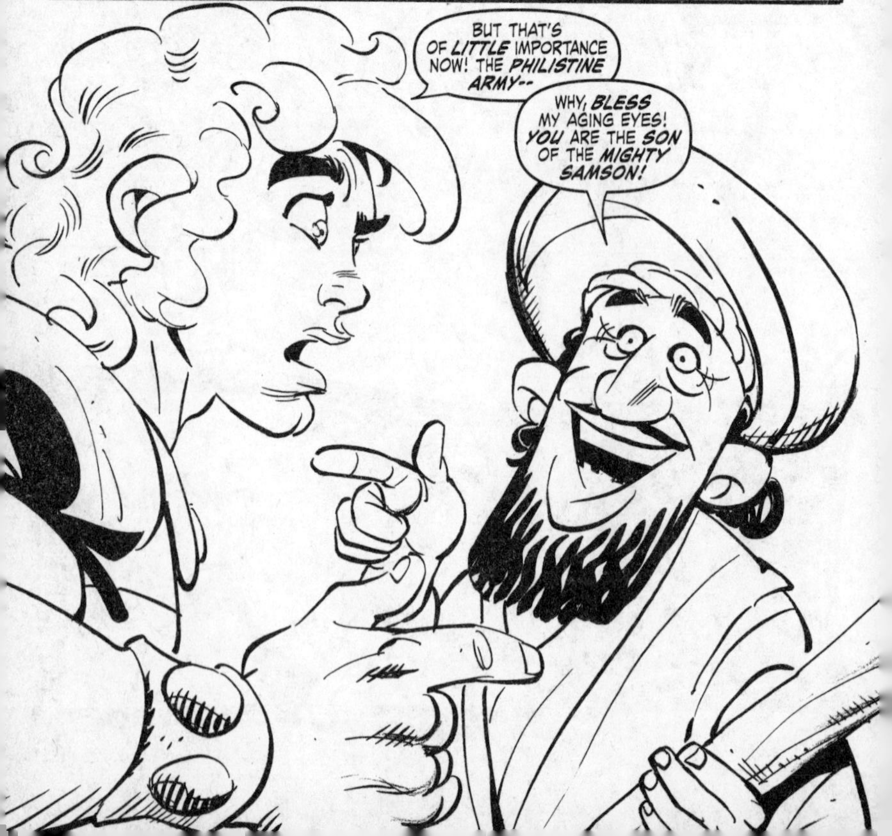
BUT THAT'S OF LITTLE IMPORTANCE NOW! THE PHILISTINE ARMY--
WHY, BLESS MY AGING EYES! YOU ARE THE SON OF THE MIGHTY SAMSON!

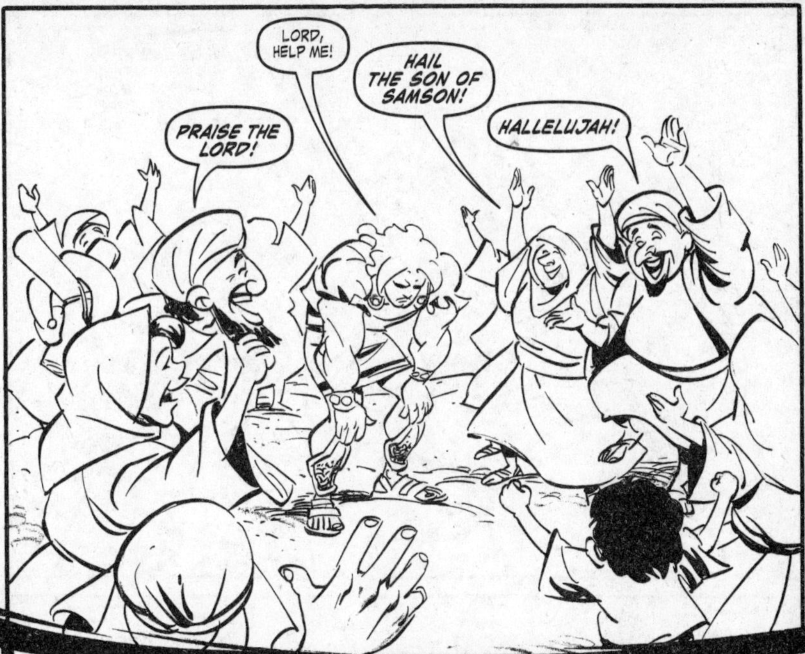
PRAISE THE LORD!
LORD, HELP ME!
HAIL THE SON OF SAMSON!
HALLELUJAH!

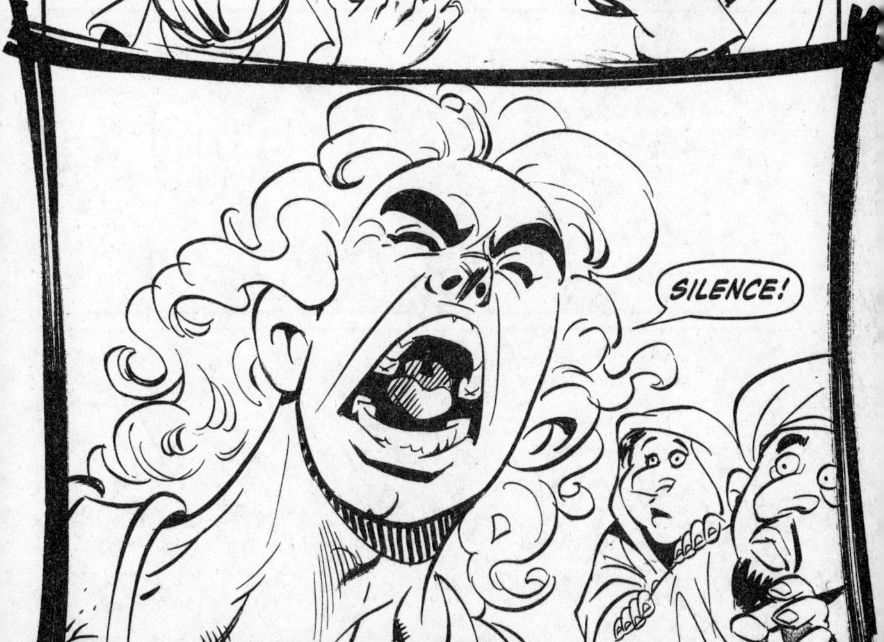
SILENCE!

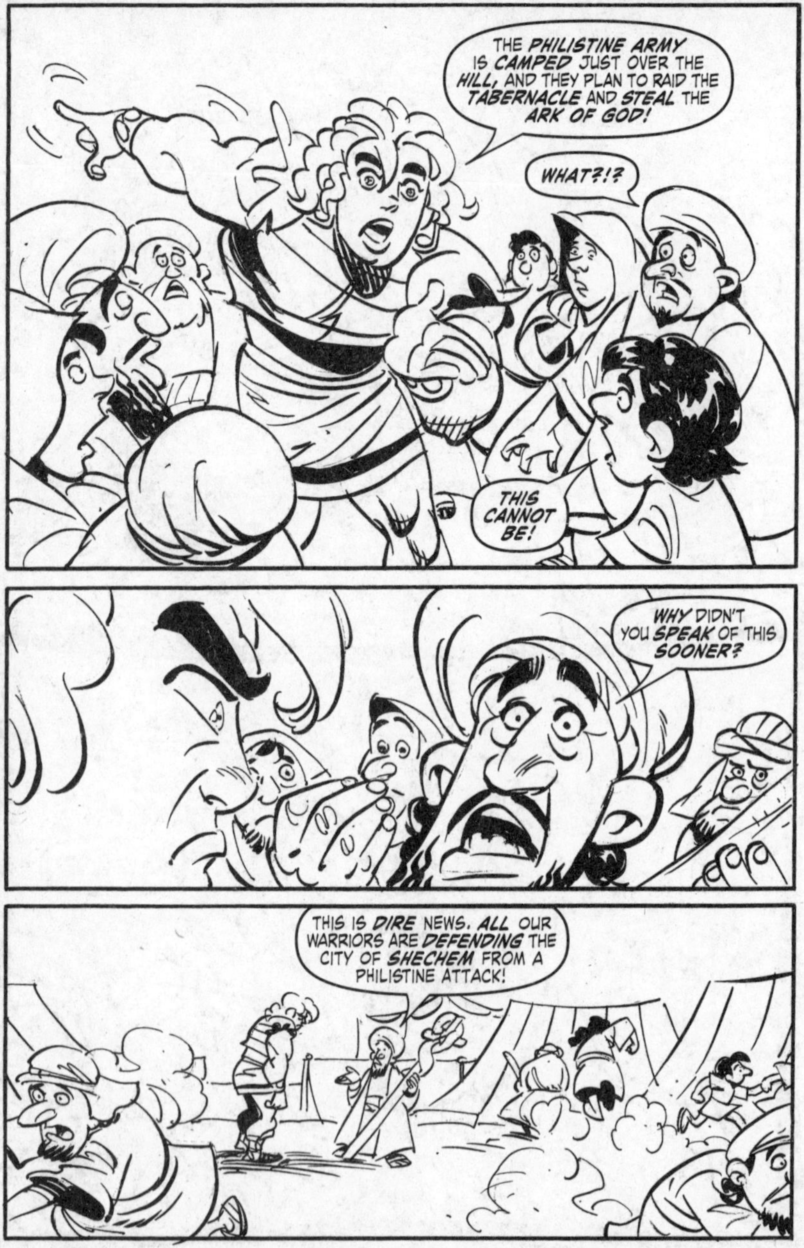
THE PHILISTINE ARMY IS CAMPED JUST OVER THE HILL, AND THEY PLAN TO RAID THE TABERNACLE AND STEAL THE ARK OF GOD!
WHAT?!?
THIS CANNOT BE!
WHY DIDN'T YOU SPEAK OF THIS SOONER?
THIS IS DIRE NEWS. ALL OUR WARRIORS ARE DEFENDING THE CITY OF SHECHEM FROM A PHILISTINE ATTACK!

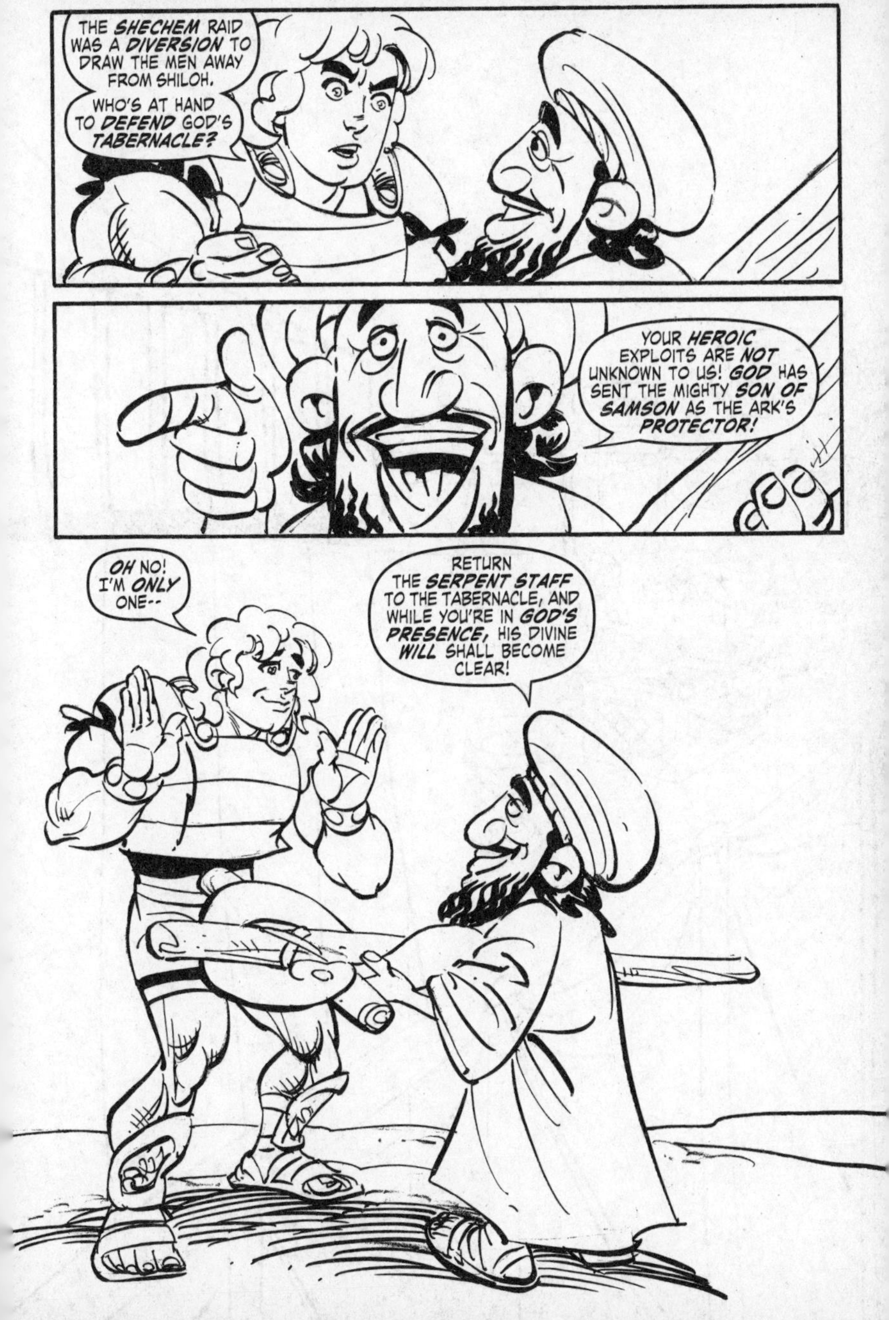
THE SHECHEM RAID WAS A DIVERSION TO DRAW THE MEN AWAY FROM SHILOH.
WHO'S AT HAND TO DEFEND GOD'S TABERNACLE?
YOUR HEROIC EXPLOITS ARE NOT UNKNOWN TO US! GOD HAS SENT THE MIGHTY SON OF SAMSON AS THE ARK'S PROTECTOR!
OH NO! I'M ONLY ONE--
RETURN THE SERPENT STAFF TO THE TABERNACLE, AND WHILE YOU'RE IN GOD'S PRESENCE, HIS DIVINE WILL SHALL BECOME CLEAR!

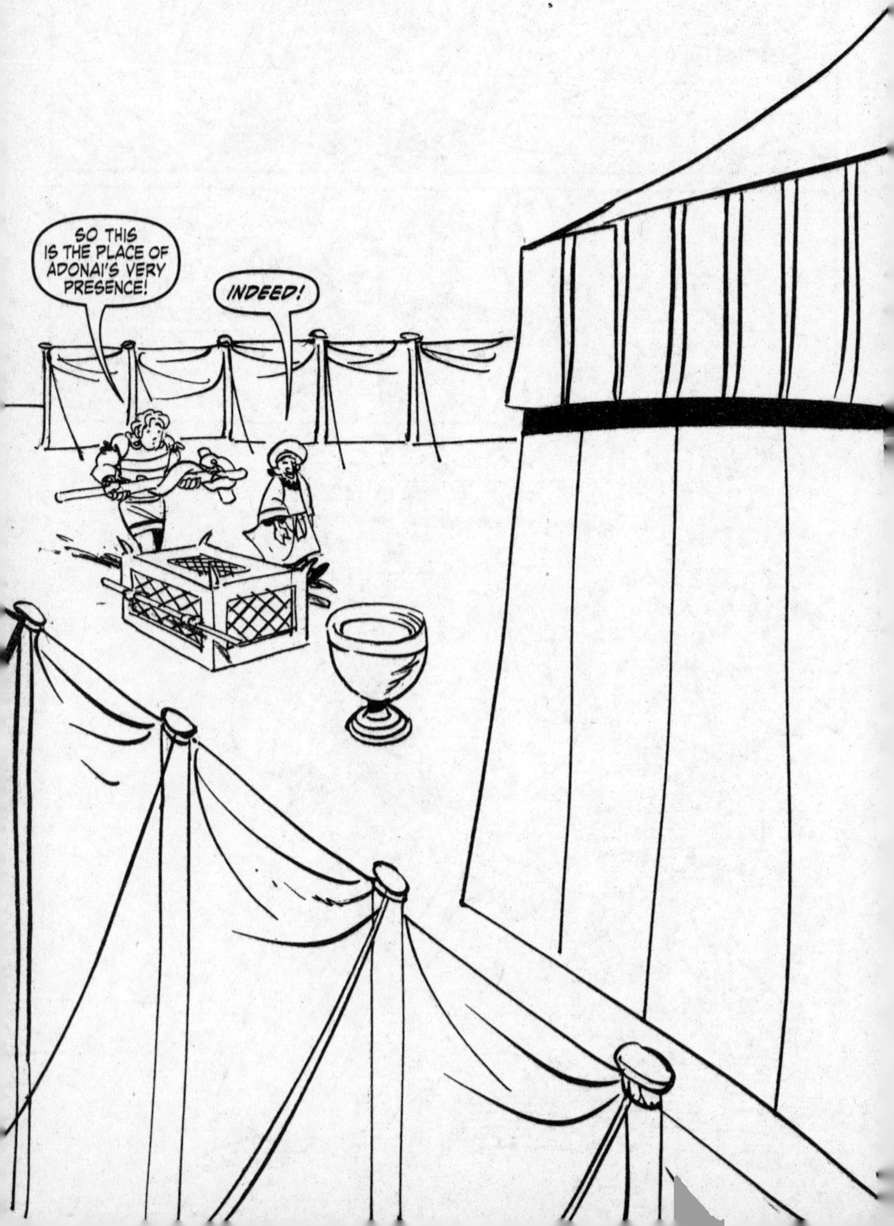
SO THIS IS THE PLACE OF ADONAI'S VERY PRESENCE!
INDEED!

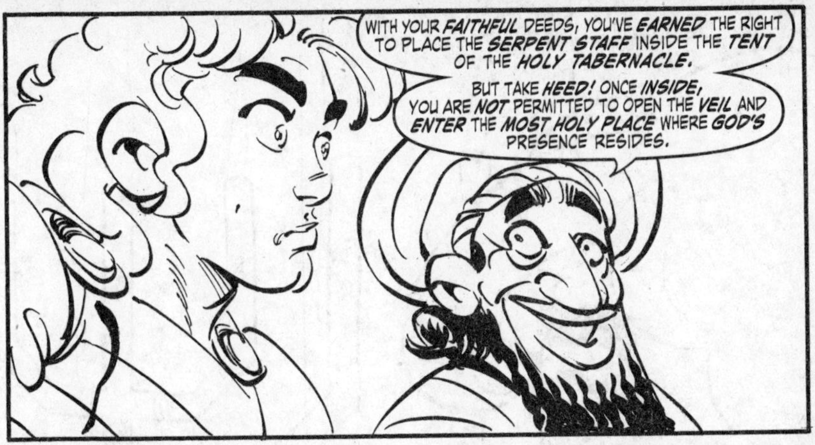
WITH YOUR FAITHFUL DEEDS, YOU'VE EARNED THE RIGHT TO PLACE THE SERPENT STAFF INSIDE THE TENT OF THE HOLY TABERNACLE.
BUT TAKE HEED! ONCE INSIDE, YOU ARE NOT PERMITTED TO OPEN THE VEIL AND ENTER THE MOST HOLY PLACE WHERE GOD'S PRESENCE RESIDES.

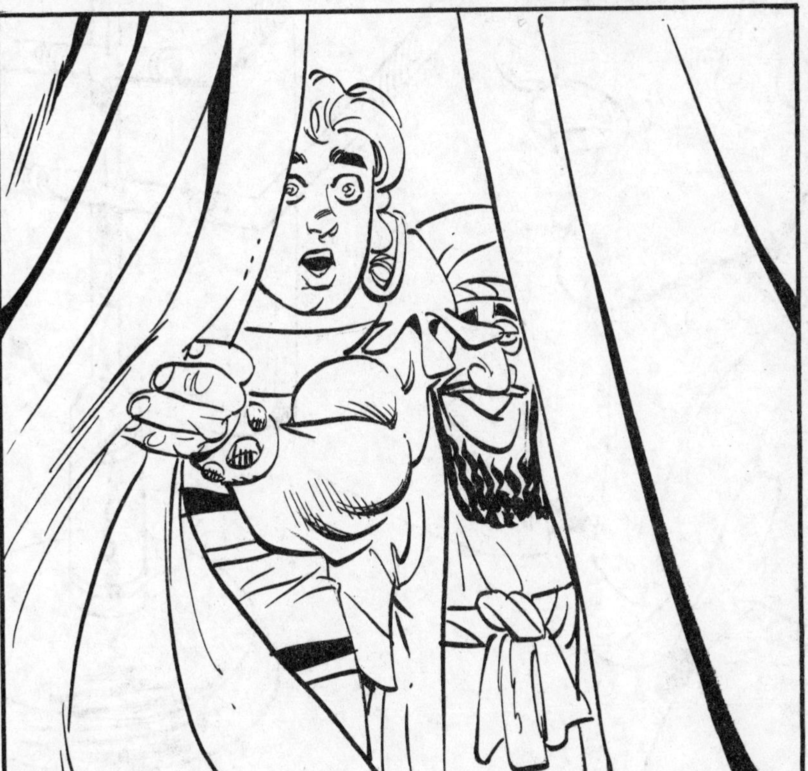

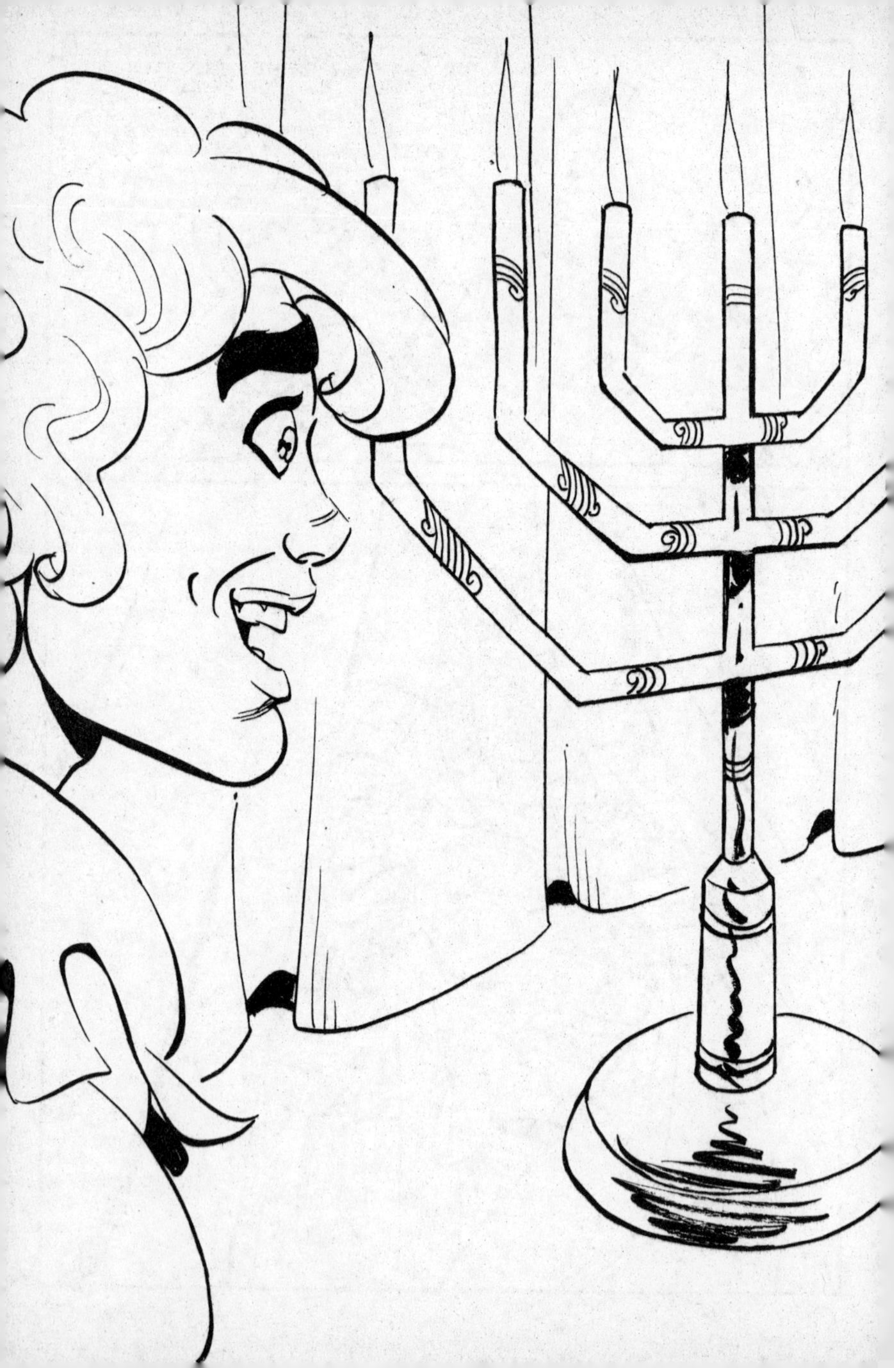

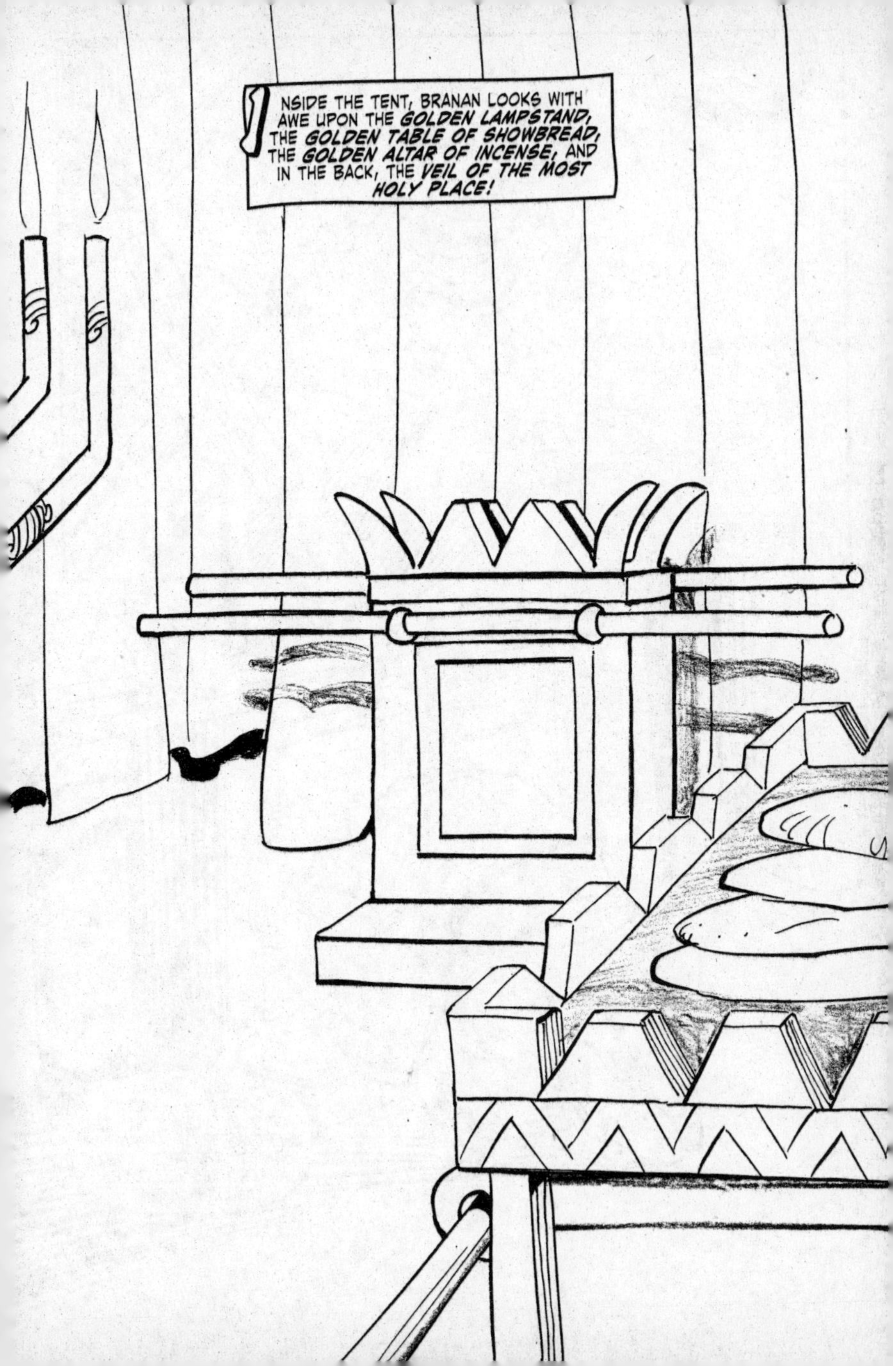
INSIDE THE TENT, BRANAN LOOKS WITH AWE UPON THE GOLDEN LAMPSTAND, THE GOLDEN TABLE OF SHOWBREAD, THE GOLDEN ALTAR OF INCENSE, AND IN THE BACK, THE VEIL OF THE MOST HOLY PLACE!

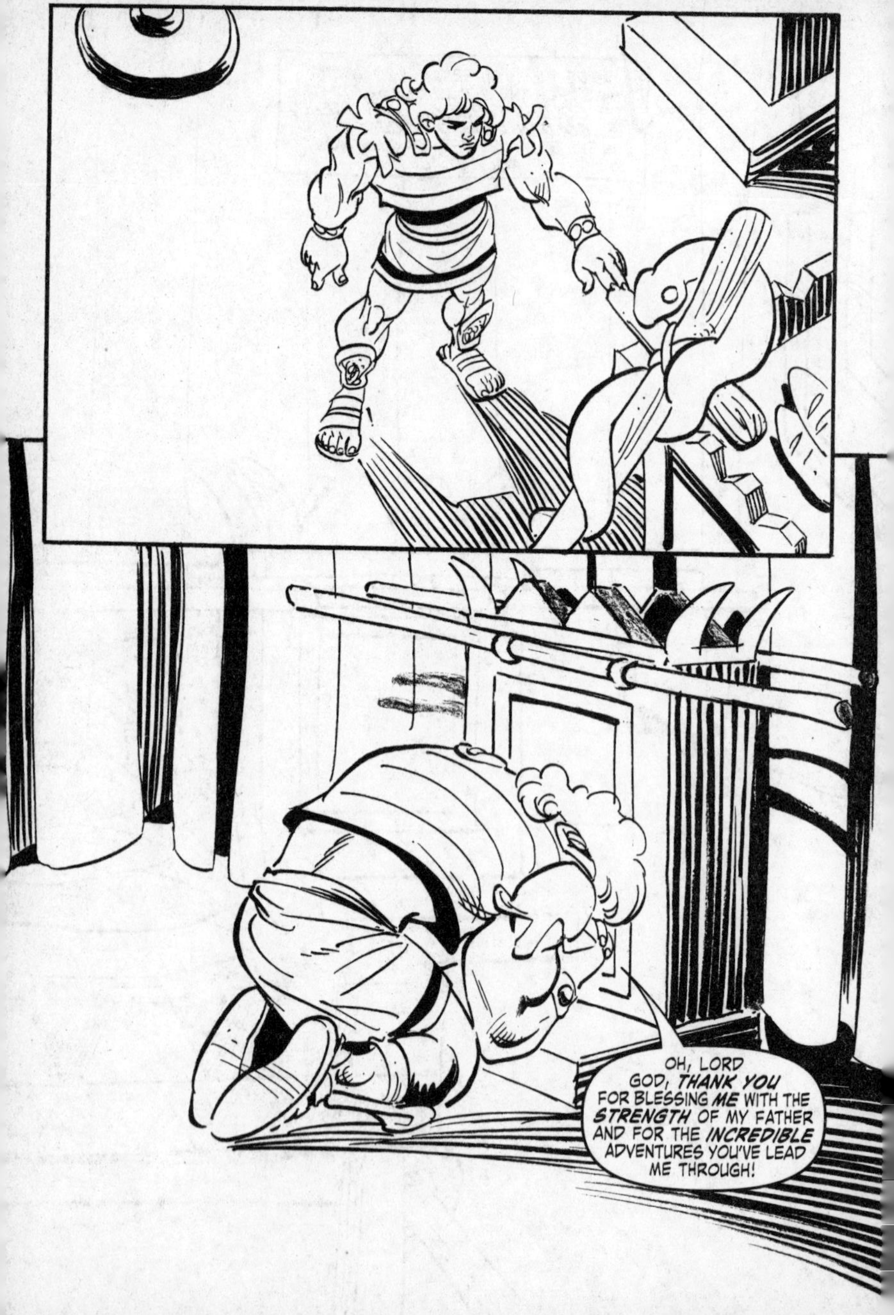
OH, LORD GOD, ***THANK YOU*** FOR BLESSING ***ME*** WITH THE ***STRENGTH*** OF MY FATHER AND FOR THE ***INCREDIBLE*** ADVENTURES YOU'VE LEAD ME THROUGH!

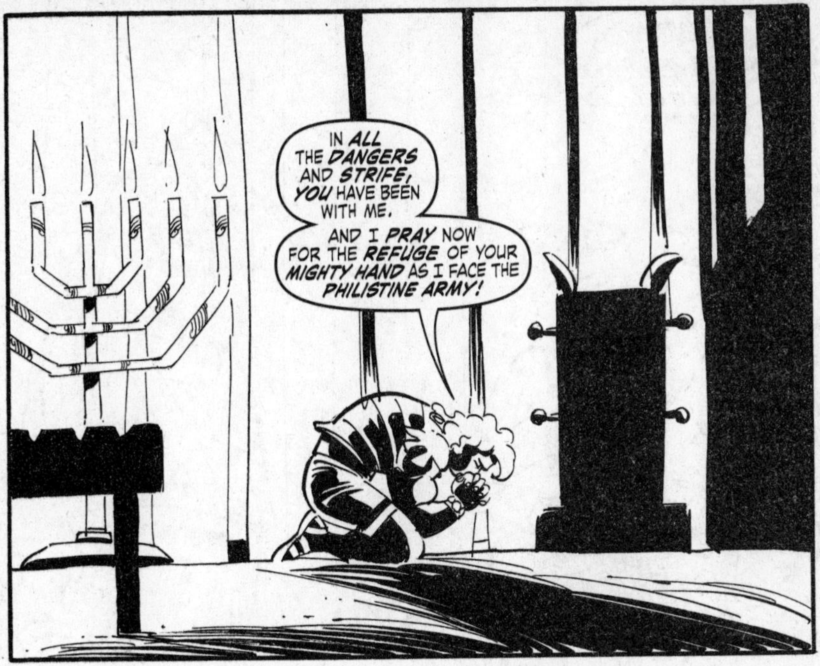
IN ALL THE DANGERS AND STRIFE, YOU HAVE BEEN WITH ME.
AND I PRAY NOW FOR THE REFUGE OF YOUR MIGHTY HAND AS I FACE THE PHILISTINE ARMY!

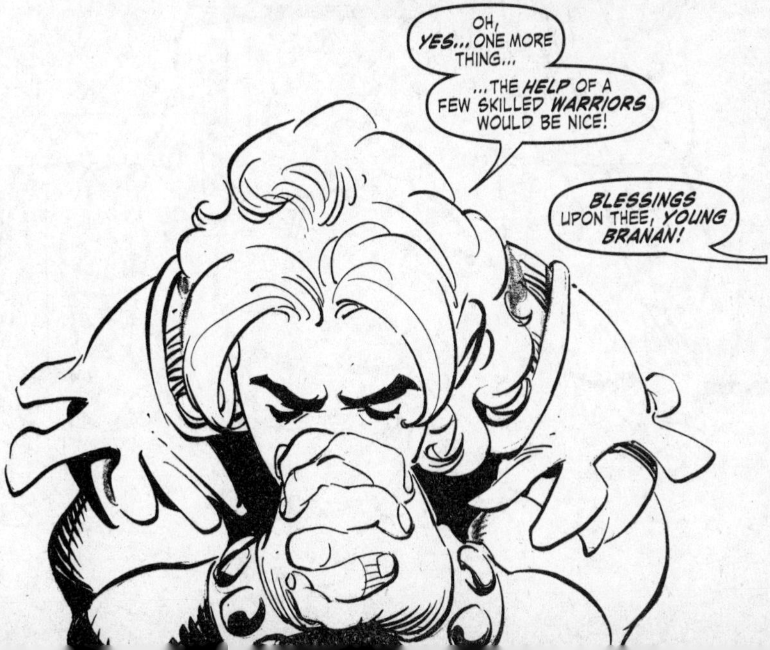
OH, YES... ONE MORE THING...
...THE HELP OF A FEW SKILLED WARRIORS WOULD BE NICE!
BLESSINGS UPON THEE, YOUNG BRANAN!

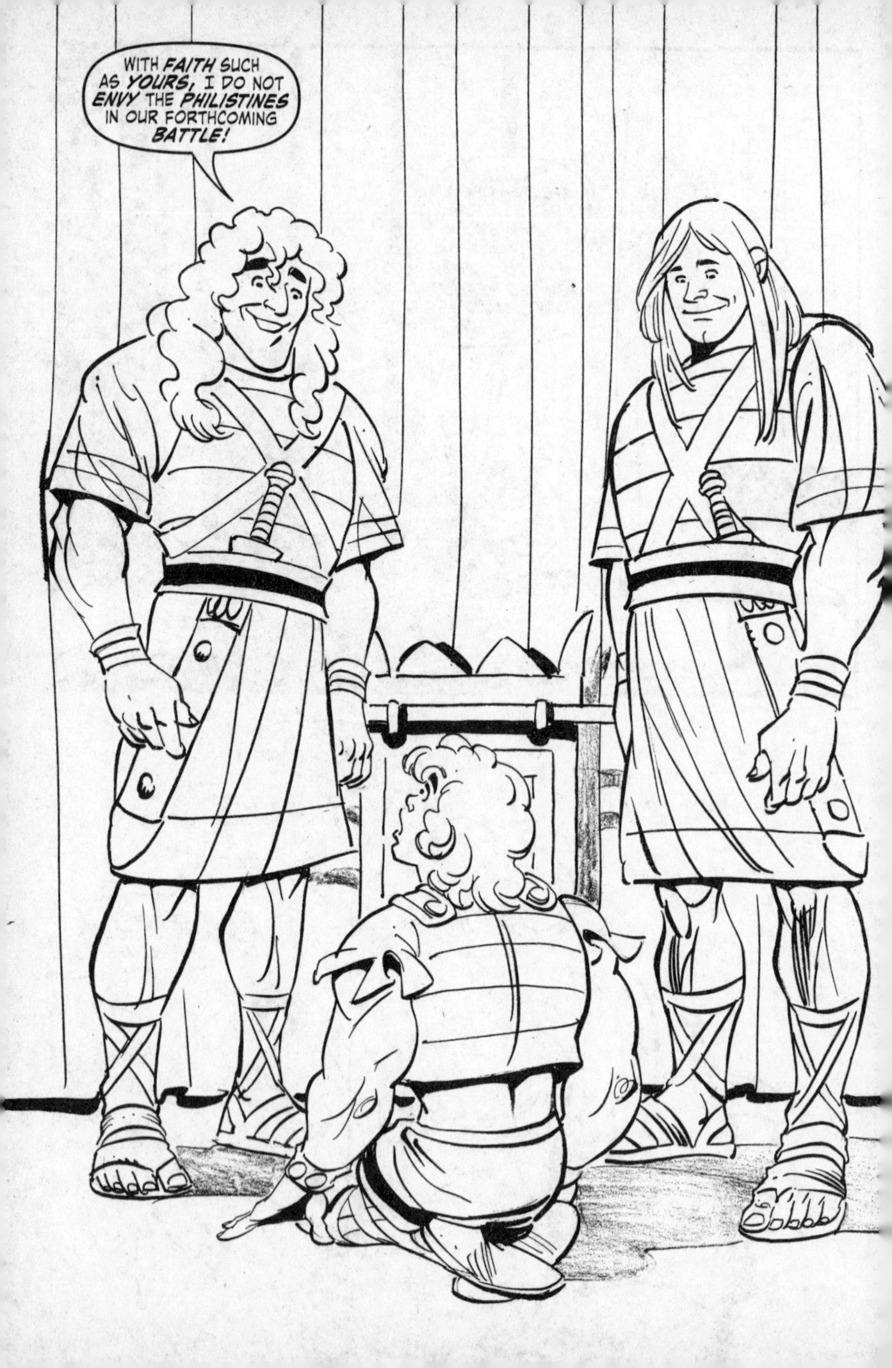
WITH FAITH SUCH AS YOURS, I DO NOT ENVY THE PHILISTINES IN OUR FORTHCOMING BATTLE!

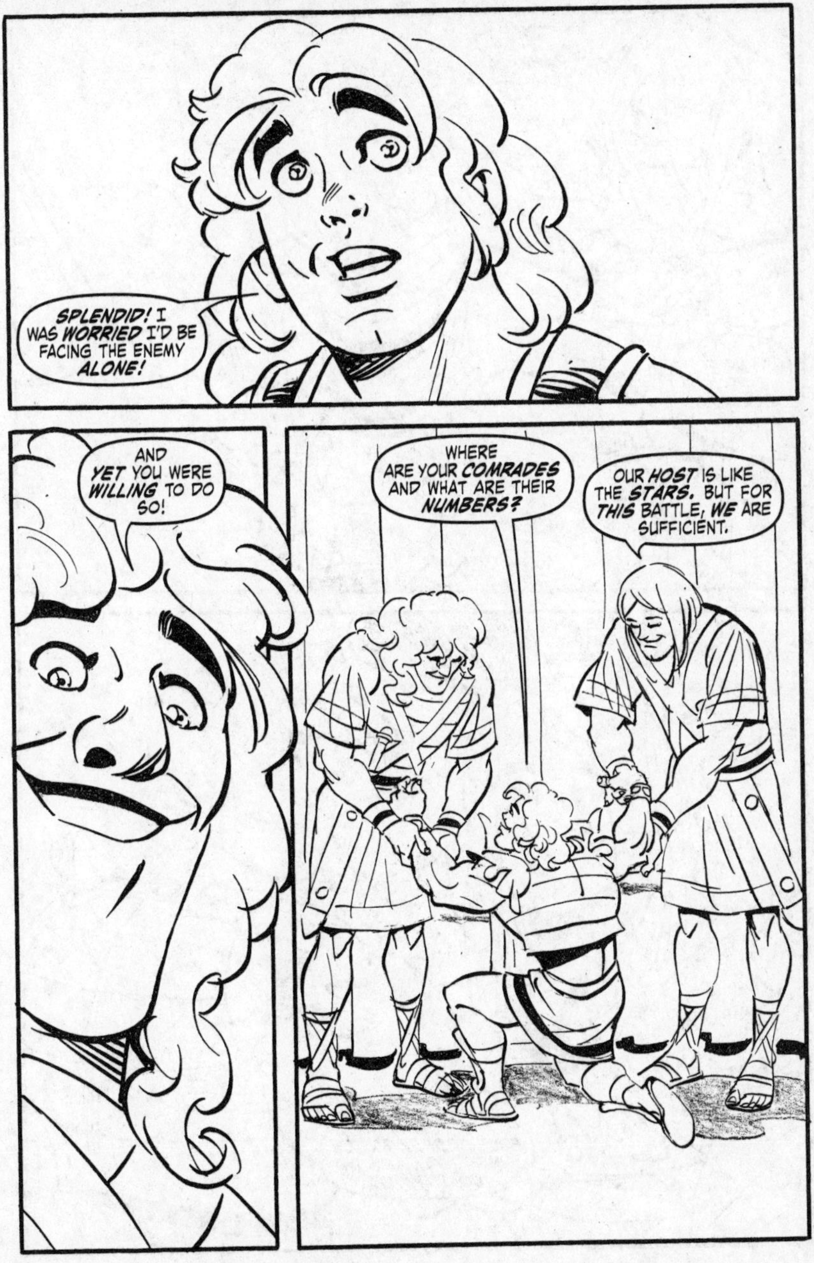
SPLENDID! I WAS WORRIED I'D BE FACING THE ENEMY ALONE!
AND YET YOU WERE WILLING TO DO SO!
WHERE ARE YOUR COMRADES AND WHAT ARE THEIR NUMBERS?
OUR HOST IS LIKE THE STARS. BUT FOR THIS BATTLE, WE ARE SUFFICIENT.

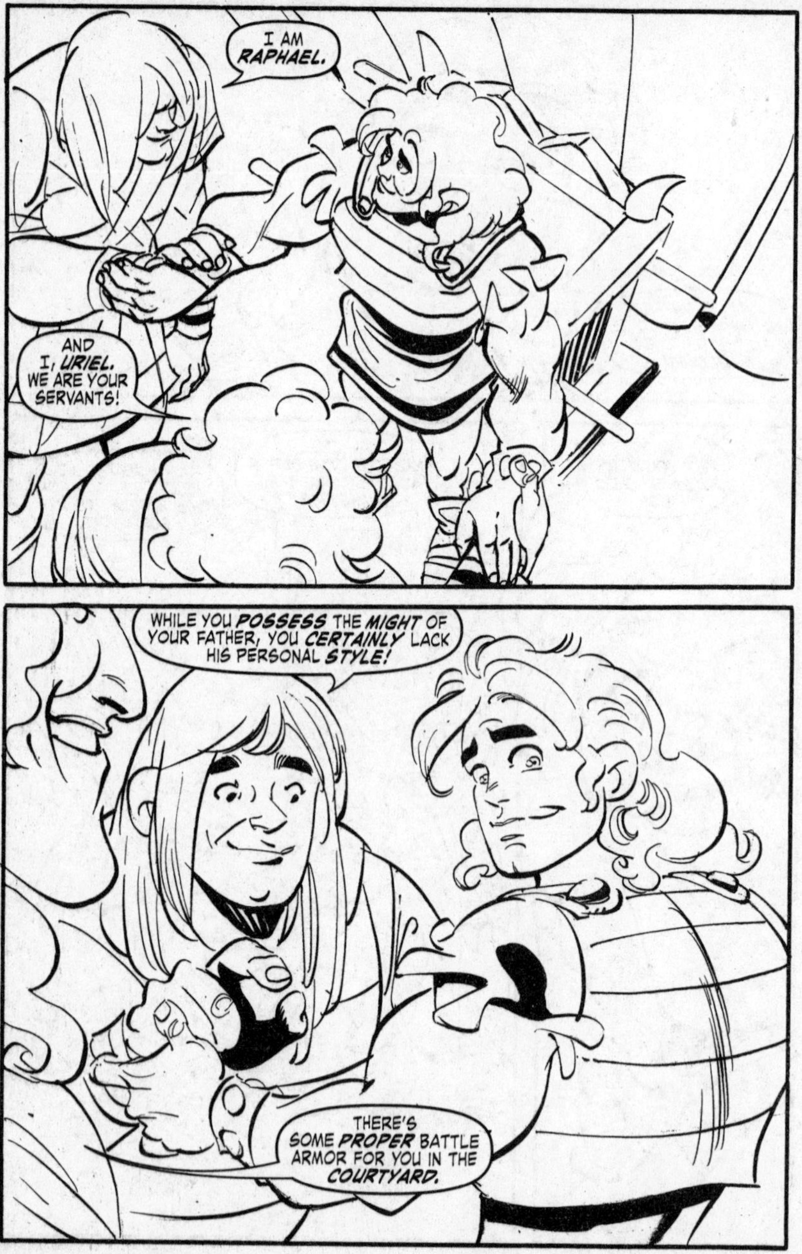
I AM RAPHAEL.
AND I, URIEL. WE ARE YOUR SERVANTS!
WHILE YOU POSSESS THE MIGHT OF YOUR FATHER, YOU CERTAINLY LACK HIS PERSONAL STYLE!
THERE'S SOME PROPER BATTLE ARMOR FOR YOU IN THE COURTYARD.

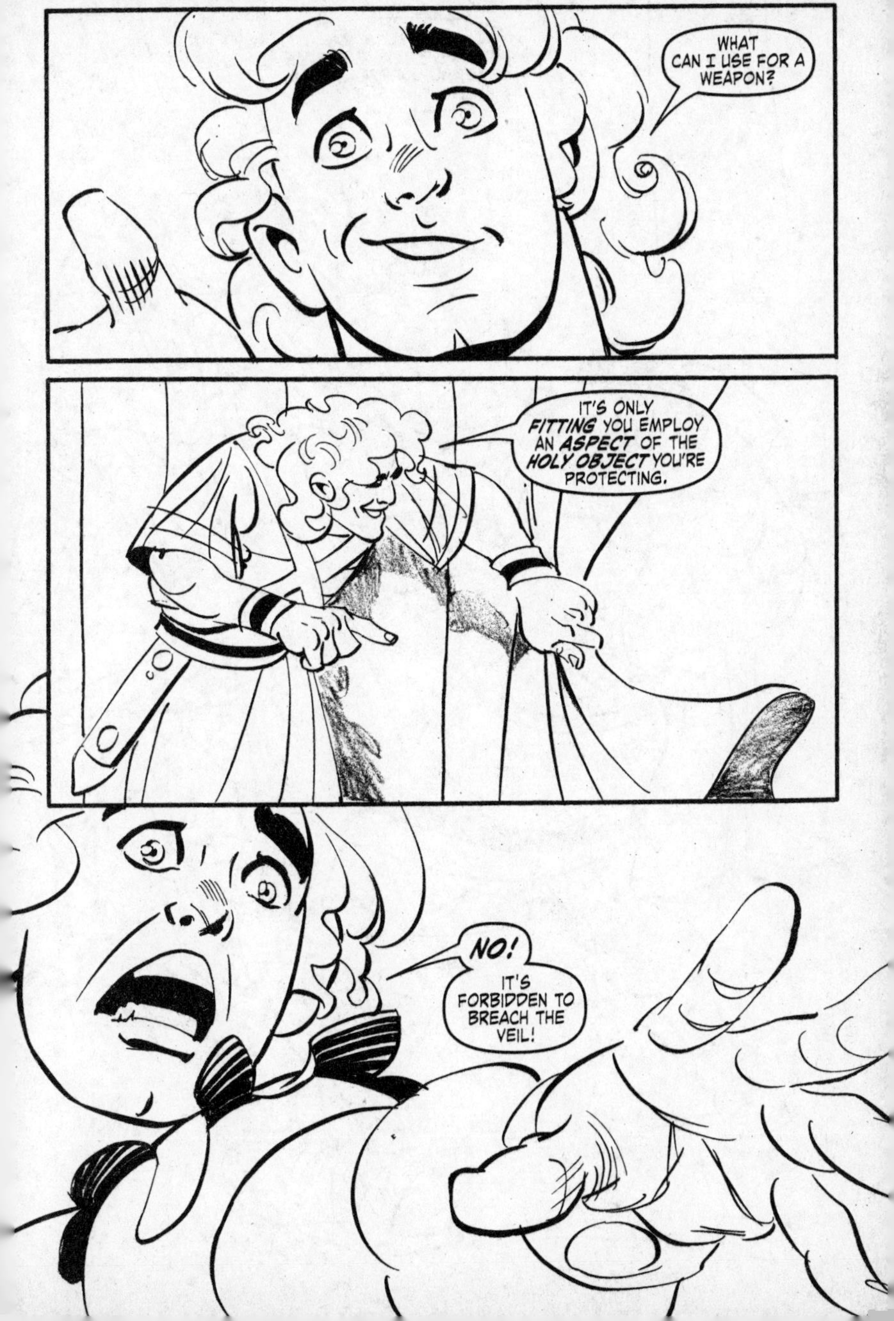
WHAT CAN I USE FOR A WEAPON?
IT'S ONLY *FITTING* YOU EMPLOY AN *ASPECT* OF THE *HOLY OBJECT* YOU'RE PROTECTING.
NO! IT'S FORBIDDEN TO BREACH THE VEIL!

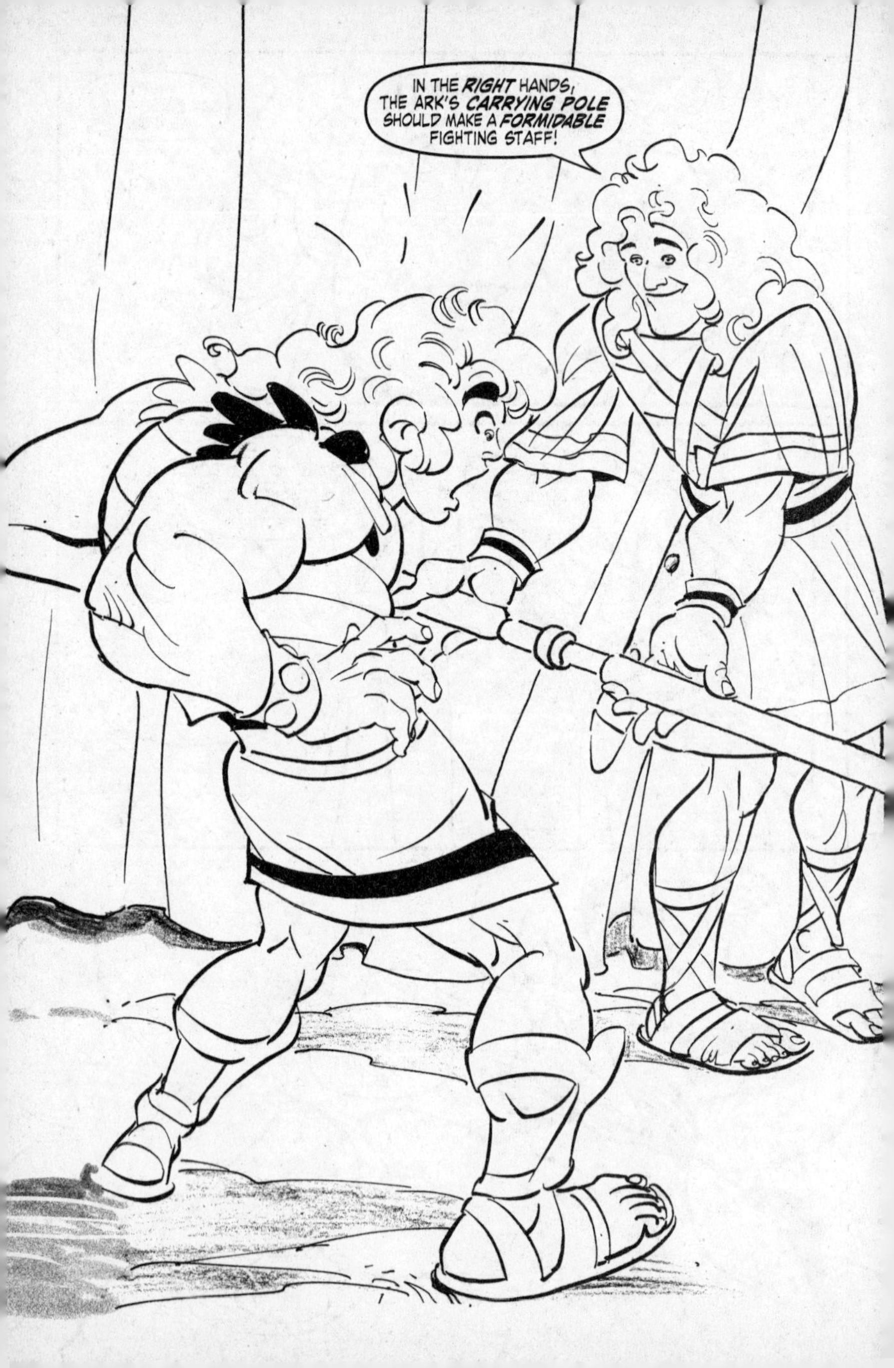
IN THE RIGHT HANDS, THE ARK'S CARRYING POLE SHOULD MAKE A FORMIDABLE FIGHTING STAFF!

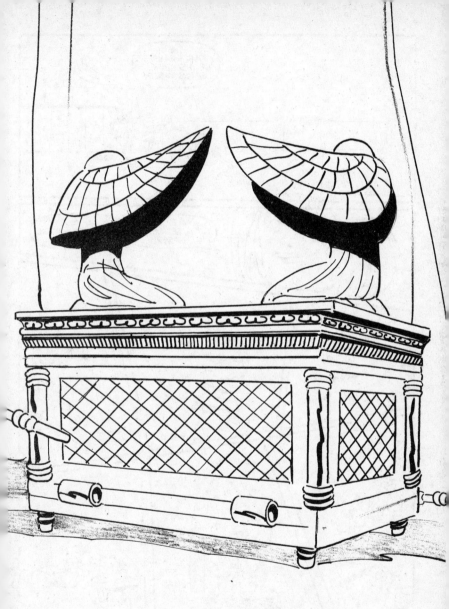

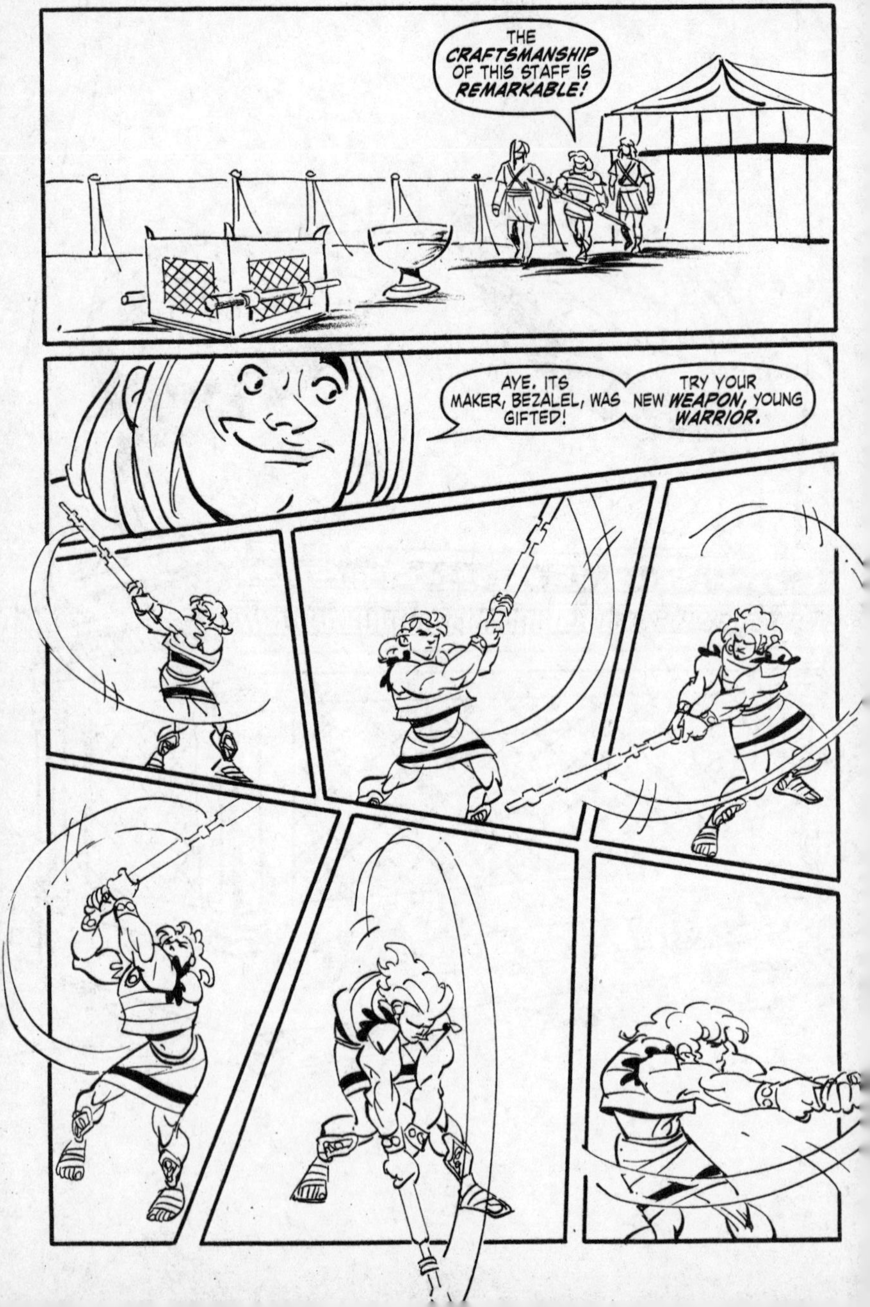
THE CRAFTSMANSHIP OF THIS STAFF IS REMARKABLE!
AYE. ITS MAKER, BEZALEL, WAS GIFTED!
TRY YOUR NEW WEAPON, YOUNG WARRIOR.

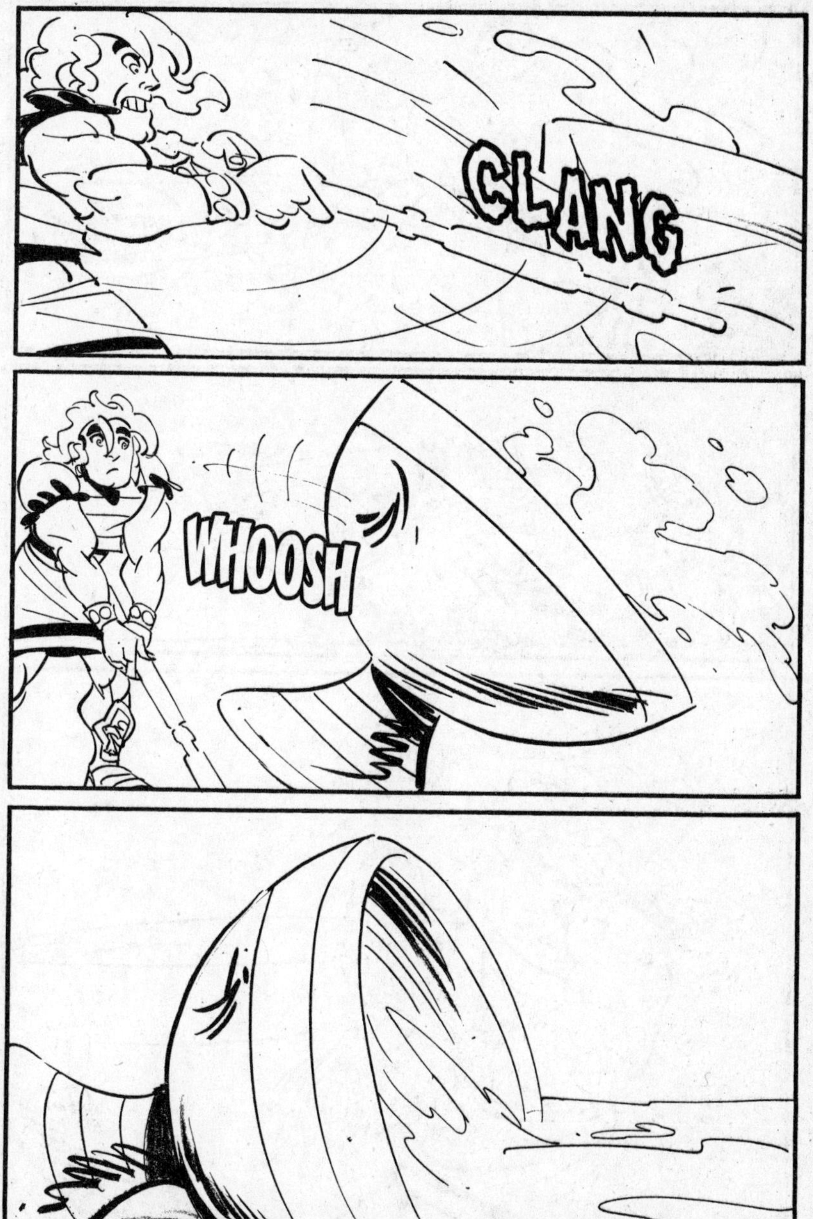
CLANG
WHOOSH

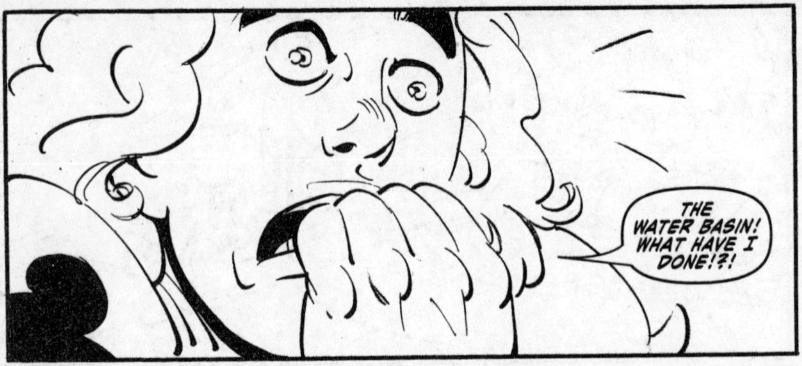
THE WATER BASIN! WHAT HAVE I DONE!?!

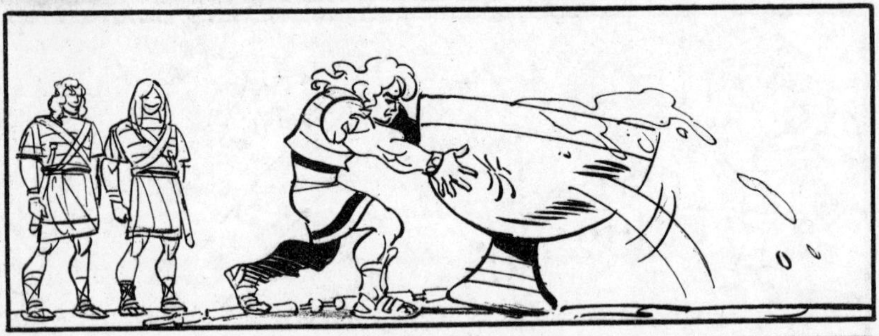

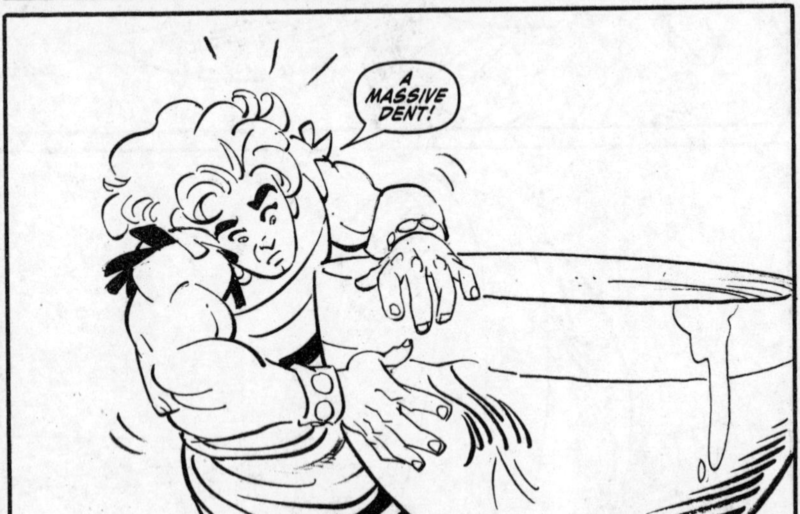
A MASSIVE DENT!

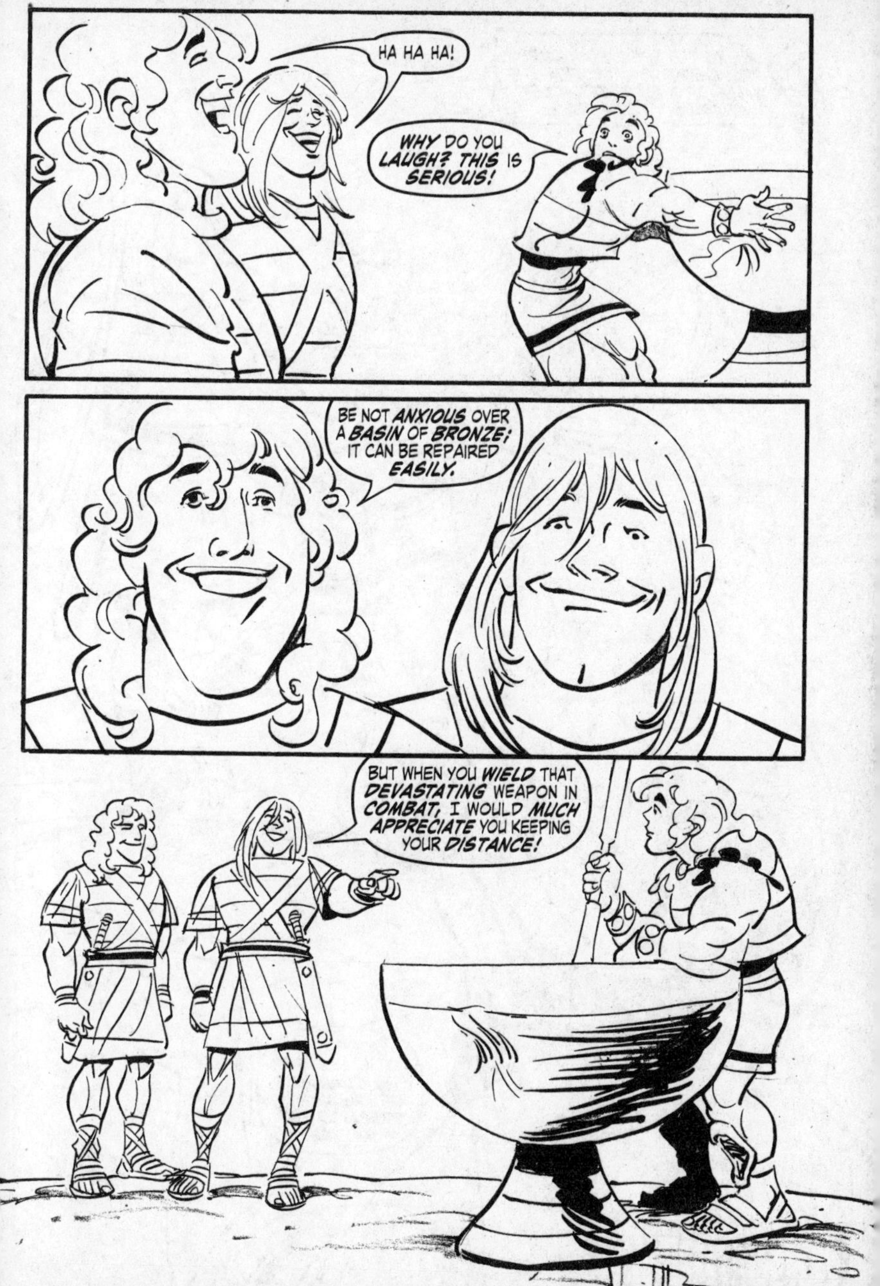
HA HA HA!
WHY DO YOU LAUGH? THIS IS SERIOUS!
BE NOT ANXIOUS OVER A BASIN OF BRONZE; IT CAN BE REPAIRED EASILY.
BUT WHEN YOU WIELD THAT DEVASTATING WEAPON IN COMBAT, I WOULD MUCH APPRECIATE YOU KEEPING YOUR DISTANCE!

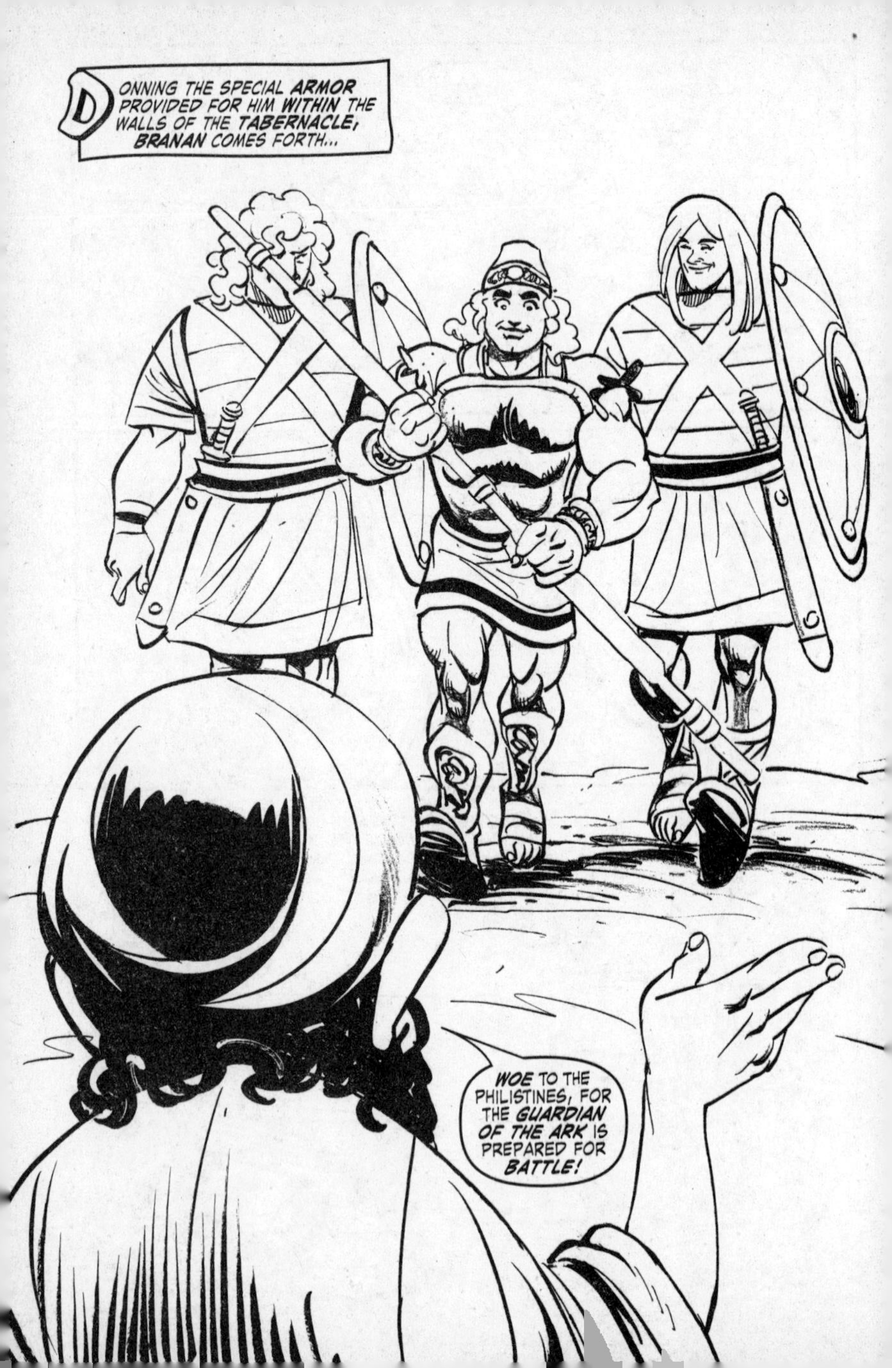
DONNING THE SPECIAL ARMOR PROVIDED FOR HIM WITHIN THE WALLS OF THE TABERNACLE, BRANAN COMES FORTH...
WOE TO THE PHILISTINES, FOR THE GUARDIAN OF THE ARK IS PREPARED FOR BATTLE!

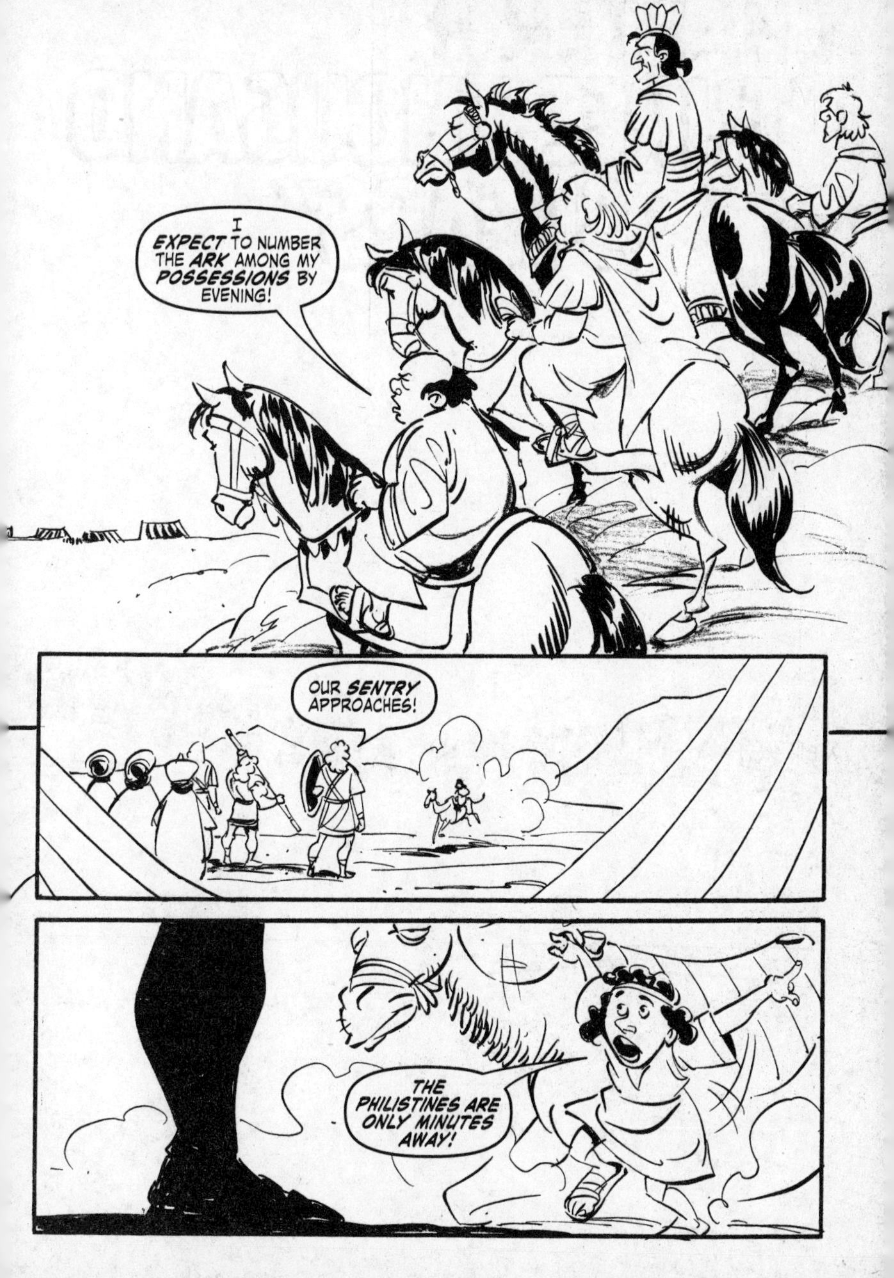
I EXPECT TO NUMBER THE ARK AMONG MY POSSESSIONS BY EVENING!
OUR SENTRY APPROACHES!
THE PHILISTINES ARE ONLY MINUTES AWAY!

CHAPTER 4
"THREE THOUSAND SPEARS"

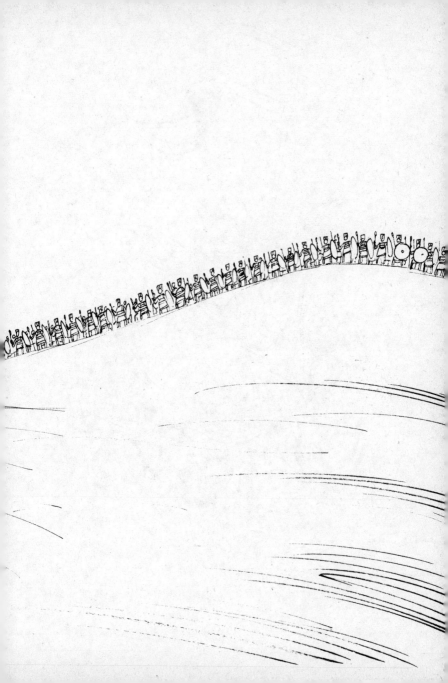

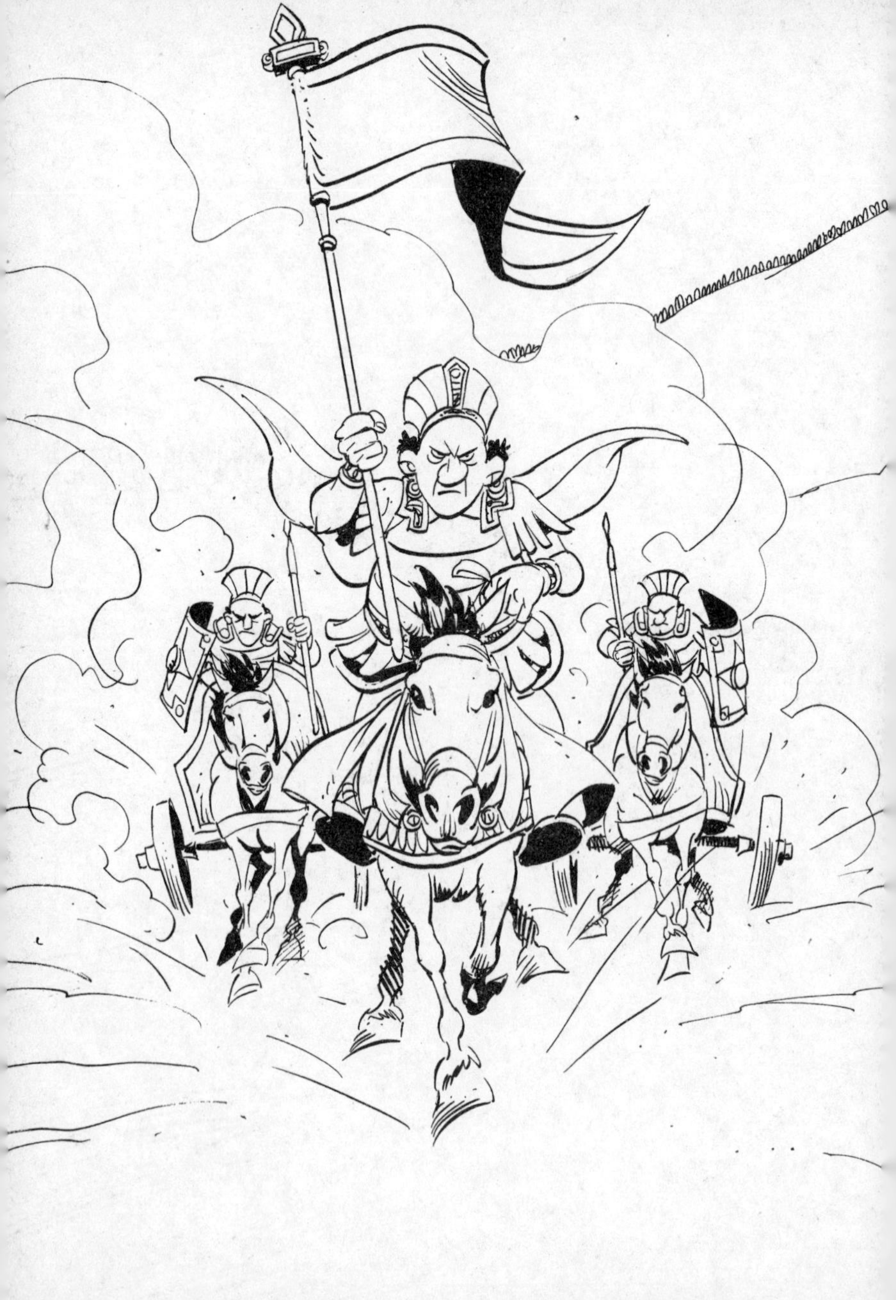

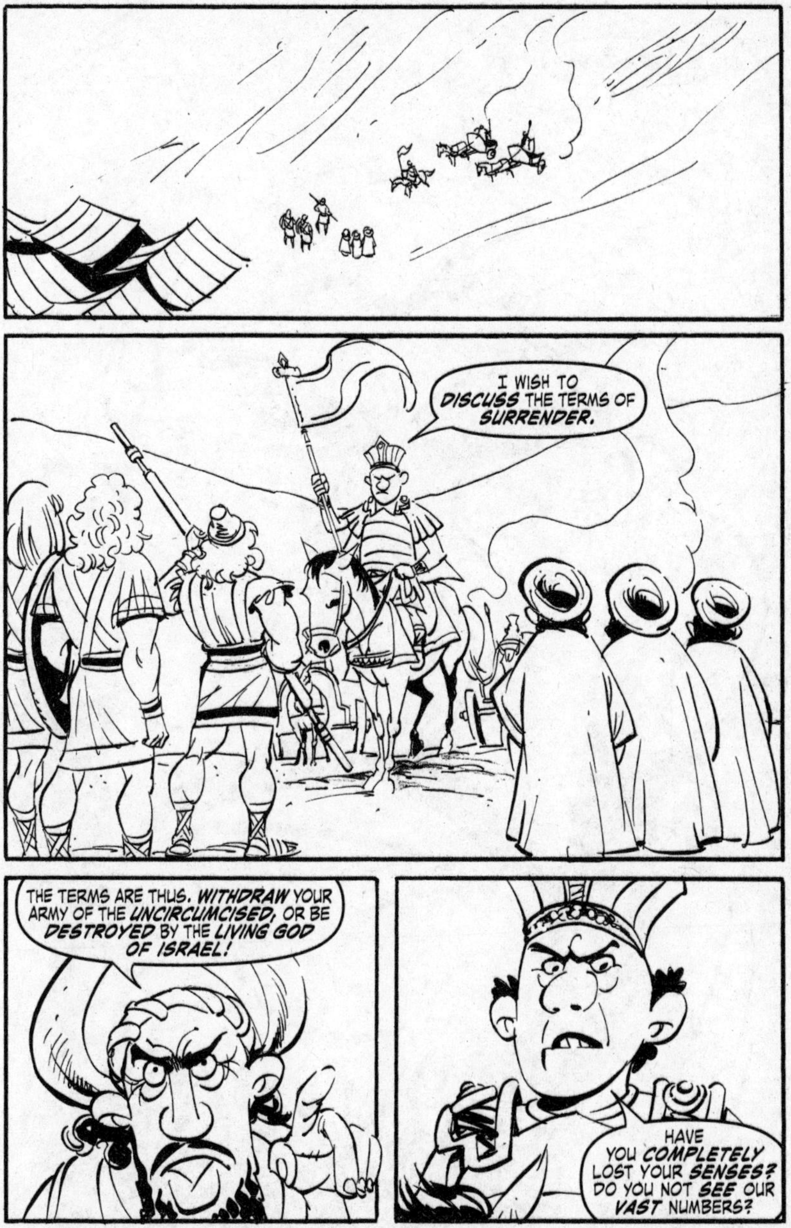
I WISH TO DISCUSS THE TERMS OF SURRENDER.
THE TERMS ARE THUS. WITHDRAW YOUR ARMY OF THE UNCIRCUMCISED, OR BE DESTROYED BY THE LIVING GOD OF ISRAEL!
HAVE YOU COMPLETELY LOST YOUR SENSES? DO YOU NOT SEE OUR VAST NUMBERS?

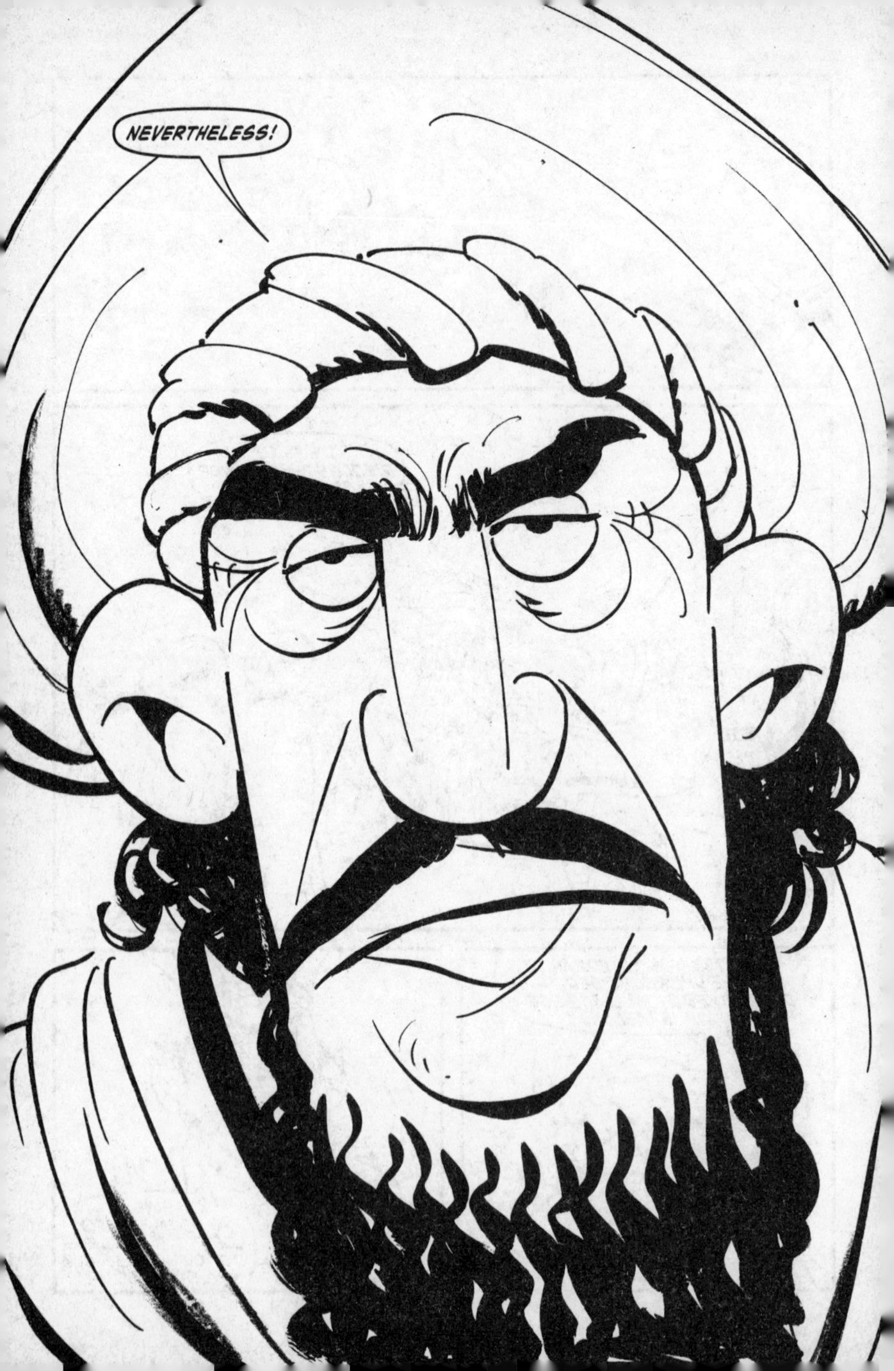
NEVERTHELESS!

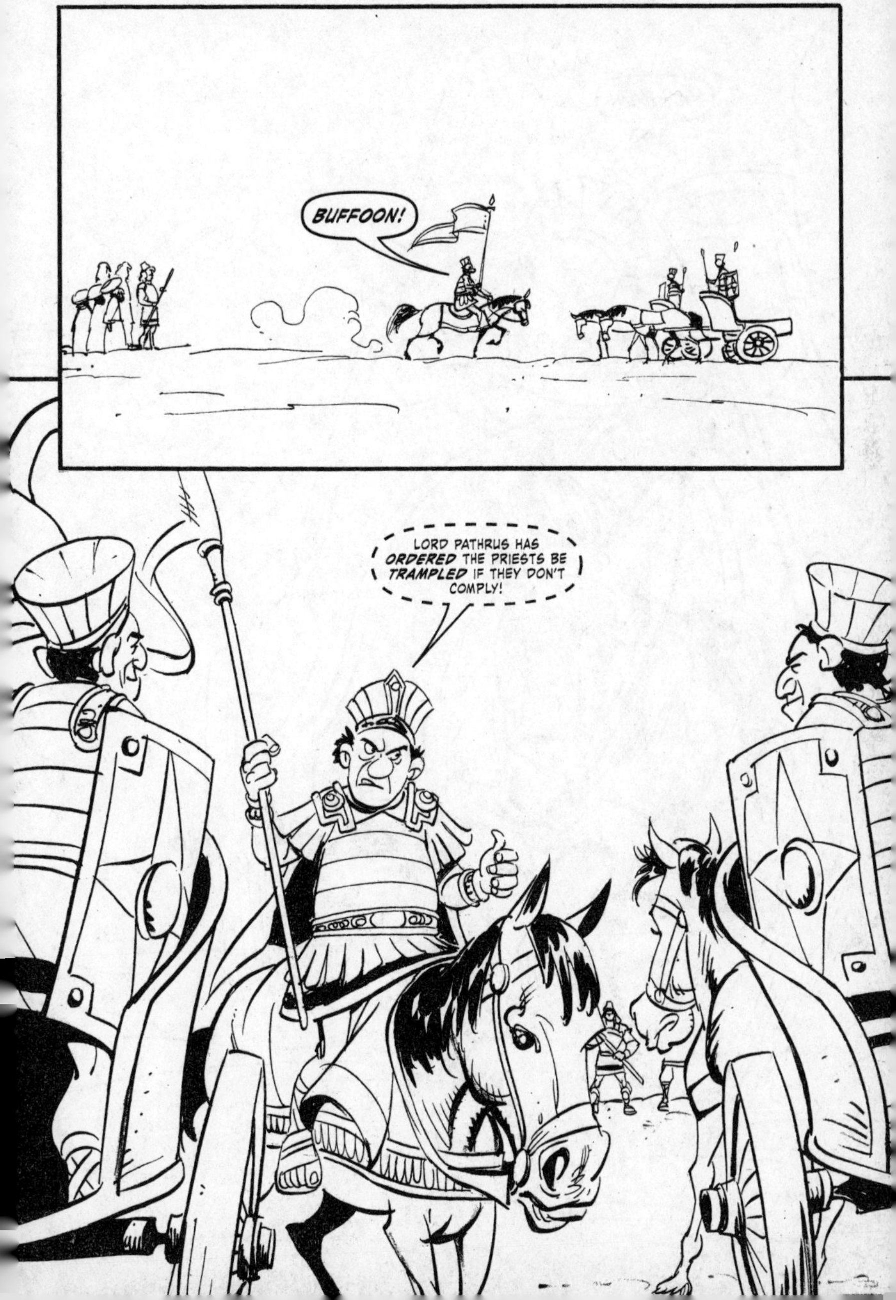
BUFFOON!
LORD PATHRUS HAS ORDERED THE PRIESTS BE TRAMPLED IF THEY DON'T COMPLY!

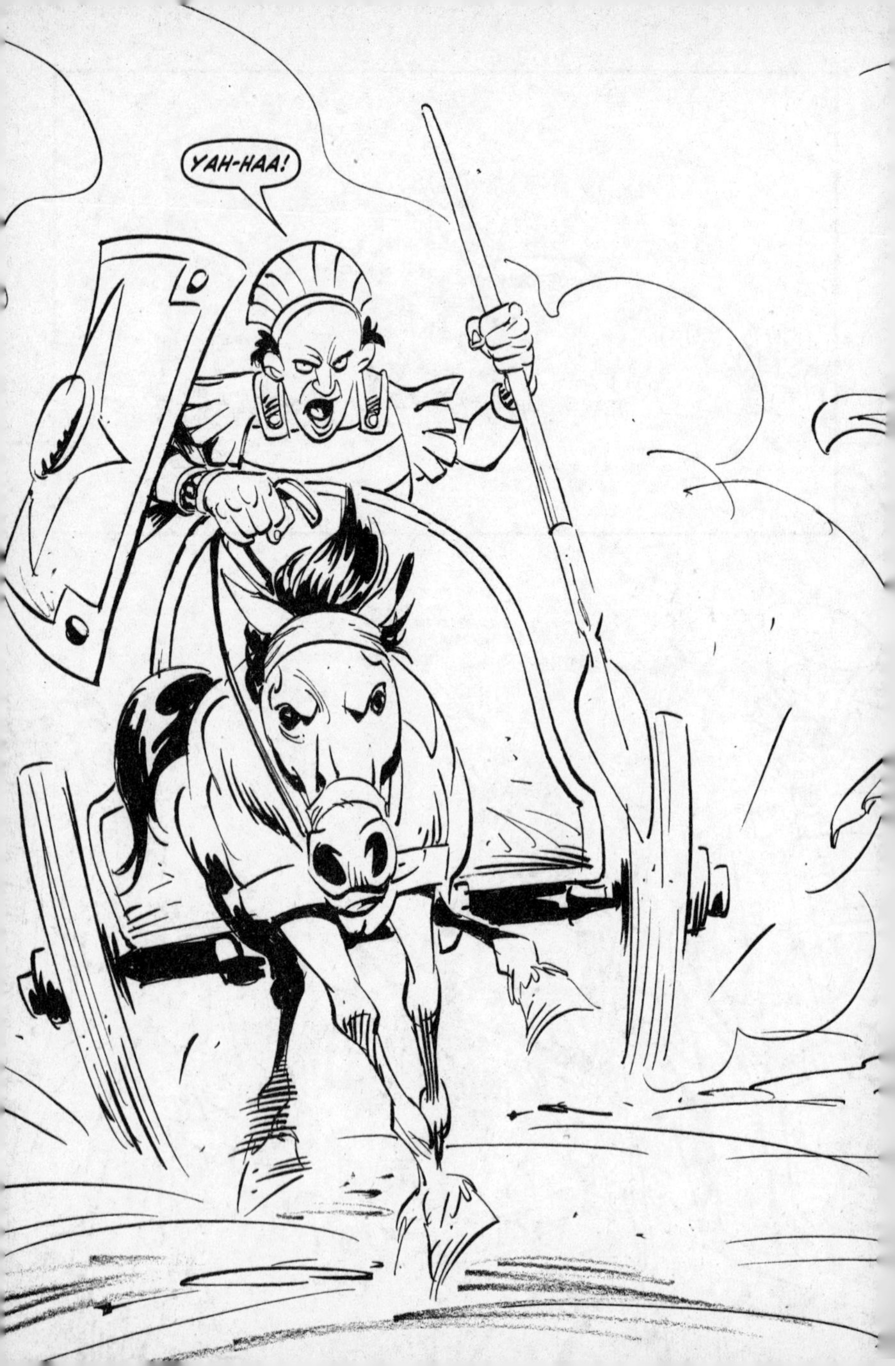
YAH-HAA!

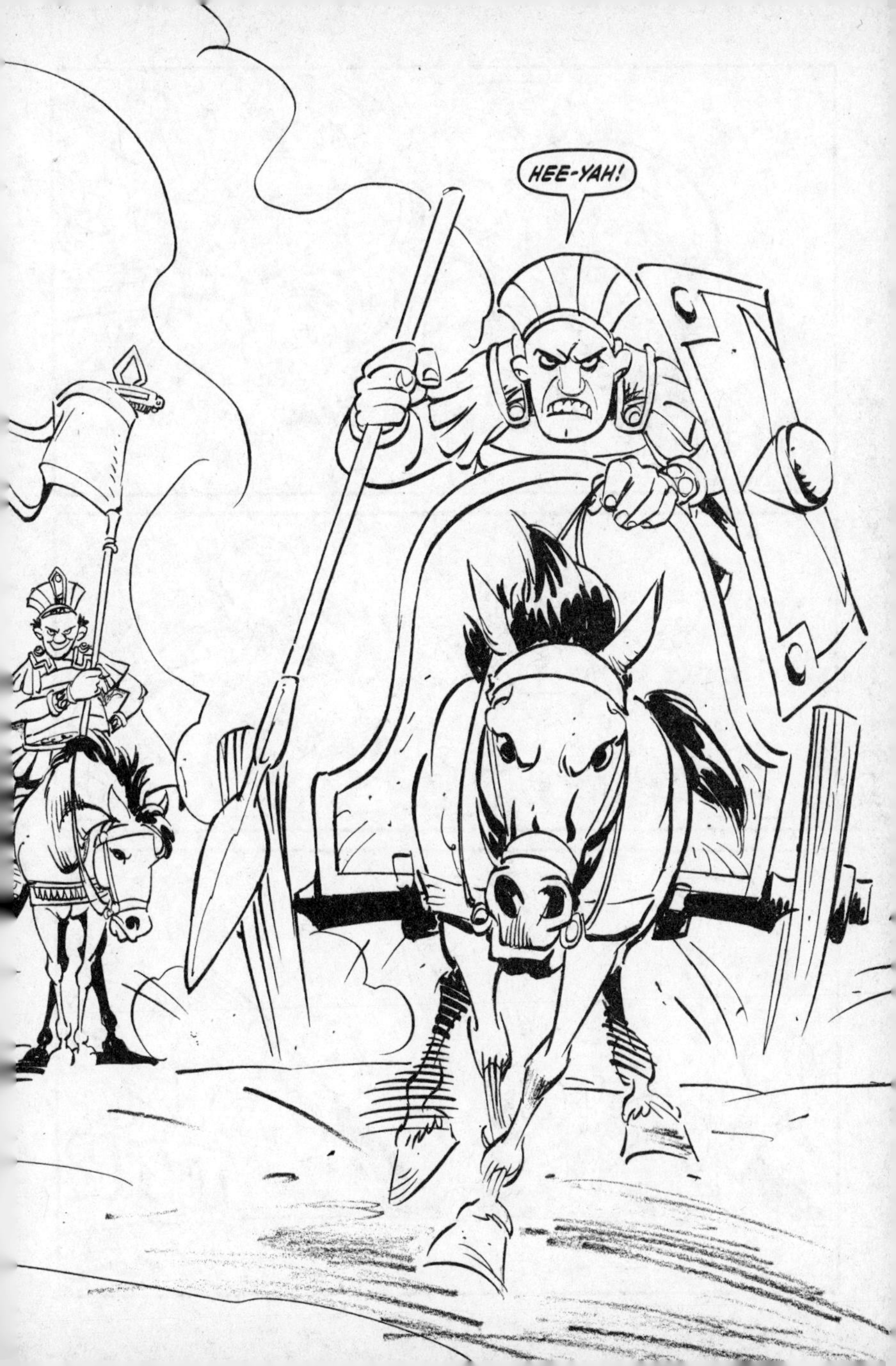
HEE-YAH!

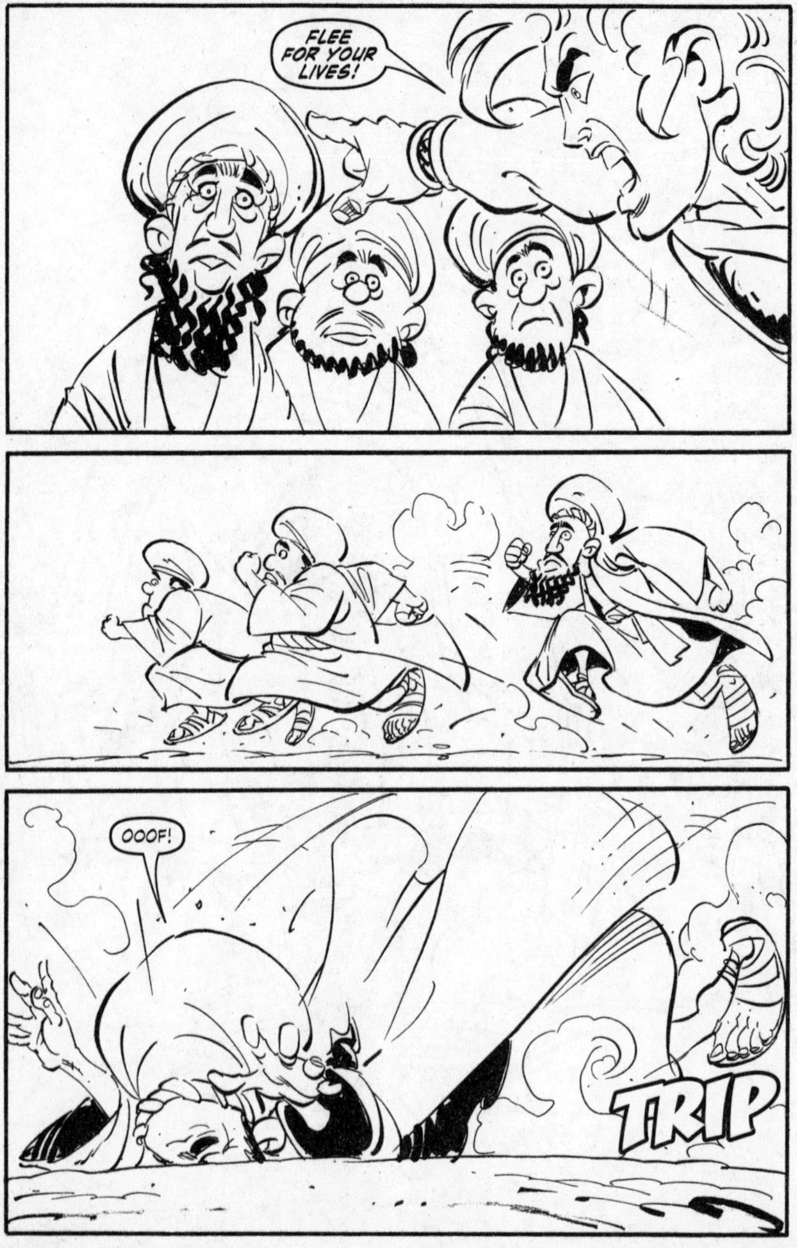
FLEE FOR YOUR LIVES!
OOOF!
TRIP

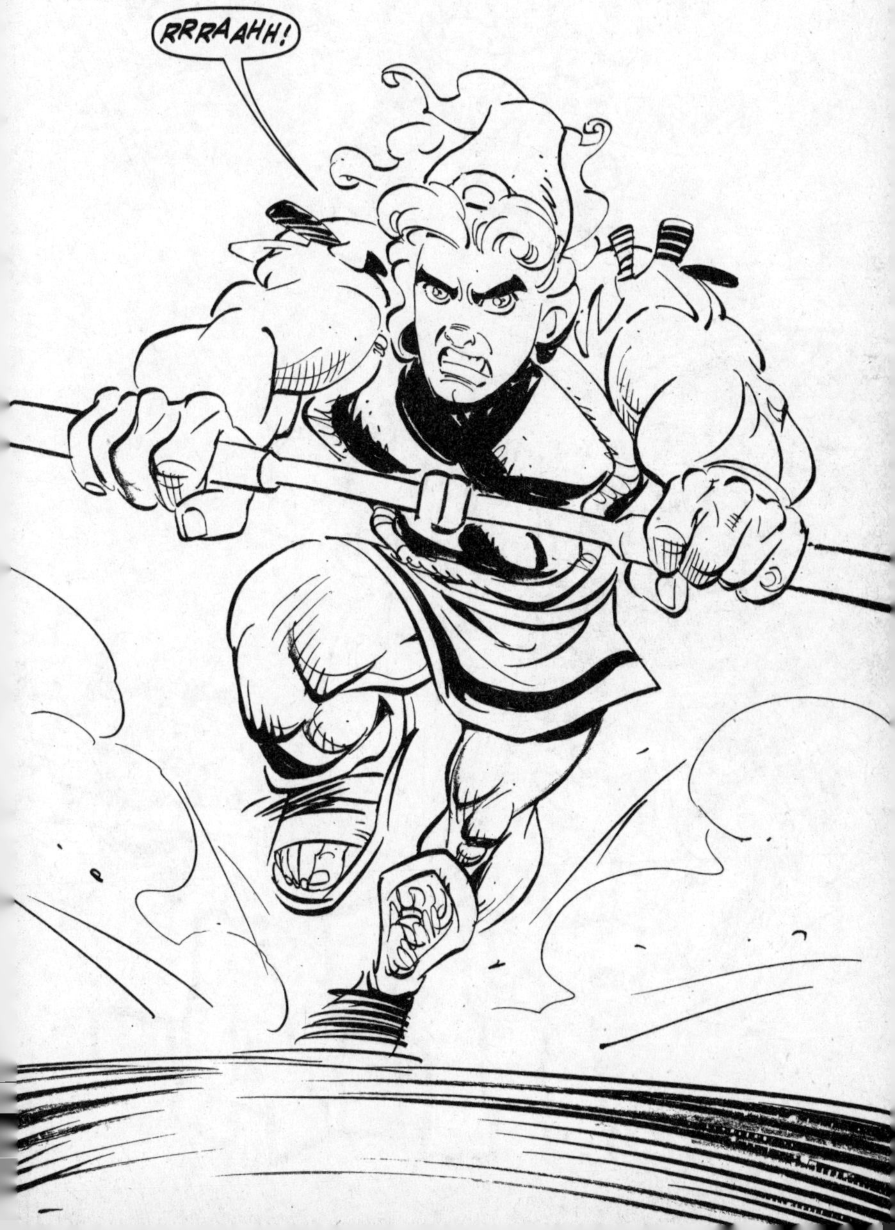
RRRAAHH!

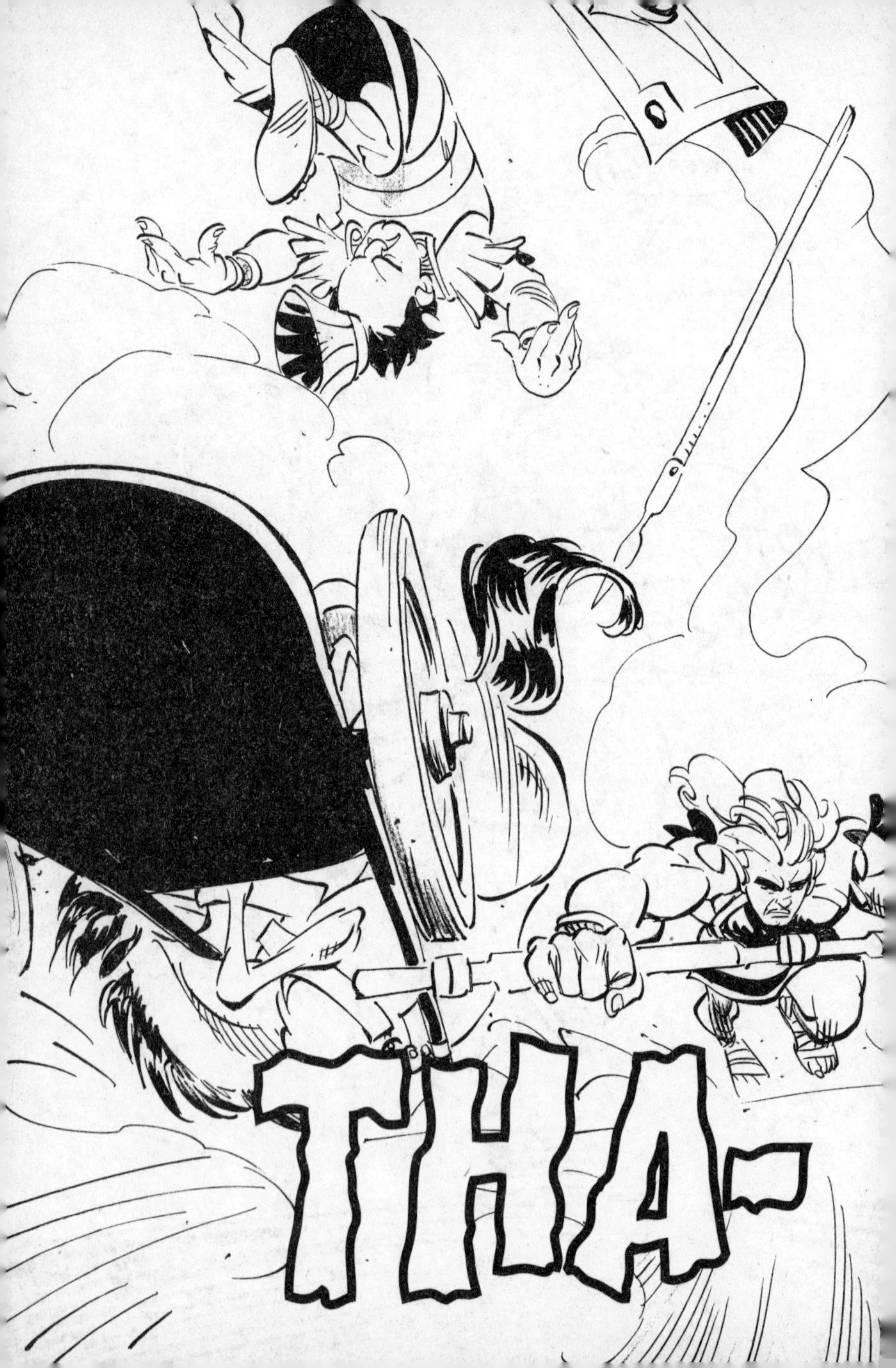
THA-

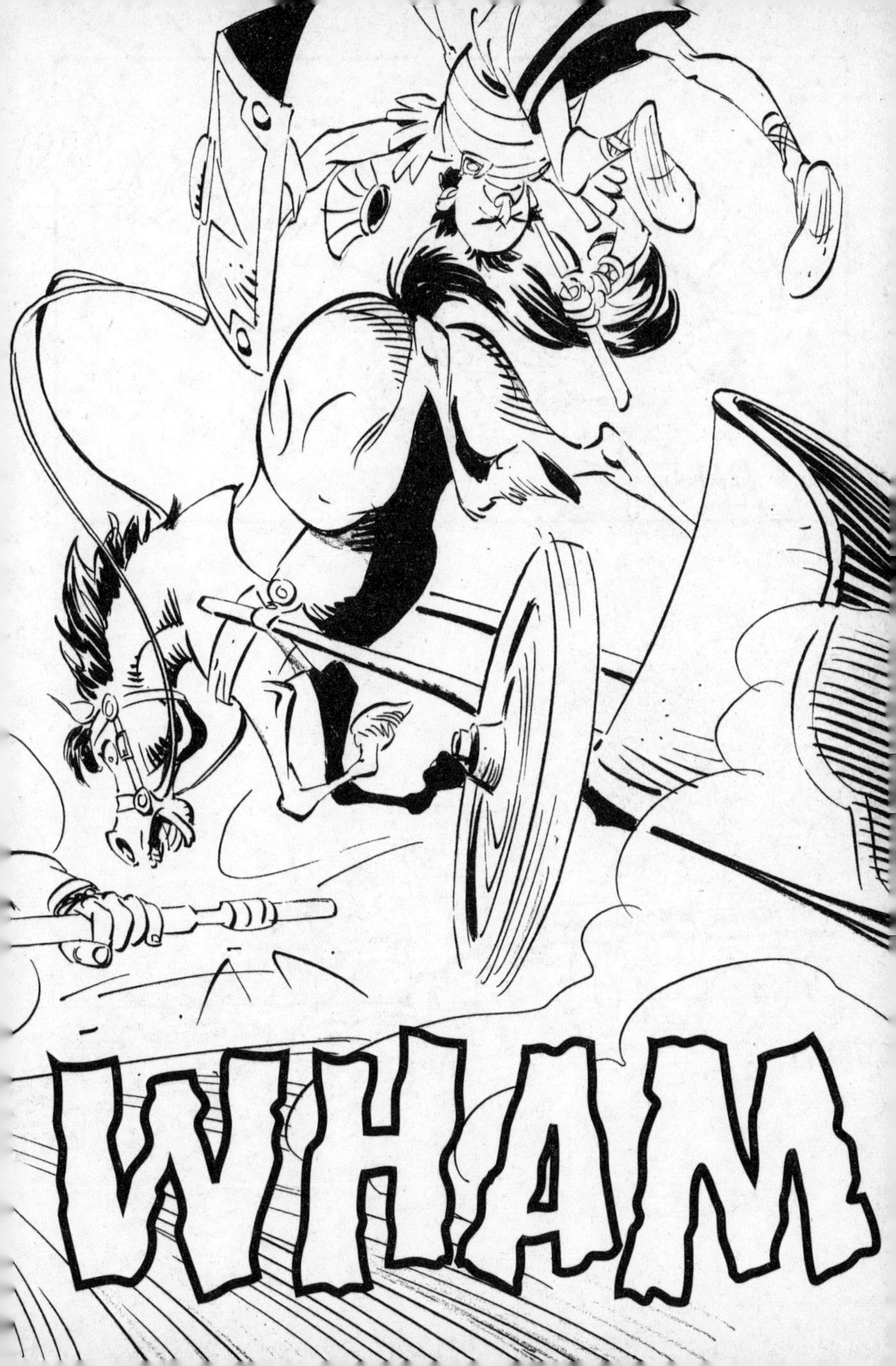
WHAM

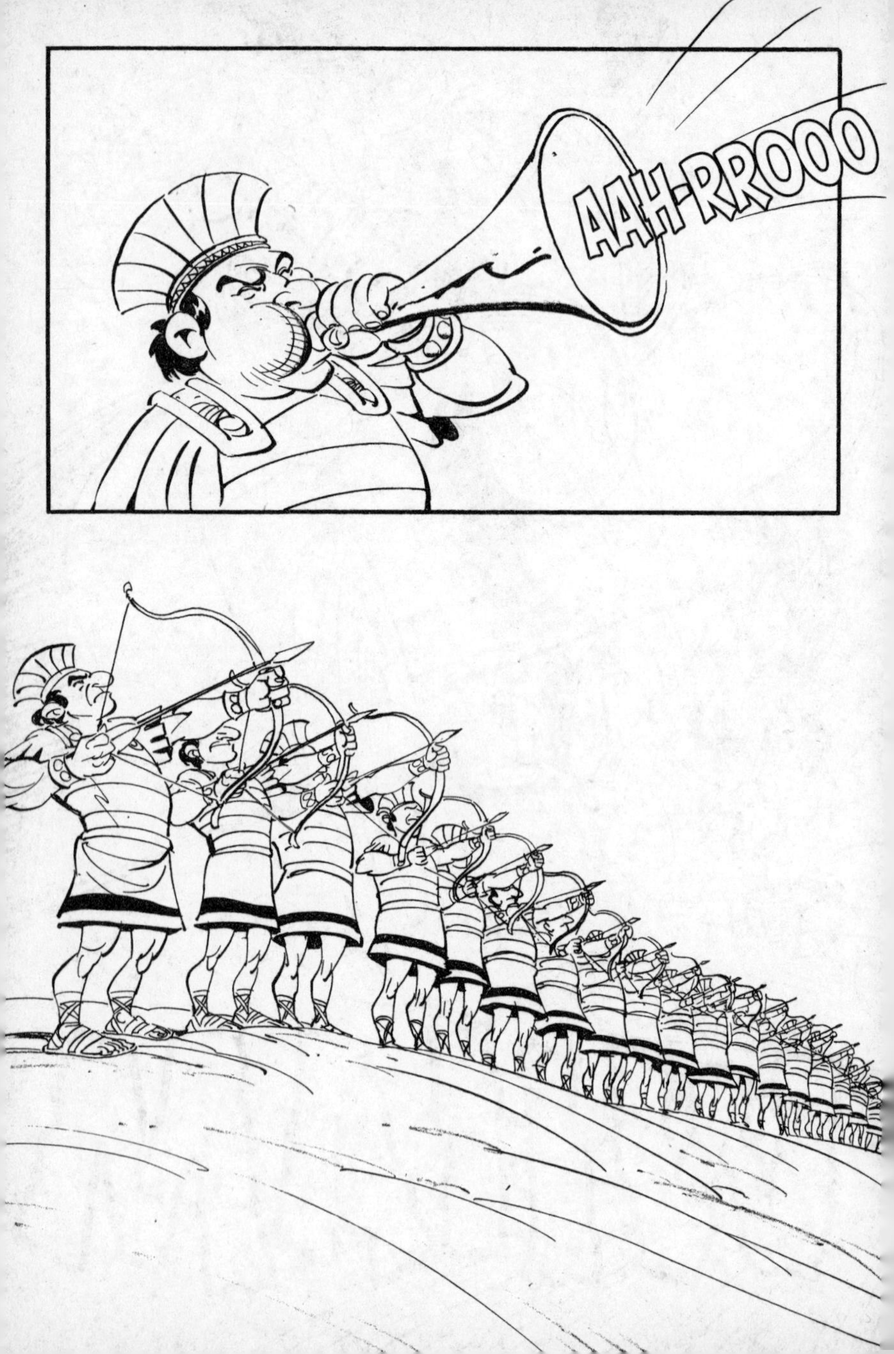
AAH-RROOO

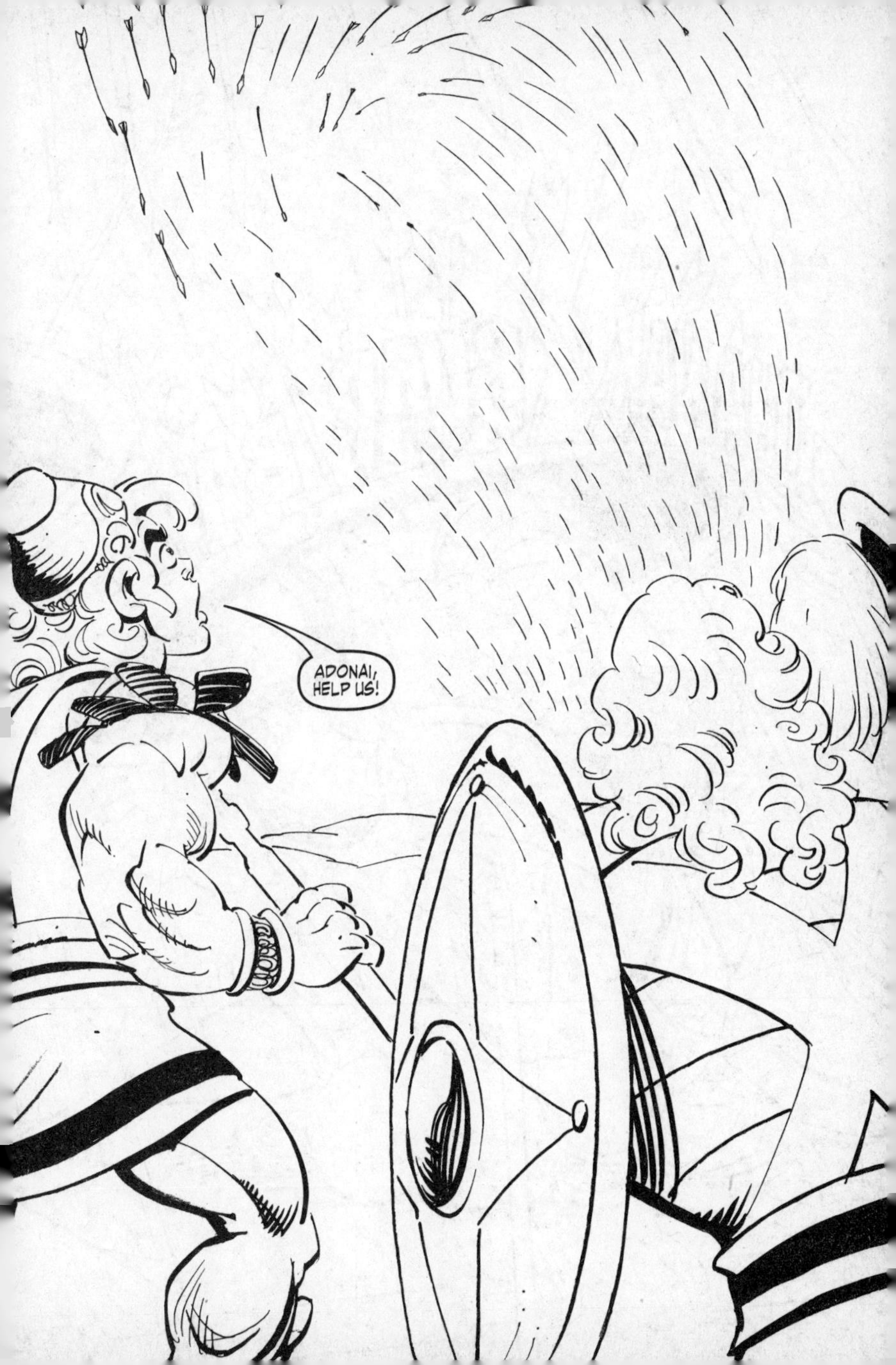
ADONAI, HELP US!

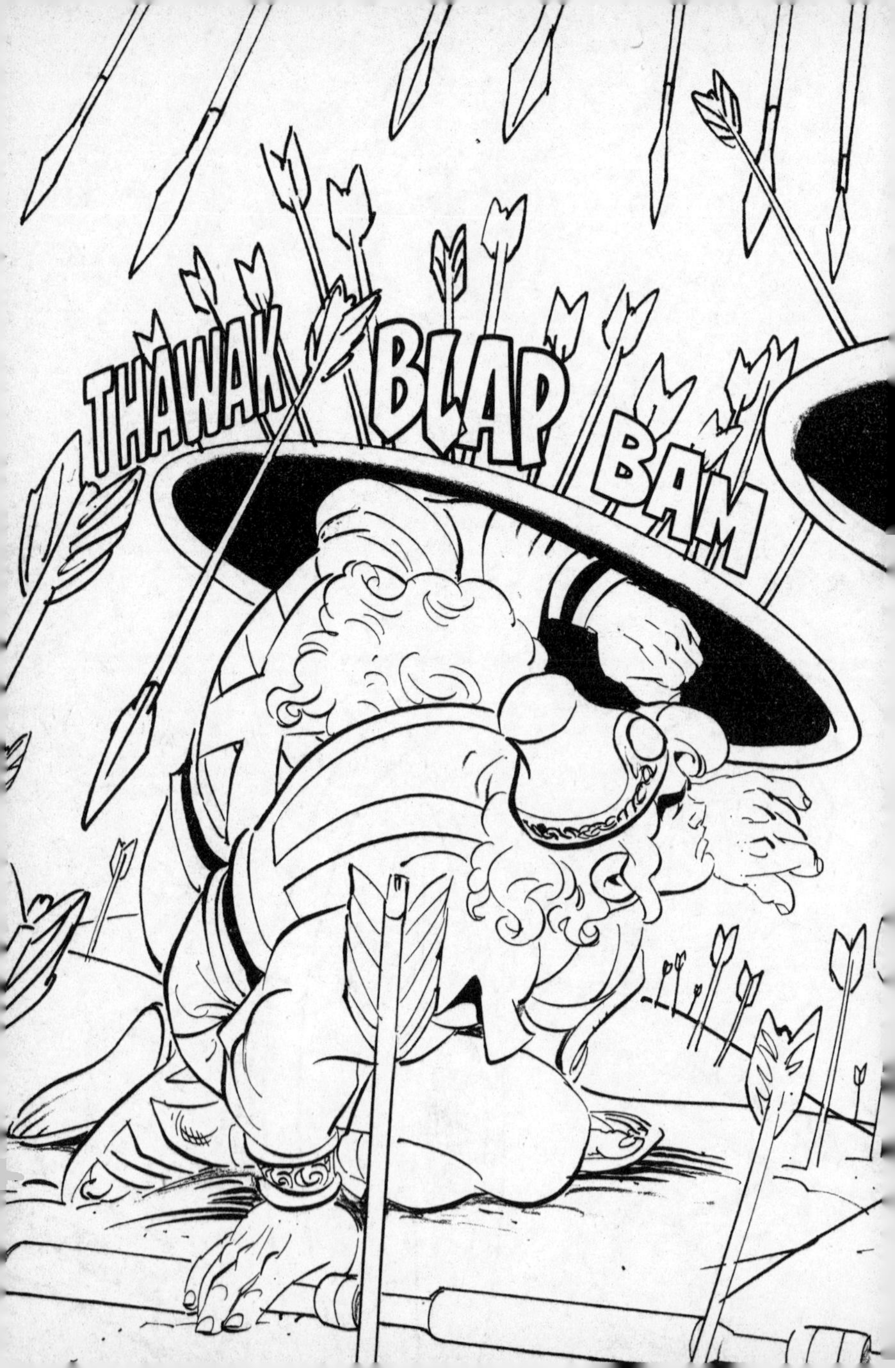
THAWAK
BLAP
BAM

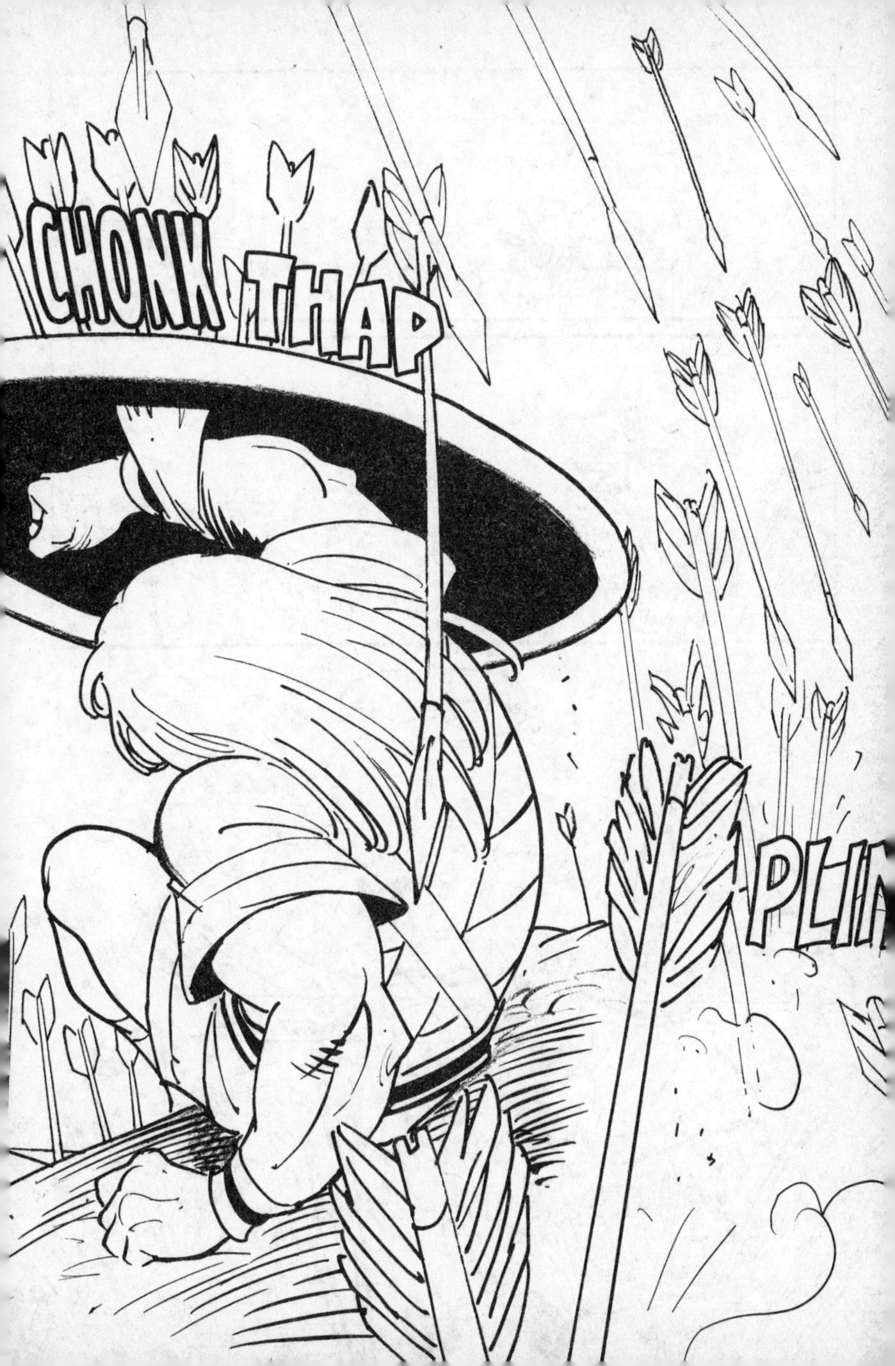
CHONK
THAP
PLIN

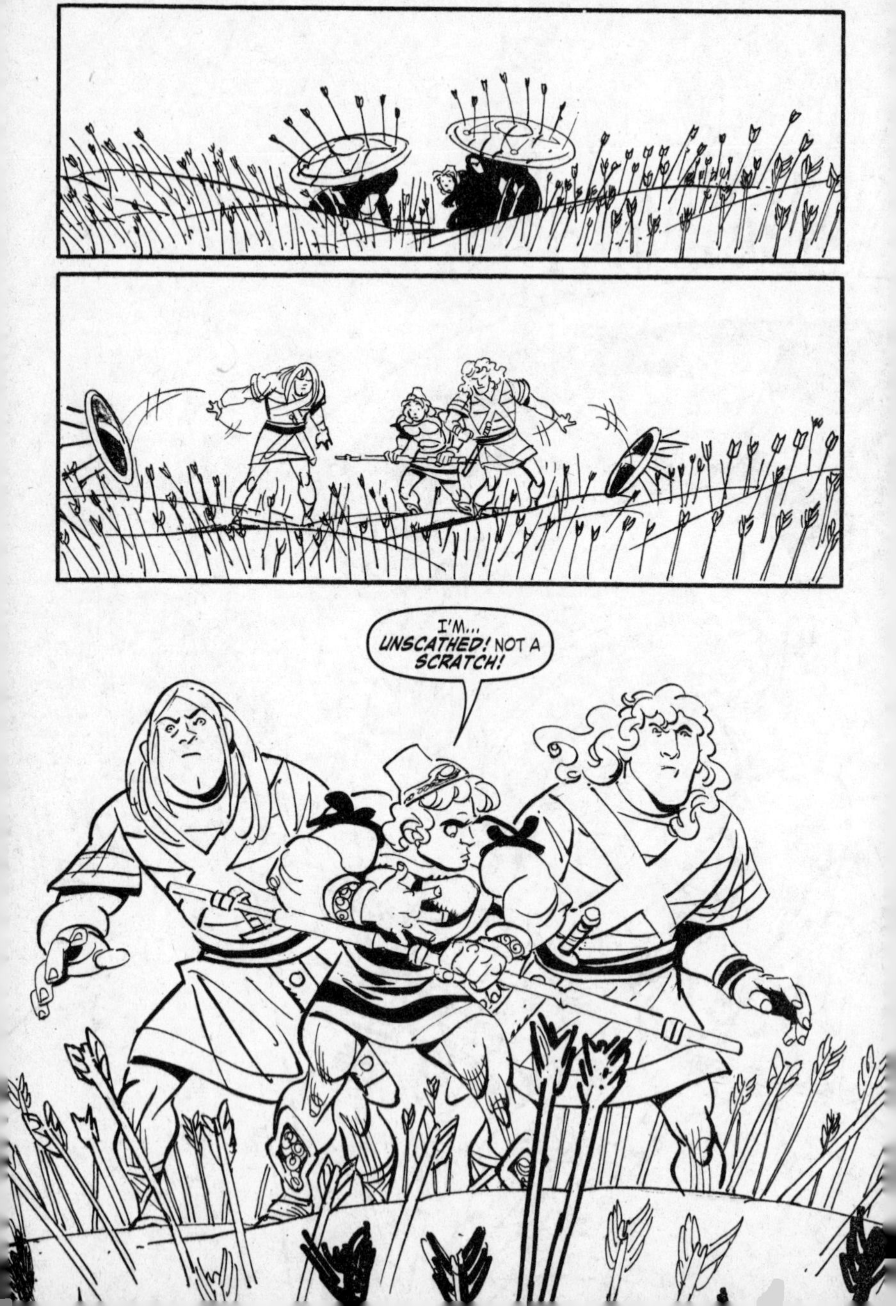
I'M... UNSCATHED! NOT A SCRATCH!

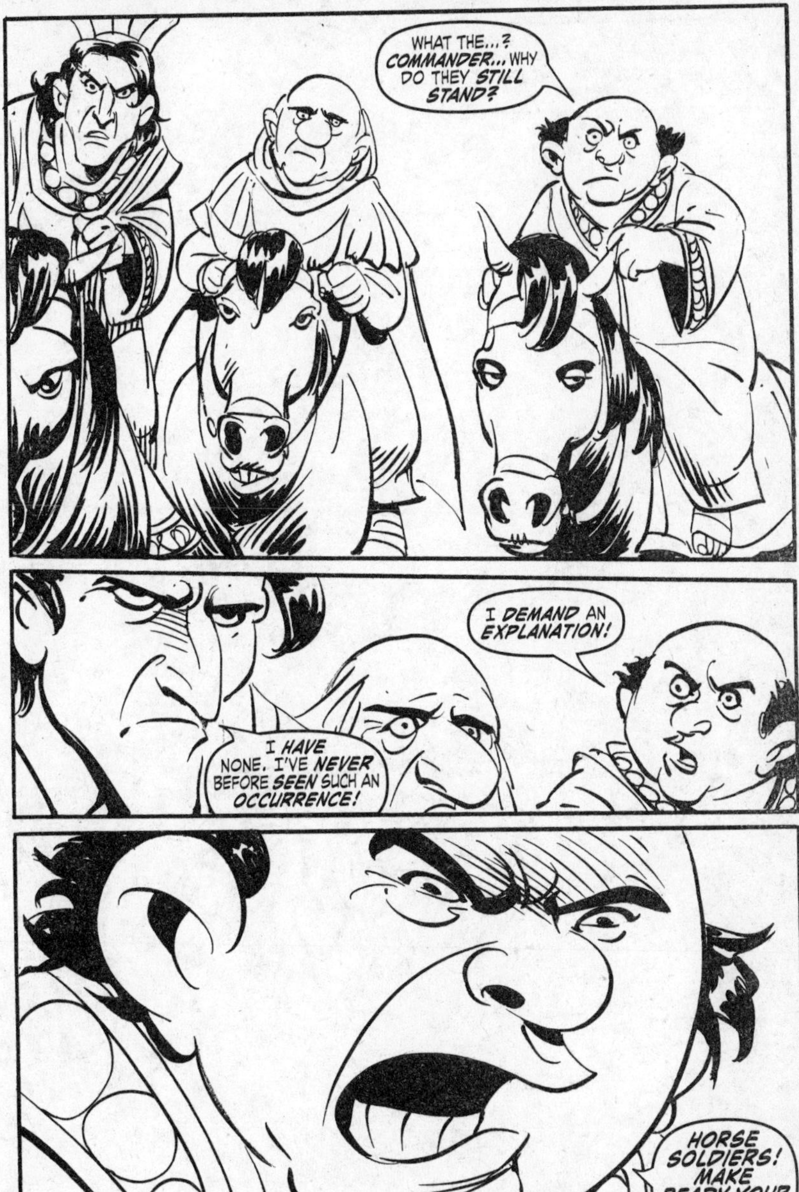
WHAT THE...? COMMANDER... WHY DO THEY STILL STAND?
I DEMAND AN EXPLANATION!
I HAVE NONE. I'VE NEVER BEFORE SEEN SUCH AN OCCURRENCE!
HORSE SOLDIERS! MAKE READY YOUR ATTACK!

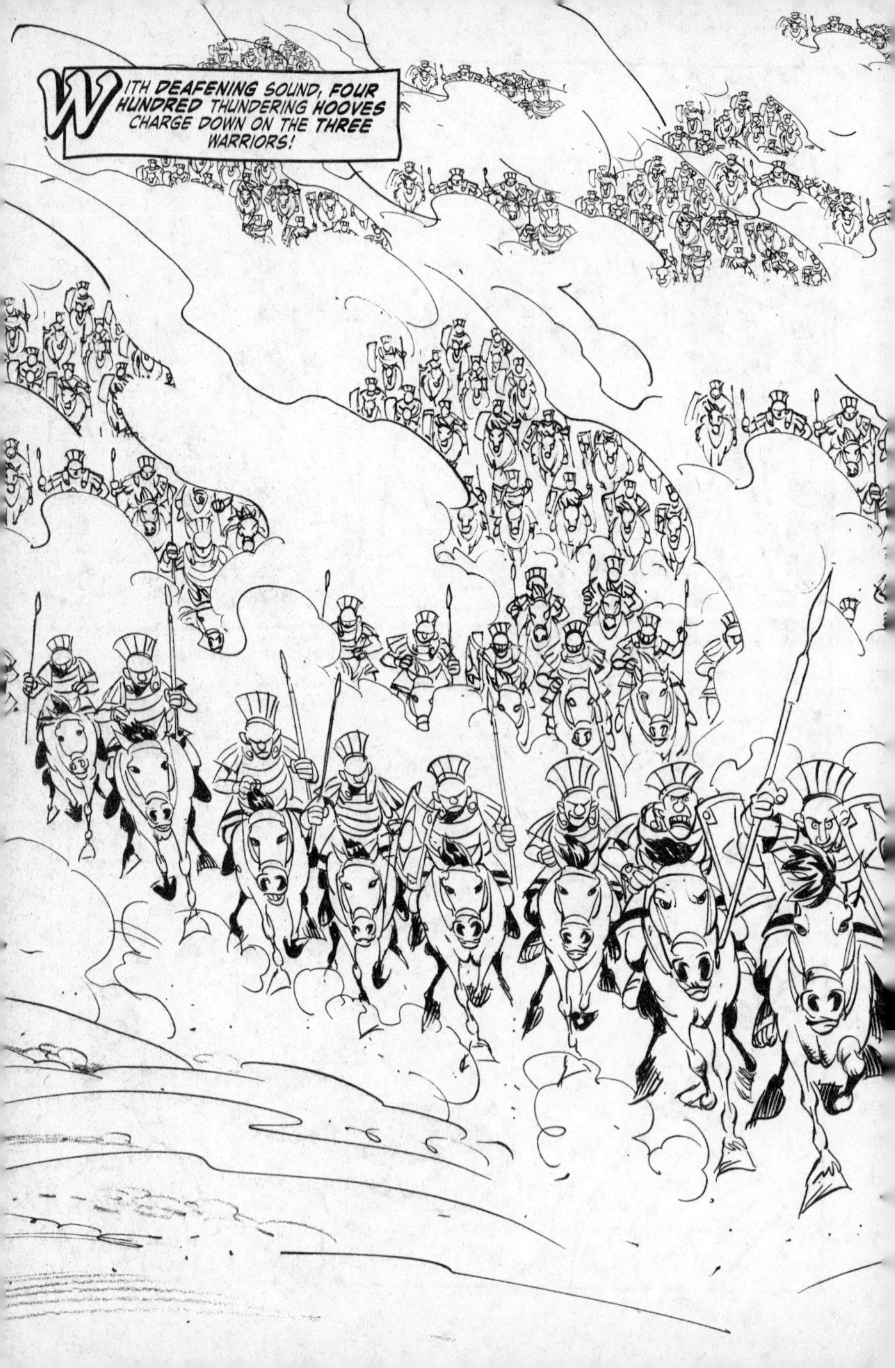
WITH DEAFENING SOUND, FOUR HUNDRED THUNDERING HOOVES CHARGE DOWN ON THE THREE WARRIORS!

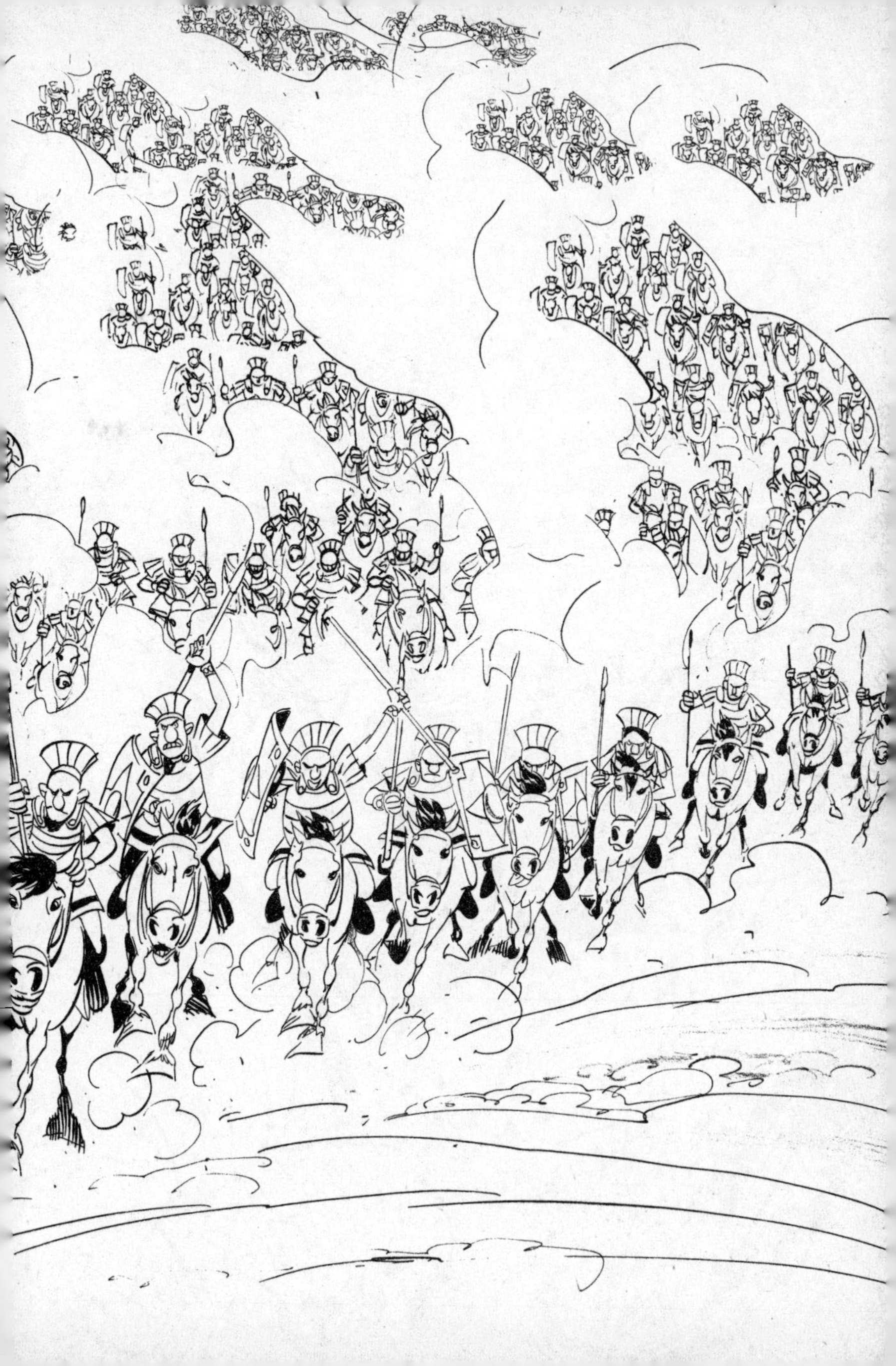

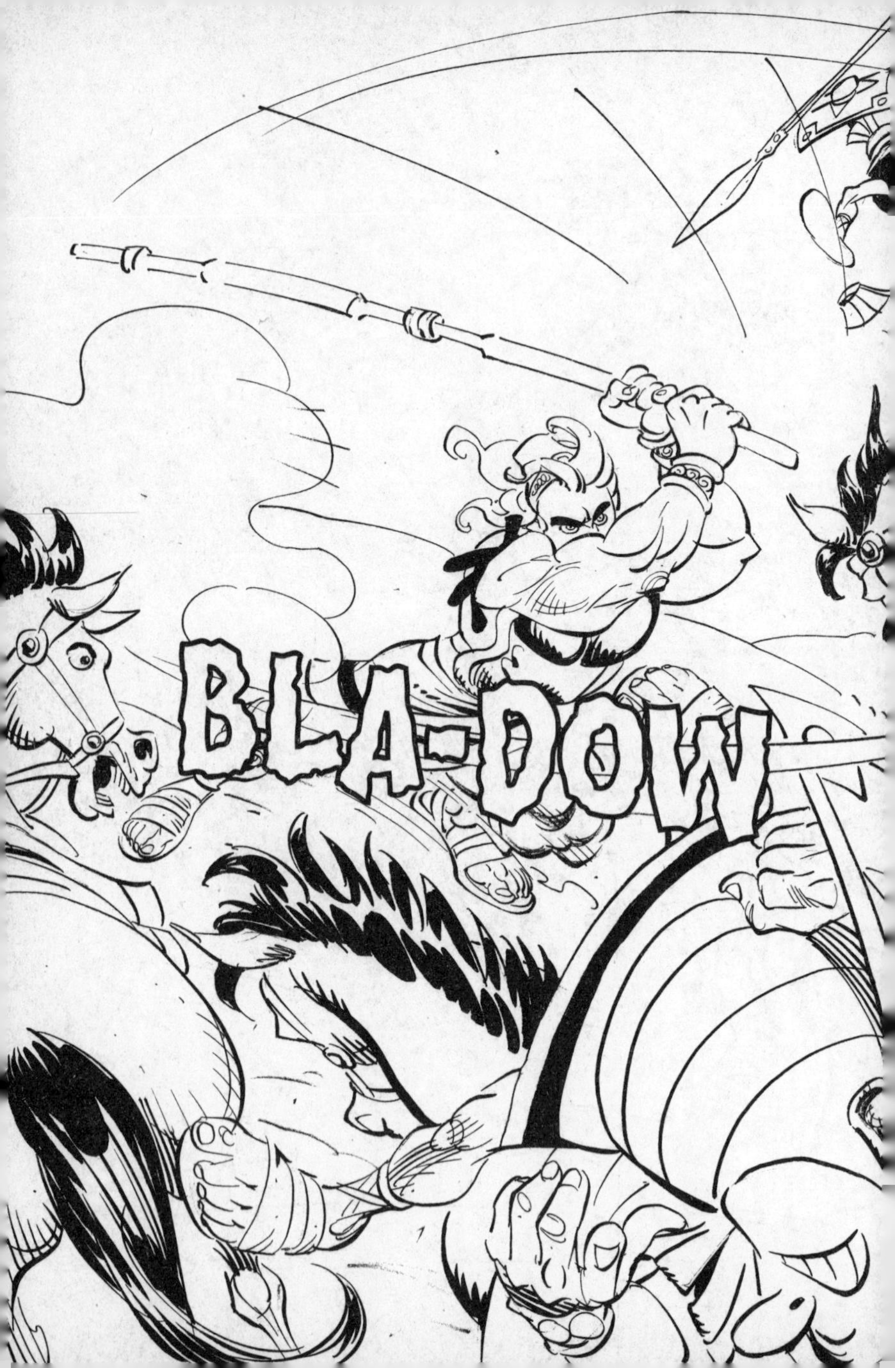
BLA-DOW

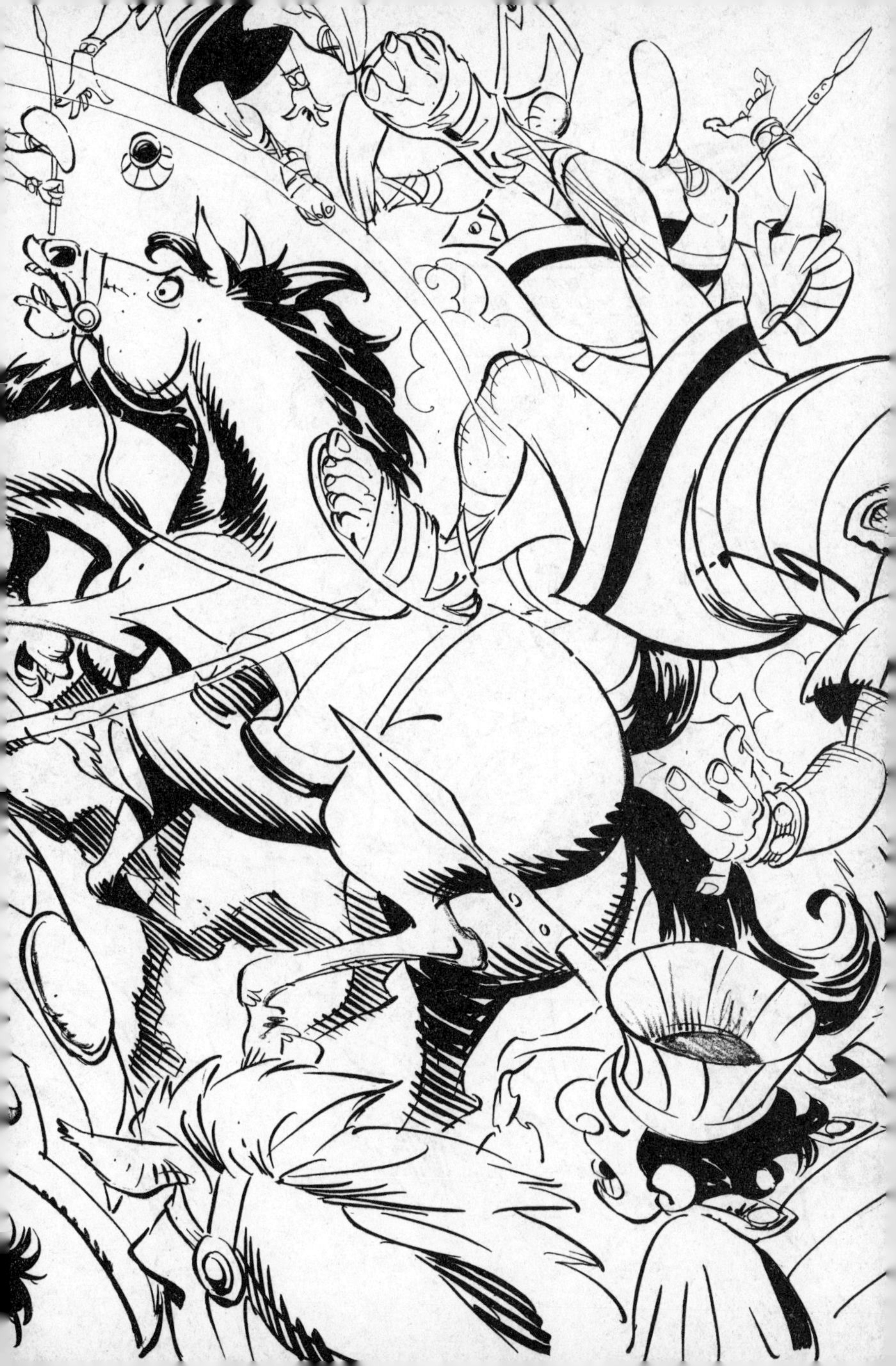

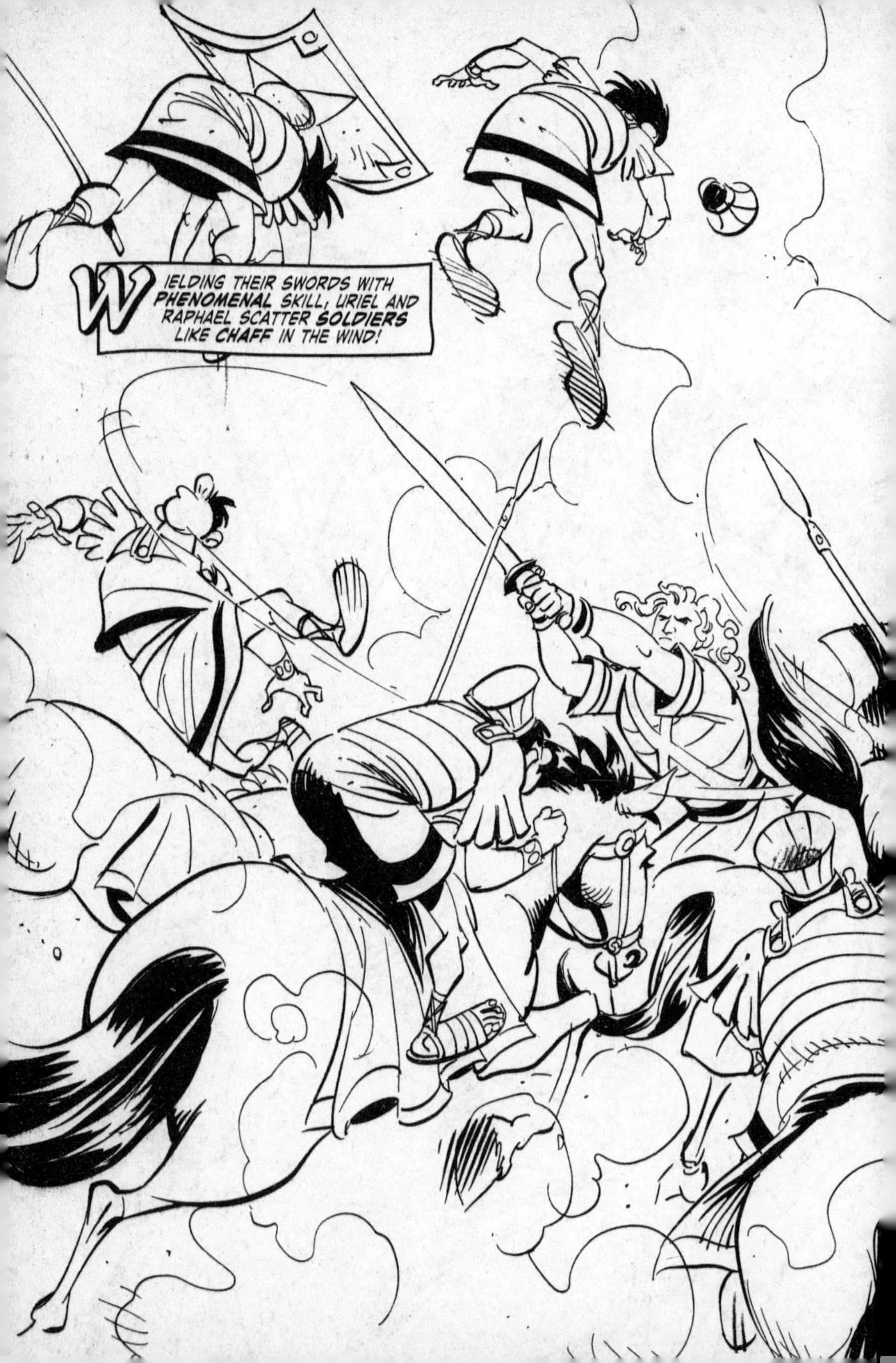
WIELDING THEIR SWORDS WITH PHENOMENAL SKILL, URIEL AND RAPHAEL SCATTER SOLDIERS LIKE CHAFF IN THE WIND!

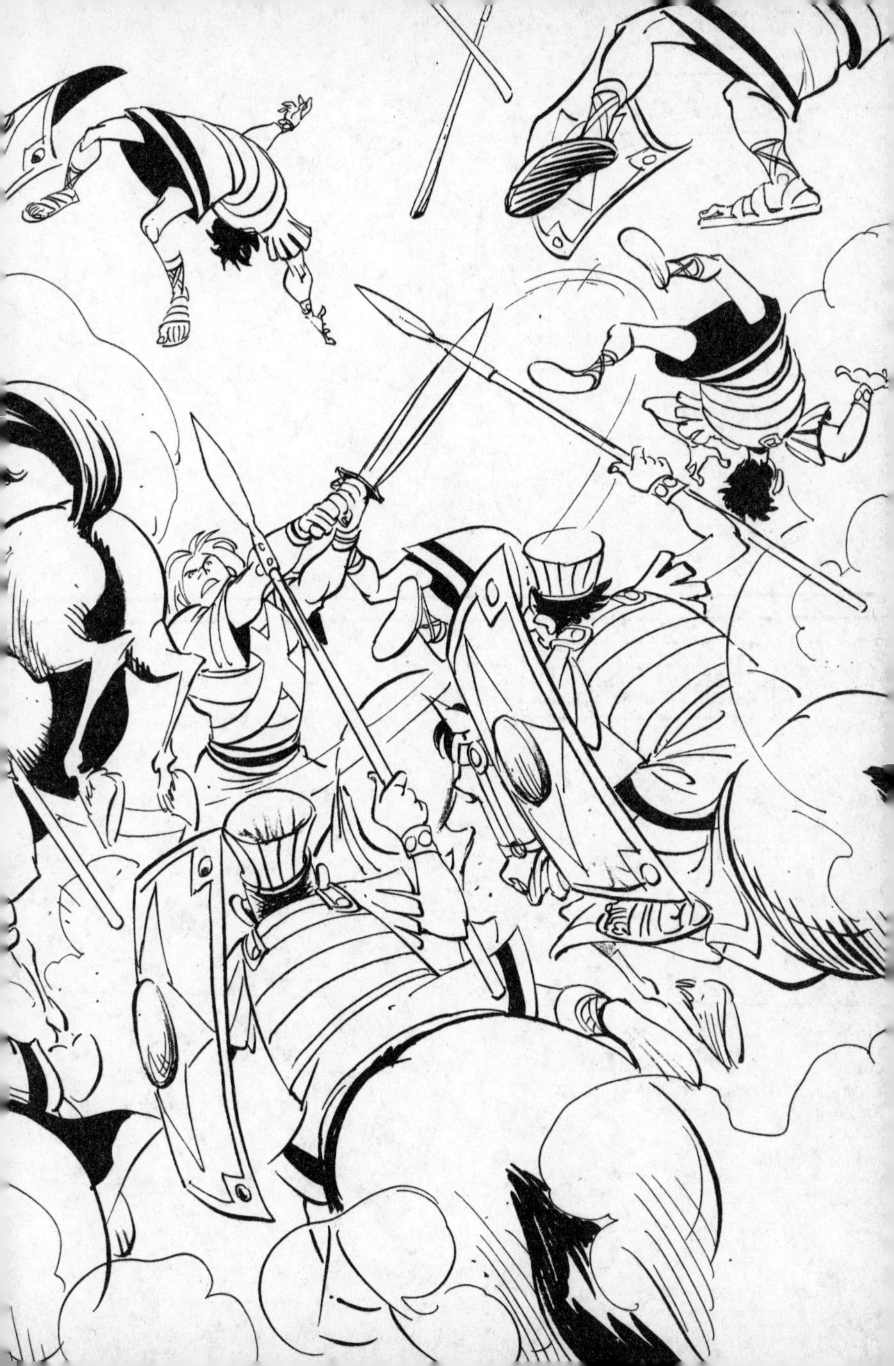

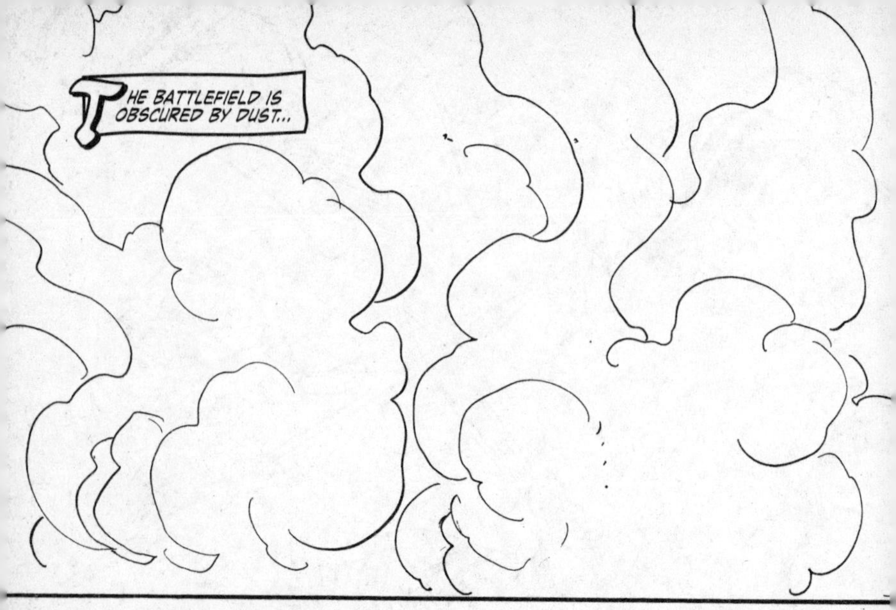
THE BATTLEFIELD IS OBSCURED BY DUST...

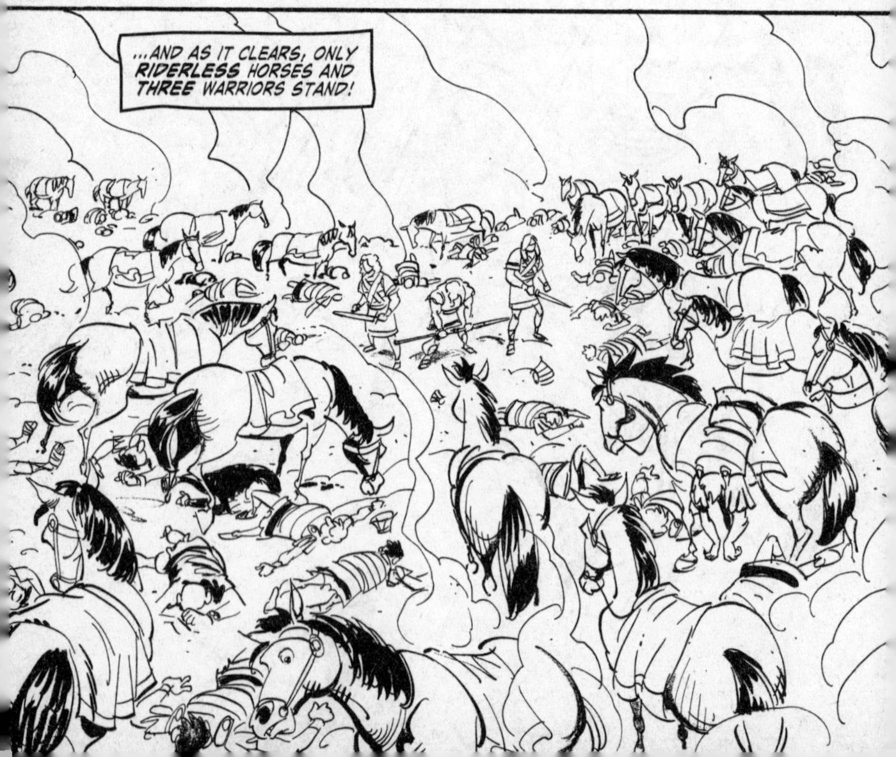
...AND AS IT CLEARS, ONLY RIDERLESS HORSES AND THREE WARRIORS STAND!

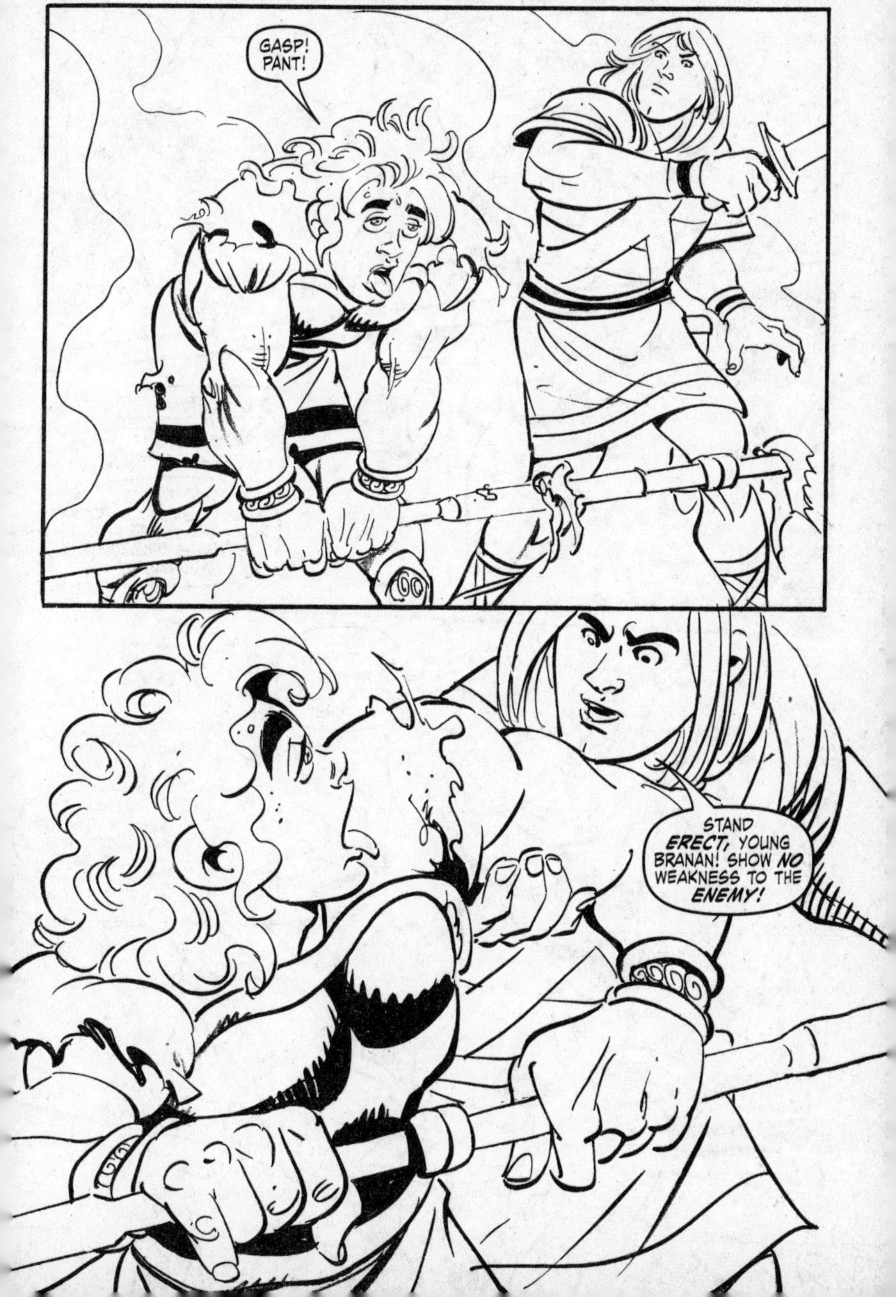
GASP! PANT!
STAND ERECT, YOUNG BRANAN! SHOW NO WEAKNESS TO THE ENEMY!

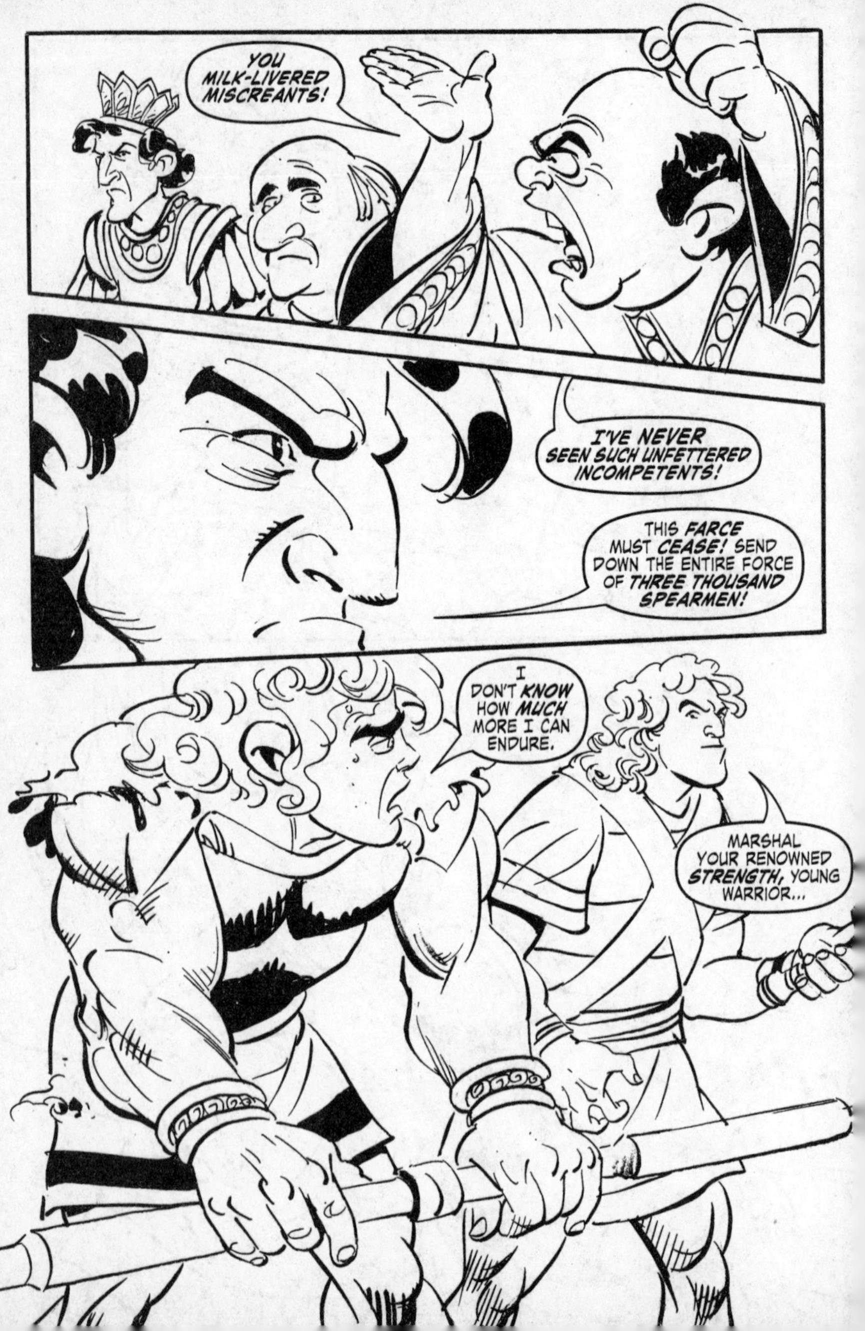
YOU MILK-LIVERED MISCREANTS!
I'VE NEVER SEEN SUCH UNFETTERED INCOMPETENTS!
THIS FARCE MUST CEASE! SEND DOWN THE ENTIRE FORCE OF THREE THOUSAND SPEARMEN!
I DON'T KNOW HOW MUCH MORE I CAN ENDURE.
MARSHAL YOUR RENOWNED STRENGTH, YOUNG WARRIOR...

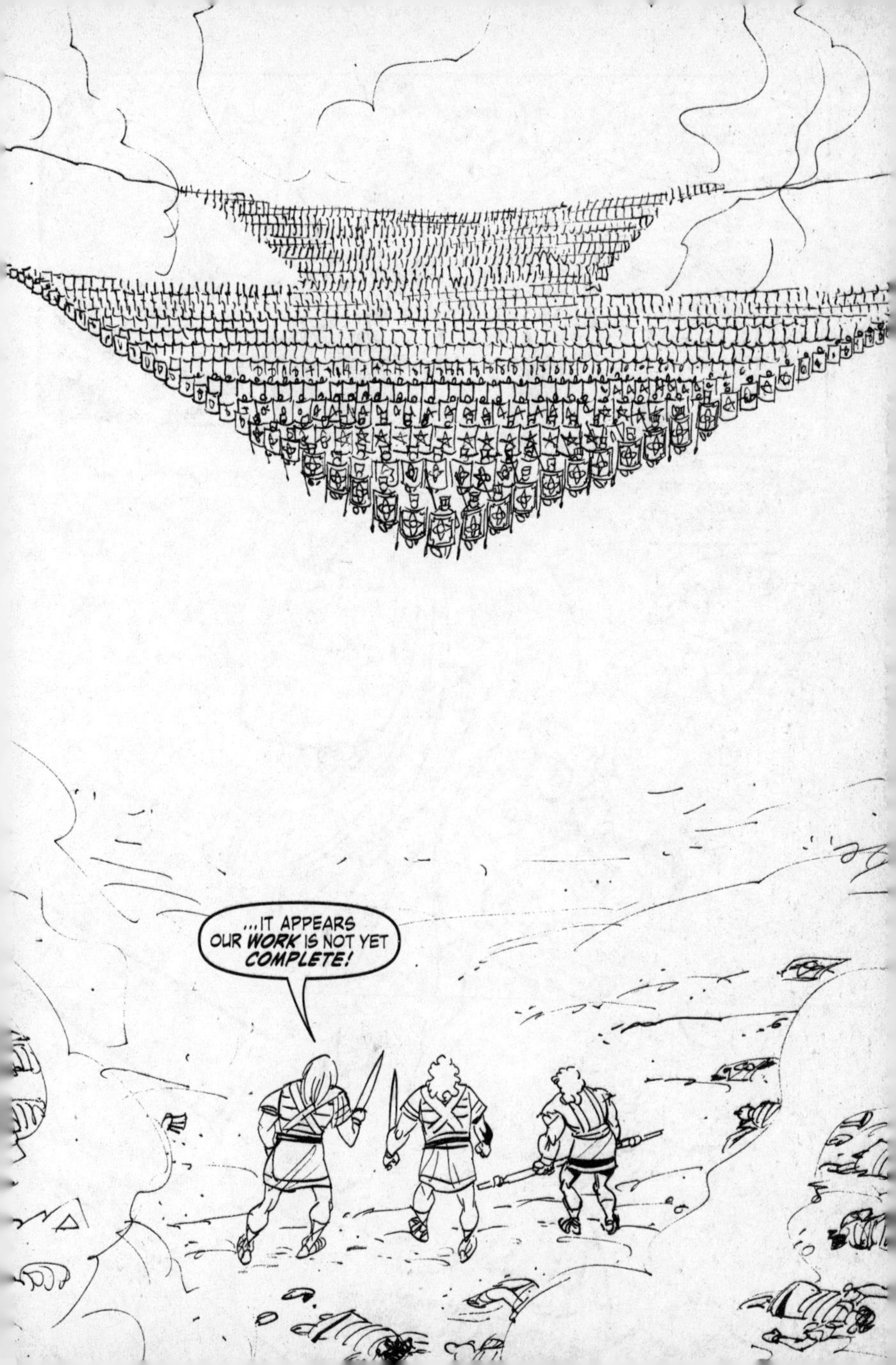
...IT APPEARS OUR WORK IS NOT YET COMPLETE!

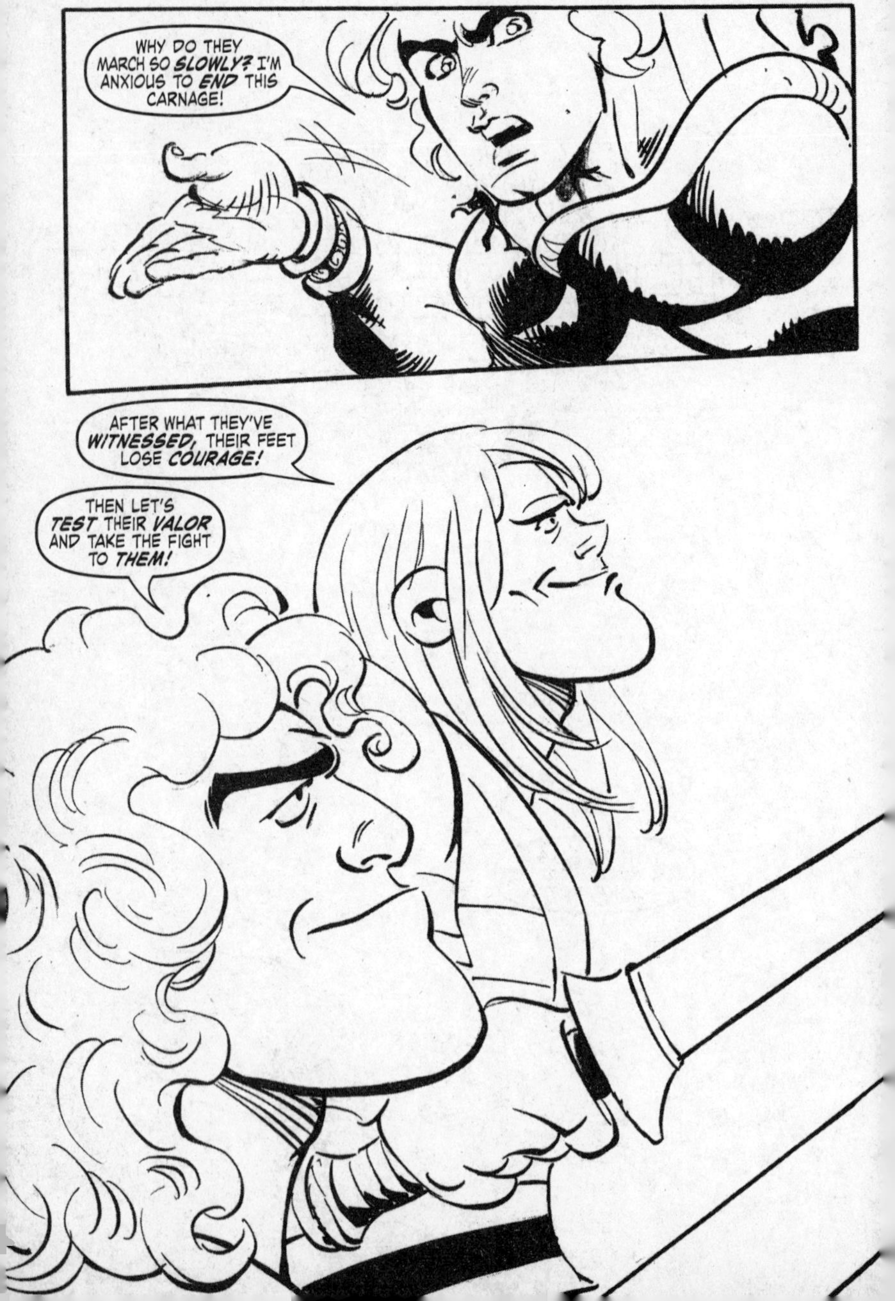

WHY DO THEY MARCH SO SLOWLY? I'M ANXIOUS TO END THIS CARNAGE!
AFTER WHAT THEY'VE WITNESSED, THEIR FEET LOSE COURAGE!
THEN LET'S TEST THEIR VALOR AND TAKE THE FIGHT TO THEM!

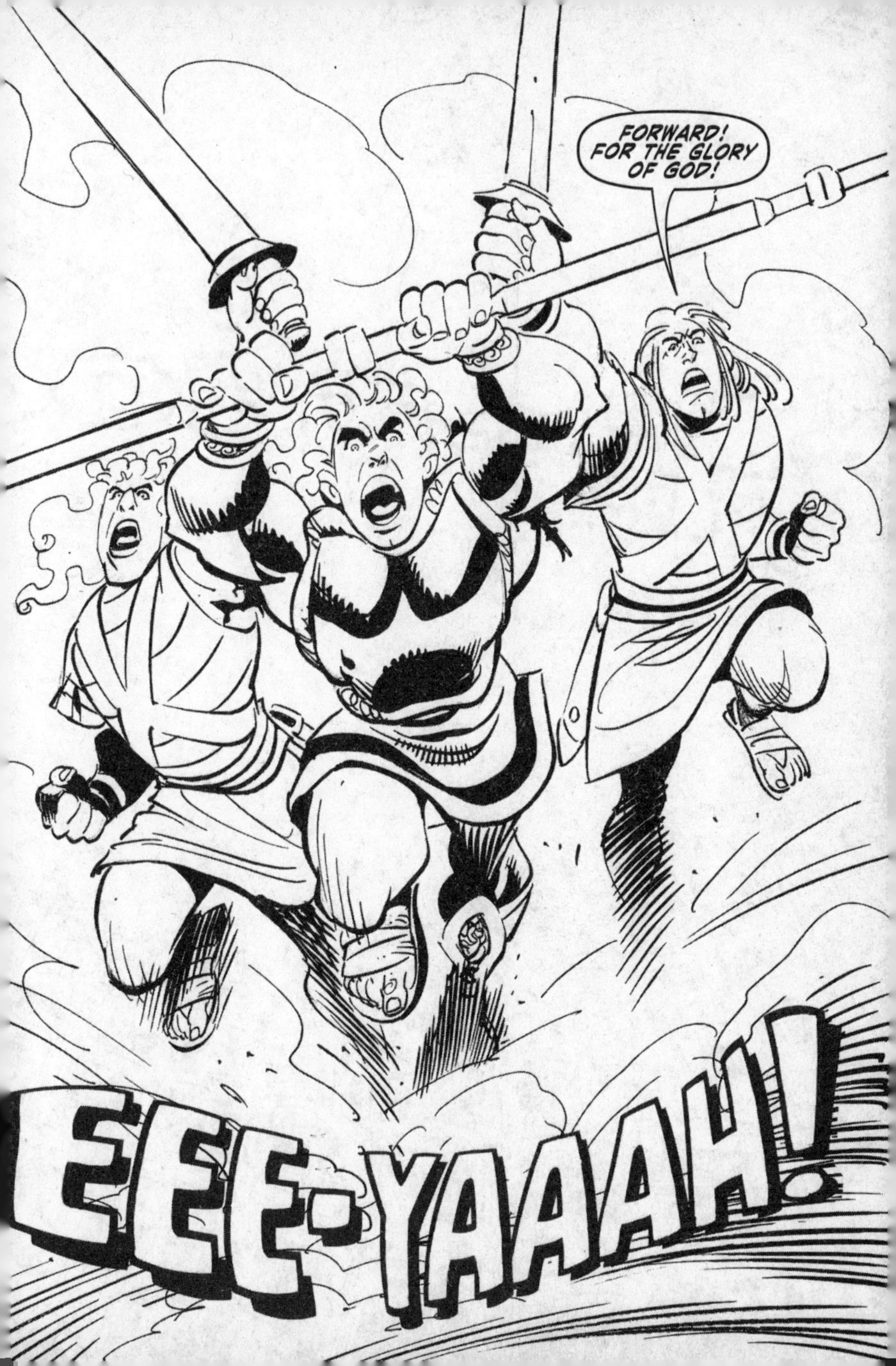
FORWARD! FOR THE GLORY OF GOD!
EEE-YAAAH!

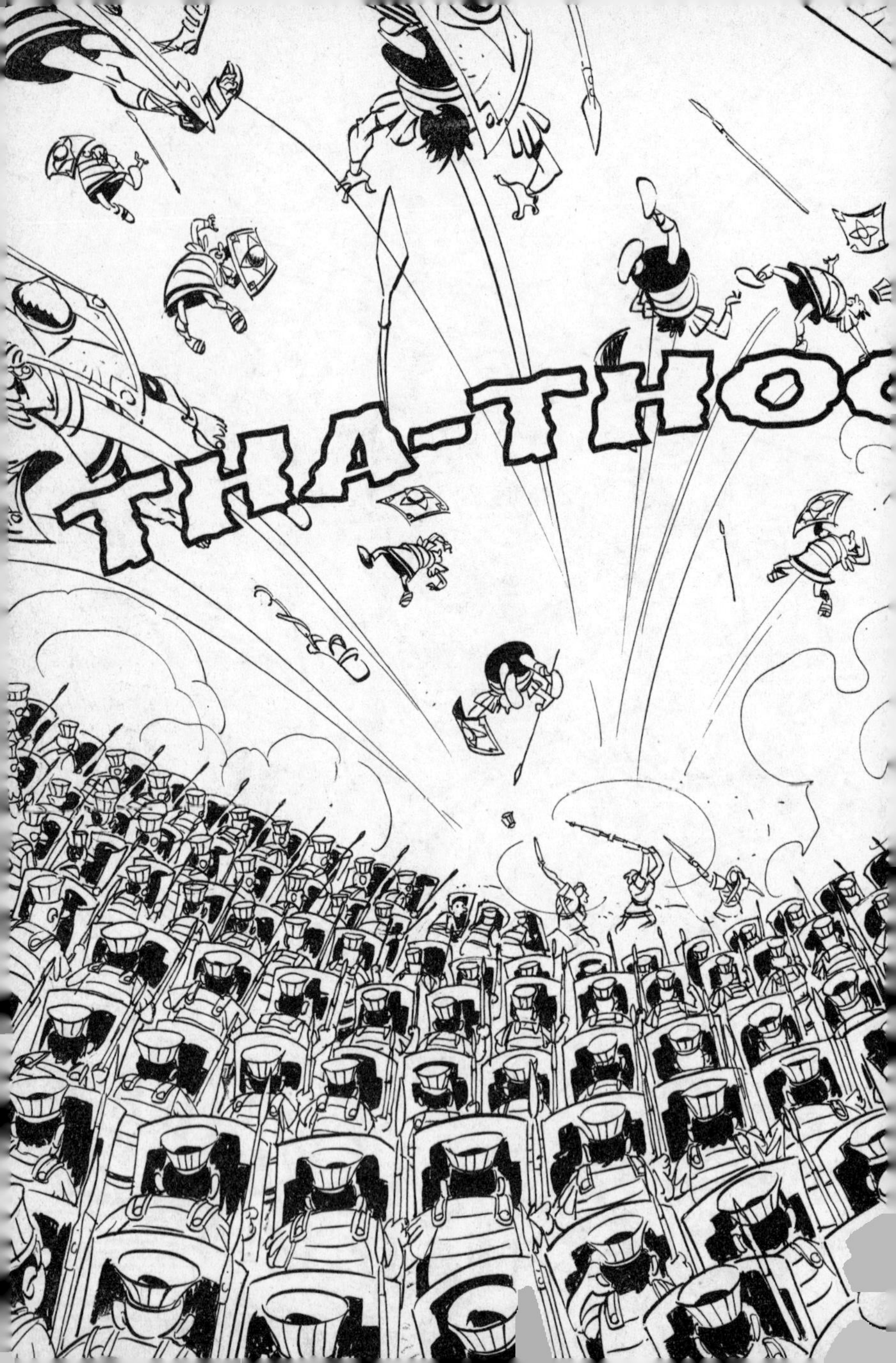
THA-THO

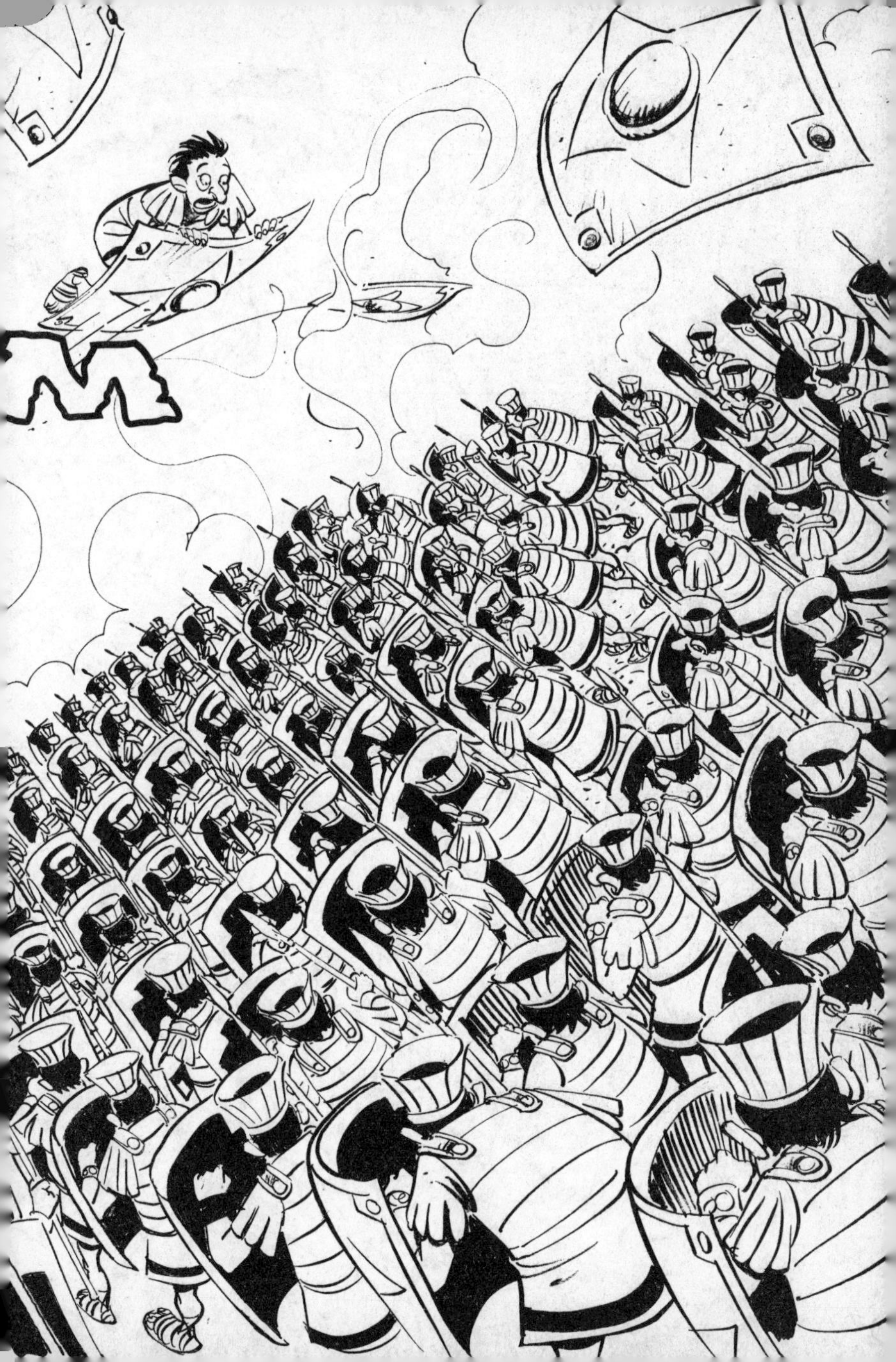

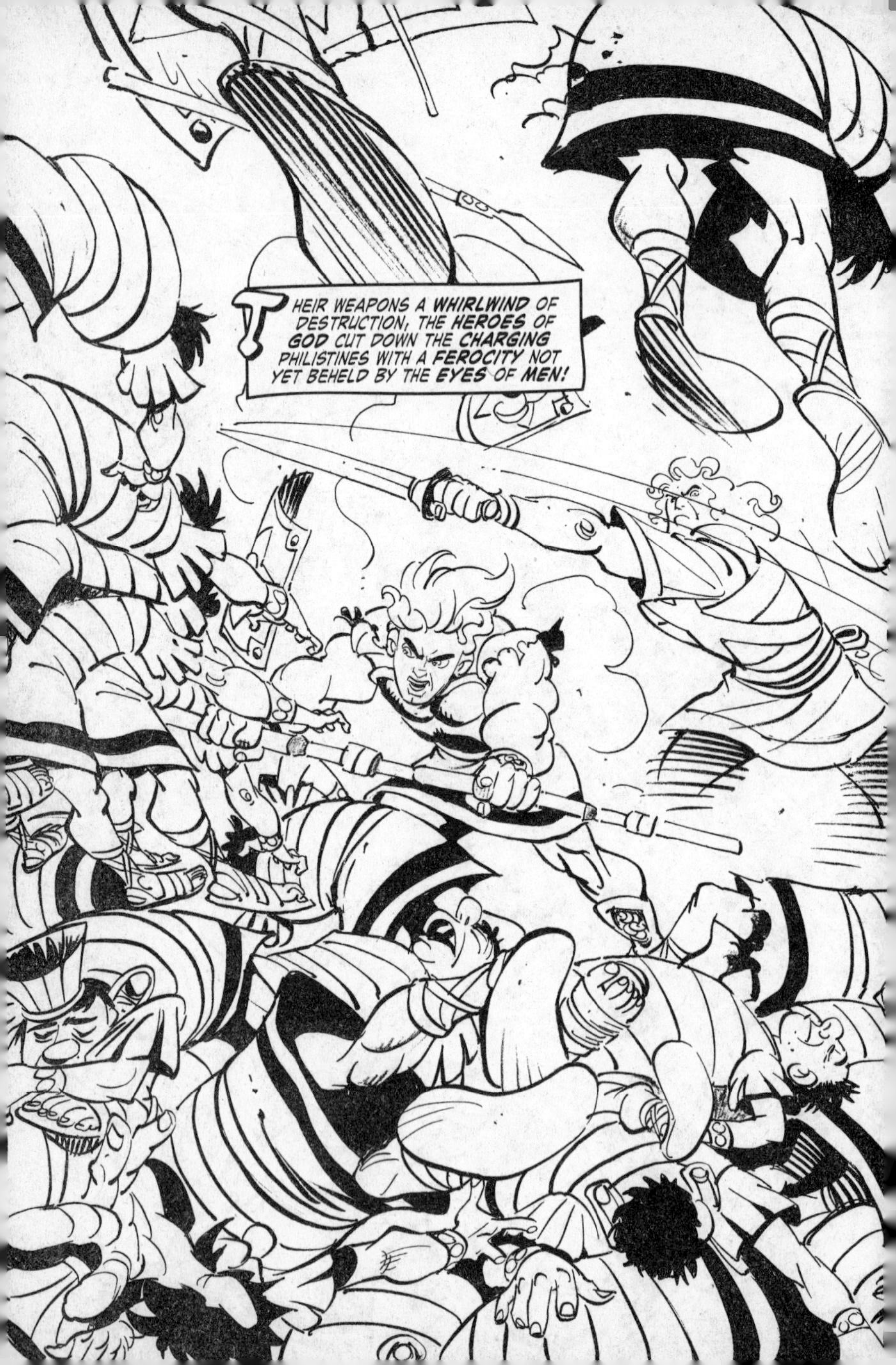
THEIR WEAPONS A WHIRLWIND OF DESTRUCTION, THE HEROES OF GOD CUT DOWN THE CHARGING PHILISTINES WITH A FEROCITY NOT YET BEHELD BY THE EYES OF MEN!

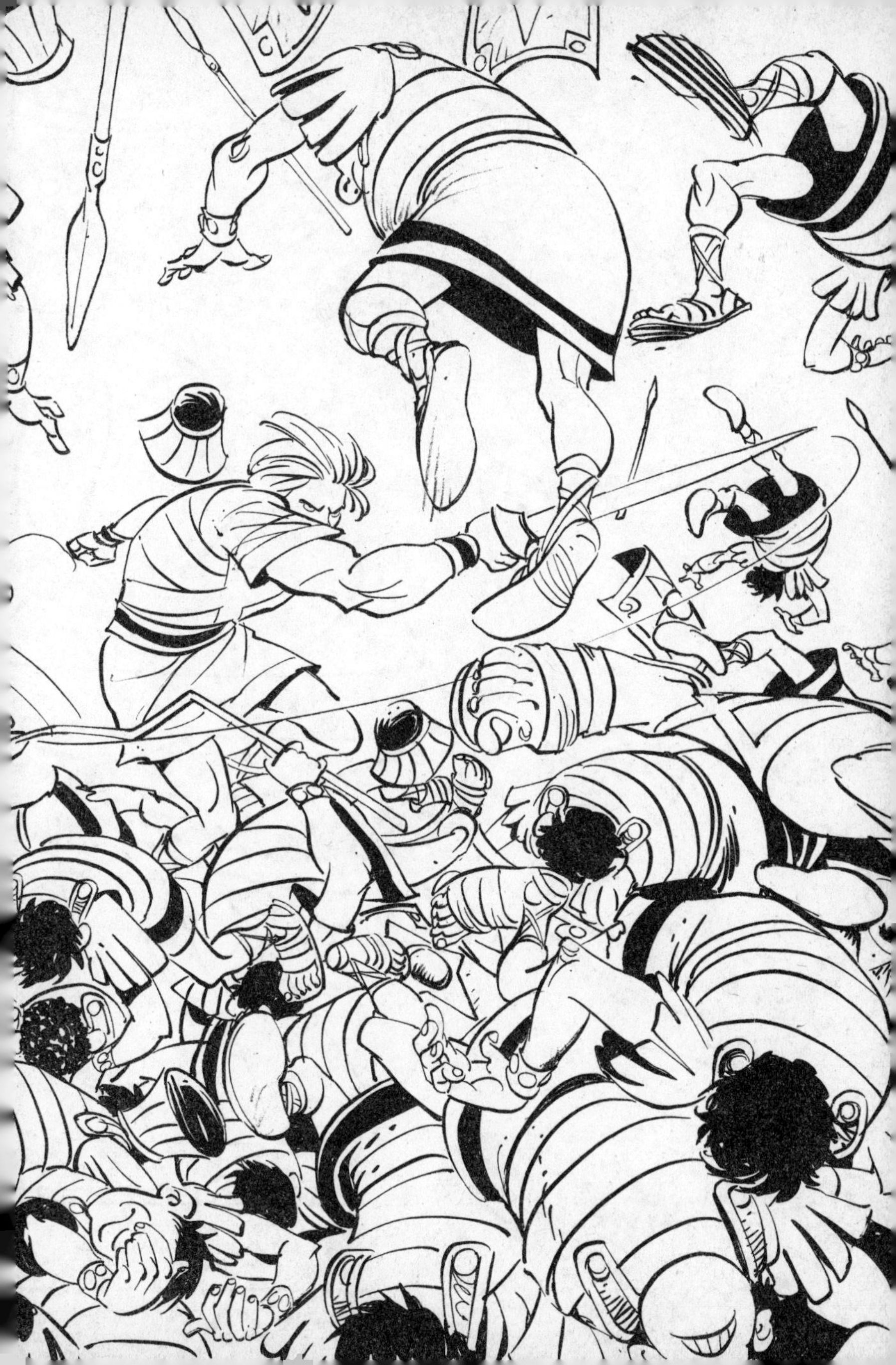

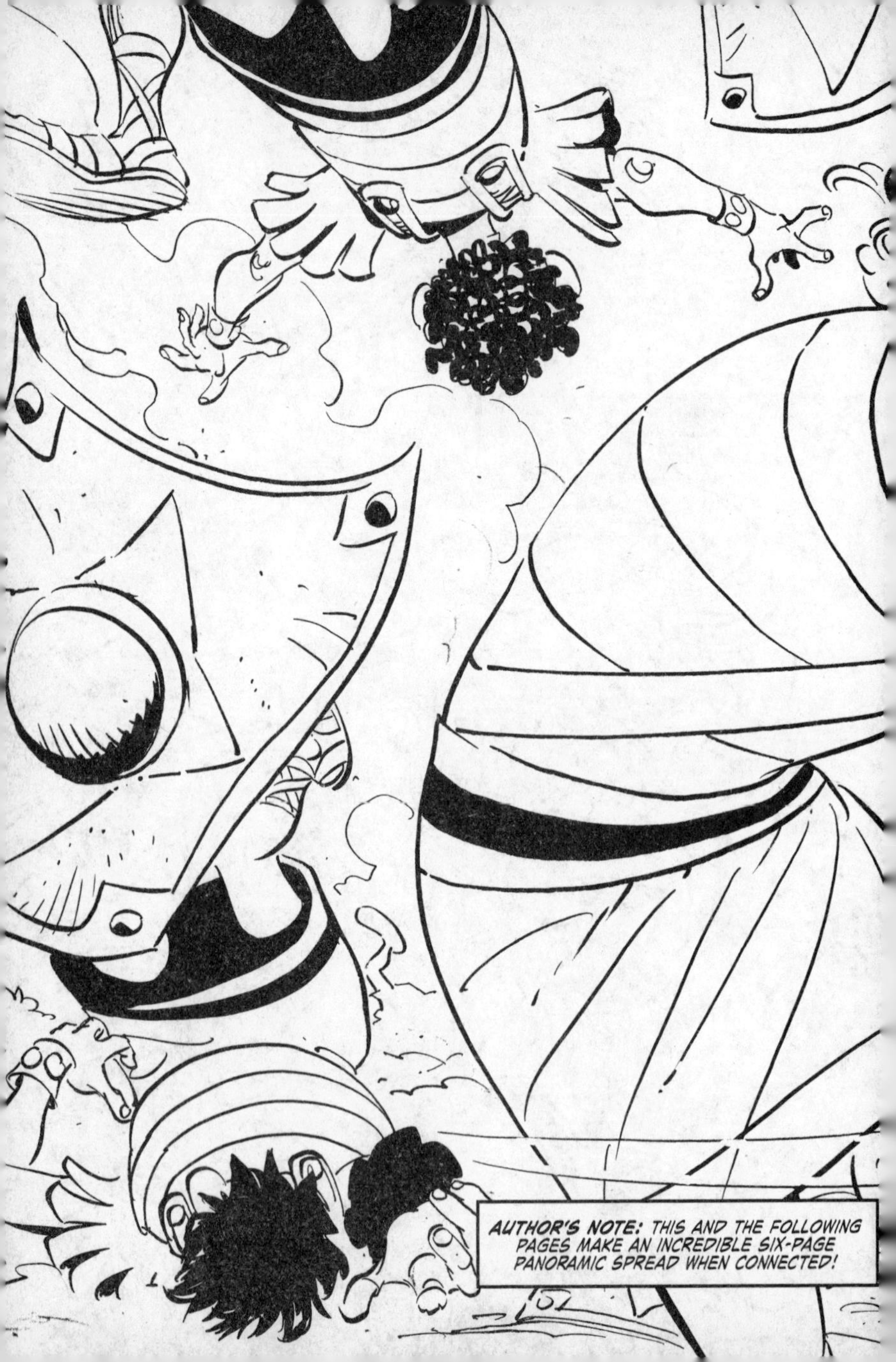
AUTHOR'S NOTE: THIS AND THE FOLLOWING PAGES MAKE AN INCREDIBLE SIX-PAGE PANORAMIC SPREAD WHEN CONNECTED!

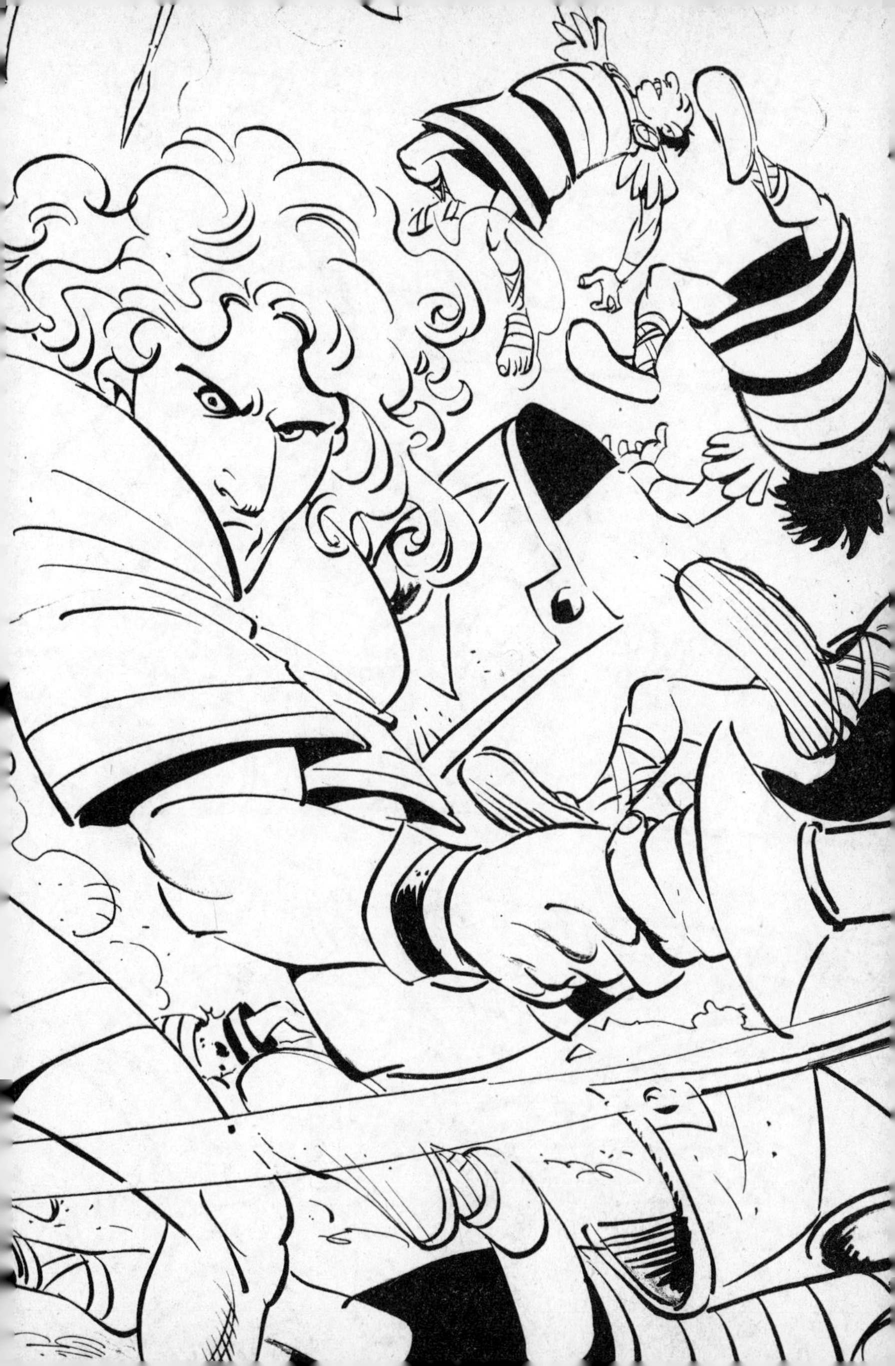

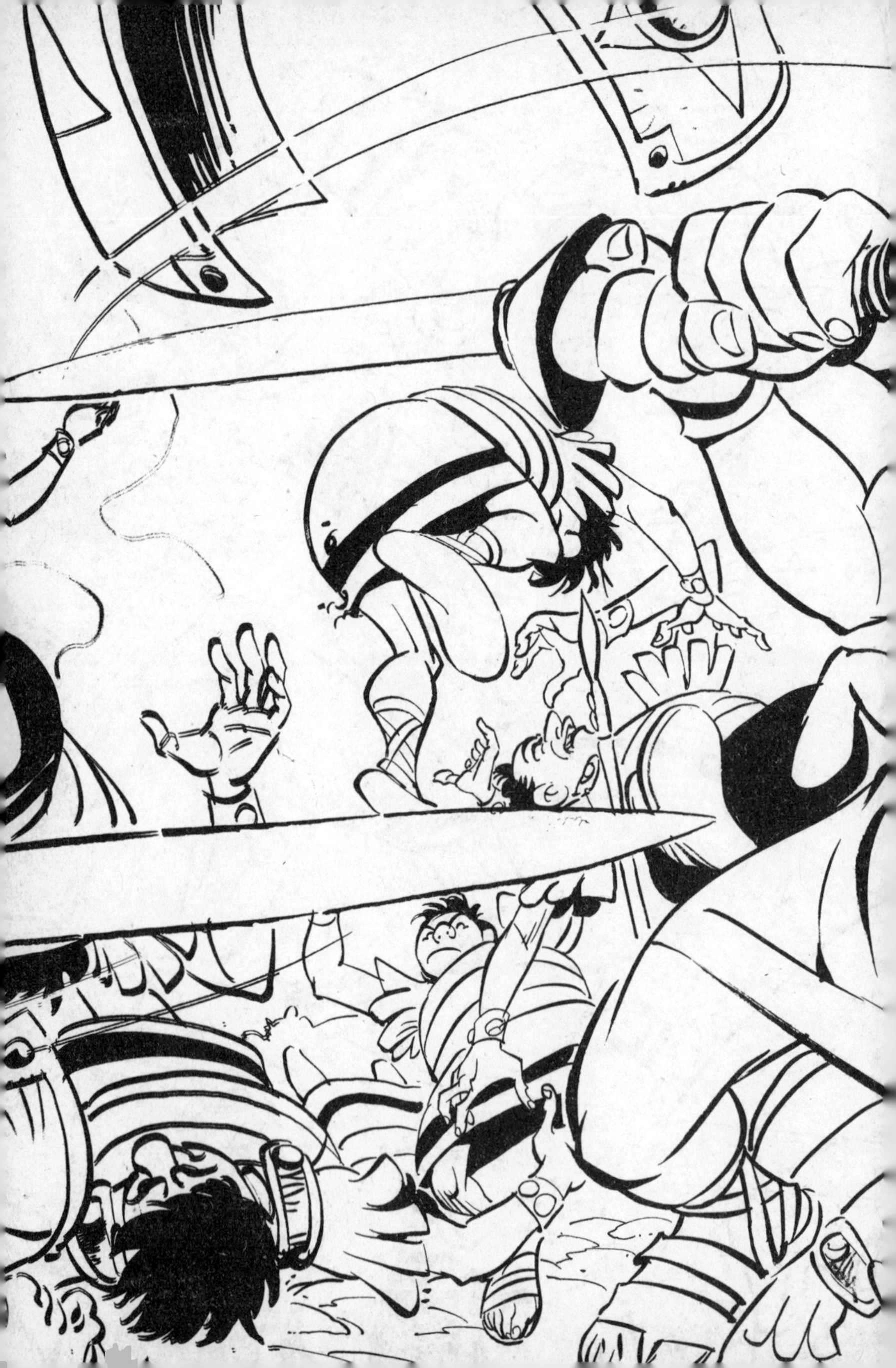

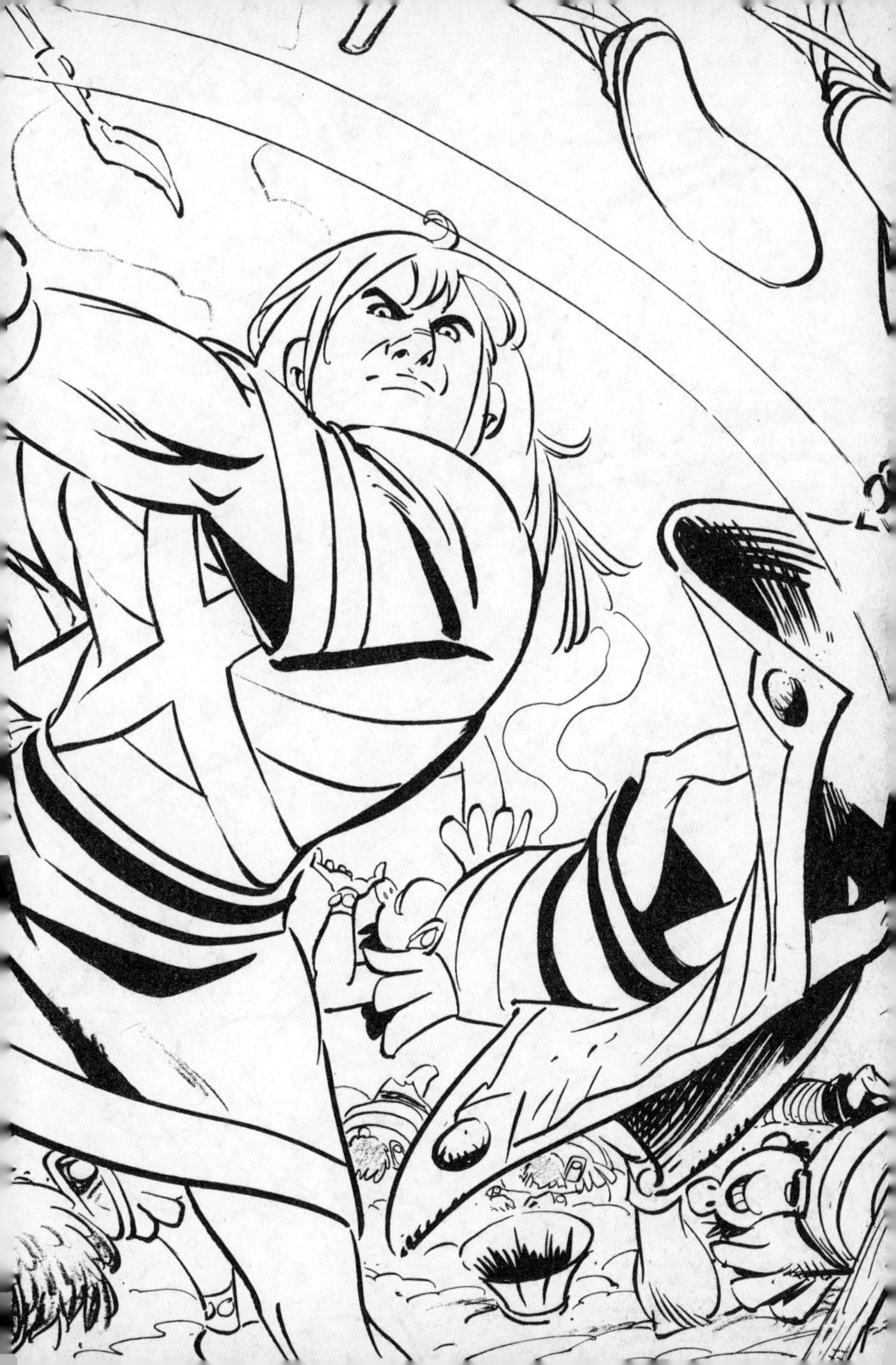

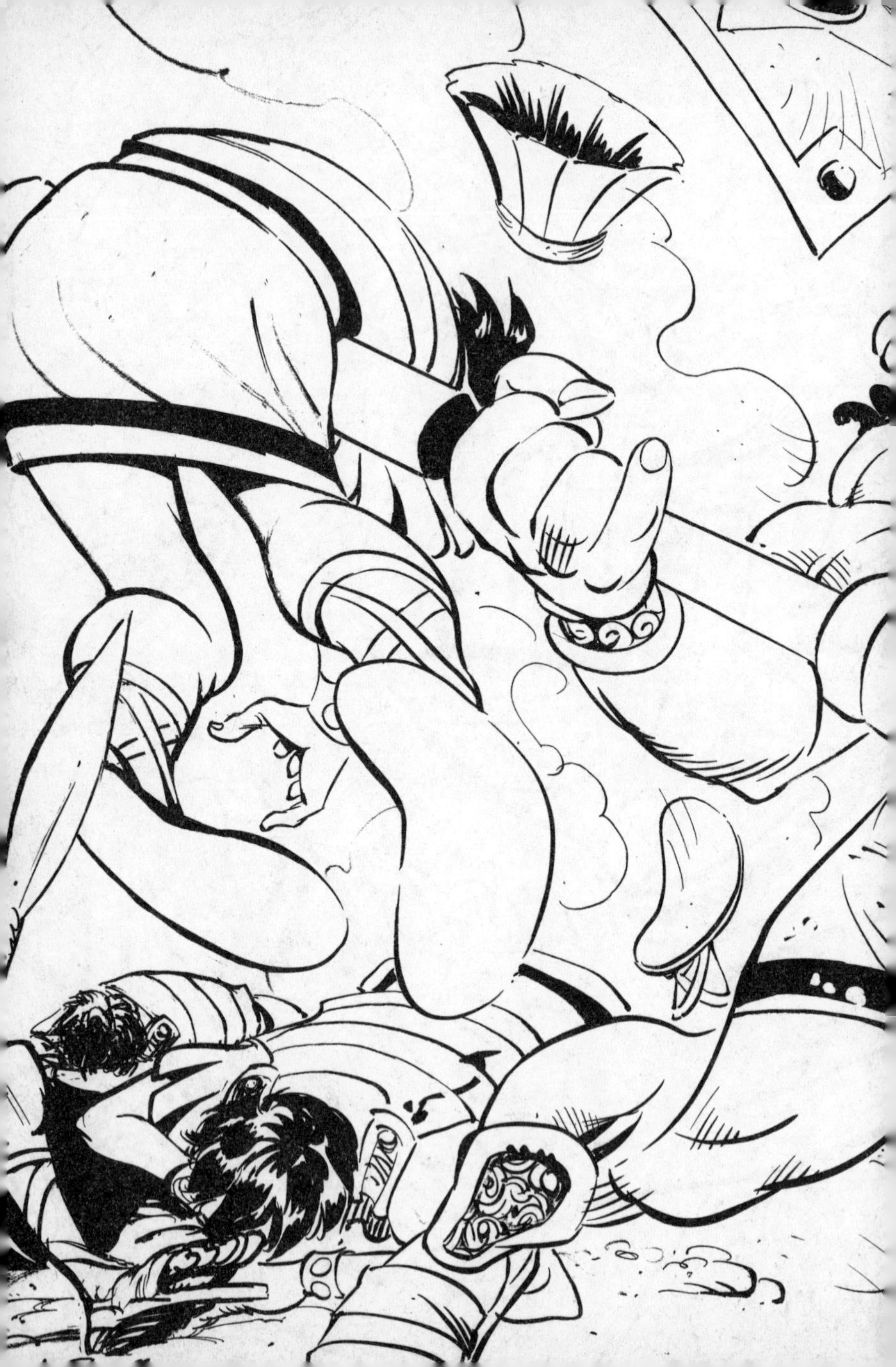

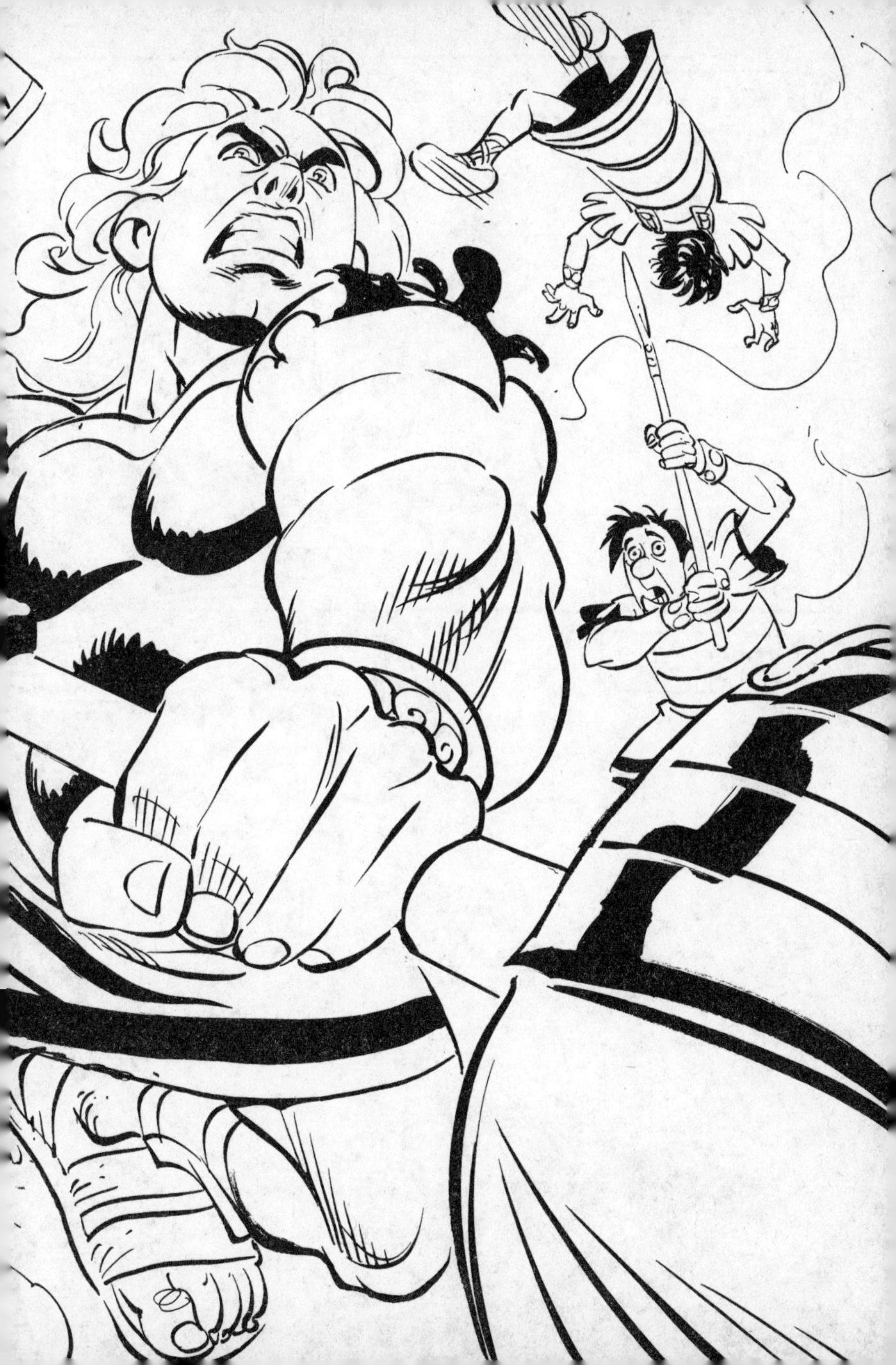

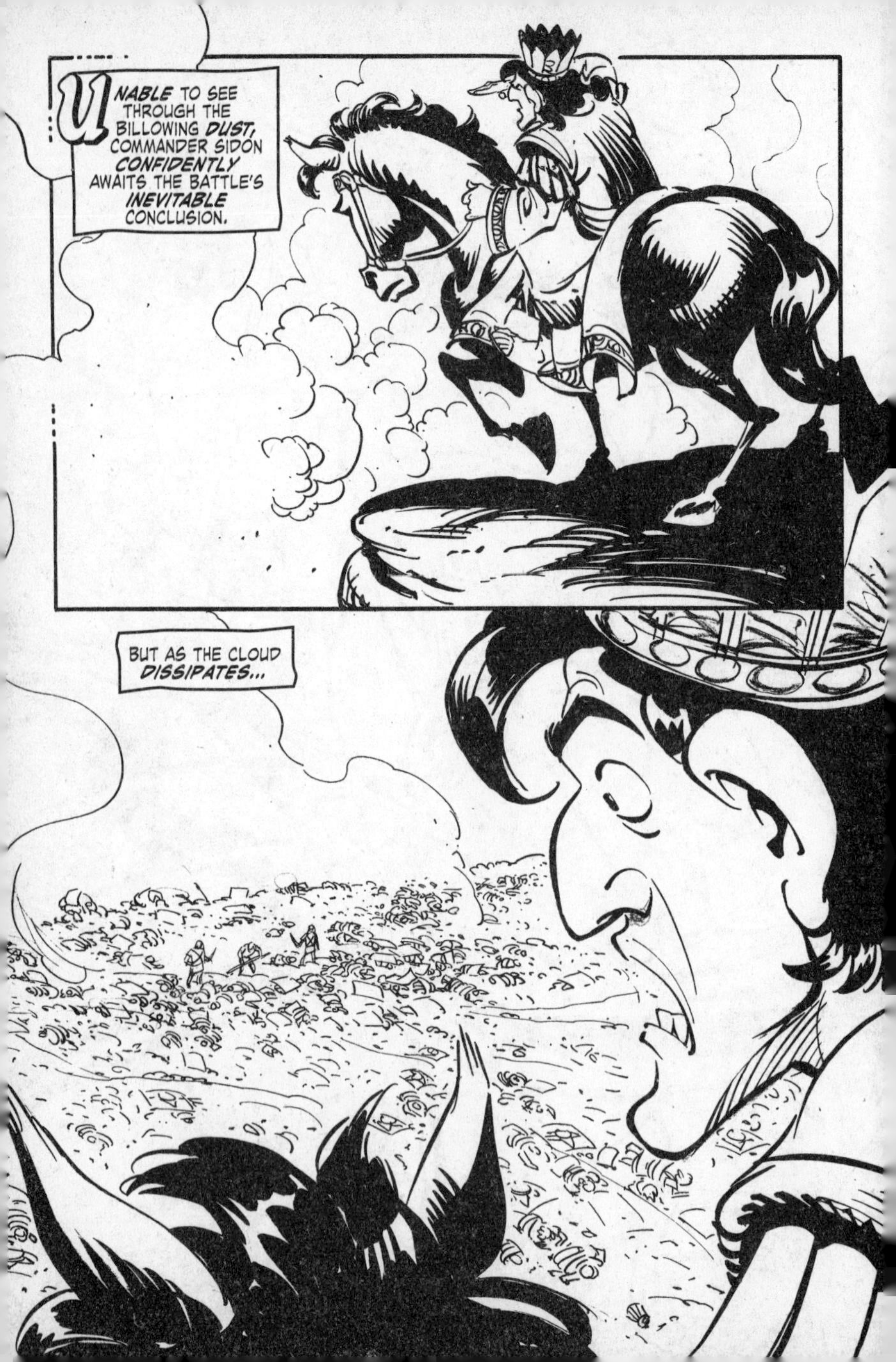
UNABLE TO SEE THROUGH THE BILLOWING DUST, COMMANDER SIDON CONFIDENTLY AWAITS THE BATTLE'S INEVITABLE CONCLUSION.
BUT AS THE CLOUD DISSIPATES...

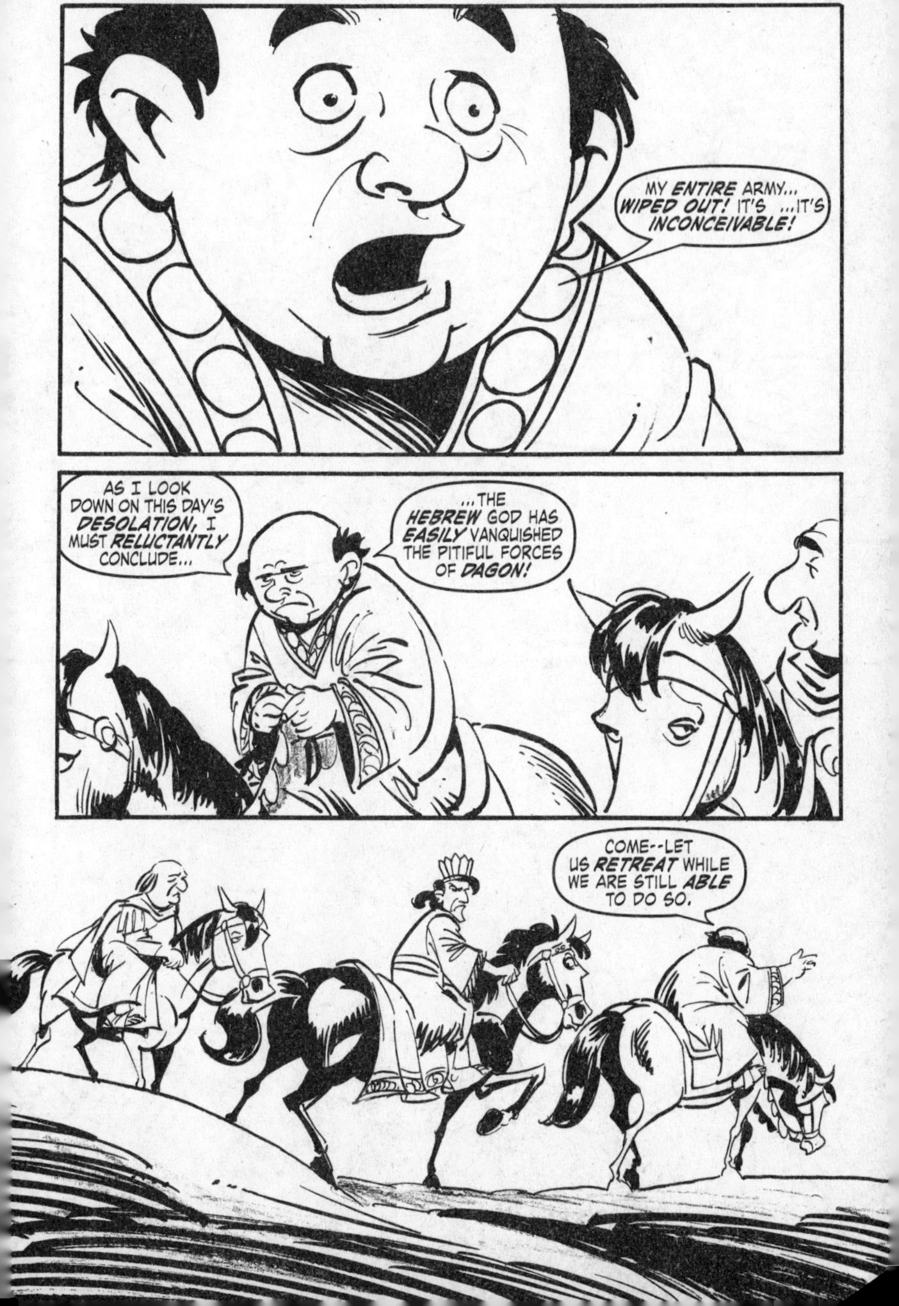
MY ENTIRE ARMY... WIPED OUT! IT'S ...IT'S INCONCEIVABLE!
AS I LOOK DOWN ON THIS DAY'S DESOLATION, I MUST RELUCTANTLY CONCLUDE...
...THE HEBREW GOD HAS EASILY VANQUISHED THE PITIFUL FORCES OF DAGON!
COME--LET US RETREAT WHILE WE ARE STILL ABLE TO DO SO.

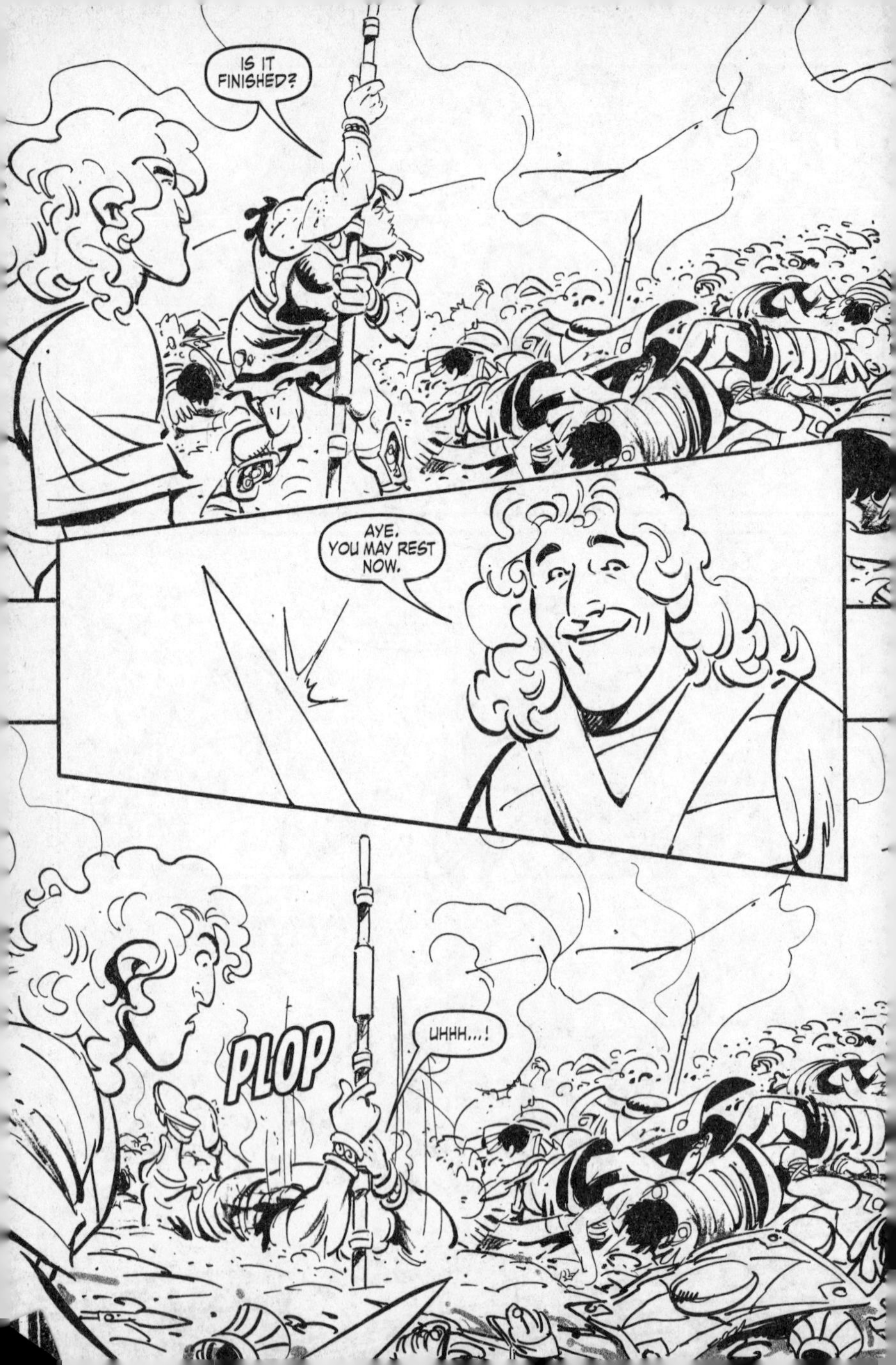
IS IT FINISHED?
AYE. YOU MAY REST NOW.
PLOP
UHHH...!

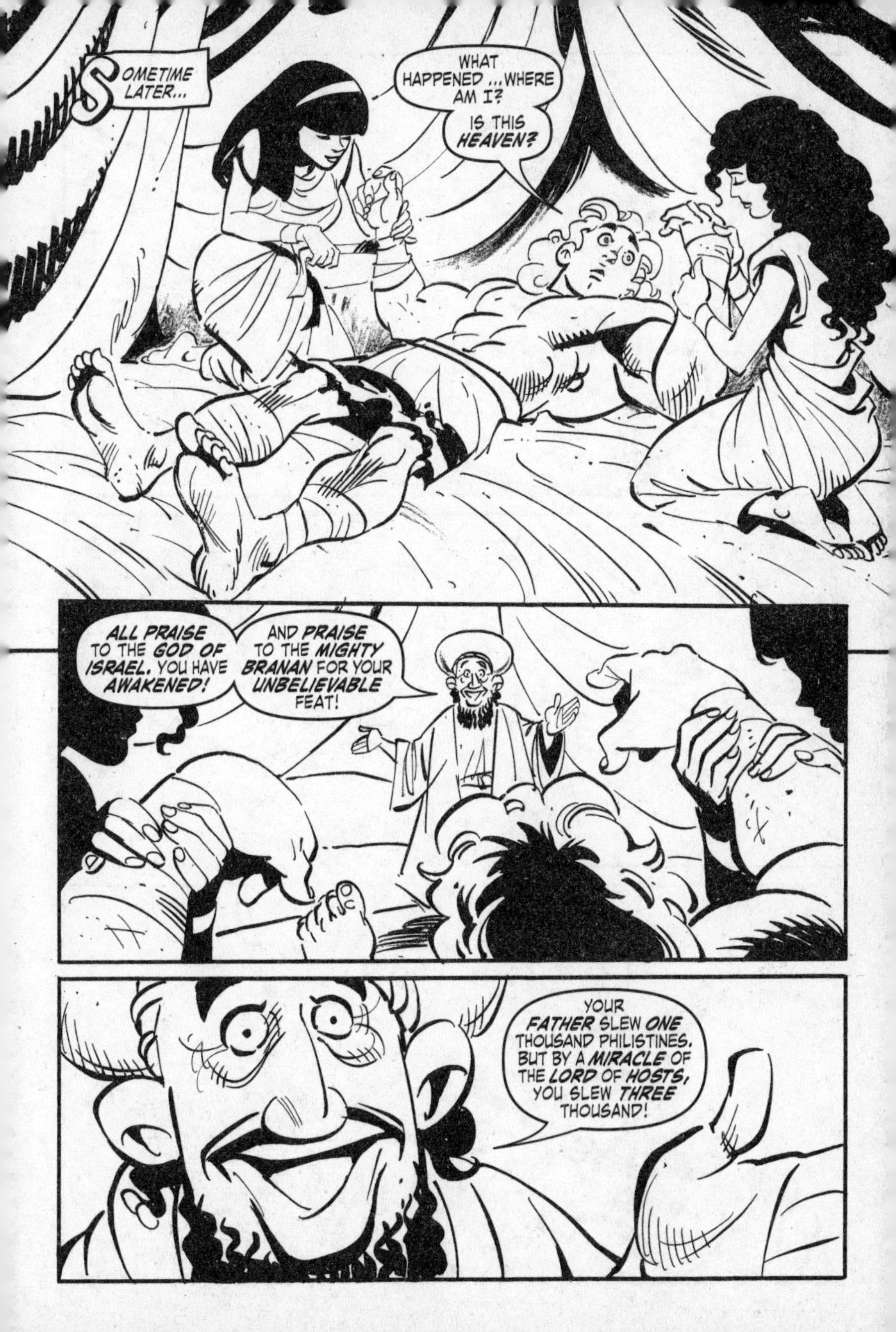
SOMETIME LATER...
WHAT HAPPENED ...WHERE AM I?
IS THIS HEAVEN?
ALL PRAISE TO THE GOD OF ISRAEL. YOU HAVE AWAKENED!
AND PRAISE TO THE MIGHTY BRANAN FOR YOUR UNBELIEVABLE FEAT!
YOUR FATHER SLEW ONE THOUSAND PHILISTINES. BUT BY A MIRACLE OF THE LORD OF HOSTS, YOU SLEW THREE THOUSAND!

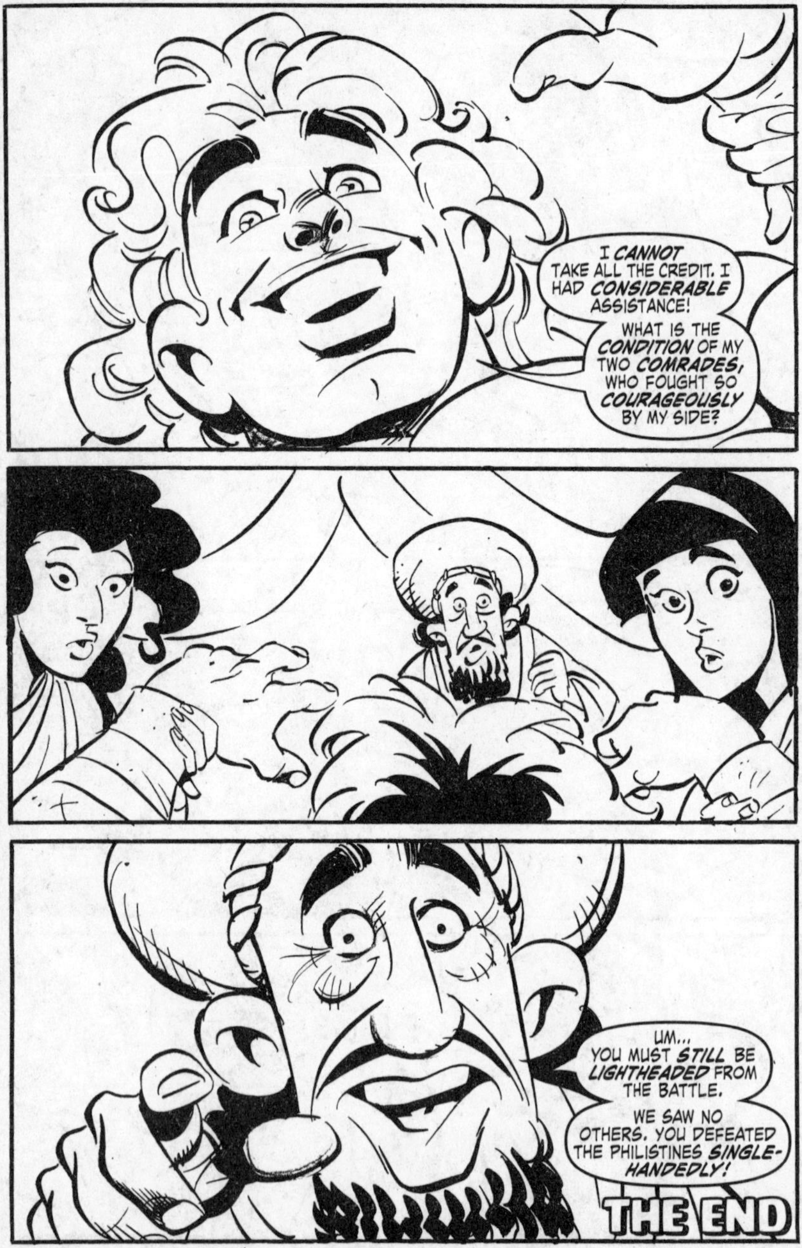
I CANNOT TAKE ALL THE CREDIT. I HAD CONSIDERABLE ASSISTANCE!
WHAT IS THE CONDITION OF MY TWO COMRADES, WHO FOUGHT SO COURAGEOUSLY BY MY SIDE?
UM... YOU MUST STILL BE LIGHTHEADED FROM THE BATTLE.
WE SAW NO OTHERS. YOU DEFEATED THE PHILISTINES SINGLE-HANDEDLY!
THE END

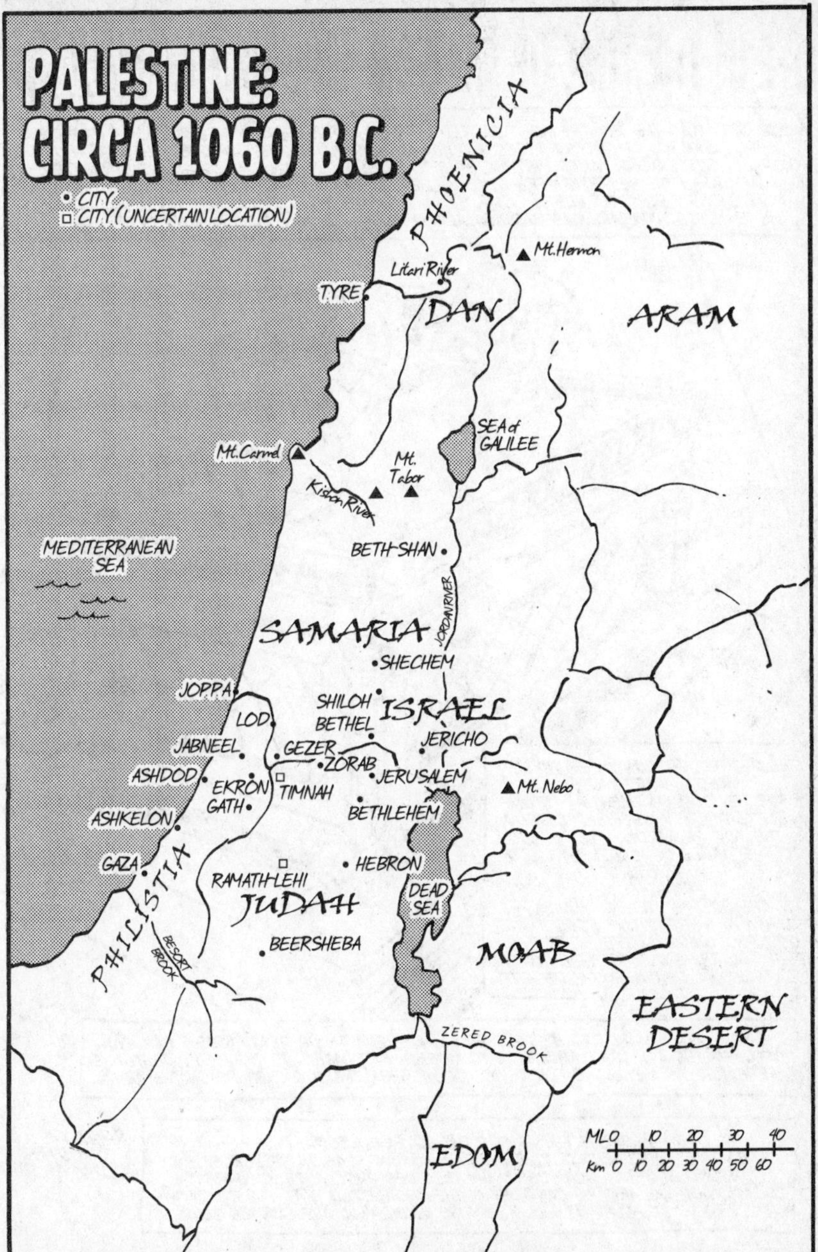
PALESTINE: CIRCA 1060 B.C.
CITY
CITY (UNCERTAIN LOCATION)
PHOENICIA
Mt. Hermon
Litani River
TYRE
DAN
ARAM
SEA of GALILEE
Mt. Carmel
Mt. Tabor
Kishon River
BETH-SHAN
MEDITERRANEAN SEA
JORDAN RIVER
SAMARIA
SHECHEM
JOPPA
SHILOH
ISRAEL
LOD
BETHEL
JERICHO
JABNEEL
GEZER
ZORAB
ASHDOD
JERUSALEM
EKRON
TIMNAH
Mt. Nebo
GATH
BETHLEHEM
ASHKELON
GAZA
HEBRON
RAMATH-LEHI
DEAD SEA
JUDAH
PHILISTIA
BESORT BROOK
BEERSHEBA
MOAB
EASTERN DESERT
ZERED BROOK
ML 0 10 20 30 40
Km 0 10 20 30 40 50 60
EDOM

LIFE IN THE TIME OF SAMSON "ARK OF THE COVENANT"

NOT ONLY WAS THE ARK THE MOST SACRED OBJECT IN THE HEBREW TABERNACLE, IT WAS THE VISIBLE SYMBOL OF GOD'S PRESENCE ON EARTH AND HIS PROTECTION OVER THE NATION OF ISRAEL. GOD GAVE DETAILED INSTRUCTIONS TO MOSES, TELLING HIM HOW TO CONSTRUCT THE ARK WHEN THE HEBREWS WERE STILL IN THE WILDERNESS (SEE EXODUS 25:10-22). ITS DIMENSIONS WERE 2 1/2 CUBITS LONG, BY 1 1/2 CUBITS WIDE, BY 1 1/2 CUBITS HIGH. (A CUBIT IS 18 INCHES.) THE ARK WAS MADE OF ACACIA WOOD AND WAS OVERLAID WITH PURE GOLD.

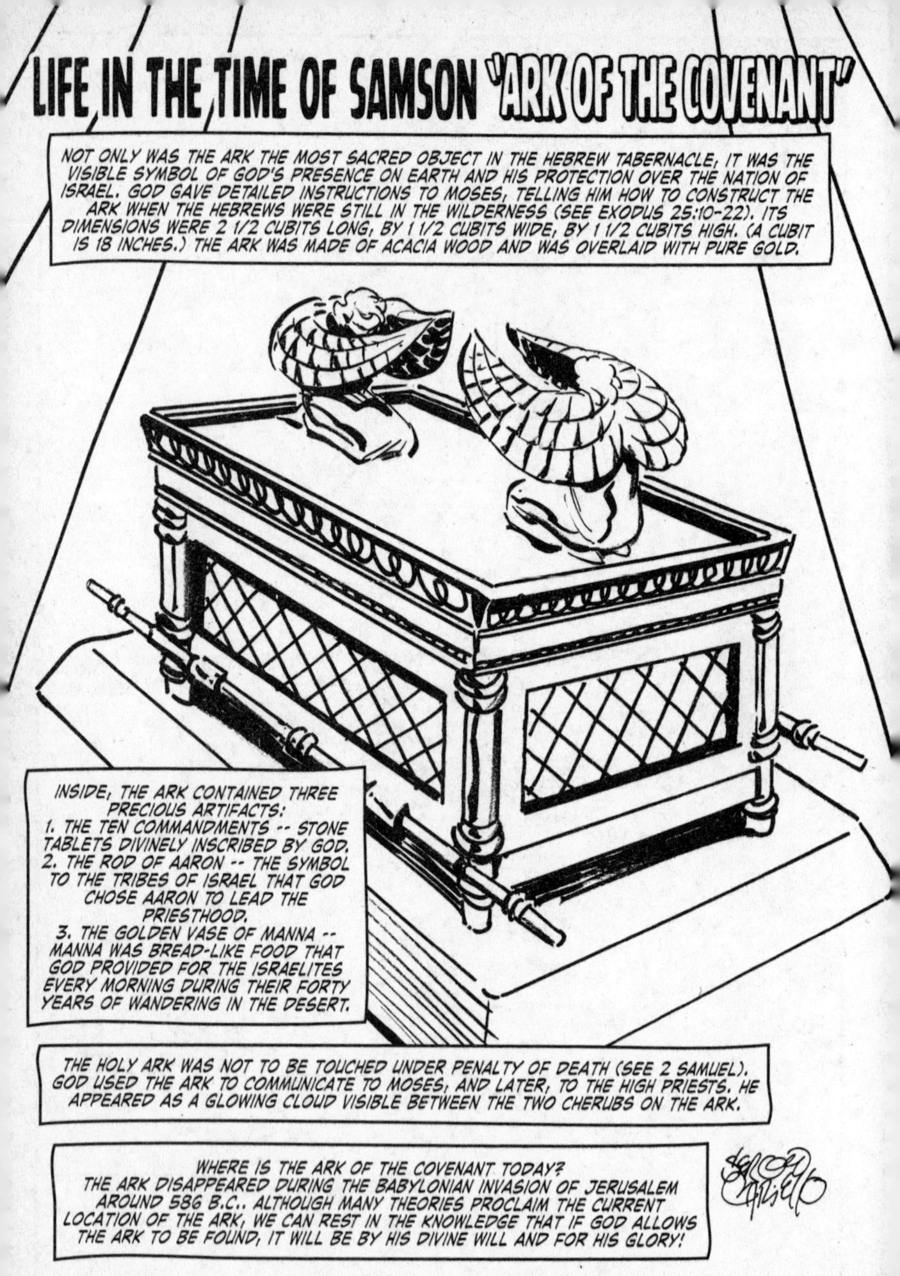

INSIDE, THE ARK CONTAINED THREE PRECIOUS ARTIFACTS:

1. THE TEN COMMANDMENTS -- STONE TABLETS DIVINELY INSCRIBED BY GOD.
2. THE ROD OF AARON -- THE SYMBOL TO THE TRIBES OF ISRAEL THAT GOD CHOSE AARON TO LEAD THE PRIESTHOOD.
3. THE GOLDEN VASE OF MANNA -- MANNA WAS BREAD-LIKE FOOD THAT GOD PROVIDED FOR THE ISRAELITES EVERY MORNING DURING THEIR FORTY YEARS OF WANDERING IN THE DESERT.

THE HOLY ARK WAS NOT TO BE TOUCHED UNDER PENALTY OF DEATH (SEE 2 SAMUEL). GOD USED THE ARK TO COMMUNICATE TO MOSES, AND LATER, TO THE HIGH PRIESTS. HE APPEARED AS A GLOWING CLOUD VISIBLE BETWEEN THE TWO CHERUBS ON THE ARK.

WHERE IS THE ARK OF THE COVENANT TODAY?
THE ARK DISAPPEARED DURING THE BABYLONIAN INVASION OF JERUSALEM AROUND 586 B.C.. ALTHOUGH MANY THEORIES PROCLAIM THE CURRENT LOCATION OF THE ARK, WE CAN REST IN THE KNOWLEDGE THAT IF GOD ALLOWS THE ARK TO BE FOUND, IT WILL BE BY HIS DIVINE WILL AND FOR HIS GLORY!

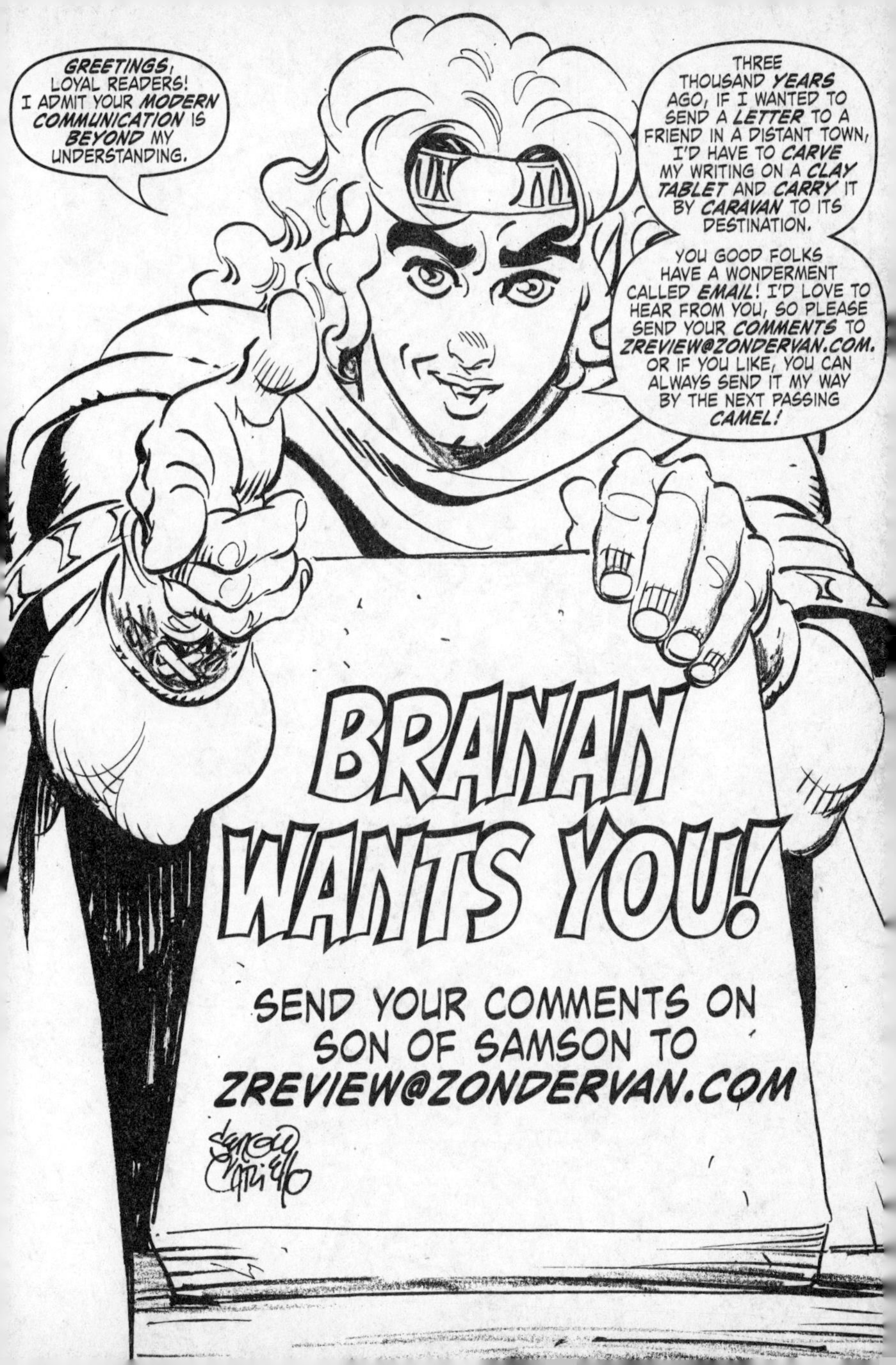
GREETINGS, LOYAL READERS! I ADMIT YOUR MODERN COMMUNICATION IS BEYOND MY UNDERSTANDING.
THREE THOUSAND YEARS AGO, IF I WANTED TO SEND A LETTER TO A FRIEND IN A DISTANT TOWN, I'D HAVE TO CARVE MY WRITING ON A CLAY TABLET AND CARRY IT BY CARAVAN TO ITS DESTINATION.
YOU GOOD FOLKS HAVE A WONDERMENT CALLED EMAIL! I'D LOVE TO HEAR FROM YOU, SO PLEASE SEND YOUR COMMENTS TO ZREVIEW@ZONDERVAN.COM. OR IF YOU LIKE, YOU CAN ALWAYS SEND IT MY WAY BY THE NEXT PASSING CAMEL!
BRANAN WANTS YOU!
SEND YOUR COMMENTS ON SON OF SAMSON TO ZREVIEW@ZONDERVAN.COM

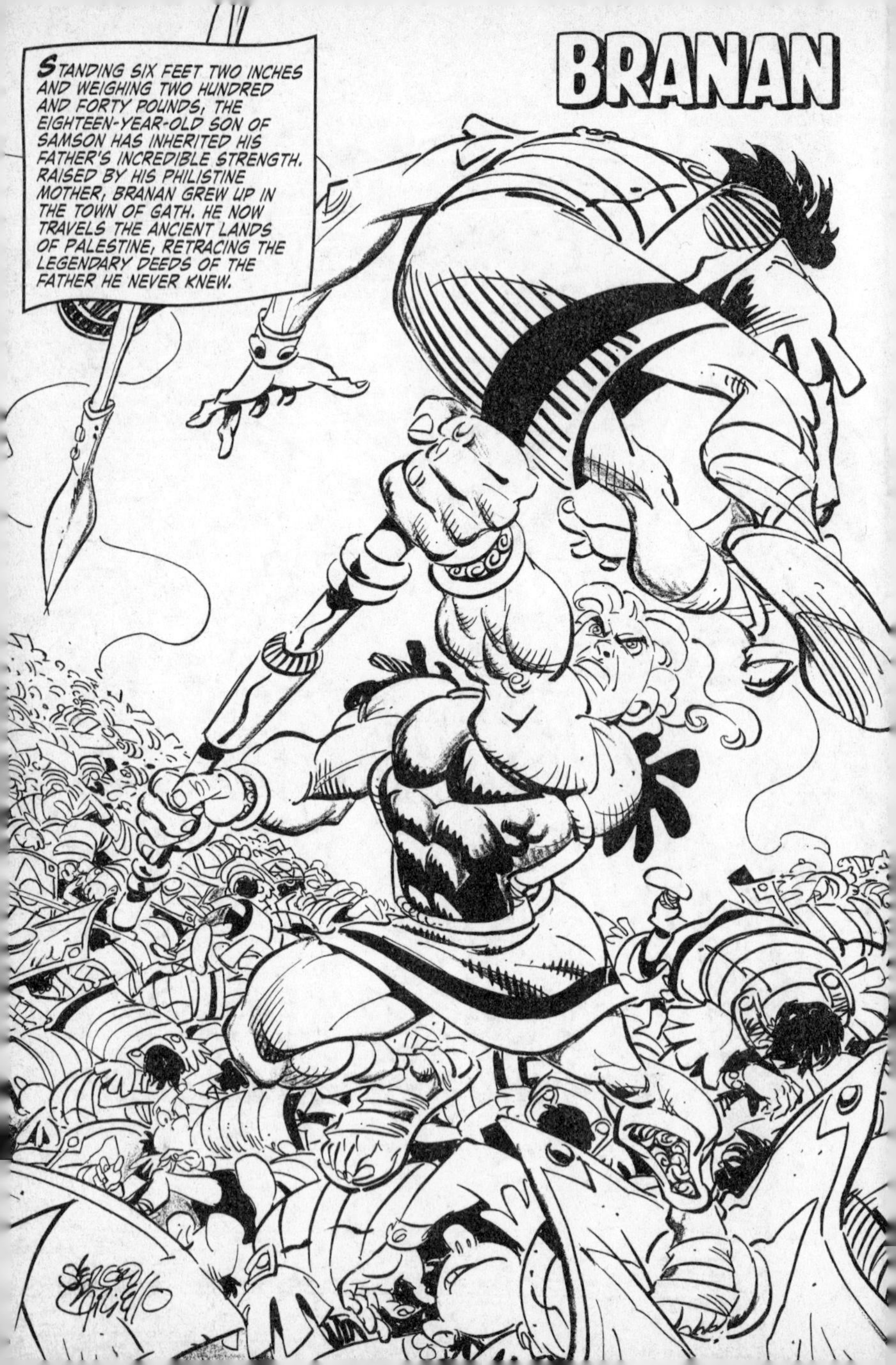
BRANAN
STANDING SIX FEET TWO INCHES AND WEIGHING TWO HUNDRED AND FORTY POUNDS, THE EIGHTEEN-YEAR-OLD SON OF SAMSON HAS INHERITED HIS FATHER'S INCREDIBLE STRENGTH. RAISED BY HIS PHILISTINE MOTHER, BRANAN GREW UP IN THE TOWN OF GATH. HE NOW TRAVELS THE ANCIENT LANDS OF PALESTINE, RETRACING THE LEGENDARY DEEDS OF THE FATHER HE NEVER KNEW.

MIZZAH AND YITZHAK

LION HUNTERS BY TRADE, MIZZAH (THE ELDEST AND MORE EXPERIENCED OF THE TWO) AND HIS PARTNER, YITZHAK, SEEM KIND AND HOSPITABLE ON THE SURFACE. BUT THEIR TRUE NATURE IS EXPOSED WHEN THEY CROSS PATHS WITH THE EVER-TRUSTING BRANAN.

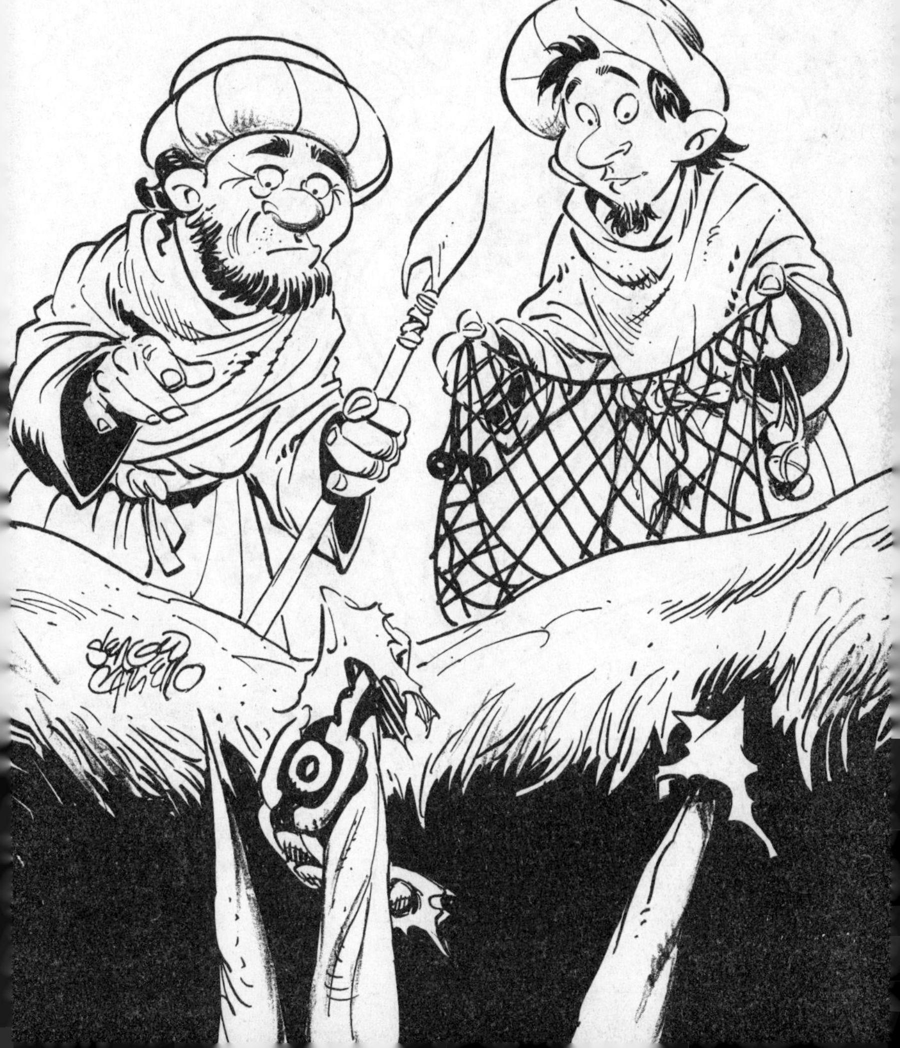

LORD PATHRUS

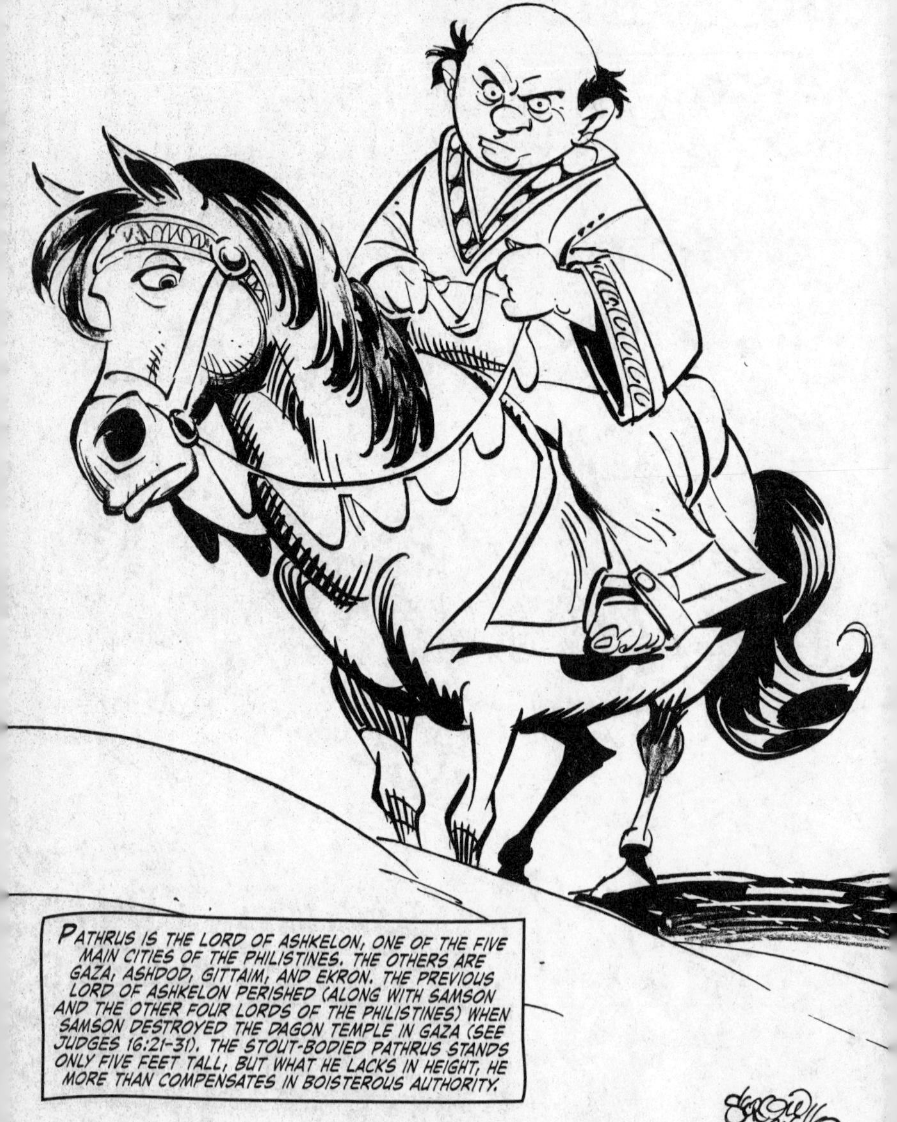

PATHRUS IS THE LORD OF ASHKELON, ONE OF THE FIVE MAIN CITIES OF THE PHILISTINES. THE OTHERS ARE GAZA, ASHDOD, GITTAIM, AND EKRON. THE PREVIOUS LORD OF ASHKELON PERISHED (ALONG WITH SAMSON AND THE OTHER FOUR LORDS OF THE PHILISTINES) WHEN SAMSON DESTROYED THE DAGON TEMPLE IN GAZA (SEE JUDGES 16:21-31). THE STOUT-BODIED PATHRUS STANDS ONLY FIVE FEET TALL, BUT WHAT HE LACKS IN HEIGHT, HE MORE THAN COMPENSATES IN BOISTEROUS AUTHORITY.

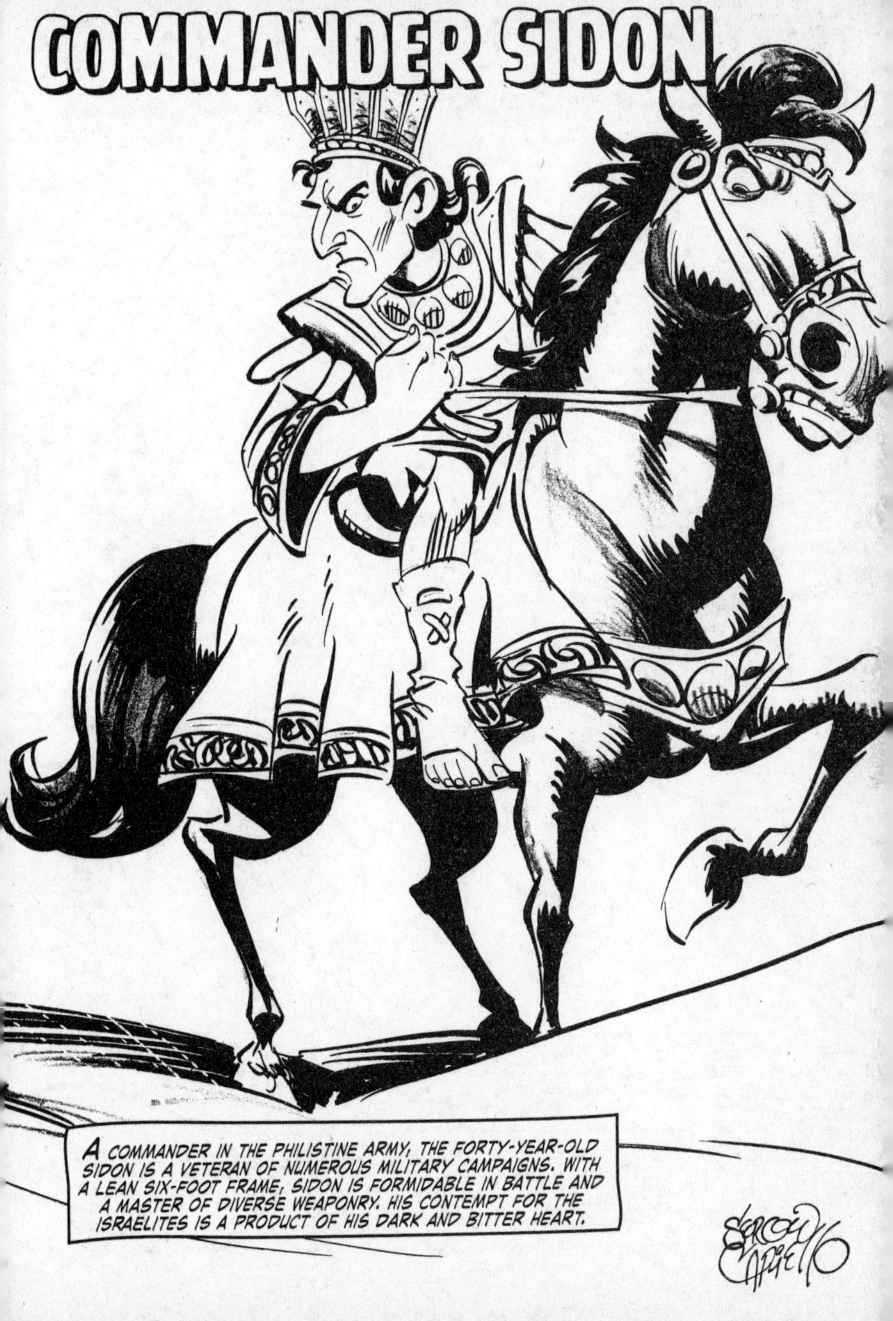
COMMANDER SIDON
A COMMANDER IN THE PHILISTINE ARMY, THE FORTY-YEAR-OLD SIDON IS A VETERAN OF NUMEROUS MILITARY CAMPAIGNS. WITH A LEAN SIX-FOOT FRAME, SIDON IS FORMIDABLE IN BATTLE AND A MASTER OF DIVERSE WEAPONRY. HIS CONTEMPT FOR THE ISRAELITES IS A PRODUCT OF HIS DARK AND BITTER HEART.

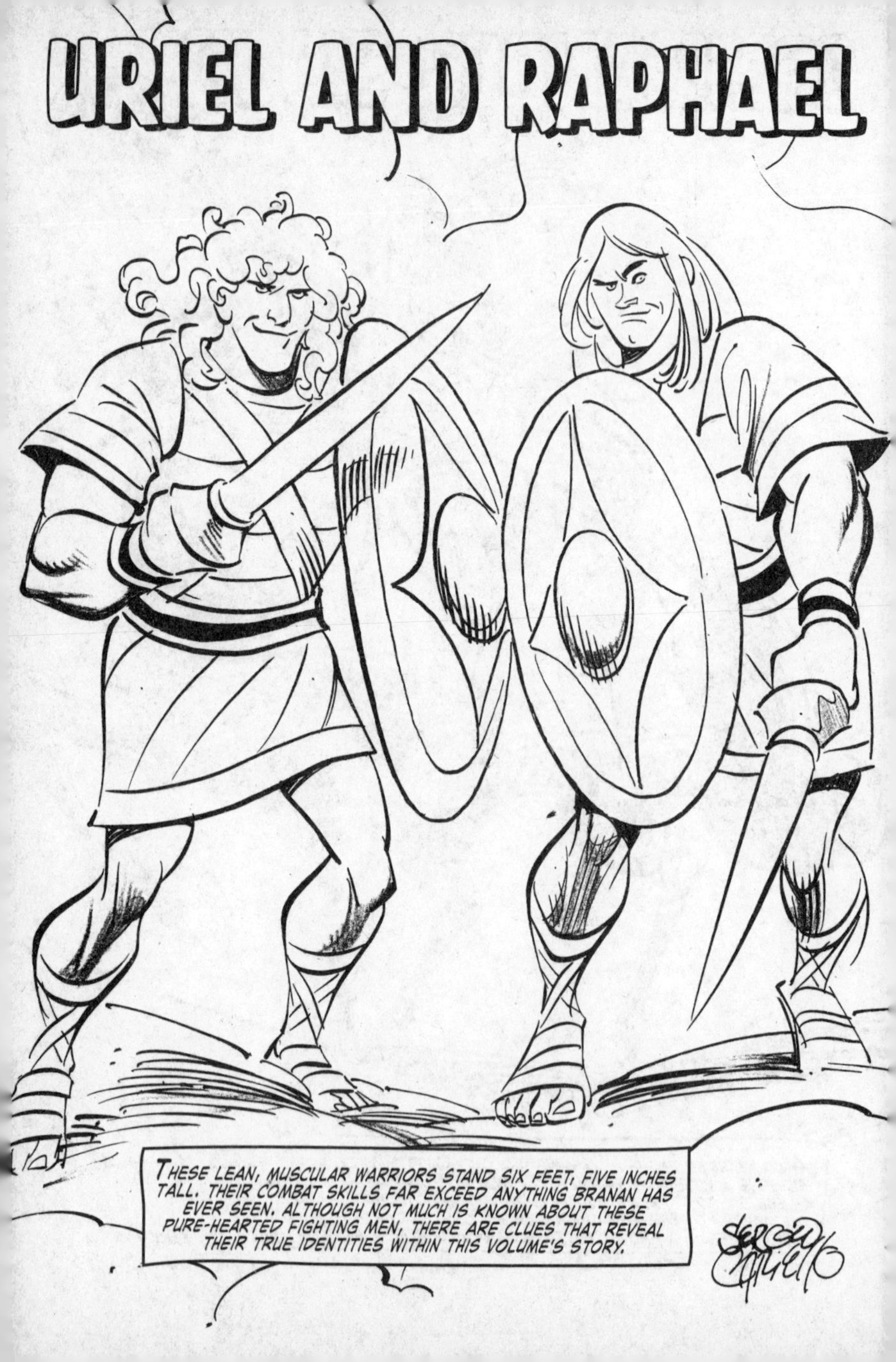
URIEL AND RAPHAEL
THESE LEAN, MUSCULAR WARRIORS STAND SIX FEET, FIVE INCHES TALL. THEIR COMBAT SKILLS FAR EXCEED ANYTHING BRANAN HAS EVER SEEN. ALTHOUGH NOT MUCH IS KNOWN ABOUT THESE PURE-HEARTED FIGHTING MEN, THERE ARE CLUES THAT REVEAL THEIR TRUE IDENTITIES WITHIN THIS VOLUME'S STORY.

SAMSON

SAMSON WAS GREATLY EMPOWERED BY GOD WITH AWESOME STRENGTH, YET HE FAILED TO FULLY UTILIZE HIS EXTRAORDINARY GIFTS FOR GOD'S GLORY. SAMSON WAS A JUDGE OF ISRAEL FOR TWENTY YEARS. THE SON OF SAMSON UNDERTAKES HIS JOURNEY OF DISCOVERY (APPROXIMATELY) TEN YEARS AFTER SAMSON'S HEROIC DEATH. (THE EXPLOITS OF SAMSON ARE CHRONICLED IN THE BOOK OF JUDGES, CHAPTERS 13-16.)

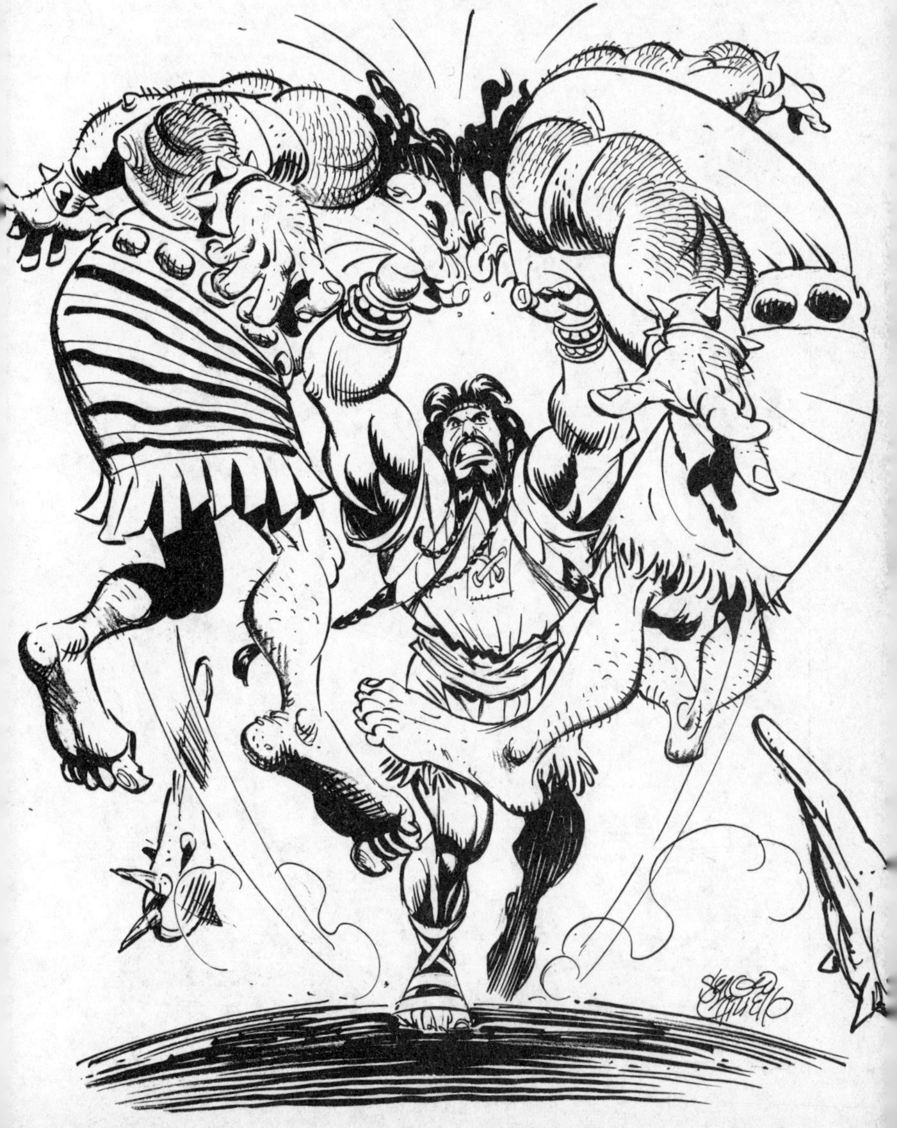

GROWING UP IN SAN JOSE, CALIFORNIA, GARY MARTIN'S DREAM WAS TO BECOME A COMIC BOOK ARTIST. AT AGE 24, HE PACKED UP HIS DRAWING BOARD AND MOVED TO NEW YORK CITY, HOME OF MARVEL AND DC COMICS. LIFE IN NEW YORK WAS NEVER DULL FOR THE CALIFORNIA BOY. EVEN A MUNDANE COMMUTE BY SUBWAY INTO MANHATTAN COULD TURN INTO AN ENTERTAINING RENDITION OF THE JETSONS THEME SONG BY AN ECCENTRIC PASSENGER. AFTER GARY'S SIX-YEAR STINT AS A STARVING ARTIST (LITERALLY), HE LANDED A REGULAR GIG AS AN INKER AND WAS ABLE TO SAY GOOD-BYE TO THE BIG APPLE.

IN 1986, GARY MOVED BACK TO THE WEST COAST AND HAS BEEN A FREELANCE COMIC BOOK ARTIST AND WRITER EVER SINCE. HE'S WORKED FOR ALL THE MAJOR COMPANIES, INCLUDING MARVEL, DC, DARK HORSE, IMAGE, AND DISNEY, AND ON SUCH TITLES AS SPIDER-MAN, X-MEN, BATMAN, STAR WARS, AND MICKEY MOUSE. GARY IS BEST KNOWN FOR HIS POPULAR HOW-TO BOOKS ENTITLED *THE ART OF COMIC BOOK INKING*. RECENTLY, GARY WROTE A COMIC BOOK SERIES CALLED *THE MOTH*, WHICH HE CO-CREATED WITH ARTIST STEVE RUDE. GARY'S HAPPY DAYS ARE NOW SPENT INKING AT HOME (IN HIS PJS AND FUZZY SLIPPERS), WRITING SON OF SAMSON STORIES, AND TRYING TO TEACH HIS LOVELY BRAZILIAN WIFE, MARIA, THE THEME SONG TO *THE JETSONS*.

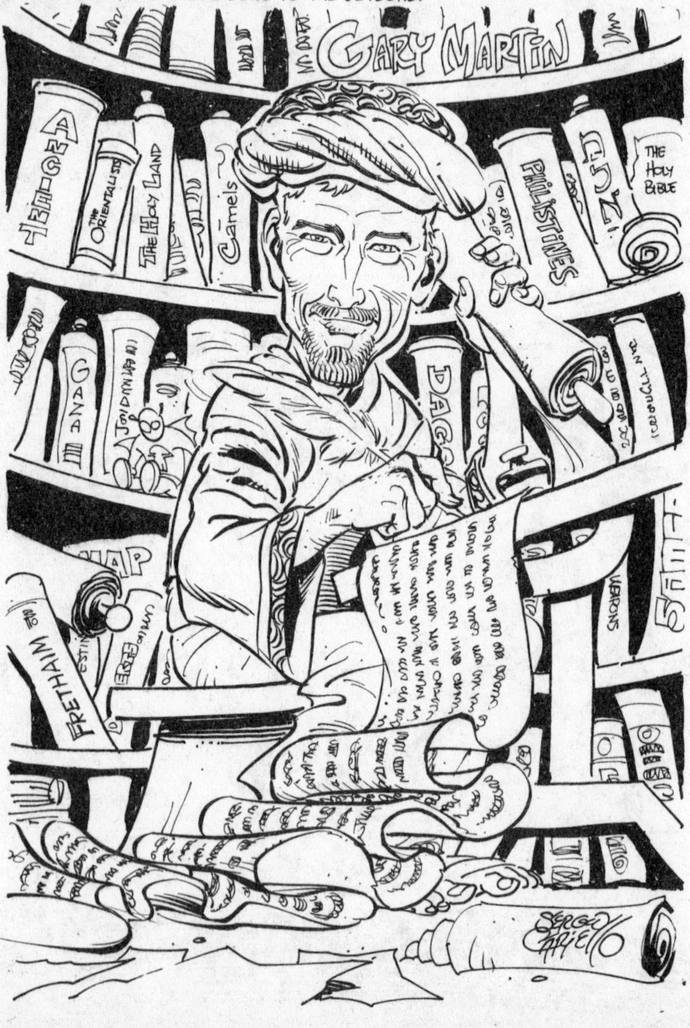
GARY MARTIN
THE ORIENTALISTS
THE HOLY LAND
CAMELS
PHILISTINES
THE HOLY BIBLE
FRETHAIM

SERGIO CARIELLO WAS BORN IN 1964. HE BEGAN HIS CAREER AT THE AGE OF ELEVEN, WRITING, DRAWING, AND LETTERING HIS OWN COMIC STRIP, FREDERICO, THE DETECTIVE, FOR A LOCAL NEWSPAPER IN BRAZIL WHERE HE ALSO DREW POLITICAL CARICATURES UNTIL THE AGE OF FOURTEEN. HE DREAMED OF ONE DAY BECOMING A COMIC BOOK ARTIST IN THE UNITED STATES. HE PAID HIS TUITION FOR LEARNING ENGLISH AS A SECOND LANGUAGE WITH DRAWINGS USED IN THEIR LECTURING BOOKS. HE MIGRATED TO THE USA IN 1985. IN 1986, HE ENROLLED AS A STUDENT AT THE WORD OF LIFE BIBLE INSTITUTE IN UPSTATE NEW YORK, WHERE HE ALSO PAID SOME OF HIS TUITION FEES WITH DRAWINGS AND CARICATURES.

IN 1987, HE ATTENDED THE JOE KUBERT SCHOOL OF CARTOONS AND GRAPHIC ARTS IN NEW JERSEY. HE WORKED ON HIS FIRST AMERICAN COMIC BOOK, DAGON, FOR CALIBER PRESS, WHILE STILL A STUDENT AT THE KUBERT SCHOOL. DURING HIS SECOND SCHOOL YEAR, HE WAS HIRED TO LETTER BOOKS FOR MARVEL COMICS, AND HE WAS QUICKLY MOVED ON TO DRAW SOME OF THEIR MAIN CHARACTERS SUCH AS SPIDER-MAN, DAREDEVIL, AND THE AVENGERS. HE ALSO ILLUSTRATED MANY OF DC COMICS' CHARACTERS LIKE SUPERMAN, DEATHSTROKE, WONDER WOMAN, THE FLASH, AZRAEL, AND BATMAN.

IN 1997, SERGIO REJOINED THE JOE KUBERT SCHOOL TO TEACH FOR SEVEN CONSECUTIVE YEARS, CONTRIBUTING TO PRODUCE MANY OF TODAY'S LEADING CARTOONISTS. HE LATER BECAME THE FIRST TO HELP JOE KUBERT AS AN INSTRUCTOR FOR THE SCHOOL'S CORRESPONDENCE COURSES. DURING THIS PERIOD, HE ALSO WORKED FOR VARIOUS PUBLISHERS, INCLUDING DRAWING A MONTHLY TITLE FOR DC COMICS.

IN 2005, SERGIO JOINED FORCES WITH ACCLAIMED WRITER CHUCK DIXON TO LAUNCH HIS FIRST CO-CREATOR-OWNED PROPERTY, THE IRON GHOST, A MINISERIES PUBLISHED BY IMAGE AND ATP COMICS. SERGIO ALSO WON FIRST PRIZE IN THE FIRST INTERNATIONAL CHRISTIAN COMICS COMPETITION FOR NO PROFIT! (A TWO-PAGE COMIC BASED ON ECCLESIASTES 5). THAT YEAR, SERGIO ALSO ILLUSTRATED AND DONATED SEVERAL PAGES TO TEMPEST, THE HURRICANE KATRINA RELIEF PROJECT PUT TOGETHER BY COMMUNITY COMICS, WHICH LED TO THE PROJECT YOU NOW HOLD IN YOUR HANDS!

SERGIO IS ALSO KNOWN FOR HIS RUN IN THE LONE RANGER SERIES FOR DYNAMITE ENTERTAINMENT, CRUX FOR CROSSGEN COMICS, THE SAINTS FOR LAYNE MORGAN MEDIA, AS WELL AS MANY OTHER PROJECTS ABROAD.

SERGIO CARIELLO AND HIS WIFE, LUZIA, LIVE IN SUNNY FLORIDA WITH THEIR ADORABLE DOG, A WEST HIGHLANDER WHITE TERRIER CALLED MONIQUE. THEY WORSHIP WITH THE BODY OF SAINTS UNDER PASTOR JOE CERRETA, WHERE THEY SERVE AS DIRECTOR OF THE CONTEMPORARY PRAISE AND WORSHIP TEAM AND KIDS' MINISTRIES, RESPECTIVELY.

LEARN MORE ABOUT SERGIO CARIELLO BY VISITING WWW.SERGIOCARIELLO.NET

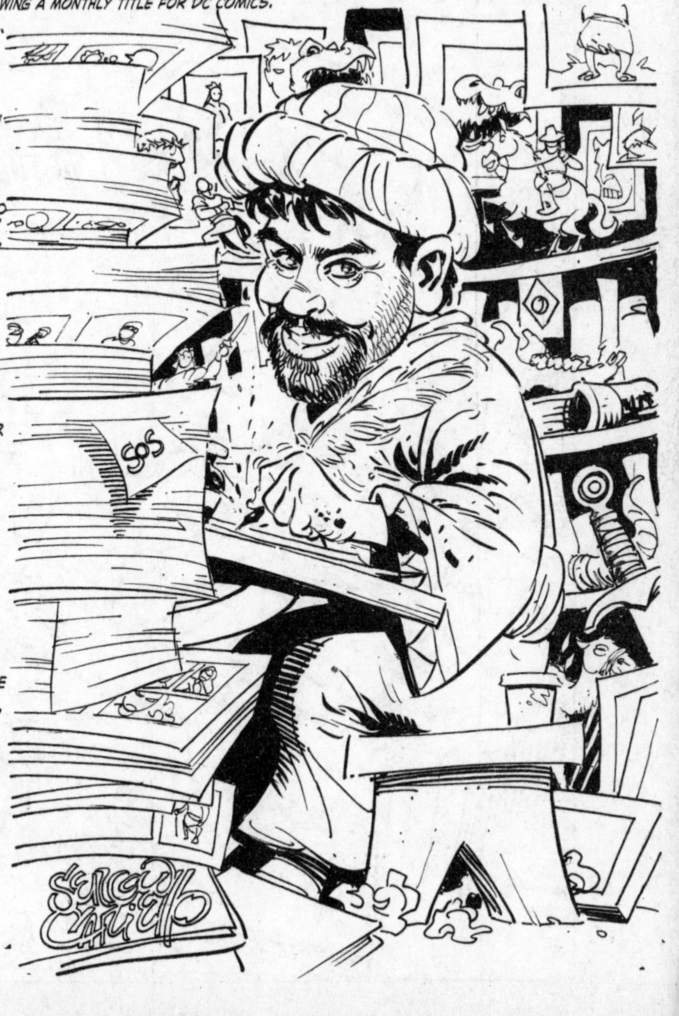
SOS

SON OF SAMSON'S LETTERER, DAVE LANPHEAR, HEADS ARTMONKEYS STUDIOS. YOU CAN FIND THEIR WORK TODAY AT MANY PUBLISHERS, INCLUDING MARVEL, DC'S CMX, DISNEY, DARK HORSE, URBAN MINISTRIES, NACHSHON PRESS, AND, VERY PROUDLY, HERE FOR ZONDERVAN.

IT'S ESTIMATED DAVE'S LETTERED OVER 40,000 COMIC BOOK PAGES, ENOUGH TO TILE THE LARGEST COMIC BOOK CONVENTION'S FLOOR FOUR TIMES. HE'S WORKED IN THREE MAJOR STUDIOS: MALIBU COMICS, COMICRAFT, AND CROSSGEN COMICS AT THEIR MOST PROLIFIC TIMES. HE'S BEEN BLESSED TO WORK WITH TALENTED WRITERS, ARTISTS AND EDITORS, COUNTING MANY AS FRIENDS, AND HAS HAD THE PRIVILEGE TO WORK ON NUMEROUS PRESTIGIOUS PROJECTS SINCE THE 1990S. HE HAS ALSO RECEIVED SEVERAL AWARDS FOR HIS LETTERING.

DAVE IS A THREE-TIME EDITORIAL CARTOON WINNER AND HAS ALSO BEEN A CARICATURIST, COMIC STRIP CARTOONIST, NEWSPAPER ILLUSTRATOR, STORYBOARD ARTIST (NOTABLY ON PBS' DRAGON TALES), MAGAZINE DESIGNER, TALENT COORDINATOR, AND PUBLISHING CONSULTANT. BUT ABOVE ALL THOSE POSITIONS, DAVE LIKES HIS CURRENT WORK BEST: HUSBAND TO HIS BEAUTIFUL WIFE NATALIE AND STAY-AT-HOME DAD TO THEIR THREE SONS.

COME READ **BEHIND THE LINES,** THE ARTMONKEYS BLOG AT HTTP://ARTMONKEYS.BLOGSPOT.COM; OR SEE THEIR GALLERY AT WWW.ARTMONKEYS.WEEBLY.COM.

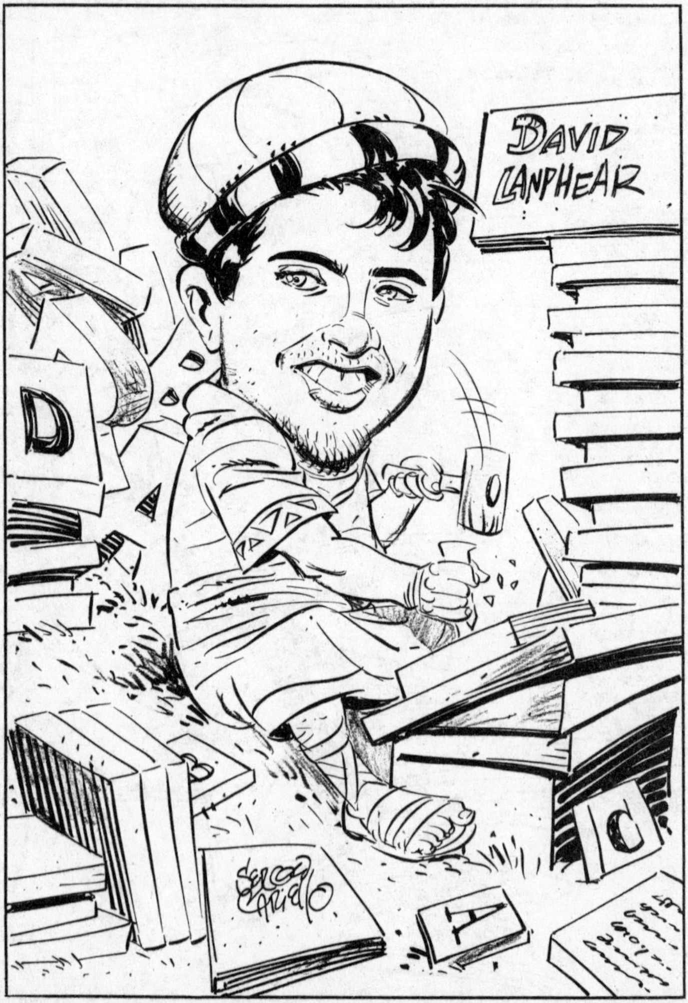
DAVID LANPHEAR

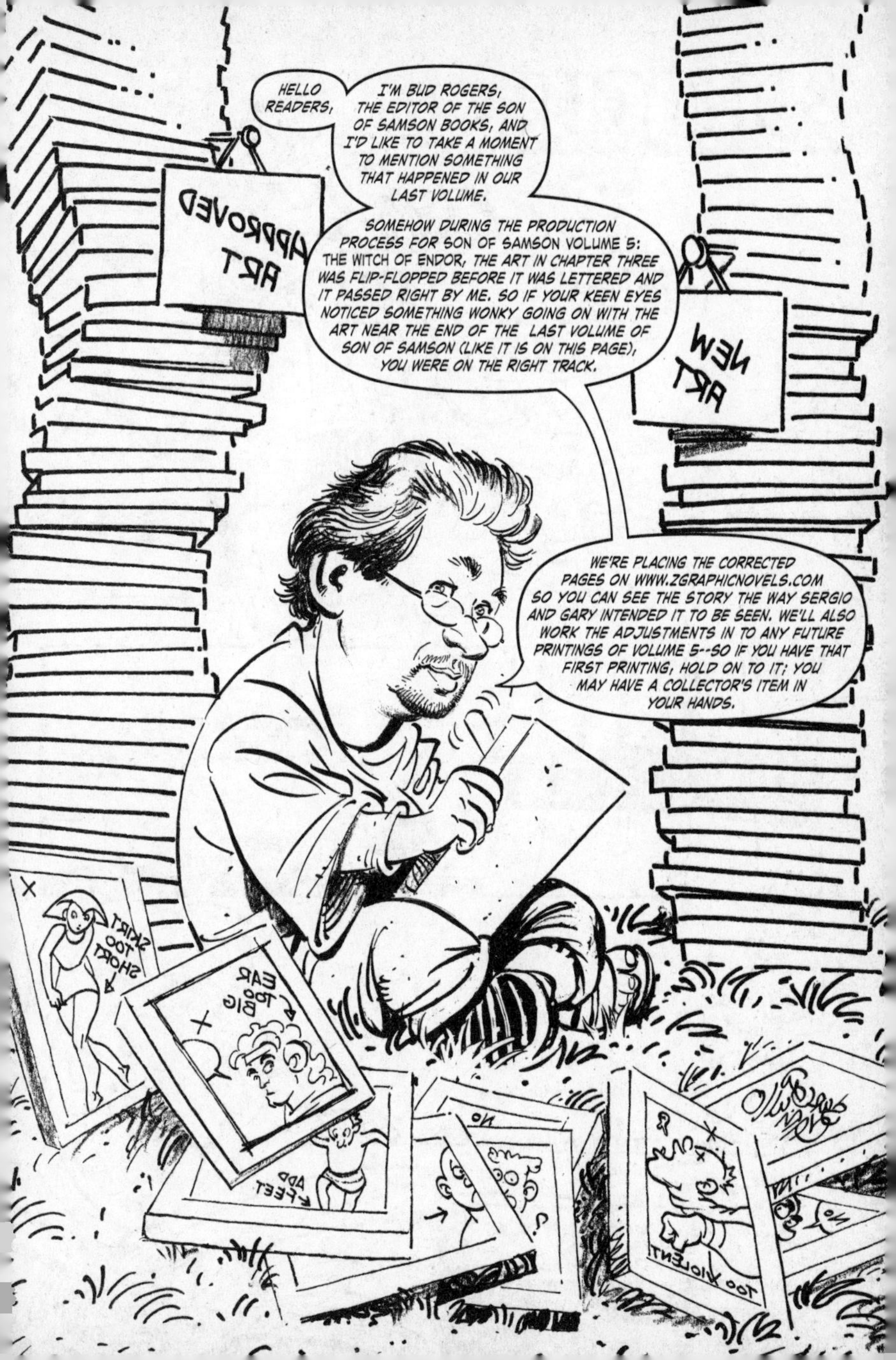

HELLO READERS,
I'M BUD ROGERS, THE EDITOR OF THE SON OF SAMSON BOOKS, AND I'D LIKE TO TAKE A MOMENT TO MENTION SOMETHING THAT HAPPENED IN OUR LAST VOLUME.
SOMEHOW DURING THE PRODUCTION PROCESS FOR SON OF SAMSON VOLUME 5: THE WITCH OF ENDOR, THE ART IN CHAPTER THREE WAS FLIP-FLOPPED BEFORE IT WAS LETTERED AND IT PASSED RIGHT BY ME. SO IF YOUR KEEN EYES NOTICED SOMETHING WONKY GOING ON WITH THE ART NEAR THE END OF THE LAST VOLUME OF SON OF SAMSON (LIKE IT IS ON THIS PAGE), YOU WERE ON THE RIGHT TRACK.
WE'RE PLACING THE CORRECTED PAGES ON WWW.ZGRAPHICNOVELS.COM SO YOU CAN SEE THE STORY THE WAY SERGIO AND GARY INTENDED IT TO BE SEEN. WE'LL ALSO WORK THE ADJUSTMENTS IN TO ANY FUTURE PRINTINGS OF VOLUME 5--SO IF YOU HAVE THAT FIRST PRINTING, HOLD ON TO IT; YOU MAY HAVE A COLLECTOR'S ITEM IN YOUR HANDS.
APPROVED ART
NEW ART
SKIRT TOO SHORT
EAR TOO BIG
ADD FEET
NO
TOO VIOLENT

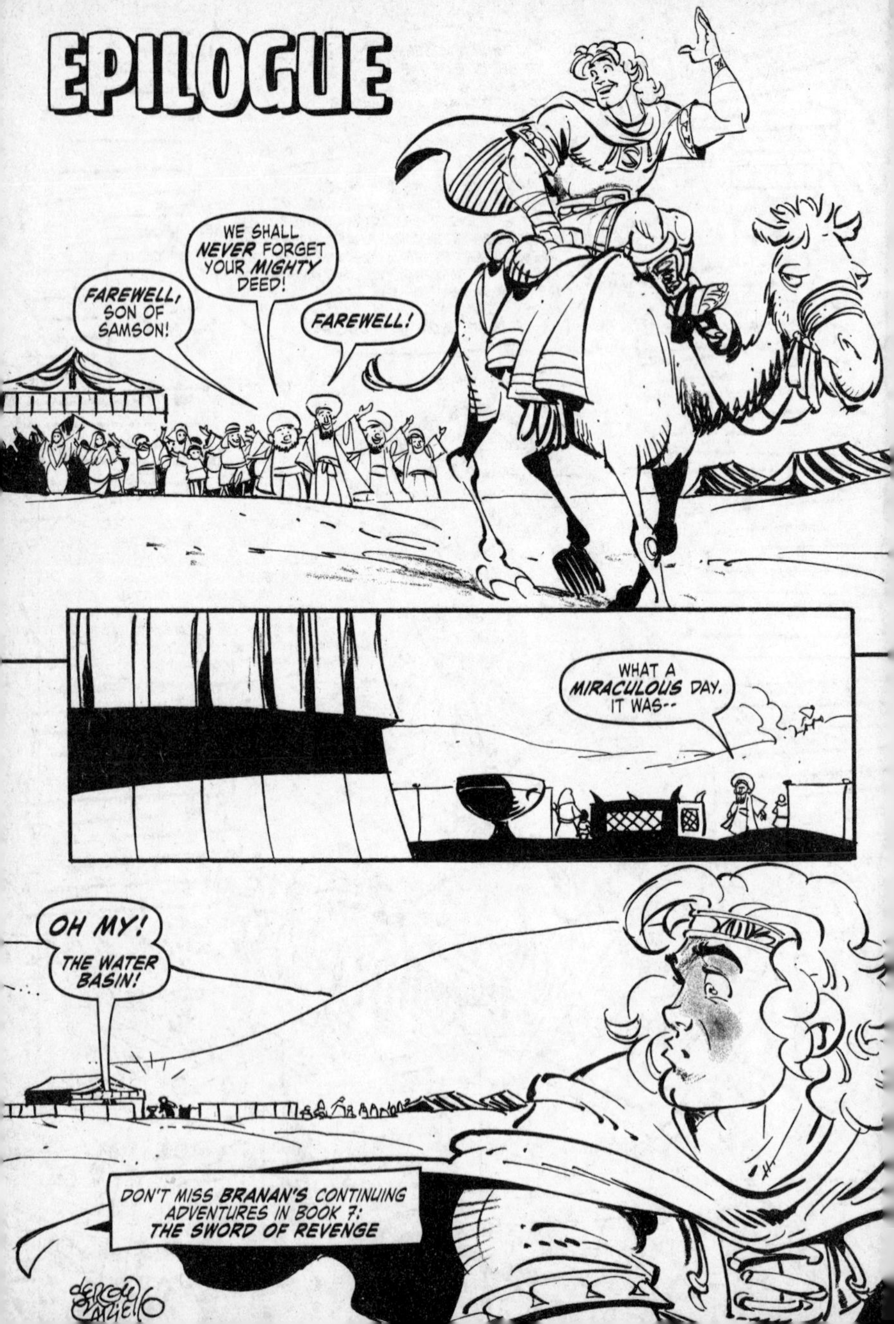
EPILOGUE
FAREWELL, SON OF SAMSON!
WE SHALL NEVER FORGET YOUR MIGHTY DEED!
FAREWELL!
WHAT A MIRACULOUS DAY. IT WAS--
OH MY! THE WATER BASIN!
DON'T MISS BRANAN'S CONTINUING ADVENTURES IN BOOK 7: THE SWORD OF REVENGE

GRAPHIC NOVELS

TIME FLYZ

SHOOM

FLYING THROUGH TIME TO SAVE THE WORLD!

Pyramid Peril

Available Now!

Turtle Trouble

Available Now!

BERLIN BREAKOUT

Berlin Breakout

Available Now!

Tunnel Twist-Up

Available Now!

POWER PLAY

Power Play

Available Now!

AVAILABLE AT YOUR LOCAL BOOKSTORE!

VOLUMES 6–8 COMING SOON!

ZONDERVAN®

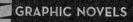

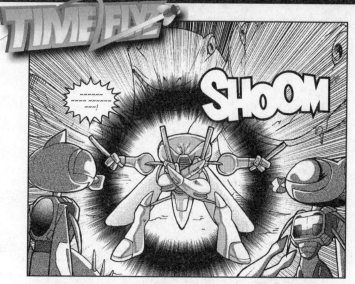

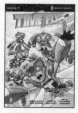

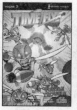

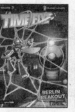

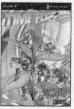

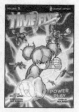

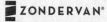